Improbable Eden

Improbable Eden

MARY DAHEIM

CAMEL
PRESS

Seattle, WA

CAMEL PRESS

Camel Press
PO Box 70515
Seattle, WA 98127

For more information go to: www.camelpress.com
www.marydaheimauthor.com

Cover design by Sabrina Sun

Improbable Eden
Original Published in 1991 by Harlequin Historicals.
Copyright © 1991 and 2016 by Mary Daheim

ISBN: 978-1-60381-369-3 (Trade Paper)
ISBN: 978-1-60381-370-9 (eBook)

Library of Congress Control Number: tk

Printed in the United States of America

Dear Reader:

FACT OR FICTION? OFTEN THERE'S a fine line between the two in my historical romances. I've been intrigued by European history since I was in my early teens. When I began *Improbable Eden,* I gave her two real—and well-known—parents: John Churchill, Duke of Marlborough, and Barbara Palmer, Lady Castlemaine. Churchill had done his share of philandering in his youth and Barbara had given birth to several of King Charles II's illegitimate children. Who'd notice one more thrown into the mix?

The result is the unfolding tale of a seemingly ill-matched "orphan" and an exiled prince. Eden Berenger and Maximilian of Nassau-Dillenburg have both been cheated by Fate. How they manage to regain their rightful places in a turbulent world of schemers and dreamers makes for what I hope is an exciting and sometimes touching adventure in late seventeenth-century England.

So sit back, relax and enjoy this romantic and sometimes rollicking ride through an era that changed English history forever.

— Mary Daheim, 2016

Prologue

Kent, 1684

HER NOSE WAS RUNNING, THERE was a smudge of dirt on one cheek, and her older sister had just dumped lemon ice on Eden's best frock. Cybele and the three other children were laughing at Eden's stricken little face, which flushed scarlet at their derision. Madame Berenger peered out from under her bright yellow parasol and scowled. "Behave yourselves," she admonished sharply from her place next to her husband on the carriage platform. "The King comes at any moment now."

Cybele, Genevieve and Etienne exchanged a round of malevolent looks before sitting up straight. Gerard grinned at them and resumed his superior air. But Eden was staring in dismay at her ruined dress. All her life she had waited to see King Charles II, that kind, humorous, charming man who held such a special place in her heart. She knew that Monsieur and Madame Berenger weren't her real parents, and that the other children weren't her real brothers and sisters. Yet no one would reveal the truth, and for Eden, there could be only one reason for such deep secrecy: her father must be a most exalted personage, perhaps King Charles himself. That idea had warmed her lonely little heart on many a cold night in the tiny bedroom under the eaves at Smarden.

And now King Charles was riding toward her, heading for Tunbridge Wells to take the waters. She had dreamed of this day, prayed for it, longed to see that tall, dark, laughing man up close and have him pick her out of the crowd and take her in his arms. He would proclaim that she was not Eden Berenger but Princess Eden Stuart, daughter of the King. And Eden would ride off with him to London or Windsor or whichever of those wonderful places her father lived in royal splendor.

A cloud of dust began to rise on the far horizon, and the faint blare of trumpets shrilled on the summer air. Nearby, spectators pushed closer to the tree-lined road. Eden watched her foster parents for a signal that they should do the same, but Monsieur and Madame Berenger remained in place on the driver's platform. It was Etienne who asked if they might stand by the road for a better view.

"From here, you have the best vantage point," Madame Berenger pointed out. "We are on a small rise, which permits us to see over the others."

Her words made sense, but Eden longed to get as close as possible to King Charles. How else would he recognize her in such a great crowd? For it seemed as if all of Kent had turned out. Shoulder to shoulder they stood, dressed in their best, a cordon of men, women and children lining the road.

Above the dust, a wavy ribbon of color evoked cheers from the onlookers. Footmen, horsemen, courtiers in carriages, ladies in open chaises, gentlemen on magnificent steeds paraded past. Never had Eden seen such spectacle. She forgot about her soiled dress and her smudged cheek. Her eyes turned darker with wonder, and her mouth formed a circle of delight.

Reclining in an elaborately decorated carriage was a fabulous creature adorned with silk and pearls and rubies. Then came another lady, raven-haired and olive-skinned, with an emerald-covered bosom, followed by a laughing, bouncing sprite with auburn hair whose conveyance scarcely seemed able to contain her high spirits. Someone called, "Nellie! We love the Protestant whore best!" and the auburn-haired nymph blew kisses with both hands.

Then Eden saw him, riding easily and exuding good humor, a tall man with a black wig and mustache that turned down at the corners as if to remind his smile that life had its serious side, too. The rest of the cavalcade faded into oblivion. Eden could see no one else. He waved and nodded, laughed and grinned, and Eden gripped the side of the carriage in fierce anticipation. King Charles was almost abreast of her now, exchanging words with a brawny yeoman. Both monarch and subject reeled with mirth. Saluting the man, Charles turned in the saddle to gaze in the direction of the Berenger carriage.

Eden could endure no more. In one swift, scrambling movement, she hoisted her little body over the side and jumped to the ground. In a flash she was running toward the road, tripping on her skirts, red hair dancing on her head like merry flames. The King was only a few yards away; Eden found herself blocked by a hefty couple who paid no heed to the small child trying to wedge between them. But at last Eden made a heroic lunge and came face-to-face with the man who would make her dreams come true.

Out of breath and trembling from excitement, she stared into the dark, ravaged countenance of Charles Stuart. He inclined his head under the osprey-trimmed hat and laid a finger next to his long nose. Transfixed, Eden watched as he winked and smiled straight into her expectant face.

And then he was gone. The tail of his fine gelding swished at the flies, and Eden felt herself being dragged away while a harsh hand swatted her backside. "You were told to stay where you were," growled Monsieur Berenger, his face suffused with displeasure. "For this bad behavior, *Maman* declares there will be no supper for you tonight."

Eden didn't hear him. Nor did she pay much attention to the snickers of Etienne and Cybele as she struggled into the carriage. The only thing that seemed real was the King, whose entourage was now a few dark specks on the horizon.

Perhaps it would have been a breach of etiquette for King Charles to seek her out among so many strangers. In a day or so, after the court was settled at Tunbridge Wells, there might be a messenger riding up to the house by the River Beult, requesting Eden's presence before the King.

She comforted herself with that thought. The King's face had been so kind. Surely he wouldn't pass by and forget her.

By the time the apples were harvested and the hops were drying in the oasthouses, Eden's fragile hope had turned to dark despair. The wind blew the season's first storms from off the channel, and in November a light snow dusted the barren trees and rolling pastures that lay to the east of the Berenger property. The yuletide season passed with bright, crisp frost.

Then, in the New Year, under glowering gray skies that dulled Nature's palette, doleful news came from London. King Charles was dead. After a fit of apoplexy, he had lingered for three days, and the words he had uttered during those final hours were well noted. With typical irony, he had apologized for taking "such an unconscionably long time a-dying," and had responded to his Queen's plea for forgiveness by begging her to forgive him a thousand-fold in return. He had remembered in particular that laughing nymph, Mistress Nellie Gwynn, and had summoned all his illegitimate children to his bedside to bid them a final fond farewell.

All except Eden. Listening to her foster parents exchange gossip about the King's demise, she had nestled close to the butter churn, out of sight and hanging on to every heartbreaking word.

"What's this?" Madame Berenger's sharp voice cut through Young the butcher's commentary about Charles's famous mistresses. "Eden! Why do you skulk in corners to eavesdrop on your elders?" Madame Berenger cuffed at Eden's ear. "Away with you! Have you no etiquette?" She loomed over Eden, her slack bosom heaving with annoyance. Her pale blue eyes narrowed as she noted the tears welling up in Eden's dark eyes. "I don't want tears. You are eight years old next week, and well past the age of crying."

Later, when Monsieur Berenger had gone out with the other children to the village, Eden heard Madame Berenger huffing around the kitchen, clattering pots and pans. Eden remained crouched on the floor in silent desolation, but after several minutes had passed, she descended the ladder of the loft where she slept along with Genevieve and Cybele. Madame Berenger's back was turned, her concentration focused on a huge iron pot into which she was peeling potatoes. For a long moment, Eden regarded the angular form with a mixture of trepidation and determination.

"*Maman?*" Eden phrased the word politely. She waited quietly as Madame Berenger wiped her hands and rolled the sleeves of her dress down.

"Eh?" She turned to gaze at Eden over her shoulder. "Here, you may peel the onions." Madame Berenger grunted as she hauled a large sack from the cupboard.

"*Maman,*" Eden repeated, less politely this time, but in a more mature voice than she usually employed. "I must ask a question."

Madame Berenger nudged the bag of onions with her knee. "Ask how many of these go into the pot."

Despite her foster mother's baleful glance, Eden persisted. "Where was I born, *Maman?*"

Madam Berenger's gaze sharpened and she waved a work-roughened hand. "Why do you ask such things? And what does it matter? You have been raised here at Smarden, in Kent, is that not so, eh?"

Eden planted her feet firmly on the kitchen's tiled floor. "It matters." She swallowed hard, desperately hoping that she wouldn't allow her tears to betray her again. "It matters to me."

Her foster mother lifted her bony shoulders in a shrug of dismissal. "*Nom de Dieu*, it cannot. It is of no importance. If anyone asks, tell them we found you under a cabbage. Come, come, *ma petite choute*, to your duties."

Reluctantly, Eden approached the bag. Hauling it over to the kitchen table, she sat down on a small three-legged stool. It was clear that her foster mother had no intention of revealing more to Eden. Yet someone had cared about her enough to see to her upbringing. If not King Charles, then who? Eden scowled as she began stripping the onions of their golden brown skin. No matter what anyone said, it must have been the King. Maybe he'd left a letter or named her in his will. After a while, Eden felt faintly cheered. When the tears began to pour down her cheeks once more, she blamed them not on disappointment, but on the ragged row of onions she had lined up on the table.

Chapter One

Kent, 1695

GERARD HAD COME HOME FROM the Battle of Namur with a stiff leg and a melancholy disposition. The yuletide season had passed all but unnoted in the Berenger household. Though English and Dutch troops had finally succeeded in recapturing an important fortress in Brabant, the victory had proved costly to the elder Berenger son.

Eden tried her best to buoy Gerard's spirits, insisting they hitch up a makeshift sleigh and ride out through the snow-covered apple orchards or slide on the north downs beyond the village. Gerard rebuffed her at first, but Eden was determined to drag him not only out of the house, but out of himself, as well.

"I need more than sheep for company," she declared, yanking at his broadcloth sleeve. "We might even ride to Romney Marsh. You've always enjoyed fishing off the spit at Dungeness."

Gerard gave her a wry smile. "That was before I got hurt. As for you, I doubt you'd be lonely in the village. Smarden's swains are quite taken with you."

Eden raised both eyebrows. "I prefer the sheep. The local lads are a glum lot, with little humor and less wit. And most are twice as gawky as you, even if they do have two good legs." She made no effort to ignore Gerard's handicap and refused to patronize him as the rest of the family did. Approaching her nineteenth birthday, Eden had learned to face life squarely—except for that still secret place in her heart that had never stopped crying out for her long-lost father.

"It's cold," Gerard protested, his voice peevish. "This weather makes my leg ache."

Eden got up from the table and moved briskly to the big open fireplace, where she turned the hissing logs with a sturdy poker. "The sun is trying to come out. I'd wager half a crown it won't snow again today."

Gerard was mulling over a suitable rejoinder when Cybele and Etienne, their faces red with cold, stomped in through the door. Cybele was a recent widow with two children; her figure had grown plump and her countenance sour.

"Where are our parents?" Etienne asked, a wary expression on his goatlike face.

"Out," Eden replied tersely, grabbing Gerard by the back of his shirt. "As the two of us will be shortly. Come, Brother, let us make our way into the village as we planned."

"Hold, Brother!" commanded Etienne with an excited wave of his hands. "We have guests coming up the walk even now! Most important business, I assure you." He gave his foster sister a shrewd look. "You, too, Eden."

"Assuredly." Cybele smirked as she hung her heavy black shawl on a peg by the door. As ever, she was galled by the sight of Eden, whose long, thick hair was the color of claret and tumbled in shining waves down her back. Her wide mouth had a smile that could light up at the very hint of humor, and the huge, dark eyes were set wide under heavy lashes and perfect, dense brows. She was slim, too, with a body growing more lush each day and with skin the color of cream. Eden wasn't much more than average height, but she gave the illusion of being taller and moved with a sprightly grace. "Not the least bit sedate," Cybele was fond of saying. The remark always struck a responsive chord in Etienne and Genevieve, who never failed to repeat it when they felt Eden was being overly vivacious. Indeed, it was Eden's exuberance and love of life that galled her family most. Even Gerard no longer found her open, expansive nature as engaging as it had seemed before Namur.

Eden was determined not to let the Berengers dampen her spirits. With a purposely winsome glance at Etienne, she started to ask what business matter could possibly concern her when their visitors suddenly materialized on the threshold. At first, the pair of newcomers appeared to be blackamoors from some exotic African tribe. But as the door closed behind them, Eden recognized the two men as Bob Crocker and his son, Charlie, their faces and hands stained by the charcoal they burned from the local iron smelters.

Etienne was greeting the Crockers warmly. With her usual frankness, Eden started to ask why they'd come but Etienne waved her to silence.

"Be patient!" he admonished. "Bring us hot cider. And rolls, too, if you baked enough this morning."

Controlling her temper, Eden went to the heavy white crock where the half a dozen potato rolls she'd baked before dawn reposed in a linen napkin.

Etienne's tone was more supercilious than usual, the well-bred accent their tutor had drilled into all five children more pronounced. The visitors were expounding on the lamentable state of the charcoal industry.

"T' bosky trees are all but gone in t' weald," Bob Crocker explained over the rim of his steaming mug of cider. "We get only half as much wood t' burn nowadays."

"A sorry state of affairs," commented Etienne, holding out his roll to be buttered. Eden slapped a knifeful against it and tried to ignore Cybele's snicker.

"Why must I stay?" Eden hissed at Cybele, who was seated at her loom, sorting different shades of green yarn. "It may be hours before our parents get back."

Cybele squinted at two lengths of pale mint wool. "Can't you guess?" Her little black eyes darted in Charlie Crocker's direction. "That great brute of a boy wants to make you his wife."

Eden stifled an incredulous cry. Only the most strenuous self-discipline prevented her from staring aghast at Charlie, whose eyes seemed to bug out at her from his soot-smudged face. "No!" she breathed, hoping for once that Cybele would show some sympathy.

But her foster sister merely looked smug. "And why not, pray? You may have come to this family with an allowance of sorts, but not with a dowry. Who did you expect to come a-courting, a noble lord from London?"

It was strange how those were the last words Eden heard before the door opened again, this time to reveal Monsieur Berenger and a man with fawn-colored hair under a modish triangular hat. It took only an instant to realize that her foster father was highly agitated. His usually impassive expression was animated, and a little pulse beat at the top of his shiny bald pate. One glimpse of the Crockers all but undid him; he stumbled across the threshold, leaving his companion at the door.

"Uh … Bob! And Charlie! *Par bleu*, I had forgotten …." He turned nervous eyes to Etienne. "Have events marched forward?"

Etienne hastily poured more cider to cover the sudden awkwardness. "No, no. We've merely been conversing. Eh, Bob? Charlie, my lad?"

Bob Crocker was too busy staring at the highborn newcomer to reply. As for Charlie, he still had his adoring gaze fixed on Eden. It was she who gestured to the stranger to enter, bestowing on him a gracious if questioning smile.

The man removed his hat and returned her smile, transmitting an aura of warmth and kindness. "Are these your children, my good Berenger?" he inquired in a light, pleasant voice while his host had the presence of mind to close the door.

"Indeed, yes! That is," Monsieur Berenger amended, making a frantic motion for Etienne to pull out another chair, "these are my sons, Etienne and Gerard, my eldest daughter, Cybele. And Eden." His head bobbed in his foster daughter's direction. "Then there is Genevieve, who is married and not here. These others, they are … old friends." He spoke the last words wistfully, as if he expected the Crockers' status to change momentarily.

"I see." The stranger's refined features wore an expression that was at once comprehending and bemused. While he had looked like a young man from the doorway, at closer range, Eden realized he was older, perhaps middle-aged. Taking note of a cat that was sniffing at his high-heeled boots, the man stooped to pick up the animal and cradle it against his shoulder. To Eden's surprise, the cat offered only token resistance before nestling contentedly into the heavy, fur-lined woolen cape.

Shifting his wiry form from one foot to the other, Monsieur Berenger cleared his throat. "My children, my friends," he said, suddenly gruff, "heed me! This," he announced all but stretching on his tiptoes in a quest for dignity, "is His Lordship, the famous and excellent Earl of Marlborough!"

Cybele uttered a bubbling gasp, Etienne's thin mustache quivered, Gerard's face showed an unaccustomed spark of life, and both Crockers swung around to gape. As startled as Eden was by the announcement, she was even more surprised to note that their exalted guest was staring at her. She faltered only briefly before remembering her manners and attempting an unpracticed curtsy.

"Charming," Marlborough said a bit absently, forcing his gray-green eyes away from Eden. "And your good wife," he went on, turning to Monsieur Berenger. "When may I have the pleasure of meeting her?"

Brushing at the lank strands of hair at his temples, Monsieur Berenger looked helplessly around the kitchen. "Of course, most certainly—but where is dear *Maman*?"

"She took some of her special medicine to Genevieve." Cybele's overbright eyes were riveted on Marlborough and she offered him an artful smile. "My sister is going to have her first baby in the early summer. I have two of my own, but the Lord saw fit to make me a widow." Her smile faded and she assumed a demure, sorrowful air.

Carefully, Marlborough set the cat on the floor, where it rubbed against his boot and purred. The Earl's face had taken on a pinched look. "May I inquire which is your foster daughter?" The gray-green eyes lingered hopefully on Eden.

Monsieur Berenger wore a pained expression, as if he wished he could foist off Cybele or even the kitchen cat. The Crockers, who had been observing the august visitor with round eyes and open mouths, swiveled in Eden's direction.

"I'm the one who does not belong." Eden spoke without rancor. "I'm not a Berenger by birth." She thrust out her chin, as if daring the others to deny what they had always been quick to maintain. "I'm Eden," she added, in case the Earl hadn't taken in all of Monsieur Berenger's introductions.

"Ah." The Earl was still pale, but his features relaxed a bit. He beckoned for Eden to come closer. "Yes," he murmured, studying her face, "I was quite certain, but …." He broke off, giving the impression that his words had been meant only for himself. "Monsieur Berenger, may I speak privately with Mistress Eden?"

Flustered, Monsieur Berenger almost tripped on the cat. "The parlor," he suggested in his anxious manner. " 'Tis humble, but tidy."

Noting how Cybele's glance raked over her with a mixture of curiosity and malice, Eden recognized the eavesdropping possibilities of the parlor and offered an alternative. "I was about to take the air. Perhaps, milord, you'd care to join me in the garden?"

Marlborough inclined his head. "A delightful idea," he remarked, though his face still wore that strained look.

In the spring and summer, the Berenger garden provided a brilliant splash of color between the river and the High Street. But now, in the dead of winter, the bare branches of the lilac tree were rimed with snow. Eden was suddenly overcome by the bleakness of her family home. Its thatched roof gave no comfort, its plastered walls offered no haven, its oak door promised no warm welcome. Eden turned her back on the house and tried to gaze levelly at Marlborough. To her surprise, the Earl seemed equally disconcerted.

"You're very lovely," he said at last, his breath puffing out before him on the cold February air. "Do you have any idea who your real parents might be?"

Startled by the suddenness of the question, Eden retreated a step. "No. I don't think my foster parents know, either." She swallowed once and frowned. "*Maman* … my foster mother … told me once that I was born in France shortly before the Berengers came to England. They're Huguenots, you see, and their kind were being persecuted by King Louis." She stopped suddenly, aware that if anyone would know every nuance of past and present politics, it would be the Earl of Marlborough. Eden felt foolish.

But Marlborough was reaching inside his cape to extract a plain linen handkerchief, which he passed over his forehead. "So. You haven't the faintest idea about your father … or mother?"

At the gate, an aged collie was nosing its way between the iron bars. "Well …." In spite of herself, the ghost of a smile touched her lips. It would hardly do to mention her childhood fantasy, how she used to dream that her father was merry King Charles and she his long-lost princess.

"No," she answered, squarely meeting Marlborough's patient gaze, "how could I?"

The Earl was dabbing at his temple with the handkerchief. Despite the freezing weather, he was sweating. Apparently Eden's concern showed, for Marlborough waved the handkerchief at her and shook his head. "Fret not, 'tis but one of my damnable headaches. They plague me most unexpectedly from time to time." Stiffly, he turned to look toward the High Street. "Where is Max?" he murmured, pressing the handkerchief against his temple. "I must return to the Bell and Whistle. We will speak again," he assured Eden. "Soon."

Even as Marlborough moved toward the gate, his step faltered. Eden rushed to his side, taking him by the arm. "Sire! Take care, you slipped on the ice!"

The Earl gave a short laugh. "Mayhap. These headaches cloud my vision. I apologize a hundredfold."

"Nonsense," retorted Eden, surprising herself by being so forthright with such an exalted personage. "Illness can't be prevented, though it often can be cured. My foster mother is well-versed in healing arts. She has taught us how to deal with sickness. Perhaps I can—"

Eden stopped abruptly, her arm still bracing the Earl. A few yards away, on the other side of the High Street, a young giant of a man, blond and lean, was scowling at them.

"Hold! What goes here?" he called, his booted feet covering the distance to the Berenger gate in scant seconds. "Leave His Lordship be! Are you trying to pick his pocket? He rarely carries money on him, I have it."

Startled, Eden stared at the blond giant. Under ordinary circumstances she would have been mightily impressed. He had an athlete's body and the face of a Norse god. And, Eden thought with outrage, the manners of a pig. "I'm no cutpurse! I was going to brew His Lordship a special tea!" she cried, refusing to let go of the Earl's arm.

"Rot." The blond giant lifted Marlborough off the ground, no mean feat considering the Earl's size and Eden's resistance. "I'll tend to him. I'm used to it. Go back to your barn or wherever you come from." He kicked the gate open and slung one of Marlborough's arms around his neck.

To Eden's surprise, the Earl summoned up the strength to defend her. "Max, this is the Berenger child. Be gentle with her, I pray you."

The man known as Max looked vaguely dismayed as Eden glowered at him from behind the fence. "As you say. But," he added as they proceeded up the High Street, "that doesn't mean she's to be trusted. This is Kent, not Kensington."

"There are more honest country folk than city folk, I'll wager!" Eden cried, gripping the iron bars and giving them a useless shake. She felt like running after the pair and doing bodily harm to the brute called Max. Eden wanted to proclaim that she knew more about medicine than he did, that she certainly had a better grasp on etiquette and that the Earl of Marlborough must be a veritable saint to employ such a rude manservant. But she held her tongue, afraid of further upsetting the Earl. He seemed like a kind man, and he must have some knowledge of her parents. Otherwise why would he have called at the Berenger cottage? Dejected, she watched the pair disappear past St. Michael's church.

Leaning on the fence, Eden surveyed the High Street, now empty except for the old collie, which was nosing around a pile of snow. How incredible that after a lifetime of ignorance concerning her real family, the one man who knew the truth couldn't convey it because he had a headache. Nor was it fair that Eden's interview with His Lordship had ended on such a sour note, with his belligerent manservant insulting her. What had begun as an intriguing visit from a vaunted noble had ended in frustration.

Eden shivered under her long cloak, watching the leaden clouds descend over Smarden. She was no more enlightened than she had been before the great Earl of Marlborough had stepped across the Berenger threshold. Trudging toward the door, she could hear Master Crocker and Monsieur Berenger discussing the price of cider and charcoal. Perhaps she could coax Gerard outside—or maybe it would be better to walk alone and collect her thoughts.

The decision was taken out of her hands by the sudden approach of Madame Berenger, muffled to the eyes and wearing a pair of her husband's boots. "What's this?" she demanded, gesturing toward the High Street. "Did I not see two strangers leaving our garden gate?"

Eden paused. She had no wish to recount Marlborough's visit to the Berenger home, and she couldn't bear to go inside and face Charlie Crocker or her foster family. "Papa will explain," Eden murmured, averting her eyes. "I must go to the cobbler's." Sidestepping Madame Berenger, Eden fled up the High Street.

FIVE MINUTES LATER SHE STOOD on the little stone bridge spanning the river. As reason triumphed over rancor, Eden realized that the Berengers could force her to marry Charlie Crocker. Her allowance would serve as her dowry. She couldn't expect any better if she stayed in Smarden; the future was as bleak as the gray skies that hung low over the village.

With a dragging step, Eden crossed to the other side. She had no choice but to go back. Her feet crunched on the frost in Water Lane; her breath rose before her like steam from a teakettle. Ahead, by the lych-gate of St. Michael's church, she saw Master Young's nephew, Adam, engaged in deep conversation with Bixby, the curate. On Twelfth Night, Adam had stolen a kiss from Eden while the Lord of Misrule had cavorted on the village green. The kiss had meant nothing to Eden, but Adam's freckled face had glowed like a beacon. Eden made a sudden turn and hurried around the nave of the church and out of sight.

She walked for several minutes without any thought to her destination until she looked up and saw the weathered sign of the Bell and Whistle. Perhaps there was the tiniest hope. What if Marlborough was waiting inside to tell her that somewhere a father and mother stood poised with open arms?

She was still sunk in thought when an eager voice called her name. Turning, she saw Charlie Crocker, his face wiped partially clean.

"Eden!" he called again, "walk wi' me t' Cloth Hall. I must fetch a bolt o' muslin home."

Eden ran an uncertain hand through her claret-colored hair. "I ... I can't." She offered him a little smile and glanced at the sign, which swayed lethargically in the wind. "I've come to inquire after Milord Marlborough," she said on impulse. "He's ill, you know."

From the baffled look on Charlie's face, it appeared he considered illness incompatible with aristocracy. "How could such as he be ill?"

"Even earls are mortal," said Eden, "and in his case, kind as well. It would be impolite not to ask after him."

"But Eden," objected Charlie, raising a smudgy hand, "we must talk. My father and me came t' ask an important question of you an' yours."

His eyes were beseeching her, yet there was also a strange glint that Eden didn't recognize. She had no wish to hurt him, but the idea of courtship—and eventual marriage—with Charlie Crocker appalled her. "Later," Eden said, hoping she sounded kind as she pushed open the door to the inn. Charlie followed her doggedly, but Eden pretended not to notice.

She stepped inside the common room and blinked several times as the smells of tobacco smoke, hot coffee, meat juices and ale overwhelmed her. Ordinarily Smarden's only inn wore an easy air, but the winter weather had driven a great many travelers into the little haven on the Beult. Indeed, at least two men, seated just a few yards away, were of the quality. Eden sensed their bold eyes on her and gave them a haughty look. The dark, rail-thin man exhaled perfect little smoke rings from his pipe, but the burly redhead with the scar over one eye roared with laughter. Flushing, Eden marched between the tables toward Master Bunn, the oversize, loquacious innkeeper.

"I wish to see the Earl of Marlborough," Eden announced with an air of importance.

Master Bunn's mouth twisted under his full black mustache. "His Lordship! I heard he'd been asking where t' Berengers live." His agate eyes fastened on her face while his enormous hands brushed at the soiled apron that covered his immense paunch. He leaned toward Eden. "Is't true that Bob Crocker's lad yonder seeks your hand? I heard t' news from someone who ought t' know."

"*Zut!*" Eden murmured the word. It was one of the few fragments of French she retained in ordinary conversation. Casting a swift glance over her shoulder at the bumbling Charlie, she forced a smile for Master Bunn. "Nothing is formalized," she said demurely. "But now I must deliver a message to His Lordship. He *is* here, isn't he?"

Bunn smoothed the bristles of his mustache. "Aye, that he is, though a shadow of his former self. Go find Mistress Bunn upstairs. She'll know the latest news—she always does."

Eden thanked Master Bunn and hurried out of the common room with Charlie at her heels. It seemed useless to discourage him.

But Charlie felt obliged to offer advice. "Eden, are ye mad? 'Tisn't proper to call on a great lord such as t' Earl...."

"He called on us," Eden reminded Charlie. Running up the narrow stairs, she all but crashed into Mistress Bunn, who was descending with a basket of dirty linen. Spare of words as well as frame, the innkeeper's wife regarded Eden's request with equivocation.

"I couldn't say," she temporized, "him bein' ill." After due consideration, she gestured with the basket toward the end of the passageway. "If he don't answer on t' first knock, go away."

Eden gave the appropriate assurances. Taking the last half dozen stairs two at a time, with Charlie thumping behind her, she reached the second floor and moved swiftly toward the door Mistress Bunn had indicated. Raising her fist to rap on the worn oak, Eden suddenly stopped. Did she really dare call on the Earl of Marlborough, hero of Maastricht, victor of the Monmouth rebellion and former Privy Councilor to the King?

Charlie answered the question by grabbing her wrist. "Hold! 'Tis madness!" He swung Eden around effortlessly, oblivious to her look of angry surprise.

"Leave me go, Charlie!" she commanded. "You've no right to follow me like a sick pup!"

" 'Tis sick wit' love for ye, I am," groaned Charlie, pulling Eden close. "I'm wanting ye for m' wife, t' sleep in m' bed, t' bear m' babes ...." He buried his face in the masses of claret-colored hair, and his big, clumsy hands clutched at her waist and hips. He groaned again and rained loud kisses on her forehead and temples.

"Stop it, Charlie!" Eden cried, pounding her fists in vain against his thick upper arms. His fumbling hands had found her breasts. Eden pulled sharply away from him, but managed only to gain enough breathing room to look up and note the strange glint in his eyes. Instinctively she recognized sheer animal lust, and she shuddered in his grasp.

"So fair, so fair," he muttered, hauling her against him, his mouth searching for hers. Eden screamed. She didn't hear the door open behind her or the curses in a foreign tongue. It was only when that voice rose to a bellow and Charlie stiffened like a pikestaff that Eden realized someone else was in the narrow passageway. Slowly, with obvious regret, Charlie relinquished her and backed away.

"Max!" gasped Eden, staring at the Norse god.

He was taller than Charlie by half a head and possessed an air of uncompromising authority. His hand shot out to snatch Charlie's shirt collar. The glance he bestowed on Eden was fleeting yet curious. "I'm not accustomed to having maidens ravished outside my door," he said in a calm, deep voice tinged with a slight accent. "Unless, of course, I'm doing the ravishing." He gave Charlie a little shake. "Get out. Now."

Charlie did just that, and Eden almost felt sorry for him. But she was relieved as well as puzzled. It would not have surprised her if this intimidating foreigner had sent her packing, too.

"It is you, isn't it?" the man called Max asked, his big frame casually leaning against the door.

"Well," replied Eden with some spirit, "I'm certainly me. Who else did you expect?"

Max appeared to reflect, and Eden took advantage of the respite to study him more closely. He was probably in his mid-twenties, with high, sharp cheekbones that suggested a hungry gauntness. Perhaps it was the enigmatic quality of his hazel eyes that gave such an impression, rather than any want of flesh. The strong jaw and chin were clean-shaven. The nose was almost straight but very likely had been broken at least once. The heavy brows were a shade darker than the sun-streaked hair with its unruly off-center part, and the wide mouth looked as if it had forgotten how to smile.

"I expected no one," he said at last, a reply that baffled Eden. "Indeed, I marvel that you had the nerve to come. Next time I suggest you leave your loutish swain on the doorstep."

"He's not my swain," Eden retorted, passing a hand over her face and noting with dismay that Charlie had left a charcoal smudge on her cheek. "I tried to discourage him."

"Without success." Max stood up straight, shaking out his broad shoulders in the plain if well-cut riding habit. Perhaps, Eden thought, elevating his status, he was Marlborough's secretary or valet. And maybe he wasn't Norse, but German or Dutch. She didn't realize that she was staring until Max snapped his fingers and made her jump.

"Well? Are you in a trance?"

"I'm in a quandary," Eden replied. "Is His Lordship available?"

Instead of answering directly, Max wheeled to the next door, opened it and went inside. She tried to peer into the room, but the opening was too narrow and the light too dim. She could barely make out masculine voices. Trying not to resent Max's patronizing manner, she reminded herself that at least he had stopped insulting her. Obviously, Marlborough had reprimanded him.

The door swung open and Max slipped into the passageway, a frown etched on his long face. "He's still in pain, but he wishes to speak with you." The look he gave Eden was frankly unenthusiastic.

"I know better than to tire out a sick person," Eden declared with a toss of her head. "Indeed, there are few people in Smarden who know better than I how to attend the infirm." She gathered up her skirts and lifted her chin as she went around Max. "I could even," she added with a sharp glance over her shoulder, "do it in Kensington."

"*At* Kensington. I referred to the palace, not the district." His tone was ironic.

Eden gripped the doorframe, considered delivering a stinging rebuke and once again reminded herself that Marlborough's well-being was more important than his valet's boorish tongue. Without so much as another glance at Max, she went into the bedchamber and carefully closed the door behind her.

The shutters were latched against the pale winter light, and a single candle burned on a small nightstand next to the bed where the Earl of Marlborough reclined, dressed in shirt, trousers and waistcoat of fine if unembellished fabric. Without his fur-lined cloak and modish three-cornered hat, he was as plainly garbed as his valet—or secretary—and as unprepossessing as Curate Bixby. In one hand he held a damp cloth, and with the other he motioned for Eden to sit in the cane-backed chair next to the bed. While his gray-green eyes were alert, his face was haggard. Eden could see the years more clearly now, and guessed him to be in his forties.

"How kind of you to come," Marlborough said after Eden sat down and began loosening the ties of her cloak. "I so hated to rush off, but this damnable headache overcame me as soon as I walked through your door."

Eden felt like telling the Earl that being under the Berenger roof was sufficient to give anyone a headache, but she held her tongue. "Have you tried the young stems of bittersweet? They're said to cure head pain."

Marlborough's smile was not without warmth. "You have an extraordinary knowledge of healing. Your foster mother's doing, I believe."

"She's quite skilled," Eden said without any grudge, though in fact she had always resented the attention Madame Berenger lavished on Smarden's sick while skimping on affection for her foster daughter.

Marlborough sat up, his stockinged feet hanging over the edge of the bed. Eden noticed that he seemed quite unruffled entertaining a young maid in such an informal atmosphere. "Your rearing has not been without some benefit," he remarked, picking up a tiny vial from the rickety nightstand and splashing a few drops of opaque liquid into a pewter cup. "I shan't ask you to share this wretched stuff, nor would you prescribe it, perhaps. There is wine in the cupboard, I believe. Prices in Kent are shockingly high for any brew save beer or cider."

Eden politely declined his offer. She was too anxious to hear what he had to say to waste time with further social amenities. Having tossed off the draft and made a face, the Earl got to his feet, casually tucking in his cream-colored shirt and flexing his neck muscles. "When I was a young man," he began gazing into the shadows, "I had to make my own way in the world. I was born John Churchill, and my father was an ardent Royalist who lost everything when the first King Charles was deposed and executed." He paused. There was a touch of regret but no sign of resentment in his expression.

"Later, after Oliver Cromwell died and King Charles was restored, this country rebelled against the harsh Puritan yoke. As will happen, an era of great licentiousness followed." The gray-green gaze was sympathetic. "You must know all this, my dear."

Eden inclined her head. "Some of it. But," she admitted candidly, "I'm not very astute at history."

The Earl looked genuinely perplexed. His interest in the affairs of his native land was so all-consuming that he found it hard to accept another's indifference. But being a tolerant man, he shrugged and took up his tale. "Into this decadent society, I brought my hopes and ambitions. A most influential— and beautiful—lady sponsored me. Her name was Barbara Villiers, Lady Castlemaine, the Duchess of Cleveland. She had been King Charles's mistress for years and had borne him several children."

Eden recalled that memorable day she had watched King Charles riding to Tunbridge Wells. Had Lady Castlemaine been one of those beauties in the royal cavalcade? Eden thought not—the name evoked a more distant era from the earlier days of Charles's reign. "I have heard of Lady Castlemaine," Eden put in, lest Marlborough think her an ignorant bumpkin. "She was very promiscuous and drank too much."

Giving Eden a rueful glance, Marlborough sat down on the bed. "Everything you've heard about her is probably true," he conceded, his face once again taking on that strained look. The fire in the grate was smoking, the glass in the window was sweating profusely, and the room had grown very close with the odor of medicinal herbs. Eden stifled a yawn and tried to keep her gaze level with Marlborough's. His anecdotes were entertaining, but not the reason for which Eden had braved the barriers of social custom.

She wanted information about her parents, not court gossip that was at least twenty years old.

"You see, Eden," Marlborough said, taking her hand in his, "Lady Castlemaine showered not only wealth and perquisites on me, but her affection as well." His mouth twisted slightly and his gaze turned melancholy. "In return, I gave her two daughters. The elder girl is a nun in France." Marlborough's grip tightened. "The younger child, my dear, is you."

Chapter Two

To the astonishment of them both, Eden laughed—a clear, sharp sound that seemed to stir the room's heavy air. The Earl's grip slackened and his forehead creased. Yet for all his bold manner in battle, he was not an impatient man. Composing his features, he waited for Eden to regain control.

Moments later, with much chagrin, Eden's shoulders slumped. "How strange," she murmured. "For years I've envisioned my father as … someone else." Her ebony eyes glistened with untapped emotion. "Are you certain? Why do you think I'm the … your child?"

Having unburdened himself, Marlborough relaxed, once again appearing younger. "I shan't try to prettify my own actions. That last night I spent in milady's arms was a mere convenience for both of us. I was in London for a brief stay, and never being one to waste money, I accepted the invitation to sleep under her roof." He averted his eyes briefly, then gave Eden the ghost of a grin. "Naturally, I ended up in her bed. I was courting my dear Sarah and had sworn over and over again that my liaison with the Duchess had ended. Then, early in the new year, I was sent to France to meet with King Louis on Charles's behalf. Barbara had flounced off to Paris the previous autumn. Imagine my shock when I learned she was about to give birth. It was most embarrassing—indeed, it could have been disastrous to my marriage plans with Sarah."

Eden was still trying to take in the enormity of what the Earl had told her. The details seemed unimportant. Distractedly, she nodded. "I should imagine," she said vaguely.

"Sarah can be the sweetest, kindest, gentlest creature in the world," Marlborough asserted, his face brightening at the very mention of his wife's name, "but she can also be jealous. Like the rest of the world, she knew about my first daughter by Barbara. But if she had discovered I'd not kept faith with her after my avowals to break off with the Duchess, I might have lost her forever. To make matters worse, my father was insisting on a match with the Sedley heiress. Sarah's family was as poor as mine, and it seemed more sensible for me to wed for money rather than love." His expression turned wry. "The problem was, you see, that Barbara wasn't inclined to take on yet another child. She was no longer young, and had seen to the other six, after her fashion. To avoid scandal, I agreed to take you."

Eden was trying to imagine the tiny baby, lying innocently in a cradle in Paris, while an infamous courtesan and an ambitious army officer confronted each other with more thought for themselves than for her. Yet Marlborough was with her now. Apparently his conscience had caught up with him. Eden gave a plaintive little shake of her head.

The Earl patted her hand. "I know, I know, it sounds most callous. Yet … there it is. I did my best, finding a suitable family to raise you. The Berengers seemed ideal—solid, hardworking, honest people who were about to emigrate to England. And after Sarah and I had started our family, I'd tell her about you."

Eden looked at Marlborough expectantly, but he was grimacing. "Life doesn't always turn out as we plan. Sarah and I had grave disappointments at first. We finally had our wonderful children, but at the time, I couldn't bear to flaunt you. And then, somehow, the years went by."

So they had, thought Eden, there in the house on the Beult with her silly dreams of being a royal princess and the taunts of her foster family and the sense of never belonging to anyone. And all the while her father had been not a king but a famous noble, and her mother a wanton courtesan with a passel of bastards. It was not the portrait Eden would have painted, but, to paraphrase Marlborough, there it was.

The Earl had finally let go of her hands and was brushing at his hair. "There can be no doubt that you are the child I gave to the Berengers nineteen years ago. Even then your hair was an amazing color, and unlike most babies, you had dark eyes when you were born." A wistful smile touched his lips. "You may not believe me, but I've carried the memory of you in my heart."

Eden did believe him. The Earl of Marlborough seemed to wear integrity as easily as he wore his fine linen shirt. But there were still many questions to be answered. "Having waited so long to find me, why now? Why ever, for that matter?" She could not restrain her customary candor even for an earl.

The gray-green eyes flickered. "Duty. Guilt. Curiosity, too. I suspect." He shrugged, then his eyes seemed to ignite, as if a fire had been lighted behind them. The transformation was so subtle yet startling that Eden winced.

Marlborough was taking a deep breath. "I need you. I need a partisan."

Eden wrinkled her nose. "A partisan? But what of your friends?"

He didn't answer her directly. "I've been on the outs with the King for some time," the Earl explained, rising from the bed and going to a cupboard, where he foraged among stacks of linen and blankets. At last he emerged with a dusty bottle of red wine, poured some into his pewter cup then scanned the room for another drinking vessel. Eden forestalled him, feeling it imperative that she remain clearheaded during this extraordinary conversation.

Marlborough stood by the cupboard and sipped slowly. "For a time I was imprisoned. King William's anger was unjustified. I'd been absolutely loyal from the start. I was even one of those who had asked him and Queen Mary to succeed Charles's brother, James." He glanced at Eden. "How much of this do you already know?"

Her face was blank. "I'm woefully ignorant, sir." Eden had not had much interest in the court or politics since King Charles had died. The Catholic James and his Dutch successor, William, had held no appeal for her.

Marlborough made a gesture with one hand, as if absolving Eden for her lack of knowledge. "I was accused of writing an infamous letter to inform James about an invasion at Camaret Bay. A ship would be waiting to bring him to England where I, along with other alleged Jacobite supporters, would put him on the throne and somehow dispose of William. The letter was dispatched, so the wretched tale ran, through the Prince of Nassau-Dillenburg's offices. All a fraud, but William of Orange believed it. I can't think why." Marlborough looked genuinely perplexed, as if gullibility and perfidy were strangers to his nature.

Some scrap of recollection surfaced in Eden's mind. "The letter was real enough, though, wasn't it? Perhaps this Prince of ...." She tripped over the unfamiliar name. "Could he—"

Marlborough laughed at the mere suggestion. "Sooth, no, he's a faithful servant to Orange, a kinsman of William's. And," he added with a diffident shrug, "a loyal friend to me."

Eden could feel a draft blowing through the shutters, carrying with it the smell of charcoal burning somewhere beyond the village. The Crockers, perhaps, though young Charlie now seemed like an echo from the past. "Where is this bogus letter about Camaret Bay?" For that matter, wondered Eden, where was Camaret Bay? Her geography was as deplorable as her history.

"I've no idea," the Earl responded. "I never saw it. If such a forgery exists, it's no doubt in safekeeping at James's puppet court outside Paris, at St Germain." He spoke mildly but was frowning at the candle, which had almost guttered out in its pewter stand. "How much would they charge for extra light here?"

The question caught Eden off guard. For a great lord, Marlborough seemed overly concerned with economy. Since he had been paying the Berengers for her keep all these years, she found his attitude inconsistent. "Master Bunn is a gracious host," she said. "Tell me, sir, have political misfortunes straitened your circumstances?"

The Earl didn't evade the candid inquiry. "As I mentioned, I grew up in virtual poverty, a state that taught me to be cautious with money. Most people are too careless. They allow their wants to exceed their needs. Naturally, the loss of my army command was a blow. Our little family would have managed badly had it not been for my wife's post as lady to the Princess Anne."

"Am I a want or a need?" Eden asked bluntly.

Small lines showed up between Marlborough's eyebrows. "Both, it would seem. More to the point, you're an investment. I firmly believe in investments."

"Oh." Eden considered his words and grew uneasy. "And how might that be?"

The Earl passed a hand across his forehead, as if charting the path of his headache. "Let me explain. Being a Dutchman, King William surrounds himself with his native countrymen. It's natural enough, but it's a mistake politically. He's a strange little fellow who, some say, prefers the company of men to women. Yet he had a mistress while the Queen was alive. Betty Villiers. Do you know the name?"

Eden didn't. She was feeling more and more inadequate as the minutes passed.

"When Queen Mary died," Marlborough continued, setting his cup on the floor, "William's conscience began to trouble him. He sent Betty away. It was probably not a sound decision for either King or mistress, but there it is. And now I believe His Majesty is a lonely man."

"No doubt." Eden couldn't reconcile Marlborough's sympathy for the King with the estrangement between them. Either the Earl was an unusual man, or the nobility possessed a different set of emotions.

"So," Marlborough went on, "it has occurred to me, what better consolation for a poor widower than a beautiful young woman to share his life?" He took three purposeful steps toward Eden. "What better future for my daughter than to be the mistress of a king?"

Eden had to grasp the arms of the chair. Her Huguenot upbringing revolted at such a suggestion. She stared incredulously at the Earl, who clearly found her reaction odd.

"Surely you don't consider my proposal shocking? Your mother was mistress to King Charles. My sister Arabella was mistress to James. It's an honor in royal circles, as revered a position as any other."

Trying to recover, Eden struggled to her feet and faced the Earl squarely.

"Milord, I must be frank. Everything you have told me this past hour has the potential to turn my life upside down. I am honored to be your daughter, but," she stated primly, "I have been brought up to respect my virtue. I will gladly be your partisan, but I'll be no man's courtesan. The very idea unsettles my soul."

Eden's words aroused no sign of dismay from the Earl. He had poured himself another cup of wine, but after a single sip, put it aside. "One of the terms of your upbringing was that you'd be educated." His smile was wry. "Obviously, you've learned to think for yourself."

"My, yes," Eden said, wondering what book learning had to do with morality. "Don't think me ungrateful or indifferent to your predicament, but …." She stopped, alarmed by the sudden change in Marlborough. His forehead was damp with perspiration; his face had turned an alarming shade of gray.

"Summon Max," he muttered, stumbling toward the bed.

Disturbed by his relapse, Eden pivoted on one foot and made for the passageway. She called out only once before Max responded.

"What's wrong now?" he asked, the top of his head almost even with the door's lintel.

"His Lordship's taken ill again. He asked for you." Eden realized that there was resentment in her tone. She was Marlborough's daughter, and he knew that she was skilled in the medical arts, yet he had asked for this arrogant foreigner. "I trust you can cure him this time," she said as Max moved swiftly to the Earl's room.

"I wouldn't have to if you didn't keep giving him a headache," Max shot over his shoulder.

Annoyed, she stomped after him but tried to cool her temper when she saw the Earl's misery. He was lying on the bed, one arm flung over his face. He didn't acknowledge their presence, but waited patiently while Max mixed and measured medicine with the skill of a chemist.

Eden's concern for the man she was beginning to think of as her father prevented her from interfering or asking questions. Instead, she waited by the cupboard while Max tended the Earl. The younger man then checked on the shutters, poked back the glowing embers in the hearth and blew out the only remaining candle. With a quick movement he signaled for Eden to follow him to his quarters next door.

"Beer?" Hoisting an enormous tankard, he indicated that Eden should join him at the square wooden table. "It's a local brew, not as good as Dutch, but it slakes the thirst when all is said and done." Max spoke nonchalantly, clearly taking his master's ill health in stride.

Having been raised by a cider maker, Eden had never tasted beer, though she'd sampled the hard drink Monsieur Berenger brewed each autumn from a portion of his apples. "Kent has some fine beer makers," Eden declared loyally. "Yes, I should like a drink."

Max poured with apparent recklessness, but topped off the mug perfectly, with the foaming suds just barely lapping the rim. Eden took a big swallow and let the beer roll around in her mouth. It tasted bitter and was too cold. She preferred cider, but refused to admit as much to Max.

"So," he said, putting his tankard on the table, "what has His Lordship told you?"

Eden shot him a haughty look. "Ask His Lordship. When you've cured him."

Shrugging, Max leaned back in the chair, his long, booted legs reaching to the opposite side of the table. "I know what he intended to tell you. I marvel that you're so calm." Despite Max's casual pose, his hazel eyes were disconcertingly intense.

Eden's full mouth pursed primly. She was unaware that a thin line of foam adorned her upper lip. "I'm not easily ruffled," she replied, and wondered why Max was suddenly smiling. "Well, do you find my encounter with the Earl a source of fun?" Taking another drink from the mug, Eden tried to look severe.

Max rubbed at his upper lip in an effort to hide his amusement. In reflex response, Eden did the same, and discovered her finger dampened by beer suds. Before she could express her irritation, Max replied, "I find anything to do with His Lordship of consequence. My future is tied in with his, after all." His long, chiseled face clouded. "The real question is, what do *you* think?"

Eden lifted her eyebrows. "That's a matter between His Lordship and me." Draining her mug, she slid it across to Max. "More. Please." She tilted her head to one side as she watched him pour, then took the mug and swung it to her lips so rashly that it spilled onto the table. Paying no heed as Max got out a handkerchief to wipe up the puddle, Eden took another drink.

Her gaze wavered as she tried to study Max's face with those intriguing cheekbones, that slightly crooked nose, the mobile mouth and the strong chin. Romantic, she thought fleetingly, though less so in a valet than in a lord. If she, Eden Berenger, was really Eden Churchill, then she was an aristocrat, far above the common class. The tedious routine of the Berenger household, the spiteful gibes of her foster family, the bleak prospect of life with a village boor would all vanish. She could even tell people like Max to go to the devil. She'd enjoy that ….

Eden swallowed more beer and closed her eyes, envisioning velvet and satin, ribbons and laces, sapphires and pearls. The gilded palaces she'd dreamed of as a child, those turreted castles and handsome manor houses flitted across the stage of her imagination. It must be true. Hadn't Eden always known that her father was someone special? She righted herself in the chair and emptied the mug. But this time when she pushed it to Max, he gave her a dubious look.

"Are you sure?"

"Certainly." Eden's haughty manner was flawed by a hiccup.

Max, who had just poured himself another mugful, remained skeptical, but finally relented.

"Thank you, Max," said Eden, in a patronizing tone. She smiled not so much at him as at her prospects, which were growing rosier with every drop of beer. "Comfort, yes—licentiousness, no." She shook her head and hummed a bit to herself. "It's wrong. And King or not, he's old." Taking another drink, she tried to fix her wavering gaze on Max's face. Handsome, she thought, incredibly so, and he knows it. No doubt he's bedded most of the wenches in Marlborough's household. Now if King William looked more like this Dutch valet …. Eden licked foam from her lips and giggled.

"Holy St. Hubert." Max was scowling as he reached out to grasp Eden's mug. Jack had proved lucky with the girl's looks, especially that insouciant quality that went beyond mere beauty. But in Max's opinion, her intelligence—or at least her judgment—was suspect. She had much to learn if she was to become an asset to the Earl. "Hold, mistress," Max commanded. "His Lordship will be annoyed when he discovers his protégée is tipsy."

But Eden had both hands clenched around the mug. "Give it back," she insisted, her dark eyes steely if unfocused. "I'm still thirsty."

Max had the mug by the handle. He appeared to surrender with a shrug, but when Eden attempted to lift her drink, he jerked it from her fingers. She lunged at him, but her elbow skidded in a pool of beer. Max burst into laughter, the handsome head thrown back.

Furious, Eden sat up, making a vain effort to recapture her composure. "You stole my beer!" she accused. "Give it back, you basty nastard!"

"You *what*?" Max could barely get the words out between hoots of laughter. He wiped his eyes, but was still grinning when he stood and placed both mugs high on a plate rail, out of Eden's reach. When he turned to face her, the grin was gone. Instead, he wore an expression of surprise, as if laughter had become an unfamiliar exercise.

Eden, however, recognized his reaction only in some dim corner of her mind. She was still furious with the Dutchman, incensed that he would have the effrontery to refuse her request. It appeared that he knew who she was; Marlborough must confide in his manservant. Surely Max ought to oblige his master's daughter, whether she was illegitimate or not.

"Max, you are a swine." She put her hands on the table to steady herself and stood up. "You've no right to take away my beer!" One arm flew out in the direction of the plate rail. "Give it back! Now!"

Any trace of humor faded from Max's face. Eden Berenger Churchill was a silly chit, unsuited for anything but life with a country dolt. A pity, since Marlborough had counted on her help. That disarming frankness would only be detrimental in the rarefied atmosphere of the court. And while her allure was undeniable, at least for a village lass, her utter lack of sophistication would prove catastrophic. Max almost felt sorry for her, but knew he must harden his heart. Otherwise, he might give the Earl bad advice.

He took four deliberate strides toward Eden and, without exerting any effort, shoved her into the chair. "Sit. Be quiet. Wait for His Lordship." But when Eden popped to her feet as soon as he stepped away, his patience snapped.

Grabbing her by the shoulders, he gave her a sharp shake. "Behave!" The hazel eyes were fierce. "Are you always this witless? Or this drunk?"

"Drunk?" squealed Eden, squirming in his grasp. The big hands seemed to scorch her flesh. It was an odd sensation, yet not painful. Fleetingly, she wished her mind weren't so muddled. Too much had happened all at once, that was the problem, and if only she could sleep for a little while, it could all be sorted out ....

Somehow, her head was resting against Max's upper arm, and while he still had his hands on her shoulders, he wasn't shaking her anymore. The room was very quiet except for the wind rattling the casements. Cautiously, Eden looked up. From this perspective, Max's face was all sharp planes and angles, formidable as the Alps. For one giddy moment she had an irresistible urge to touch the long, lean jaw that jutted out above the linen shirt collar.

"I don't drink. I never drink beer. I never had until ...." She gasped as she realized his hazel eyes seemed to be devouring her. Was he still angry? Was he trying to frighten her into proper behavior? No, it was something else, a foreign emotion that Eden had glimpsed somewhere before but couldn't quite recall ....

"Never mind." Max's words came out in a growl. Before he could say anything further, noises erupted in the hallway. Puzzled, Max turned toward the door, though his hands remained on Eden's shoulders. A woman called out above the deeper voices of some men, then a door banged.

"Jack!" exclaimed Max, letting go of Eden. He grabbed his sword and dashed into the passageway.

Trying to shake off the fog of drink, Eden followed. In the corridor, Mistress Bunn was berating a half dozen uniformed men who were already charging into Marlborough's bedchamber.

"King's men," she said under her breath to Max as he tried to cross the threshold.

Three of the soldiers had the Earl of Marlborough under guard. While his face was still haggard, his color had returned and his composure seemed unruffled. "My waistcoat, please," he said in his usual mild tone. "Surely you don't expect to arrest me in a half-dressed state at this time of year?"

One of the soldiers hurriedly brought Marlborough's waistcoat, along with his hat and cloak as well. To Eden's surprise, the man bowed deferentially before handing over the apparel.

Another man—the senior officer, judging from his age and amount of decoration—was not so obsequious. "What of these others?" he demanded, gesturing with a pudgy hand at Max and Eden.

Marlborough's gray-green eyes flickered over the pair with feigned indifference. "Leave them be," he said. "They're of no consequence."

The commander's eyes rested on Eden, unabashedly ogling her engaging if disheveled appearance. Then he raised his eyes to Max, scanning the great distance from the top of his blond head to the tips of his booted feet. "You're armed. Hand over that sword."

With a shrug, Max obliged. The commanding officer still stared hard at the tall foreigner. "I don't know," he muttered. "I could swear I've seen this one at …."

She wasn't precisely sober, but Eden's state of inebriation had ebbed considerably. "We're servants," she blurted, jabbing at Max. "This here's Max the Dutchman, His Lordship's valet."

Eden's affected county accent might have fooled the pudgy soldier, but Max's impressive size gave him away. "Owr …" the commander rumbled, casting a baleful glance at Marlborough. "Do ye take me for a fool?" He pointed a stubby finger at Max. "I know this one, it's His Highness, Prince Maximilian of Nassau-Dillenburg."

"Ta! And I'm the Queen of Spain!" retorted Eden, clapping her hands and noting with relief that they made contact. She looked at Max and made a wry face. "Great heavens," she whispered, "how inventive is this soldier!"

Max's first reaction was to ignore Eden's remark, but the color was rising in his high cheekbones. "It was my parents who were so inventive, God rest their souls." Without further ado, he moved toward Marlborough and his captors. "Never mind, Jack," he said with a careless lift of his shoulders. "It's an honor to be arrested in your company. By the way, what's the charge?"

Marlborough was adjusting the *steinkirk* at his neck. "A fancy one, I'm afraid, Max. High treason." A truncated laugh escaped his lips. "Someone thinks I tried to kill the King."

Eden's brain was reeling from more than the beer. It had been a day of shocks, and this latest blow rendered her speechless. All she could do was stare blankly at the departing backs of Marlborough and the alleged Prince Maximilian. But even as she tried to sort out the jumble of astonishing events, a strong hand took her by the wrist.

"You, too, Mistress," growled a florid-faced soldier not much taller than Eden. "For all we know, you *are* the Queen of Spain."

It was useless to protest. Eden's world had spun out of control. Without a word, she let herself be hauled away, a suspected conspirator in a plot to murder the King of England. In less than two hours, she had gone from being the unwanted child in a Huguenot household to the daughter of an English earl. But instead of going to a warm welcome at court, Eden Berenger Churchill was headed for prison.

Chapter Three

EDEN'S FIRST GLIMPSE OF LONDON came after dark, through patchy fog, as a cumbersome barge pulled up to the Tower's infamous Traitors' Gate. Until they reached the river, the journey from Kent had been made on horseback, with little opportunity for conversation. Never at ease in the saddle, Eden was sure she'd be killed before they reached London. At their only resting stop, the Earl of Marlborough had expressed his brief, if sincere, apologies to Eden.

"I'm sorry, my dear," he'd said, with fatigue in his eyes. "I had no idea this was going to happen. The King thinks I came to Kent to light a bonfire at Dover, signaling that an assassination had taken place. Absurd, of course, but there it is."

It was more than absurd to Eden, it was incredible. But then it had been such a turbulent day, with one astounding revelation after another. That Max should turn out to be a Dutch or Flemish prince made Eden feel mortified at the way she'd treated him. Between her high-handed manner and her drunken behavior, she understood why he thought she was a foolish country simpleton.

But regret was replaced by fear as Eden was propelled up the lichen-covered steps to the Tower. In front of her she could make out Max's blond head, turned to gold by a torch hanging on the dank wall. Eden paused and shuddered on the top stair. Terrifying tales of the ancient prison had given her nightmares as a child. Briefly she closed her eyes, wondering if she'd ever taste freedom again.

A rough hand shoved her forward, and she almost slipped on the slimy stones. In a weary daze, Eden watched a dignified Tower official speak in low tones with Marlborough. The exchange was civil, even amicable. And then the Earl was taken away, while she and Prince Maximilian were led in another direction. The corridors and stairways seemed to wind on forever, like an endless stone maze. At last a cell was opened and Max disappeared inside. Eden felt a surge of desperation and strained forward, but her guard put out a beefy arm.

"In here," he muttered, gesturing toward an open cell.

She froze, seeing only darkness and feeling a raw draft at her back. Her captor cuffed her smartly on the temple, and Eden stumbled then lurched into the cell and slumped to the floor as the iron door clanked behind her.

She sat for a long time, huddled against the cold, feeling miserable and alone. Finally, Eden struggled to her feet and looked out through the narrow barred window. Cold, wintry stars studded the blackness of the night, and though there was no moon, the fog had lifted so that she could make out an expanse of grass patched with snow. Eden saw clusters of buildings where lights burned behind some of the windows. Tower Green, she guessed, and wondered dolefully how many hapless souls had ended their lives on the notorious block. Directly below, two men in flowing capes moved leisurely along the limewalk. Their freedom made Eden acutely aware of her confinement.

Just as the church bells tolled eight o'clock, the sound of the cell door opening made her jump. A guard stood before her, holding a tray with two covered dishes and a mug of ale. Eden stared at the repast, then turned away. She was ravenous, but the sight of the ale upset her stomach.

"I prefer water," she said, her back turned. The guard, a squat man with eyebrows like a crow's wings, had set the tray down on a little stool.

"It's ale ye got and ale ye'll drink," he asserted, starting to leave but pausing when he saw Eden whirl around in annoyance. "Well, who might ye really be? The Prince's doxy?" He was rocking back and forth, boldly studying Eden with voracious eyes.

"Hardly." She held her head high, her back straight. "Surely there is water in the river?"

The man cocked his head. "There is. But it don't bring itself in here. What'll ye pay for a cup, Princess?"

Eden shot him a scornful look. "Go away."

The guard snorted. "Fancy, eh?" Someone was coming along the passageway and he quickly retreated from the cell. Eden didn't turn around until the sound of his footsteps had faded.

She ate little of the underdone mutton, less of the stale bread and drank none of the ale. The church bells chimed nine and ten and then eleven. At last Eden lay down on her lumpy pallet, her heavy cape wrapped securely around her. Despite her fatigue, she couldn't sleep. Somewhere out there, Eden thought dismally, there is music and laughter and excitement …. There is all of London and the court and the King.

There is freedom, too, Eden told herself just before she fell asleep. The one thing she had possessed upon waking that morning in Smarden was freedom. In the hours that had followed, glittering promises of a new life had been dangled before her. But as London's lights dimmed, Eden's future seemed as empty as the night. She slept dreamlessly, as if the theft of her liberty had also robbed her of illusion.

EDEN HAD BEEN AWAKE FOR some time when the squat guard showed up with what passed for breakfast in the Tower of London. A crust, a piece of cheese and another mug of ale were placed before her. Eden gazed bleakly at the unappetizing meal but said nothing.

The guard was not so reticent. "Well? Might ye be accustomed to gold plate and crystal goblets? Eh?" Eden chose not to reply. But the guard wasn't giving up so easily. "No curiosity and no appetite! Tsk! Tsk!"

When she remained unresponsive, he touched the claret-colored waves of hair at her neck. "Eh, doxy, pretty doxy …."

Eden pulled away and held up a hand. "Wait!" The seed of an idea was taking root in her mind. She gestured at the breakfast tray. "I asked for water last night, I ask again this morn." The haughty glance she threw him was softened by the hint of invitation in her eyes. Noting slow if unmistakable comprehension spread across the guard's blunt features, Eden grew specific: "A large amount of water, in a great heavy basin, so that I may not only drink, but also—" she flicked her tongue over her lips in the most provocative manner she could muster "—bathe."

"Ah!" The guard all but danced at the prospect, then he was gone, scurrying down the passageway.

Eden moved on wobbly legs, trying to make herself limber by the time the guard returned. It never occurred to her that the scheme she'd just concocted was wildly imprudent. For Eden, brought up on the strict Huguenot code of right and wrong, the King's men had acted unjustly by imprisoning Marlborough and Prince Maximilian. Clearly, neither was guilty of plotting against his sovereign lord. Marlborough had said as much, and it must be true. Even more outrageous was her inclusion in the arrest. Thus, since the night had passed with no apparent effort to release them, Eden had decided to take matters into her own hands.

The guard was panting with a mixture of exertion and anticipation when he arrived with a much-dented tin tub and a big pewter jug. Fighting repugnance, Eden reached out to take the water. But the guard had no mind to wait for the niceties. He banged the jug down so hard that some of its contents splashed onto the rushes. Eden's attempt to play the coquette was foiled. The guard lunged across the narrow room and fell upon her, almost knocking them both into the tub. Jarred, Eden gasped for air and was about to try reasoning with the wretched man when he began ripping at the muslin of her bodice.

"Hold," she breathed, fighting to keep panic out of her voice. "I must bathe first!"

The guard's answer was to rip her gown on the diagonal, then paw at her thin chemise. Eden wiggled beneath him, trying to escape his greedy hands. The game had gone badly; her inexperience had disqualified her from the start. The protest that rose to her lips took on a shrill note as the guard yanked down the chemise to reveal her full breasts.

"Damn!" he whistled between the spaces in his teeth, "now there's a lovely sight!" To prove his point, he covered her breasts with his sweating palms, squeezing and flattening them as if they were bread dough. Eden's cries were strangled in her throat; her entire body throbbed with revulsion. Was this what men and women did when the kissing was done? She couldn't imagine it, couldn't equate such bestial savagery with the smug faces of Cybele and Genevieve after their wedding nights.

Eden stretched out one arm so tautly she was sure it would snap. But a great, straining effort permitted contact with the pewter jug. Squirming under the guard, she wrapped her fingers around the handle and brought it down on his bald head with a resounding thud.

She did not see the stupefied expression on his face, for the water cascaded over them both. His groping fingers fell away, his squat body went limp, and Eden kicked free. Struggling to her feet, she brushed the water out of her eyes with one hand while she tried to fasten her bodice with the other. At her feet lay the guard, a nasty red bump swelling on the top of his head. She marshaled her thoughts, then leaned down to remove the heavy iron loop that held several keys. She hurried out into the passageway and was relieved to find that it was empty.

She had no plans other than to escape the guard and her cell. Having accomplished both, she puzzled over what to do next. Locking the door behind her with the proper key, she decided to turn to her right. The guard had come from the opposite direction; his post must be avoided.

Moving on tiptoe, she noted that the three other cells in this part of the Tower were unoccupied, though she knew that Max was being held somewhere nearby. She hesitated, unsure of where to go next, then froze in place. From around the corner of the corridor's bleak stone walls, she could hear the approach of brisk footsteps.

Terrified, Eden glanced around her. There were no hiding places, no privy stairs, no recesses of any kind. She would have run, but it was too late. The other person came around the corner, all but tripping over her cringing figure.

"Eden!" Max grabbed her by the arm to make sure she didn't topple over. "What in the name of St. Hubert are you doing here?"

Eden swayed, then put a hand on his chest to steady herself. "Well, now." She swallowed hard, feeling awkward in her torn dress, embarrassed by the disrespect she had shown him earlier, but most of all, conscious of his solid presence, which she found surprisingly reassuring. Her long lashes dipped with chagrin. "I escaped."

Max was staring at the top of her head. "So it seems." He checked an urge to laugh, and marveled at himself. This grim fortress was scarcely the place for merriment, yet even within these cold walls the silly chit managed to provide more amusement than he'd known in the past four years. To his dismay, he found that it took an effort not to place his big hand over the small one that rested on his chest.

She was looking at him with those wide, dark eyes. "And you? You are no longer locked up, either?"

"That's true." The high cheekbones displayed just the hint of a flush. "They released me. There are, it seems, some advantages to being a foreigner in England."

Eden's hand fell away. "You mean that His Lordship is not free?"

Max was vaguely embarrassed. "My ... friends have not been able to secure Jack's release. As soon as I'm out of this wretched place, I shall see to it." He paused, securing his cloak more tightly around his neck. "Indeed, I must be off to get this matter straightened out."

"Wait!" Eden all but pounced, stopping Max in the act of turning away. "You can't leave yet." Was he abandoning her because she had been so pert? In truth, it would serve her right. "I have these," she said, brandishing the keys she'd purloined from the guard. "Can't we free His Lordship and rectify this injustice?"

With one swift movement, Max snatched away the keys. "This isn't Kent," he said grimly, ignoring Eden's spurt of resentment. "You'd only make a bad situation worse. You don't understand court politics."

Eden considered briefly. He was right, and she had no choice but to agree. After all, Marlborough had expressed great confidence in the Prince, both as a friend and patriot. Though she had known Max but briefly, despite his aloofness there was something about the man that evoked her trust. "Please," she begged, a tremor in her voice, "then at least see that I get out of here safely."

Max shifted his considerable weight and looked anxious. Accepting responsibility for Jack's illegitimate daughter made him uneasy. Max had never been convinced that the Earl's plan was feasible, and after meeting Eden, he questioned her ability to play the part Marlborough had written for her. Yet she was an appealing little creature, and he could hardly abandon her to an unknown fate in the Tower. "Yes, of course. Jack would want me to," he added, more to himself than to Eden. "All right," he said brusquely. "Let's hurry. The guards might try to detain you, no matter what I tell them."

With a sigh of relief Eden clutched at her torn dress, gathered up her cloak and hurried after Prince Maximilian. She felt like a newborn foal chasing a sure-footed stallion. With a pang of remorse at the thought of her father still languishing in a cell somewhere inside the Tower, Eden came out into the sunlight and took in a dizzying breath of freedom.

UNDER A PALE WINTER SUN, the tumult of London sprawled westward into the City itself, and beyond to their destination of Westminster. Skirting Billingsgate Market, where the odor of fresh fish hung heavy in the air, they passed London Bridge on their left. Eden would not have guessed that the crowded edifice was anything but another street. Max had to point out to her that for centuries the bridge had been no mere river crossing, but host to a variety of commercial ventures, including some of London's most famous shops.

"Strange, wondrous strange!" marveled Eden as Max warded off a pretty hawker of hot baked pears and pippins. A cartload of bricks rumbled by, splattering dirty snow on Eden's skirts. Now that they were out of the Tower, her emotions were in a jumble. Even though she scarcely knew Marlborough, she felt guilty about leaving him in the cheerless prison. As for Prince Maximilian, he had not exhibited much enthusiasm for taking her with him. His height made him seem aloof, yet Eden sensed that he was a private person by nature and that he wore detachment like armor.

"You must think me an ignorant bumpkin," she said at last as they approached Blackfriars.

"What?" Max glanced at her, then pressed forward into the crowd of street vendors making their way up Ludgate Hill to St. Paul's. He shrugged. "You are what you are. That's true of us all."

"But …" Eden took a deep breath and forged ahead, fearful of getting separated from Max in the throng. "Who *are you*?" she asked as the crowd began to thin out near the church.

He was gazing at the skeletal spires that Christopher Wren had designed to replace the old edifice, which had been destroyed in London's great fire some thirty years earlier. "I'm Max. What else I am is not important. At least," he added dryly, "not in this country."

Noting a hint of bitterness, Eden started to question Max further, thought better of it and stared in the direction of St. Paul's. Workmen perched and pigeons fluttered along the unfinished walls, but even in its uncompleted state, the new church seemed immense. Indeed, everything about London struck Eden as larger than life—and noisy and crowded and dirty and foul-smelling. There were painted women with their bosoms all but exposed, rouged gentlemen wearing more lace than a Kentish bride, blackamoors with colorful turbans, stodgy merchants speaking in foreign tongues, shrieking children wearing rags, and dozens of strange smells, from coal and smoke to bread and oranges to musk and gin.

"Dumplins! Dumplins! Diddle, diddle, dumplins, ho!" cried a mammoth woman who looked as if she'd eaten more of her wares than she'd ever sold.

Eden edged closer to Max and noted that their surroundings had taken on a calmer, less oppressive air. She wished he'd smile more often; humor made him much less intimidating. But Max was solemn, his long, purposeful strides taking them into a broad avenue flanked by many new buildings, some of which were still under construction. "It's all so different," she sighed. "In Kent I could never imagine what London must be like."

"You speak well for a country lass," Max remarked as a splendid coach rolled past. "You have little accent."

Eden was surprised to discover that Max's comment pleased her. "My foster parents hired a tutor who had no accent. They felt it would be to our advantage to speak like proper folk. Being French," she added seriously, "the Berengers thought we should acquire our new language in its purest form."

Max was looking at her with bemused eyes. "Then you must find my errant English harsh, Mistress."

"Oh, no." Eden shook her head and realized it had begun to rain. " 'Struth, you speak well for a Dutchman."

"I'm not exactly Dutch," replied Max, his mouth trying to rebuff a smile. "I'm Flemish." Without waiting for Eden to respond, he gripped her by the arm as they crossed the broad avenue, dodging horses, more coaches, finely clad strollers and a three-way dog fight.

"Your manners are atrocious, of course." He spoke with nonchalance, then blinked against the chilling rain and looked speculatively at Eden. "Do you still speak French?"

Eden bristled at the reproach but kept her temper in check. "I used it little at home, but can converse with perfect …." She stopped, awestruck by the splendid rain-blurred vision before her. They were on a tree-lined street, the bare branches trembling in the wind with elegant dignity. Beyond stood a phalanx of new buildings, each several stories high, with row upon row of windows that seemed to stare at Eden like so many haughty glass eyes.

"Many of the courtiers live here," said Max, amused at Eden's openmouthed wonder in spite of himself. "The houses face St. James's Square, and the palace lies there. Come, you'll have time to gawk later. We're getting drenched, and I'm starving."

"Houses!" exclaimed Eden. "*Houses*! I thought they *were* the palace! How grand they are! Does Milord Marlborough live here?"

"He plans to build in this neighborhood," Max replied, steering Eden across another wide thoroughfare where more mansions with imposing, if fallow, gardens lay behind wrought-iron fences. "Before you conceive of any grandiose notion about my residence, let me warn you that it's quite modest. I'm not a rich man."

Only now did it dawn on Eden that Prince Maximilian was taking her to his house. Somehow, in the back of her mind, she'd had a vague idea that they must be headed for Marlborough's home. But of course the Countess might not welcome her.

"I'm trespassing," she said, and turned glum. "I should not have asked you to take me with you."

Max lifted one shoulder in an indifferent manner as the wind chased them around a corner and into Clarges Street. "No, it's my duty to Jack. If it weren't for him, I'd be hawking holland socks at four pairs a shilling like a common peddler."

Poverty and princes seemed an unlikely combination to Eden. Yet she knew that during their exile, both King Charles and his brother, James, had wandered the Continent like virtual beggars. Without comment, she struggled behind Max, fighting her skirts and cloak, which whipped at her weary legs.

Max didn't break stride as he took the stairs two at a time to the bright blue door of a trim sand-colored house. There was a fan-shaped window above the lintel and a brass knocker wrought in the form of a boar's head. Max walked in. Eden took a deep breath and craned her neck to absorb her new surroundings. The hallway was narrow, with the morning gloom dispelled by a small spiral chandelier. Eden shook out her cloak and ran a hand through damp claret tresses. Max was calling to someone in his native tongue. When a half-dozen servants converged upon the hall, he greeted them with brief, seemingly concise instructions before he turned to Eden.

"My housekeeper, *Vrouw* de Koch, will see to you. I shall deal with specifics later."

Bewildered, Eden watched Max turn on his heel and disappear into the recesses of the hallway. Most of the servants followed him. Only the stout Dutch housekeeper remained, her lively eyes studying Eden with unconcealed curiosity. She hitched up her petticoats and grimaced.

"For you, he wants a room?" *Vrouw* de Koch's jowls jiggled with what Eden took to be disapproval. "What is on his mind now? Why is he so unpredictable?" She shook her head, her tall, tufted *fontange* cap swaying precariously.

Eden was as mystified as she was indignant. "His Highness and I were released from prison only an hour ago. We—"

Vrouw de Koch made a sharp, chopping gesture with one hand. "Pah! With himself, it's always something! Prison, duels, war, women!" Though her tone was testy, the keen eyes softened. "I raised him, I ought to know. What was it this time, a coffeehouse row?"

Eden was prepared to offer a complete explanation, but *Vrouw* de Koch cut her short with another chop of her hand. "Never mind, you're wet through and look like a ragamuffin." She started up the central staircase, her stout body listing like a ship loaded too heavily on the starboard side.

Three doors flanked the upper hallway. *Vrouw* de Koch reached for the cut crystal knob at her left, then shook her head. "What am I thinking of?" she murmured in consternation. She turned to the opposite door, opened it and ushered Eden in with a mock flourish. "There's clothes, brandy in the cupboard, maybe perfume."

The handsomely proportioned chamber was furnished from an earlier era, except for the oak bracket clock with its ebony veneer and a lacquered cabinet displaying a motif of Chinese pagodas. Eden was so impressed that she didn't hear all of *Vrouw* de Koch's explanation of the household routine. The most she took in was that Max had a *hofmeester* named Jan Van de Weghe, who seemed to be in charge when *Vrouw* de Koch permitted it. As for Eden, bathwater and food were on the way. Concluding her recital, *Vrouw* de Koch listed her way out the door, closing it firmly behind her.

Overcome with fatigue, Eden flopped down on the bed with its deep blue hangings and faded counterpane embroidered with yellow and purple pansies. As she closed her eyes, a sense of guilt overwhelmed her. She had left Smarden without a word to her foster parents, she had abandoned Marlborough in the Tower and she was encroaching on Prince Maximilian's hospitality. It was not her fault that she had been dragged off to London, and no doubt the Berengers, except perhaps for Gerard, wouldn't expend undue concern over her. Monsieur and Madame Berenger would be inclined to embarrassment rather than worry if the news got out that Eden had been arrested.

As for Marlborough, Eden was powerless to help him. Max must have influence, or at least allies. She must speak to him again about her father's release. It was likely that the Prince was already engaged in an effort to free his friend and mentor.

Now that she was in Max's house, she supposed he'd had no choice but to let her tag along until Marlborough was out of prison. With any luck the Earl would join her in a day or two. Eden knew that Max had been reluctant to bring her home with him; she would try not to make a nuisance of herself. She'd already behaved in a most disrespectful manner, gotten tipsy and otherwise made a fool of herself. The sooner she was free from Prince Maximilian's supervision, the better.

Oddly enough, that thought disconcerted her. She must be overtired, Eden decided, and closed her eyes as the prelude to a much-needed nap.

Chapter Four

Her deep slumber was interrupted by a twittering mite of a girl who was accompanied by two youths carrying an ancient wooden bathtub. The girl's size made her seem no more than a child, but up close she appeared to be nearer Eden's age.

"The water's coming," the girl announced in an odd, faintly accented voice. She pointed to herself, a dimpled smile lighting up her round face. "I'm called Elsa." Her lips formed the name very carefully.

"I'm Eden. Eden Berenger. Or actually …." She stopped, confounded as to what she should call herself and ignorant of how she should be addressed by a servant. Elsa, however, was waving her hands at the two youths, who were now bringing in the water jugs.

"Mayhap," suggested Eden, "you could simply call me—"

Elsa was shaking her head vigorously, and though she smiled as widely as before, she pointed to her ears. "I can't hear. I'm quite deaf."

"Oh!" To hide her embarrassment, Eden moved to the tub and tested the water. "Just fine," she shouted. Then, getting no response save the dauntless smile, she dipped a hand into the tub and nodded her approval.

"May I help?" asked Elsa as the youths went out, empty water jugs slung over their shoulders.

Since the only attention Eden could recall having received while taking a bath were the attempts of the other Berenger children to drown her, the offer came as a pleasant surprise. Dispensing with modesty, she allowed the maid to assist her, and at last relaxed in the soothing water while Elsa carried on a chirruping monologue.

"My father was a Dutch sailor, my mother English. Poor Papa drowned, and Mama married again, a farmer from Dedham Vale in Suffolk. The land there is like Holland, flat, low, but pretty. Some days I miss it. But Prince Max, he is kind, and oh, so handsome, hey? Yet he's a melancholy sort, with sadness in his eyes … such a pity."

Elsa's description of Max piqued Eden's interest, but she didn't know how to put a question to the little deaf maid. As Eden wrapped herself in a fleecy towel, Elsa explained that she could read lips if a person spoke slowly and clearly.

"Or," she said, making motions with her hands, "you do this. It's sign language, so people who can't speak or hear can talk. Clever, no?"

Eden had never heard of such a thing, but found the idea intriguing. "You must teach me," she said, forming the words with great care.

Again, Elsa beamed at Eden. "Of course. We will have many fine talks together." With a decisive nod, she quit the chamber, hauling the bathtub behind her.

Left by herself, Eden sat at the Venetian mirror and frowned at her image. The damp tangle of her claret curls nestled on her bare shoulders, her skin glowed from its recent scrubbing, and the lavender peignoir that Elsa had found looked well with her coloring. Yet she was not content with her appearance. The brief glimpses she'd had of London ladies made her feel inadequate. Their clothes, coiffures, and jewels enhanced even those on whom Nature had skimped. Eden rearranged the peignoir's folds this way and that, artfully posing for the best effect. With an audacious tug, she pulled the fabric down just enough to reveal a hint of décolletage. Madame Berenger would have been scandalized by such a blatant display; Eden giggled in spite of herself. She didn't hear Max open the door.

"A pearl hung in that valley would be even more alluring."

Eden yanked the peignoir up to her neck and whirled to see Max's tall, athletic figure leaning against the door frame. She expected to find mockery in his eyes, but he was quite serious. "How long have you been standing there?" she breathed. "Didn't you knock?"

"The door was ajar. And," he added, making his leisurely way into the room, "it *is* my house."

Eden turned to the mirror and swallowed. "True," she said, watching their images in the glass. Max was standing directly behind her, one hand resting idly on the back of her chair.

"That shade is good, although I suspect your skin has too much color, and your hair needs taming." He was eyeing her critically, his hand holding a thick tress up to the candlelight. "I don't know much about fashion or fripperies, though. You shall have to be given advice by experts."

"For what?" Eden's face puckered. Max was still toying with her hair; the gesture unsettled her. "I thought we were going to get His Lordship released. What difference does it make if my skin has too much color and my hair looks like a haystack?"

Max didn't reply immediately, but continued to study the shimmering strand that lay across his big palm. "Haystack? What?" He let go of her hair and backed off a few paces, then scowled. "We can't get Jack out. He's being formally charged this very afternoon. King William, damn his stubborn Dutch hide, is convinced that Marlborough is a Jacobite supporter and has been up to his ears in plotting to bring James back to England. Here," he said, pulling a folded piece of paper out of his linen shirt. "This message just came from the Tower. You can read, can't you?"

Eden snatched the paper from Max's hand. "Like a proper Sunday parson," she retorted, but lost her verve as she skimmed the letter. "This is from His Lordship!" she exclaimed, heedless of how the lavender peignoir had managed to slip off one shoulder. "He minimizes the seriousness of his plight, yet it's quite clear that this is a grievous matter. What shall we do?" She turned anxious eyes to Max.

Max's lips twitched. "We?" His glance strayed to the naked shoulder, then fixed resolutely on the letter Eden held in her slim hands. Having taken on the responsibility for her, he must maintain a proper distance. Eden was far too inclined to familiarity, a natural result of her background. Ironically, Max considered himself a very informal person. The situation was awkward at best, even dangerous. Indeed, Max told himself as he made a conscious effort to avoid staring at the tempting rise of her breast above the lavender silk, if he considered Jack like an older brother, then he must think of Eden as a cousin. Or better yet, a sister. "You're right, of course," he agreed. "It's a mutual endeavor. Jack also sent this." He extracted another, smaller piece of paper. "In his absence, I am assuming the task of your tutelage. Considering the gravity of the situation, we must waste no time."

"Doing what?" Eden asked testily. Her bare feet had grown cold, and she stood up, keeping the peignoir clutched tightly against her body.

Max hesitated, his eyes unable to avoid the soft curves under the clinging peignoir. She was unschooled in courtly manners, but he should be pleased that she was at least a delectable little morsel. Her enticing appearance would make his job much easier. Once she was groomed to seduce the King, he could forget about her and concentrate on Marlborough. And on his own future, he reminded himself, and was annoyed to discover that he had lost his train of thought.

"Well?" demanded Eden, slipping into a pair of black satin mules and sitting down on a little bench that had feet that looked like lions' paws. Deliberately she yanked the hem of her peignoir out of Max's way. "You haven't answered me. Sir," she amended hastily. Despite Max's imposing presence, Eden was having trouble remembering that he was socially superior, even to Jack Churchill's daughter.

"Your lessons, of course." Max became brusque, taking the letters from Eden and putting them inside his shirt. His scowl reappeared, and he sampled a plate of smoked salmon that *Vrouw* de Koch had left on a small chased silver stand. "Music, dancing, riding, how to dress, deport yourself, engage in courtly banter …."

"All that to entice one scrawny man?" Eden tossed her damp hair over her shoulders, discovered that the peignoir had slipped and decorously tugged it into place. "If I'm to be a concubine, why don't you teach me how to … to …." Face reddening, Eden broke off, her Huguenot upbringing not allowing her to complete the thought. "What else does a courtesan need to know?" she added.

The scowl deepened as Max downed another slice of salmon and fixed Eden with a glacial stare. "You *are* a bumpkin. You know nothing of life among your betters. Being mistress to the King is a great honor."

Eden sniffed. "Not according to *Maman*. She says it's only vile Papists and their imitators who make adultery fashionable. She also says they'll go to hell in a hand basket."

Polishing off the last bit of salmon, Max kept his level gaze on Eden's righteous face and wondered how anyone so beguiling could be such a dunderhead. "Do you think King Charles went to hell?"

Eden thrust out her lower lip. "No. But Charles was different."

"Nonsense." He plucked up the linen napkin that had been resting on the silver stand and wiped his hands. "Charles, like most great men, indulged himself. Look at James in exile, or Louis of France. The women fairly fight for places in their beds."

The image Max had created conjured up a far different picture than he had intended. Eden giggled, envisioning Europe's greatest beauties scrambling around in various royal boudoirs, beating each other over the head with satin bolsters while the object of their affections sat in majestic comfort, awaiting the evening's victor.

"Eden …." Max made no effort to keep the exasperation from his voice. "You must be more serious."

"Oh, my … yes, but …." She gasped, bringing her laughter under control. "I'm afraid I'm not a very serious person."

"I realize that." He sighed, taking in the merry, gamin features and the dark dancing eyes. Suppressing Eden's ebullient nature was going to be difficult. William of Orange was a solemn sort, not given to mirth except when drinking late into the night with his Dutch cronies. But for Max, the hardest part was his discovery that Eden's good humor was contagious. For a man who had seldom laughed in the past four years, the revelation came as a not entirely welcome shock. It did not seem right that any form of happiness should intrude upon his grief.

"As you will," he conceded. "Amorous conduct can have its comic side. But Jack's predicament is grim. He expects you to help him."

Composed at last, Eden nodded. "I know. I'm to blame, in a way, having been what drew him to Kent and into suspicion." Guiltily she cast around for a way to prove her good intentions. "Can anyone else help us? What about my ... mother? Should I call on her?"

Max stifled his initial reaction. It had always appalled him that such a notorious harlot should have dared to mate with that model of honor and refinement, Jack Churchill. Yet, on the heels of his lecture to Eden, he could hardly admit as much. "Let's see how Jack feels about that," he temporized.

"If you say so," agreed a more docile Eden. Max and Marlborough had to be right. Being the King's mistress must be a prestigious post. As a child, she had witnessed firsthand the approval bestowed upon Charles's favorites. Only in the straitlaced confines of her Huguenot home would such a vocation be considered immoral. And Marlborough's future, if not his very life, was at risk. She owed him her very existence. Still, the idea of those tedious tutors hung over her like a dead weight, especially the riding lessons.

"I don't like horses," she began, but was stunned into silence by the crash of the window casement across the room.

Eden screamed as Max leaped to his feet. Amid the shards of glass and bits of wood, a man tumbled onto the carpet, blood streaming from his hands. Max instinctively went for his sword, only to discover that he hadn't bothered to put it on. In three great strides he had reached the intruder and set a foot on his neck.

"What knavery is this?" he demanded, glancing at the window to make sure no one else was about to descend upon them. "Speak, man!"

"Stay!" gasped the interloper, trying to move his neck from under Max's heel. "Mercy! My life is in danger!"

"It is indeed," muttered Max, but he took his foot away and reached down to haul the man into a sitting position. Slivers of glass fell to the floor, along with a few wood splinters. Max frowned as he recognized the uniform of a King's cavalryman. "Well? Who are you? And why this violent entry?"

The man stood, and managed on shaky legs to reach the chair by the dressing table. "Captain Thomas Craswell at your service, sir," the man said, still fighting for breath. "I was being pursued along the rooftops. I ..." he stopped, closed his eyes and covered his bloodied face with trembling hands.

Max went to the door and called for brandy. Master Van de Weghe was already on the scene, apparently having heard the crash. "Later," Max said tersely in response to his *hofmeester's* inquiry about the noise. Turning, Max noted that Eden was busying herself with a basin of water and strips of linen.

"Sit still," she told Craswell quietly, wincing at the drops of blood on the exquisite embroidered cushion.

Craswell suffered her ministrations with only a grimace or two, but opened his eyes when Max proffered the brandy. *Heer* Van de Weghe, upon his master's instructions, had gone outside to look for any suspicious strangers. Craswell, meanwhile, had been overcome with a coughing fit as he drank the strong liquid.

Eden raised the man's hands high above his head and gazed vexedly at Max. "He drank too fast. Some of that brandy should be applied to his cuts. It helps, you know."

Max ignored her comments and turned to Craswell, who had got himself under control. "Come now, Captain, who was pursuing you—and why?"

Small blue eyes focused under sandy brows, then shied away from Max's compelling gaze. " 'Tis terrible ... terrible," muttered Craswell, before darting another glance in Max's direction. "I was on my way to see Milord Bentinck, the Earl of Portland—though how that may be when he's as Dutch as Edam cheese, I'll never—" Craswell caught himself and made a feeble effort at a sheepish grin. "Pardon, Your Highness, I forgot you're a foreigner, too."

"But no relation to Bentinck. Yet," Max added under his breath, provoking a curious stare from Eden. "Go on."

"There was a plot," Craswell continued, "hatched by the Jacobites to assassinate King William. It was known that he hunted every Saturday, returning by way of Turnham Green. He'd be done in, as it were, when he crossed the river. Simple, eh?" Craswell spread his now bandaged hands, the snifter propped up between knees and chest.

Max reined in his impatience. "I've heard some of this already. What has it to do with you? Or with me, for that matter?"

Craswell stroked his sharp nose. "I was among the conspirators." He shot Max a defensive look. "I worked for Sir John Fenwick. But another of us, one Pendergrass, went to Milord Bentinck and warned him in the nick o' time. Now I'm duty-bound to tell my part, too. As for your friend, Marlborough, he's innocent. *I* was at Dover to light the signal fire to alert King James."

Max folded his arms across his chest and looked as inflexible as steel. "Will you so testify before the King?" Max queried.

Craswell wriggled uncomfortably. "Isn't it enough to tell Bentinck? I almost died for my noble sentiments."

"No." Max was emphatic. "You must tell His Majesty face-to-face. That's the only way to convince him of Marlborough's innocence. Who was chasing you over the rooftops of Westminster?"

Craswell shrugged. "Except for Fenwick, you wouldn't have heard of them. Jacobites all, but small fry. Mostly northerners from Yorkshire and Northumberland, the usual Papist dupes."

Max poured brandy for himself and looked thoughtful. "Where is Pendergrass now?"

"Gone to ground, I suppose, waiting to see which way the wind blows. He doesn't know yet if he's a villain or a hero, same as me." The immediate fear for his life apparently on the wane, Craswell spared an appreciative glance for Eden. "Her Ladyship here, I take it, is privy to Marlborough's business?"

"Yes." The single syllable erupted between Max's lips like a rifle volley. Flushing, Eden turned away and busied herself with putting the stopper in the brandy decanter. No one spoke until Master Van de Weghe appeared, announcing Rudolf, Count Hohenstaufen of Swabia.

Max muttered an oath at the prospect of seeing his loathsome cousin and downed his brandy in a gulp. "What's he doing here?" He set down the glass and gestured at his *hofmeester*. "Keep him below stairs, in the withdrawing room."

But Max was too late. Rudolf cruised over the threshold, brandishing a gold and ivory walking stick. He was almost as tall as Max and possessed the same fair coloring, but his features were less defined. He had a tenaciously boyish air, though Eden guessed him to be close to thirty. If Max seemed disinclined to laughter, Rudolf looked as if his smile had been applied with permanent paint. Despite herself, Eden cringed when the Count looked her way.

"Such excitement, cousin! Imprisonment in the Tower, Jacobite conspiracies, and now, I'm told, visitors streaming through the windows. Pray introduce me, Max, you know how uneasy I am among strangers."

Eden thought she could detect Max grinding his teeth. "Milord," she interposed, dropping as deep a curtsy as she could manage in the lavender dressing gown, "you've caught us in dishabille! Allow me to introduce myself and my brother. I'm Eden Berenger, and this," she went on with an airy wave at the mystified Craswell, "is Gerard. He was wounded at Namur."

"And more recently than that," murmured Rudolf, taking in the bandages on Craswell's hands and face. "This fellow," he asked pointedly, "is your *brother*, Mistress?"

Eden beamed at the Count. "He followed me from Kent. We're a very close family." She edged closer to Craswell and put a hand on his shoulder. "Naturally, he was upset to learn I'd been arrested."

"Naturally," remarked Rudolf dryly. Despite the smile, his blue eyes were hard as he studied Craswell, then turned to Max. "It appears your charity is boundless when it comes to offering shelter to members of the—what's the name? Berenger?—family, Max."

"There are rather a lot of them," replied Max, casting a swift glance in Eden's direction. "I may have to open up the attic."

"Well, you've certainly opened up the windows." Rudolf grimaced at the shattered casement, then resumed his boyish air. "Such a pity you're so preoccupied with all these fine country folk, Max. I'd hoped we might have our own family discussion today. I'd hate to see you get arrested again before we can sort things out."

Max's hazel eyes snapped with what Eden perceived as outrage before he regained control and gave Rudolf an overly hearty slap on the back. "Forgive me, it can't be helped, Rudi. Later, perhaps." Even as he spoke, Max was propelling his cousin into the hallway.

"You may have waited too long already," Rudolf called back before he disappeared from view.

Eden was distressed by the threat in Rudolf's voice, but she was not prepared for Max's irate expression when he returned.

"Well? What was the meaning of that outrageous lie to Count Rudolf?"

Discomfited by his anger, she forced herself to look at him, wishing that he were at least half a head shorter. "I'm not sure. It seemed prudent to lie. The Count doesn't strike me as a very nice man."

Max's gaze moved from Eden to Craswell and back. "He's not. He's an unscrupulous villain." The anger was abating, replaced by a grudging sense of gratitude. While Max found himself surprised by Eden's perception, he was even more amazed at how much he savored having her as an ally. "Rudolf and I have often been at odds," he admitted, though there was an evasive note in his voice. "The reasons aren't pertinent now. He's grasping. Even as a child, he was spoiled and selfish."

Eden saw the shadows surface in Max's eyes and knew that he was touching upon well-guarded ground. She wondered if he would have said more had Craswell not been there. Instead, he retreated behind his customary cool facade and gestured at the injured captain. "I'll see that *Vrouw* de Koch makes up one of the empty rooms in the servants' quarters."

"Isn't there an extra room on this floor?" Eden asked, remembering the third door.

The flesh over Max's cheekbones tightened and the hazel eyes frosted over. "No." He bit off the word as if it were deadly poison. "The servants' quarters will do." He left the room in chilly silence.

WITH THE AID OF *VROUW* de Koch, Eden saw to the settling in of Captain Craswell, who expressed gratitude to them both. "The cuts and such will mend," he said as the housekeeper plied him with stewed chicken and Eden changed his bandages. " 'Tis facing the King that bothers me most."

"It will ease your conscience," Eden replied, plumping up the pillows and arranging a thick comforter, "For now, you must rest."

Craswell gave her a grateful smile as fatigue overcame him. Eden and *Vrouw* de Koch tiptoed from the room, assured that their unexpected guest would spend a peaceful night.

When the housekeeper bustled in the next morning with breakfast, Captain Craswell was gone.

Chapter Five

B Y THE TIME EDEN LEARNED of Craswell's disappearance, Max was already out searching for his missing guest. *Vrouw* de Koch, however, was less than sympathetic.

"No need to fuss over the likes of a knave who smashes half the house trying to get in," she huffed, setting Eden's tray next to the bed. "At least he didn't wreck the other half getting out."

Eden picked up a mug of hot chocolate and glanced across the room to the window, which a hastily summoned glazier had repaired the previous night. "I wonder," she mused, but said nothing more since she had no idea how much Max had confided in his housekeeper. *Vrouw* de Koch might dismiss Craswell's departure without a pang, but Eden was upset. He might have convinced the King of Marlborough's innocence. The Earl would have been set free, and with his name cleared of implication in the assassination plot, the two men might have reconciled. But with Craswell's disappearance, Eden's hope for her father's future suffered a severe setback.

Despite the distraction caused by Craswell, Max had not neglected his responsibility for Eden. Before she could finish her hot chocolate, one of London's most fashionable dressmakers arrived at the house in Clarges Street. While she was still worn out from the rigors of the past two days, one glimpse of the dressmaker's wares picked up Eden's spirits. There were a dozen bolts of glorious fabric, reams of ribbons, piles of petticoats and high-heeled shoes with pointed toes. Beaver hats, fringed parasols, painted fans, jeweled buckles and fur capes made Eden's eyes sparkle. At home in Smarden, her plain linen, muslin and wool gowns were usually brown or gray or tan.

Making selections was far less taxing than the fitting process. After almost three hours of standing still, Eden was weary. *Vrouw* de Koch and the dressmaker were without mercy. There were still many outfits to be tried and even a corset of whalebone. At the latter, Eden balked.

"I'm not in the least bit stout," she asserted, indicating the slim curve of her waist. "Why must I wear something that looks as if it should gird a Crusader?"

"Then you must wear a busk instead," *Vrouw* de Koch insisted.

The dressmaker, an exalted creature of French origin, nodded at Eden. "*Regardez*, it is the long look you wish to achieve—trim, *très élégante*." She surveyed Eden's chemise-draped form critically, tapping one finger against her cheek. "A fine body, *c'est vrai*, but still, a corset or busk is mandated by fashion. Do you prefer horn or wood?"

Eden was aghast. "Horn or wood? Am I being dressed or constructed?"

The dressmaker exchanged knowing little smirks with *Vrouw* de Koch. "Both," the Frenchwoman replied. "*Alors!*"

Eden's lack of enthusiasm did nothing to stem the tide of pins and bastings. But the afternoon's ordeal didn't end with the fittings. Eden still had to face Master Cloudsley Clavell, a hairdresser whose pointed features reminded Eden of a ferret.

"Gorgeous, marvelous, eminently opulent hair!" Master Clavell enthused, tugging Eden's tresses this way and that. "The opulence, oh, the opulence!"

"It's all my own, at any rate," Eden remarked crossly, remembering how Max had also fingered her hair. Though he might have made her nervous, his touch had not annoyed her.

"Excellent, wonderful!" Master Clavell was oblivious to his client's sensibilities. "Now," he began, suddenly more businesslike, "a center part, then high curls on either side of the forehead—We'll have to do some snipping— there's really more hair here than we can handle." He clicked his fingers, and a youth wearing a powdered wig so large that it seemed to be wearing him, rushed forward with a long pair of shears.

"Stop!" ordered Eden, leaning as far away as she could in the chair without falling on the floor. "Don't you dare cut off even one tendril!"

Master Clavell was shocked. "You'll lose the effect, you'll look positively frizzy, like some Nubian attendant in a pasha's seraglio! It's unthinkable!"

Somehow a compromise was reached. Eden permitted a few discretionary snips, while Master Clavell altered his basic design to accommodate more hair than he felt was necessary.

"It is your choice," he pouted, but when the coiffure was completed, Master Clavell grudgingly admitted that Eden looked quite comely. "I suppose," he remarked, hand on chin as he studied her reflection in the mirror, "it does say something about the inner you. A bit of a rebel, eh?"

"Perhaps." At least he hadn't said "bumpkin," Eden thought as she scrutinized the courtly styling. Indeed, she looked most fetching, with the gleaming claret curls piled at her temples and the long coiled tresses trailing over her shoulders and down her back. "Can Elsa manage this?"

"*Ja, ja,*" replied *Vrouw* de Koch, "Elsa can manage anything with hair. Like a good baker, just give her the ingredients and she makes wonderful concoctions."

Relieved that she wouldn't have to learn the art of hairdressing along with everything else, Eden collapsed on the bed after Master Clavell and his assistant had departed. The day's activities had left her keyed up. She was restless in the sudden vacuum of activity and wanted to go for a walk, but it was growing dark and had started to sleet. She wondered when Max was coming home, and realized with a sense of shock that she missed him. Never in her life, with the exception of waiting for Gerard coming home from the war, had Eden anticipated anyone's return. Aimlessly, she began to walk through the house, her ears attuned for the sound of Max's voice or the tread of his boots in the hallway.

The main floor consisted of a handsome drawing room with lovely old Flemish tapestries, a dining room in the Italian style that could seat no more than twenty, the kitchen area, which Eden avoided, a study with finely bound books in tall oak cases and a small parlor with a trio of wonderful landscape paintings. She admired the pictures for some time, particularly a snow scene in which rosy-cheeked children skated on the ice and a portly gentleman tumbled downhill after his runaway dog.

Upstairs she paused at the first of two doors. The one at the end of the hall must belong to Max. Having no wish to be caught invading his privacy, she tried the door opposite her own. The latch gave at once. Eden discovered that the furniture was covered in dust cloths and the draperies were tightly closed. There was a stale, musty smell, indicating that no one had used the room in a very long time.

An easel stood in the middle of the floor holding a partially hidden canvas. Carefully Eden plucked at the cloth and found an unfinished portrait of what was probably a very beautiful blond woman. The curls were the color of honey, the eyes a brilliant blue. But the mouth was only sketched in, the nose a mere stroke and the rest a blank. Eden pondered her identity and wondered why the artist had given up his task. Preoccupied, she made her way out of the room and ran straight into Max.

He was wearing a light gray riding cape and held his three-cornered hat in his hand. He wore no wig, and Eden wondered if he ever followed fashion.

"You're in the wrong room," he barked, taking an awkward step backward.

"I know," she admitted. "I went exploring. I found an unfinished portrait in there. Who is she?"

The high cheekbones darkened. "What idiotic questions! Why do you pry?"

Eden shrugged, trying not to let Max know how much his volatile temper unnerved her. "I was restless, and it was too foul to go outside." Her lashes dipped in apology. "Forgive me."

Max was having trouble controlling his emotions. The pulse in his jaw twitched, and his big hands played havoc with his hat. "You ought to be sorry," he growled. "Why aren't you studying something?"

"I was," Eden replied defensively. "I was studying your house." She watched his glower deepen and decided on a more placating approach. "The landscapes in that little parlor downstairs—they're lovely. Who did them?"

Max's hands grew still and his voice became controlled, if tense. "One is by Abraham Storck. Another by Aert van der Neer, who died some years ago. They both have a genius for water scenes. The one with the skaters is mine."

"Oh!" Eden clapped her hands together, ignoring Max's disgruntled look. "But it's wonderful! Those charming children and the dog running down the hill and the little village .... Wherever did you learn to do that, Max?"

He was as oblivious as she to the use of his Christian name and was already swinging past her, the gray cape snapping at his calves. "It was merely a hobby." One arm jutted toward the door to the vacant room. "Don't go in there again. Ever."

"Max!" she cried, distressed at his harsh words. She was even more jarred by the note of reproach in her own voice.

"Well?" He turned, still scowling.

Eden swallowed hard and tried to strike a conciliatory note. "Did you find Captain Craswell?"

"No," snapped Max. Why couldn't the wench leave him alone? It was one thing to have her under his roof, but quite another for her to invade his life. She should have had the good sense to keep to her place. Instead, she strolled around his house, poked into his private rooms, scrutinized his paintings and acted if she had every right to treat him like an equal. That, Max knew, was the problem with comely lasses—they felt free to take advantage. But he was well-armored against such feminine onslaughts. "Craswell has disappeared into thin air," he said in a less heated, if distant, manner. Perhaps he couldn't treat her like kin; maybe he should act as if she were the enemy. Yet, he reflected, that was often what kinsmen were.

"How strange." Eden put a hand to her hair, hoping Max would notice the transformation of her coiffure. "Maybe he was kidnapped," she suggested.

"Of course he was!" Max started to turn away again.

Eden's hand froze on the cluster of curls at her temple. "Truly? Who would do such a thing?" She knew, of course; her father had relentless adversaries.

"Whoever it is, I intend to find out," Max assured her, giving the doorknob a twist. "By the way, are you wearing a wig? I hate wigs."

"It's my own hair! Master Clavell did it this afternoon." Eden was defiant. "You sent for him, did you not?"

Max shrugged, but came forward to study the hairdresser's art more closely. It was his duty to approve her appearance, after all. "I sent for somebody. The name would mean nothing to me." He tipped her chin up, then to one side. The shining curls smelled like honeysuckle, and Max was reminded of summer days on the Rhine. "Well. It's rather becoming, if contrived. I'm not sure I didn't like it better the other way."

"Fashion demands artifice," Eden averred, finding Max's touch warm and not unwelcome. "Could a peasant seduce a King?"

"A number of them probably have," Max replied, apparently still absorbed in the intricacies of Master Clavell's creation. "Not William, but others. Such as Charles." His hand fell away, and he shifted rather uncomfortably. "I must give Jack a favorable report. The swifter your progress, the sooner he will be free."

Eden's ebony eyes were questioning. "You mean how quickly I can get the King to …?" She averted her gaze so abruptly that the gleaming curls bobbed on her shoulders. It was one thing to talk about seducing William in the abstract; it was quite another to contemplate the grim reality.

"Holy St. Hubert," sighed Max, "don't tell me you've suddenly gotten tongue-tied?" Grooming Eden for the royal boudoir was difficult at best, but it was certainly compounded by her reluctance and naïveté. How, Max wondered, could the wench provide companionship for a king when it was so obvious that she herself needed looking after? "The truth is," he said in a rather uneasy voice, "I'm not much good at courtly manners myself."

"But you're a prince!" she protested, her hands nervously working to restore her coiffure to Master Clavell's pristine perfection.

"A prince without a principality, a man without a home," he replied with a wry expression. "Except for this house, which is leased from Lord Godolphin, to whom I owe the past three months' rent. Stop that," he exclaimed, grabbing Eden's wrist, "you've got hairpins all but sticking from your ears!"

Eden stood motionless while Max did his clumsy best to rearrange her hair. In truth, though she couldn't see the results, she had the feeling that his efforts were no more efficacious than her own. She suffered his ministrations without protest, however, and discovered that she liked the tickling sensation of his fingers on her skin. Though he insisted she look straight ahead, Eden darted an occasional glance at his chiseled face and wondered what it would be like if Max leaned down and kissed her. Surely not like Charlie Crocker or Adam Young or the guard in the Tower.

"There." Max nodded and stepped back. "Much better. Don't let them put those silly patches on your face."

"But they're all the rage," Eden declared, not wanting to admit that she, too, found them somewhat ridiculous, at least when used in profusion. "I thought you wanted me to be a proper courtesan."

"What I want doesn't matter!" Max exploded, shocking them both with his vehemence. He was standing stiff as an icon, fists clenched at his sides. Embarrassed, he looked away for a moment, struggled with his composure and finally brushed one sleeve across his forehead. "Why should it matter?" he muttered before regarding Eden with a stony expression. "Except for Jack, of course."

"Of course," Eden agreed, forcing lightness into her voice. Max's moods continued to unsettle her. In Smarden she could at least predict the various ill humors that persisted among the Berengers.

"So." Max was undoing the tabs of his cape. "I must delve further into this Craswell affair. And you must practice your French."

He wheeled, this time heading not for his chamber but for the stairs. Eden stared after him and called out in a voice that dismayed her with its querulous tone, "I told you, I already speak excellent French!"

But Max had disappeared down the staircase, leaving Eden alone.

THAT WEEK THE MUSIC MASTER arrived, followed in due course by a dancing instructor, a professor of languages, a gourmet and a riding teacher who took a very nervous Eden riding in Green Park. The days were long and full, stretching through cheerless February and into dreary March. Meanwhile Marlborough languished in the Tower. Others had since been arrested, including the Earl's doughty old friend, Lord Ailesbury. The Duke of Berwick, James's son by Arabella Churchill and thus Marlborough's nephew, had been implicated but had fled to the Continent. Ironically, Craswell's crony Pendergrass had been rewarded by the King and had gone abroad. Sir John Fenwick remained at large.

The first day of spring brought a gray drizzle. Eden sat at the inlaid desk in her boudoir to write a letter to her father. She began on a positive note, regaling him with her small successes but concealing her larger failures. Halfway through, however, she confessed her loneliness and frustration: "Having found a Father, and being so hastily deprived of his Comfort, I am driven in my Duties only by the Thought that somehow my poor Accomplishments can aid in releasing you from Prison."

Eden stared at the writing paper, wincing at the many blots she had made. A fortnight ago she had written to her foster family in Smarden, advising them of her whereabouts. That piece of correspondence had been virtually flawless. Why could she not have done half so well by her father?

Dispirited, Eden scrunched up the parchment and threw it across the room. Words, however neat, would do the Earl little good. Even now Max was abroad, looking for Captain Craswell. When the missing man had not turned up in London after a two-week search, Max had decided that Craswell must have been spirited out of the country. The house on Clarges Street seemed to echo with emptiness in Max's absence, and Eden felt cast adrift.

On impulse she made up her mind to visit her father. She had to make an eloquent gesture to prove to him that she had his best interests at heart.

Snatching up her new cloak with its miniver trim and matching muff, she called for Elsa and ordered Master Van de Weghe to send for two sedan chairs. In less than an hour, she was confronting Sir Edmund Greene, the Lord Lieutenant of the Tower, and asking for permission to see Milord Marlborough. To her surprise, the request was readily granted.

"Milord Marlborough," said the bluff Lord Lieutenant with a wink, "has certain privileges."

He also had a fairly commodious cell, complete with scarred but comfortable furniture. There were books and the remnants of what had been a full meal, and at least one complete change of clothes. Still, the Earl's excellent complexion had turned sallow, and he was thinner than Eden remembered him.

"Eden!" he exclaimed, hurrying to take her hand and kiss her cheek. "What a delightful surprise!"

"Albeit a tardy one," she responded ruefully. "I had no notion 'twould be so easy to call on you here. I' truth, your lodgings are well-nigh luxurious."

Marlborough, who had been studying Eden's metamorphosis with approval, gave a quick look over his shoulder at the familiar surroundings. "Sidney Godolphin insists on bribing the gaolers. You'd think a man who had been Lord Treasurer of England could devise better ways to spend his money." The Earl shook his head at the thought of such extravagance. "Sidney, bless him, is a good and generous friend."

"For the sake of your comfort, I'm glad he is," Eden declared, trying not to smile at her father's penurious streak. She still had difficulties reconciling his expenditures on her behalf with his frugal nature. "Have you any news from the King?"

Marlborough was lifting the lid of a small teak chest. He extracted a dusty bottle, presumably of wine, and reached for a mismatched pair of pewter mugs. "A toast, my dear? To our success?"

Eden eyed the wine bottle uncertainly. A few drops wouldn't hurt, now that she knew it was unwise to down too much too fast. In any event, she must become accustomed to strong spirits, since she understood that the courtiers drank little else. "Indeed, sir," she replied, realizing that, as with Max, she had no idea what form of address to take with Marlborough.

The Earl had noticed her sudden consternation. "I believe in respect," he remarked, handing her one of the mugs, "but we are family, after all."

Family, Eden thought as she held onto the mug with both hands. The word had taken on a new dimension, though it still didn't seem quite real. Yet there was Marlborough, standing not three feet away, as easy of manner imprisoned in the Tower of London as he would have been in the House of Lords—or the Berenger kitchen. Any notions Eden might have had about the haughty arrogance of English aristocrats was given the lie by her father's comfortable egalitarian manner.

"I can't call you Papa, I called Monsieur Berenger that. And Father sounds so formal ...." Eden's earnest face wore a puzzled expression.

"What about Jack?" suggested Marlborough. "That's what my friends call me."

"Jack?" She'd heard Max refer to the Earl in such a way, but somehow it seemed too ordinary, even common. Yet, Eden had to admit, he looked more like Jack than milord or Pater or even Father.

"Jack." Eden turned the single syllable over on her tongue, then brightened and put out her hand. "Yes—Jack! I like that, it's so friendly."

He squeezed her fingers and smiled broadly. "So 'tis, dear Eden. And I should very much like us to be friends. I hope you would like it, too," he added with touching candor.

"Oh, indeed I would, sir! *Jack*," Eden corrected, laughing gaily. "You know," she said, suddenly serious, "I've had a papa before, but I've never had a friend."

Marlborough leaned down and gently kissed her forehead. The keen gray-green eyes met the eager ebony gaze. "Everyone has parents, but friends are hard to come by. Remember that, Eden, no matter what you do or how high you climb." His smile washed over her like balm. He raised his pewter mug. "To more than kinship—to friendship, as well."

Eden touched her mug to his, then took a small sip. Though the dark amber liquid was harsh on her tongue, it went down easily enough. For some time they were both silent, savoring the bond that blood had forged and feeling had intensified.

"The sun is coming out," Eden remarked at last, gazing through one of the cell's two narrow windows. "It must be spring after all."

For the first time since Eden had met Marlborough, she saw him look grim. "I wonder how many seasons will pass before I'm out of this confounded place."

Eden regarded Marlborough with sympathy. "Max tried to explain why you needed my help. But if the King relies so much on his Dutchmen and Flemings, why doesn't he listen to Max?"

A lesser man might have been vexed by Eden's lack of political acumen, but the Earl merely smiled indulgently. "Because Max is my friend. And because he has enemies of his own."

"Who?" Eden queried bluntly.

But her father shrugged off the question. "Max is a private sort of man. In any event, enmity can be bred at home and abroad. We English have become so intertwined with the Dutch that when Queen Mary was asked to rule in her father's place, she made William not only her consort, but King, as well. After she died, Parliament declared that while William could remain as sovereign, the Crown would pass to Mary's sister, Anne, rather than to any heirs he might have by a second wife."

Eden blinked at the Earl. So, she thought, that was why a mistress, rather than a wife, was required. But aloud she spoke not of herself but of Mary.

"I felt sad when the Queen died," said Eden, recalling that bleak winter day over a year ago. "She had smallpox, did she not?"

Marlborough's cool gaze held no emotion. "She did. But I must be candid. Her Majesty never cared for either my dear Countess or me. Perhaps it was because we had always been so close to the Princess Anne."

Even in Smarden, Eden had heard bits of gossip about the Princess and the Countess—how devoted Anne was to her dearest friend, Sarah Churchill. Eden could see that such an attachment might cause resentment between any pair of sisters.

"Frankly," the Earl continued, offering Eden more wine, which she politely refused, "I don't know what we would have done without the Princess's generosity. Except for my investments, Sarah has been the sole support of our family. Of course, my lack of employment has given me an opportunity to spend more time with our children while Sarah is away. Now," he said with an affectionate smile, "I shall also get to know you."

"I'll do my best to win the King's ... ear," Eden promised. "Though I wonder if he'll believe me when he learns I'm your daughter."

Marlborough was bemused by her naïveté. "A woman, especially a pretty one, has all sorts of advantages in convincing the unconvincible. Remember, William is lonely. He was never a demonstrative man, yet he was devoted to the Queen and misses her enormously. He also, I'm sure, feels lost without Betty Villiers."

Marlborough was so reasonable that Eden could almost believe in the possibility of success. Her doubts about the morality of what she was being groomed to do had begun to fade in the wake of the Earl's dispassionate explanations. Lulled by his easy manner, she nearly forgot their surroundings and the very real danger that hung over them both.

"Have you heard about Captain Craswell?" Eden asked.

Marlborough looked unwontedly grave. "Yes. Max came to tell me before he left England. I hope no mischief has overtaken Craswell. If only Pendergrass would admit that neither I nor Lord Ailesbury were involved in the confounded plot." He paused and shook his head. "Yet to give the devil his due, at least Pendergrass had the courage to inform Bentinck about the assassination plans. I mustn't judge his other motives too harshly."

Eden marveled at her father's fair-mindedness. There was so much about him that goaded her into wanting to please him. "I try to learn from my instructors," she said truthfully, "but sometimes it's very hard."

"I've much confidence in you," he said, standing up on limbs that had grown stiff from lack of exercise in the Tower.

In the corridor, a guard was clearing his throat. Marlborough looked beyond Eden and nodded at the man. "Yes, yes, Norton, our visit is concluded. We thank you for your patience." The Earl gave Eden his hand, assisting her from the chair. "They do like to keep to a regimen here."

"I understand." Eden smiled warmly at her father, but her words were wistful. "I waited so long for you to come for me. How I wish you were free so that we might enjoy each other's company."

Gently, Marlborough squeezed her hand. "The burden of my freedom lies with you, my child. Godspeed, dearest daughter."

His words fell sweetly on her ear. How she had yearned for kin, for blood ties, for a sense of belonging! Tears welled up in the great ebony eyes, but she willed herself not to shed them. "I swear to do whatever I must to bring us together. I scarcely know you, yet it seems I always have." Her tongue flicked over her lower lip. "I love you, Jack."

"Well!" The Earl beamed at Eden, his expression a mixture of surprise, diffidence and paternal pride. In the corridor, the guard drummed his fingernails against the iron bars of the cell. "How enchanting you are," Marlborough said softly. "How fortunate a father am I!"

He bent to kiss her cheek, then she was gone.

Chapter Six

THE CHANGE IN THE WEATHER inspired Eden to walk to Clarges Street, at least as far as the Strand. Elsa, who had been trying to teach Eden the new way of talking with her fingers, was bursting with questions about her mistress's visit to the fearsome Tower. The little maid knew her place, however, and refrained from posing any impertinent inquiries.

"I sat out on the Green," she twittered as they approached bustling London Bridge. As ever, the Thames was littered with every sort of craft, from sleek yachts with billowing sails to small wherries, each propelled by a single oarsman. "There were ever so many handsome soldiers marching about! Who do they guard, do you think? Is anyone going to be executed on the block?"

Eden suppressed a shudder; treason was a capital crime. Failing in her effort at signing, she turned so that the deaf girl could watch her lips. "I hope not. It's too cruel."

"Cruel?" Elsa wrinkled her little nose. "But necessary with bad people."

Eden couldn't imagine anyone that bad. Some naughty boys had once set Master Young's black cat afire on All Hallows' Eve, and there were always tales about beer being stolen from the brewery at Wye, but otherwise, Eden knew little of evil. She was trying to compose her reply when they noticed two sturdy King's men carrying a large sack up the embankment while a gaggle of London citizenry trailed behind.

"Make way!" one of the King's men shouted. "Make way!"

The traffic that had been streaming westward from London Bridge stalled rather than parted. Ballad singers, fishwives, muffin-men, rag sellers and even a pair of gentlemen applying snuff pushed forward to see the diversion. Elsa was gazing questioningly at Eden. "What passes here, Mistress?"

Eden shrugged, wondering why the Londoners seemed so excited over two soldiers carrying a lumpy bundle. She was trying to figure out a way they might circumvent the crowd when a rangy hawker of pancakes informed his companion in gleefully ghoulish tones that, " 'E was stabbed through the 'eart, 'e was—murder most foul!"

Grasping Elsa by the arm, Eden started to retreat in the hope of avoiding any gruesome sights. But at that moment one of the King's men fired a volley into the air, scattering the eager crowd. Elsa, of course, heard nothing and held her ground despite a fierce tug from Eden.

"It's a man!" Elsa exclaimed, breaking away from Eden and moving quickly toward the inert form that lay on the cobbles.

Eden caught a hostile gleam in the eye of one of the King's men as he approached Elsa. "She's deaf!" Eden called. "Leave her be, I'll take her off!" Gingerly, Eden went to Elsa and plucked the other girl's sleeve. The soldiers were watching them with suspicion that was only partly mitigated by admiration. Avoiding the miserable bundle that had once been a living creature, Eden forced Elsa to face her. "We must go. Now!"

But Elsa's cheeks had grown very pink, and her delft-blue eyes were overly bright. "Who is this man?" she demanded of Eden, her high voice filled with concern.

Eden shook her head. "I don't know. But we must go." She gestured at the soldiers, who were shifting impatiently.

Still Elsa persisted, one small hand fluttering excitedly toward the dead man. "Look, look! He wears Prince Maximilian's monogrammed linen!"

Suddenly more afraid of Elsa's rampant tongue than of the corpse, Eden clasped a hand over the girl's mouth. She glanced at the crowd. It appeared to Eden that no one had paid any attention; they were all caught up in their own reactions to this latest grotesque sensation. With great reluctance, Eden forced herself to look at the dead man. Despite the bloated body, the empty sockets where gray eyes had once darted and the ravaged face that had served up a feast for the fishes, Eden knew at once that this was Captain Craswell.

She also knew that she was about to be sick. Her grip tightened on Elsa, forcing a little shriek from the other girl. "Forgive me," Eden begged, as she hauled her companion away. They headed for a side street, stopping at an inn marked by the sign of three spotted cows. Oblivious to the passing porters and carters, Eden leaned against a splintered timber and managed to keep from retching. A few moments later, as Elsa watched her mistress with marked concern, Eden shook herself and announced that they could proceed. She was unsteady and very pale. Soon they espied the scaffolding of St. Paul's new dome.

"Who is he?" Elsa asked, no longer able to restrain her curiosity.

Eden was concentrating on finding a hackney coach for hire. They were outside the Temple, where law students scurried around, carrying sheets of foolscap and unbound legal tomes. Distractedly, she signed to Elsa that the dead man was a former Jacobite who wanted to help Prince Maximilian and the Earl of Marlborough. It was clear that Elsa hadn't known about Craswell's noisy arrival in Clarges Street. She could not have heard the crash, and for whatever reasons, neither *Vrouw* de Koch nor *Heer* Van de Weghe had revealed the soldier's presence to the rest of the staff. As well, Eden reflected, sighting a row of carriages for hire in Drury Lane, such knowledge could be dangerous.

"This way." She motioned to Elsa and hurried toward the waiting vehicles. Surrounded by throngs of shouting, cursing, babbling hawkers, peddlers and workmen, Eden glanced at the proud new skyline of raucous London and felt very alone.

AS MUCH AS SHE WISHED to, Eden couldn't ignore Craswell's death. She considered an immediate return to the Tower to tell Marlborough, but there was little he could do from his prison cell. Max was away, looking in vain for Craswell on the Continent when all the time he'd been at the bottom of the Thames. Lady Marlborough sounded like a resourceful woman, but Eden felt it unwise to approach her father's wife unannounced. The only other person she knew to be a friend of the Earl's was Sidney Godolphin.

"He's at Newmarket," Elsa said glumly. "He has fine Arabian horses that he'll be racing when the season comes. Everyone is talking about his amazing animals."

It struck Eden that London's denizens seemed more interested in livestock and dead men than in the plight of one of their greatest heroes. "Who, then?" she muttered.

Though Eden had not spoken directly to Elsa, the little maid had caught the words. "Bentinck's niece, Lady Harriet Villiers. She lives nearby, in Piccadilly. Milord Bentinck's wife was a Villiers. But of course you know that Lady Harriet is—"

But Eden cut her off. Without further ado, she leaned forward and banged on the panel separating them from the driver. The Villiers family was very prominent, though Eden wasn't sure exactly how they'd acquired power. Betty had been William's mistress, this Harriet's aunt had married Milord Bentinck, and somewhere in the dim past there had been a duke or two. Clearly, they were well-connected, both with the English and the Dutch. Eden couldn't wait to seek Lady Harriet's help.

Within ten minutes they stood before the open gates of a large, ornate stone mansion off Windmill Street. Beech trees lined the short drive, and the gardens were bursting with spring blooms. Eden summoned her courage and marched up the short flight of steps to a dark green door with a knocker shaped in the form of Eros.

A liveried servant, stiff and correct, surveyed Eden's fur-trimmed cloak and proper accompaniment of a demure maid. "May I?" he inquired in a squeaky voice that contrasted with his stately demeanor.

"Yes, you may," replied Eden, not having the least idea what the man was asking. "My name is …" she paused, uncertain whether or not to present her Churchill credentials. Not yet, she decided, and gave the manservant her most engaging smile. "I'm Mistress Eden Berenger, newly arrived from Kent. I should like to speak to Lady Harriet Villiers." Eden took a breath, pleased with herself for presenting her request with such aplomb. At her side, Elsa nodded approval.

The servant had pursed his lips, but before he could respond, an exquisite young woman with raven-black hair and a perfect cupid's bow mouth floated down the spiral staircase in a haze of silken ruffles and foamy lace. She stopped upon seeing Eden. "Who are you?" she asked in a lilting voice. Her lovely green eyes held a spark of curiosity that skewered both newcomers on the spot.

For all her newly acquired finery and artful coiffure, Eden felt indecently inadequate next to this cool, confident creature. "I'm Mistress Eden Berenger," she repeated. "I've come to speak to you about a matter concerning … politics, Lady Harriet." She chose the word carefully, not wanting this worldly noblewoman to think she would come calling on any lesser pretext.

"Politics?" The thick black lashes fluttered in apparent bewilderment, though at the subject or the speaker, Eden was not certain. She dismissed the servant with a languorous wave. "Surely you mean to see my brother, Sir Edward Villiers?"

"Edward?" It occurred to Eden that the branches on the Villiers family tree must look like the Berenger orchard at harvesttime. "Actually, I've come on behalf of Milord Marlborough. I live in Clarges Street with Prince Maximilian of Nassau-Dillenburg."

If Eden had said she was the bride of Satan, she could not have wrought a more radical change in Lady Harriet. The green eyes narrowed, the cupid's bow twisted into a snarl, and the length of her lithe body seemed to coil up like a snake. "You *what*?" Harriet demanded, leaning toward Eden with a menacing attitude.

Eden sensed Elsa's sudden consternation but didn't understand it. "I live in Clarges Street," Eden repeated, wondering if she hadn't made herself clear. "Prince Maximilian is Flemish, and he—"

"Get out!" Harriet's arm lashed at the door. "Get out! How dare you come here with your gutter talk!" She whirled, scanning the hallway for any sign of a servant. "Armbruster!" she shouted, and her voice was suddenly shrill, a far cry from the melodious lilt she had affected only moments earlier. The serving man appeared from one of several doors along the corridor. "Throw this baggage and her whoring maid out of here! At once!"

"Just a moment," interposed Eden as Armbruster made for the two unwelcome guests. "I came here asking for help, Lady Harriet." She put up a hand to allay any show of force on the servant's part. "I meant no insult."

Lady Harriet's wide green eyes flared at Eden. "Such drivel! You came to flaunt yourself!" She gestured with clawlike hands at Eden's fur trim. "Look at you, no doubt wearing finery paid for with credit from my dowry! How should I react to a strumpet who declares she's living with my betrothed?" Harriet spun on Armbruster. "You heard me! Away with them both!"

Harriet's words had rooted Eden to the spot. Captain Craswell's murder receded into the background in the face of this startling revelation. Surely Max couldn't be affianced to this shrieking virago! But she was very beautiful—and apparently rich as well. She was also a Villiers, and therefore part of a powerful family alliance that spanned the Channel. What better match for an impoverished foreign prince?

Eden didn't need to be thrown out. Brushing aside the somewhat befuddled Armbruster and shooting Harriet Villiers a scathing glance, she yanked Elsa across the threshold. She left Lady Harriet standing in the doorway, shaking a fist and shouting vile imprecations.

"I hate her," Eden muttered as they turned into Piccadilly. "I don't even know her and I hate her."

But of course Elsa didn't hear a word her mistress said.

DEPRESSION SETTLED OVER EDEN LIKE a black shroud. She had failed to find help for Marlborough, and she was appalled at the prospect of Max marrying Lady Harriet. She could not understand why he hadn't told her he was betrothed. The simplest answer was that it was none of Eden's business and that Max was a man who kept his private affairs to himself. But that explanation comforted her not a jot. She was convinced that Max had made a bad match. Lady Harriet might be rich and beautiful, but she was also a bad-tempered witch who would make his life miserable. Had she been otherwise, Eden would not have been so upset. Or so she told herself.

Despite the fullness of her days, Eden found the time dragging. Max had been gone for almost a month, and if Eden had known him longer or better, she would have sworn she was desolate without him. That was nonsense, of course. More likely she was homesick, if not for the Berengers, at least for the rolling green fields of Kent. For the first time in her life, Eden's natural exuberance deserted her.

Still, Elsa's companionship was a comfort, and *Vrouw* de Koch had warmed considerably. The housekeeper, in fact, had taught Eden to play cards. It had begun one dreary evening when the fog was so thick that Eden swore she could taste it inside the house. Grumbling that such was probably the case, and that the air in Amsterdam was as pure as a baby's breath, *Vrouw* de Koch had suggested they pass the time with a game of two-handed ombre. Eden had discovered a knack for cards and had quickly picked up the game.

On the Monday after Easter, as Eden was trying to sort out her lessons so that she might find time to visit Marlborough again, Max came home. His manner was as casual as his worn shirt and tan riding breeches. When he encountered Eden at the end of another of her interminable fittings, he addressed her as if he were picking up some conversation they had just dropped in midsentence.

"I'm growing accustomed to Master Clavell's artistry with your hair," he said, casting an appraising eye in Eden's direction. He was sitting in a chair of Spanish leather with one long leg slung over the sturdy oak arm. "Have you learned to powder and decorate your face yet?"

"Have you?" Eden shot back. Inexplicably, she was rankled by his casual attitude. "It's as much the fashion for men as for women, you know."

Max shrugged and picked an apple from a bowl that sat on a white marble pedestal. "I'm not much for beautifying myself. And I'm too damned tall to go about posing like a statue, as so many fine fellows think they must." He took an impressive bite of apple and chewed thoughtfully. "Craswell's dead, I hear."

Eden was taken aback by the unexpected remark. Obliquely she studied Max's face—the chiseled features, the high, gaunt cheekbones, the not quite straight nose, the strong, lean jaw. Despite the shadows behind those sharp hazel eyes, Eden perceived that this was a face that invited trust. It was also, she realized with a sudden sense of giddiness, a face that asked much more. Exactly what, she wasn't sure—or at least didn't want to know. Not yet.

"Some soldiers fished him out of the Thames," she said. "I was there. With Elsa. It was quite awful." She shivered in spite of the mild April day. "I think he'd been in the river a long time."

The heavy brows drew together as Max paused, the apple midway to his mouth. "You were there? Why?"

As concisely as possible, Eden explained her visit to Marlborough. "Elsa and I just happened along. It was a coincidence." She heard the defensive note in her voice and was annoyed with herself. "I' faith, I wish I'd not seen any of it."

Max reduced the apple to a scrawny core and flung it across the room into an empty porcelain bowl. "Pendergrass remains abroad. I doubt he'll risk his hide to return and exonerate Jack." Max rubbed thoughtfully at his long chin. "Are you prepared to meet the King?"

Eden stiffened, but forced her voice to sound lighthearted. "I can dance my feet off and make gay repartee. What more could any man want?"

Max's gaze was fleetingly cynical, then enigmatic. "What indeed? In William's case, I expect he wants companionship. Someone who will listen, as Betty Villiers did. But it's all too rare a quality in most women."

"I listen to you," Eden replied with a lift of her chin. "And speaking of the Villiers tribe, I met your fiancée the other day. She wouldn't listen to me at all."

Somehow, Eden had hoped Max would deny any knowledge of a fiancée. Ridiculous, of course, but reason couldn't conquer feelings. With raised eyebrows Max listened to her brief recital of how she had gone to the Villiers mansion in Piccadilly. When she came to a faltering stop, he frowned.

"I prefer keeping Harriet out of these intrigues. She's a delicate creature, given to—"

"Temper fits!" exploded Eden, leaning on the edge of her chair. "She tried to have me thrown out of the house! She called Elsa a whore! You call that delicate?"

Dumbfounded by Eden's reaction, Max frowned again. "She did? That's odd. Perhaps she had a fever."

Eden shot out of the chair. "Then it's chronic, if you ask me! I went for help about Craswell and she carried on as if I'd come to kidnap her!"

The entire episode sounded strange to Max. Yet it might explain why Harriet hadn't been in when he'd called on her that morning. He could have sworn that the Villiers coach was in place behind the yew hedge, and Harriet seldom went anywhere without it. He'd insist on seeing her tomorrow and try to sort out this misunderstanding. By nature, women often shaped the facts to suit themselves; Max had a feeling Eden was doing precisely that.

Eden was standing with her arms folded across her breast, glaring at the fruit bowl. She tried to envision how Lady Harriet would look roasted, with an apple in her mouth. "When," she asked archly, "do you plan to wed?"

"I'm not sure. Autumn, maybe, or at Christmastide. It depends on how events proceed."

Eden moved her head just enough to catch Max's expression. He seemed quite unruffled, even bemused. "What events?" she inquired breathlessly.

Max unwound himself from the chair and stretched his long legs. "Many things, here and abroad. It's complicated, but I don't want to come to Harriet empty-handed."

Why would it matter, Eden wondered fleetingly. Harriet must love him, and she had money of her own, so what difference would it make if Max were as poor as a parson?

For one brief irrational moment, Eden hoped that Max would never find the fortune he was seeking—or trying to regain. "Why didn't you tell me about Harriet?" she blurted, turning to face him.

Max looked genuinely surprised. "To what point? My marriage plans in no way infringe on your pursuit of the King. Jack knows I'm betrothed to Harriet. He sees no conflict of interest. It should be an ideal match, since Harriet has both English and Dutch connections."

His recital sounded so dispassionate that Eden was momentarily assuaged. But it occurred to her that Max viewed her campaign to win the King with equal detachment. To Eden, that viewpoint was askew. She could not so easily set aside her personal feelings. Nor could she put her sentiments into words. A silence fell between them like a sad old song. Max was retreating into himself, while Eden moved around the room, toying with a vase of daffodils, sampling an orange, fidgeting with the clasp on a strand of the newly fashionable artificial pearls at her neck.

It was Max who finally spoke, and his words were unexpected. "I hear you're quite a cardplayer."

Eden smirked, though her reply was couched in modesty. "I'm passable. Would you like to play? Any game, you name it," she added magnanimously.

Max studied the frayed cuff of his leather riding boot and considered. "Why not? How about basset?"

"I' faith, that's a great favorite of mine," Eden exclaimed, hurrying to remove the cards from their ivory case. The deck, which was already worn, featured various crowned heads of Europe as well as famous battle scenes. Eden pulled up the little Oriental table and offered the cards to Max. "You deal first." She regarded him with pleasure and confidence, which caused Max to smile in spite of himself.

"What shall we play for?" he asked, shuffling the deck with practiced mastery.

Eden frowned, chewing on the end of her finger. "I have no money. What about pins?"

Max lifted his eyebrows. "Pins? That's a pitiful stake, even for a pauper prince and a country wench." He saw Eden start to bridle and grinned at her, "Don't be so touchy, you don't look like you're from the country anymore." Indeed, as she relaxed in her chair and concentrated on her cards, Eden could have passed for a wellborn young lady who lived in the precincts of St. James's. Not, Max noted with an inner grimace, that she didn't possess her own unique style and quirks. But on the other hand, they only added to her unusual allure.

The heavy brows were drawn together, the full mouth was pulled down, the cluster of claret-colored curls trailed over her silk-clad shoulders, the ebony eyes were candid, yet so deep that they concealed her most private thoughts … If she had any, he reminded himself. He realized how little he knew of this lass from Kent with her ingenuous air. It was imperative to keep Eden in perspective. Max must think of her not as a person but as an instrument to liberate Marlborough. As the man entrusted to watch over that instrument, Max must see to her well-being, but remember to what purpose she was being honed.

"Treats," exclaimed Eden, jolting Max from his reverie. "If I lose, I shall bake you something tasty. If I win," she went on, looking supremely smug, "you must escort me to the chophouse of my choosing."

To Max, the suggestion sounded fair—and safe—enough. The game seesawed for half an hour, then began to tilt toward Max. Eden's aplomb was shaken but not destroyed. Scooting to the edge of her chair, she willed Max to play a diamond. He did, and Eden took it neatly with her trump, then gathered in the next trick as well and waited triumphantly for Max's last card. To her horror, it was also the last trump. He flipped the cards into his pile and leaned back, hands entwined behind his head. "Well? What shall I demand? A cheese tart? A ginger trifle? A perfect rice pudding?"

Chagrined, Eden stared at Max. "You may ask for anything, but I do apples best." She was quite serious, but still couldn't believe she'd lost. "You didn't cheat did you? No, you're not that sort." Pensively, she chewed her finger. Outside, the afternoon sun had broken through the morning fog, and a halo of golden light bathed the room. A carriage rolled by, the coachman calling for a stray dog to get out of the way. A woman's laughter floated up to them, followed by a deep muffled voice. Max unfolded himself from the chair and went to the window.

"Holy St. Hubert," he muttered, peering between the draperies, "it's Harriet!"

Eden got up, too, but didn't move from her place by the little table. "I don't suppose Lady Harriet has come to apologize."

Max didn't seem to hear her. He was moving uneasily around the room, pushing at the full sleeves of his lawn shirt until they almost reached his elbows. "Women," he groaned, and came to a sudden stop in front of Eden as he caught the sound of approaching footsteps. Eyeing the door as if he expected it to be splintered at any moment by a battering ram, Max motioned for Eden to keep quiet. "We won't answer," he whispered, as Master Van de Weghe called from the corridor.

Observing Max's big motionless form, Eden had to bite her lips to keep from beaming at his deception. At last, when the *hofmeester's* tread had faded away, she erupted into a giggle. "Oh, won't she be vexed! You're very brave, Max!"

Max made a face. "I'm craven, to let that woman cow me." He gave Eden a sheepish look. "I don't know why, but I didn't feel like facing Harriet just now."

Eden's glee evaporated at the recognition of Max's helplessness. It struck her as strange, even incomprehensible, that a man who had fought in some of the fiercest battles of the past decade should be intimidated by his fiancée. "No doubt," she said without thinking, "you didn't want Harriet to know we were playing cards."

Max scowled at Eden. "Rot. Why should Harriet care about that?"

To Eden, the answer seemed obvious. Max's denial stung. Did he really not consider her a worthy rival to Harriet Villiers? But why should he? Harriet was wealthy, aristocratic, beautiful and admired. As for Eden, though her bloodlines might be as exalted as Harriet's, she was still a bastard from Kent. Max didn't take her seriously, and it hurt.

"You find me negligible, don't you?"

Max looked genuinely puzzled. "No. How could I, and still promote your cause with the King?"

What had begun as a pout spilled over into anger. "Oh! That's cruel! Must you think of me only as some sort of pawn, as ammunition for your political arsenal? What about me—Eden? I'm a person, not just the product of lessons and coaching and pretty clothes!"

Taken aback by her outburst, Max put out a placating hand. "I know that," he soothed, trying to rein in his impatience. "Eden, you must cease harping about my regard for you. It's my commitment to Jack that counts. Were he not in the Tower, he would be supervising your preparations. By chance, the responsibility has fallen to me, and I'm doing everything I can to help." Watching her unhappy face, Max knew he wasn't explaining himself very well. Yet every word he spoke was the truth. Why couldn't Eden understand the awkward position he'd been put in by her father's arrest? Some men would have forsaken her from the start. Others would have taken advantage of her helplessness. But he was doing his best not to, despite the temptation to do otherwise. "If you're angry because I went abroad, that couldn't be prevented. It wasn't just because of Craswell, but on orders of the King. I was destroying a French arsenal at Givet."

Eden brushed aside his military adventures with a careless hand. "I'm not talking about what you do when you're not here," she cried, "but what you do when you are! You worry so about Harriet's precious feelings and give not a dandiprat for mine! Or do you think because I'm a country bumpkin that I don't have any?"

Max was torn between exasperation and repentance. She was right, in her way. He had behaved rather highhandedly. Fearing that she might cry, Max put an arm around her shoulders and gave her a little hug. "I've had many distractions," he admitted, and was surprised when Eden made no attempt to pull away. "The war on the Continent, searching for Craswell, the charges against your father, some plaguing family quarrels over property—" He was speaking much more rapidly, and freely, than usual. Suddenly he stopped, his chin resting on the top of Eden's head.

"You serve too many masters," Eden interjected, allowing herself the luxury of leaning against Max's chest. "I' truth, I'm sorry you had to inherit my poor suit, as well."

"But I don't mind," he protested, his voice dropping a notch as his hand slid down the heavy green silk that covered her back. "This house is a happier place with you in it."

"Oh!" Eden gasped with astonishment and stared at Max. She could hardly believe he'd uttered such gratifying words.

Judging from the embarrassed look on Max's face, neither could he. "It's more like … ah, family," he explained a bit clumsily, his hand straying to the curve of her waist. "Not that my relatives were a kindly lot. But then you've met Rudolf."

Eden gazed up at Max and blinked in confusion. What she beheld in those hazel eyes startled her. She could have sworn that she saw more than sadness or anxiety. A yearning, perhaps, or some other need that she couldn't recognize? She was still trying to solve the riddle when Max claimed her mouth in a tentative, exploratory kiss. Taken by surprise, Eden's mind registered a protest, but her body melted pliantly into Max's embrace. The kiss deepened, driven by that unleashed hunger she had unwittingly glimpsed.

To her amazement, Eden responded with an eagerness that was as foreign to her as it was intoxicating. She felt Max's hands caress her back as he kissed her chin and the curve of her throat. Resting in his arms with her head tipped back, she hazily noted that the door was opening. A moment later, Max froze then released her so abruptly that she stumbled against the little inlaid table.

"Harriet!" Max exclaimed, pushing back his hair and attempting a weak smile. "I thought you had left."

"I can see that." Harriet's eyes could have chilled the sun. "I intended to, but I sensed you were at home." She gave a brisk tug at the velvet mantle draped over her shoulders. "It seems I was right. If ever a man was comfortably settled in, it's you, Max."

The brittle note jarred Eden as she tried to recover from Max's kiss and concentrate on Harriet. As for Max, his valiant effort to regain his composure was only a partial success. "Will you stay and sup with me?" he invited, moving in swift, long strides to help Harriet with her mantle. "I can explain everything over a succulent pheasant."

Harriet's glance flickered over Eden. "It's the succulent *peasant* that concerns me," she retorted. She shook off Max's hand and whirled, the mantle's lace-edged tails swinging behind her like angry butterflies.

"Harriet ..." Max began, but was silenced by the frosty glare she threw him from over her shoulder.

Eden, however, was not so easily quieted. "La, Milady, it seems I've won my wager, after all. Now Max owes me *three* kisses." She stood in the middle of the room, her fingers laced behind her back, her hips swaying slightly under the gimped silk skirts.

"What wager?" demanded Harriet, her voice more shrill than brittle.

Eden glanced from a bewildered Max to an irate Harriet and shrugged. "I bet Max a kiss that you were the most unreasonable woman in London. He argued and argued and finally convinced me otherwise. So," she added, unlinking her fingers and raising her hands, "I had to pay him with a kiss. It's part of my training, you see."

Harriet's perfect dark eyebrows arched. "Training? To do what?"

Eden tilted her head to one side. "To please. To charm. To captivate. Isn't that so, Max?"

Max's expression was somewhere between stunned and apoplectic. But it was to Harriet, not Eden, that he turned. "It's true, she's being groomed for the court. It's Marlborough's idea," he averred, and winced at his disclaimer.

"If Jack weren't in the Tower, I wouldn't be here," Eden chimed in, affecting a careless manner as she patted Max's arm in apparent commiseration. "But, Milady, you must be very proud of Max for defending your disposition. Foolish as I am, I'd let my own eyes and ears deceive me. Max made such a persuasive case on your behalf that I came to believe you were indeed a most agreeable person, right up until you walked through that door."

The lovely oval of Harriet's face grew yet more pale. "You're impudent," she said through clenched teeth. "As for you," she went on, waving a gloved finger at Max, "for the sake of our future, I should like to take as truth what this creature says, though common sense tells me otherwise. I will not stay to sup, but shall expect you to call on me early tomorrow." On that imperious note, Harriet departed, banging the door behind her.

Eden's glee was dashed by the stormy expression on Max's face. Having overcome his shock at Harriet's ill-timed intrusion, he turned wrathful. "Why," he demanded, shaking Eden by the shoulders, "didn't you keep quiet? Why didn't you just disappear? I told you before, I'm in charge in this house!"

Eden felt like a rag doll in his grip; the strand of pearls snapped, and little beads spilled all over the floor. "I thought I was helping you!" she cried as he noted the broken necklace and let go of her. "You just stood there like a stick!"

Max said nothing, but stomped to the window where he stood with his shoulders slumped. His hand went to the drape, but he made no attempt to pull it back. After a painful silence, he turned on his heel, brushed past Eden and headed for the door. "How can you pretend you helped," he growled from the threshold, "when in fact you hindered?"

Angry and humiliated, Eden let loose her reply a fraction too late. "I didn't ask to be kissed!" she called after him, but the door had already closed in his wake. Fighting back tears as she bent to collect the scattered pearls, Eden spoke again, though this time in a whisper: "I didn't, I swear it!"

But somewhere deep within her, a small voice said she lied.

Chapter Seven

MARLBOROUGH'S LONGTIME FRIEND LORD AILESBURY had barely escaped going to the block on Tower Hill. Other accused conspirators had not been so lucky. The King's justice had been meted out. But rumors persisted that neither William nor Bentinck was satisfied. At home and abroad, there were still Jacobites plotting to restore James. As for Marlborough, his trial date had been postponed, due to insufficient evidence.

Eden had visited him on two other occasions, but the second time she found his quarters moved to a cramped cell without amenities. The gaoler had been much more punctilious about the length of the visit, hustling her away after a brief ten minutes. Despite her father's optimism, Eden had left the Tower precincts in a somber mood.

As was often the case these days, Max was not at home when she returned. He seemed to have a number of pressing engagements concerning his inheritance on the Continent and his appeasement of Harriet. Unable to express her anxieties about Marlborough to Max, Eden cast discretion to the wind and entrusted her innermost fears to *Vrouw* de Koch. As it turned out, the housekeeper knew a great deal more than Eden had realized.

"This is too small a house to hide much," she told Eden, plying her with freshly baked current buns and strawberry jam. "Himself tries to keep his little secrets, but I know him too well."

"You were his nurse?" Eden ventured, toying with a warm currant bun.

Vrouw de Koch shrugged. "Of a sort. I was his mother's confidante. She was a pretty thing—smart, too. Catharina of Anhalt-Dessau, daughter of the Elector of Saxony. She married Prince Frederick of Nassau-Dillenburg, Duke of Brabant." The housekeeper paused to take another bite of the buttered bun she held. "Happy they were, all things considered."

"Such as?" Eden murmured innocently.

Vrouw de Koch was too shrewd to be duped. "It's not just tittle-tattle. You talk of Jan and Jana from the farm—that's gossip. But when you're speaking of German Electors and Flemish Princes, that's history. Remember," she admonished, wagging a buttery finger, "you heard it here. Prince Frederick was killed in the war, at Huy. Princess Catharina wasted away. A broken heart, maybe, but more likely one of those sicknesses that takes people young. They had only the one child, Maximilian. The others were stillborn, which was very sad. You'd think Prince Max would be spoiled, eh?" She didn't wait for Eden's answer, but gave a firm shake of her head. "Not a bit of it! Sometimes I thought they blamed him for living when the others didn't."

"You mean they were unkind?"

"Oh, no. But hard. They expected much of him. It was as if they wanted him to make up for all the others." *Vrouw* de Koch's round face softened. "A pity they didn't do more to help him. The rest of his family are worthless, especially that meddlesome Rudolf."

Eden reflected briefly, then risked asking the question that had been taunting her for weeks. "What about that unfinished portrait in the other bedroom? Who is she?"

Vrouw de Koch suddenly seemed absorbed in brushing errant crumbs from the white whisk that covered her bosom. "I've never seen it. His grandmother, maybe."

Eden sensed the other woman's evasiveness, but had no opportunity to press the matter. *Heer* Van de Weghe had burst into the room, his usual aplomb ruffled. "An invitation has come, from His Majesty. There is to be a levee at Whitehall two days hence."

Even though the royal summons was anticipated, Eden didn't feel ready. Anxiously she watched the *hofmeester* scurry off, tufts of hair standing straight up on his balding head like the feathers of an agitated canary.

Almost two hours later, Eden finished her singing lesson, leaving *Signor* Macarelli with his usual severe headache. His eager departure was interrupted by Max, whose entrance all but knocked the little Italian down.

"*Scusi*," Max murmured, setting the music teacher on his feet and grinning at a startled Eden. "At last! King William's keepers are allowing him to go out in public!"

"I don't know ...." Eden gulped and passed an uncertain hand over her forehead. "Max, I'm afraid. I've not been an apt pupil. I have no sophistication. I shall embarrass Jack, and you, as well."

Max gave her arm a little squeeze. "Rot. You're wonderfully real and disarmingly honest. William will appreciate that. Just don't talk much."

"Ooh …." Eden's expression was withering, even as she clung to Max's fingers on her arm and wondered if he remembered their kiss. "You think I'm an imbecile, don't you?"

"Of course not," he answered in a reasonable tone. "You've had only a short time to learn history and politics, that's all." Max took her hand in both of his. "Don't fret, you'll probably have only the briefest conversation at this first meeting."

Fleetingly, Eden glanced at her hand, imprisoned in Max's long fingers. She felt uneasy, yet comforted by his touch. "You're not still vexed with me?" she inquired wistfully, thick lashes shielding her eyes.

Max looked vaguely puzzled. "Vexed? Oh." He shrugged. "Not anymore. I've made amends to Lady Harriet, though it cost me almost two months' rent. I must beg Dame Chance's help when next I dice at the coffeehouse."

Gritting her teeth, Eden withdrew her hand. "You bribed her! What sort of love is that?"

"What business is it of yours to ask?" Max barked, no longer puzzled or benign.

Eden thrust out her chin in a pugnacious manner. "I need to understand this 'love' business, as carried on by the nobility. It's certainly not the same in a village."

Max's face grew dark, though his eyes held an ironic expression. "If that lout at the Bell and Whistle was an example of how you've learned about love, you know nothing about the subject."

Eden made an angry slashing gesture with her hand. "*Zut!* At least Charlie Crocker isn't mean-spirited! I can't imagine how you could learn of love from Lady Harriet, who seems about as warm as February frost!"

Max reached for Eden as if he intended to shake her, but then restrained himself. "I didn't say I learned to love from Lady Harriet," he said with quiet dignity before turning to take his cloak from the newel post. His hazel eyes had an intensity that conveyed both searing heat and chilling cold. "I learned all I could ever need to know about love from my wife."

Eden's jaw dropped, but no sound came from her mouth. With a deliberate step, Max ascended the staircase.

THE PALACE AT WHITEHALL HAD been the seat of English monarchs since the reign of Henry VIII. William of Orange, however, preferred the country air of Kensington. Plagued by asthma, William found London's reeking atmosphere unhealthy, but deferred to his English subjects by holding court at least once a week at Whitehall. Often these were public appearances, with the King playing the gracious host in the beautiful banquet hall designed by Inigo Jones.

There had been a damp chill in the spring twilight as Eden and Max set out for the palace in a rented coach, a strained silence between them. She had not yet recovered from the shock of learning that Max had had a wife. No doubt that unfinished yet lovely face on the canvas in the empty bedroom belonged to the woman Max had married. There had been no opportunity to question *Vrouw* de Koch during the hectic hours of preparation, but Eden assumed that the poor creature had died. Certainly that would explain a great deal about Max that had puzzled Eden until now.

Nervous and on edge, Eden tried to concentrate on the handsome homes along the way. Almost all of them had been built some thirty years earlier, after the great fire. She gawked openly at the gold and rose-colored brick, the fine wrought iron, the row upon row of windows, the balconies and arches, the colorful parterres.

Whitehall, with its jumble of buildings from a bygone era, struck her as a dowdy matron set among a bevy of fresh-cheeked maids. The company, however, was another matter. Lackeys in green, gold-laced livery held candelabra on the stairs, pages in blue satin trimmed with crimson and gold scurried to satisfy the guests' every whim, musicians in ivory silk played Scarlatti, and footmen in purple and silver served tasty delicacies from gilded dishes.

But it was the noblemen who evoked the greatest gasps from Eden. Not only did they far outnumber the women, but their apparel overshadowed that of the fairer sex by far. Shut up in Clarges Street these past two months, except for her unnerving riding lessons and her visits to the Tower, Eden had only glimpsed the mincing beaux who decorated the better parts of London. Here in the banqueting house at Whitehall, she was confronted by a sea of silk and satin-clad men, as exotic as rare tropical birds. It occurred to her that the elaborate wigs dictated the posing attitudes of their wearers, because they restricted movement of both head and shoulders. Preening on high-heeled shoes, with a gem-studded snuffbox in one hand and a lace handkerchief in the other, many had highlighted their powdered faces with tiny stars, crescents or triangular patches. Eden was relieved that neither Max nor Marlborough aspired to the height of fashion. Max was plainly garbed in his dove-gray breeches with buckles at the knee and a long blue coat decorated with three rows of silver braid. Yet he still appeared ill at ease in his court clothes.

As it turned out, his lack of enthusiasm for dressing à la mode was shared by the King. Indeed, had William of Orange not been sitting in the chair of state, Eden would never have picked him out as her sovereign lord. Though he affected the formal wig, it was unpowdered, and there was no suggestion of the much admired furling horns on either side of the center part. William's nod to fashion was a light shade of brown, which, Eden judged, was probably not unlike his own hair. His eyes were an intense brown, his mouth stern yet malleable, the brows even and well etched. But it was the nose that dominated William's face, large and beaklike, evidence of the aggressive side of his character and strength of purpose that reposed in his frail frame.

The King was a small man, thin and wiry, with an air of weariness about him. Though Eden knew he was the same age as Marlborough, William could have passed for the Earl's father.

At last Eden dared to broach a comment. "He looks so … insignificant," she whispered to Max behind her fan. "Somehow, I thought he'd look more like Jack. Or even you," she added, unable to take her eyes off the King, who was listening to an animated monologue by a handsome young man at his left.

Max was accepting a glazed cherry tart from a tray proffered by a buck-toothed page. "He's never been robust," Max admitted, his tone even but distant. "I fear he's aged greatly since the Queen died."

"Sad," Eden sighed, thinking it was also a pity that William should be so puny and unattractive. But most of all, she fretted over Max's impersonal attitude and his lack of moral support. If ever Eden needed words of encouragement, it was now, when she was about to make the most important impression of her life. Tentatively she put a hand to the claret-colored curls whipped into a gleaming confection by Elsa. "Max," she began, as the King laughed so hard that he started to cough, "do you think I look … passable?"

Max, however, was looking not at Eden but at the young man who had so amused the King. "That's Joost van Keppel. He's signaling that we may be introduced to His Majesty. Are you ready?" His eyes skimmed over Eden, exhibiting neither approval nor censure. The tight rein he held over his emotions bordered on physical pain. In Clarges Street, she had descended the staircase in a cloud of copper-colored silk and black lace mesh, the candlelight catching the threads of silver in her petticoats and the shimmering curls. Her full ruffled sleeves were decorated with perfect black bowknots that inched their way across the top of the bodice to nestle against her creamy breasts. On her feet were silver slippers with topaz stones set in tiny buckles, and on her hands she wore gloves of spidery black lace. If Max had always considered Eden disarming, on this night he found her utterly breathtaking. But of course he had no right to say so.

Eden's hand tightened around her China fan. Her legs felt weak, and her stomach turned over. "I asked you," she breathed, her eyes enormous, "how do I look?"

Though he winced inwardly, Max seemed to give her no more than a cursory glance. "Satisfactory. How else after all these weeks of planning and great expense?"

With what felt like all her strength, Eden lifted the lace mesh and silk skirts so that she could turn her back on both companion and King. She could not face the one without the sustenance of the other. If she had cherished Max's kind words before, she hungered for them now. Without his support, her cause—and Jack's—was lost. "I want to go home," she whispered. "Send for the coach."

Max was genuinely stunned by her attitude. "Eden—don't be a diddlewit. You're just nervous."

But she was already pushing through the crowded room, oblivious to the satin toes she trod on and the velvet sleeves she crumpled. She had spent over two months getting ready for this moment, and Max had ruined it with his cold indifference! He was a false friend to Marlborough and a traitor to her cause. Eden hoped he hadn't bothered to follow her from the banquet hall; she preferred not to speak to him ever again.

Tinkling laughter, grating voices and clattering china all but drowned out the musicians playing a lively Italian air. The colorfully costumed courtiers were a blur as she sought the nearest exit. Eden would have achieved her goal had she not suddenly been forestalled by Lady Harriet Villiers, a vision in green and gold.

"La," exclaimed Harriet, plying her fan in the most acceptedly languid manner, "I could scarce believe my ears when Max told me he was letting you tag along to meet the King! Did my darling realize how rashly he was behaving?"

No greater change in Eden could have been wrought had Harriet drenched her with a bucket of ice water. Tossing her curls and squaring her shoulders, Eden met the other woman glare for glare. "I was about to take some fresh air," she retorted, trying not to let the heat rise in her voice, "but now that I know what is so badly spoiled in here, I might as well rejoin my escort."

Harriet's fine brows shot up like bird wings, and an angry flush filtered through her heavy powder. Before she could counter Eden's remark, Max had joined them, a firm hand on each of their shoulders.

"I see you two are having a gossip." His smile was almost convincing. "The King heads this way. Joost has put him in a fine humor, I might add."

Harriet regained her temper at a visible cost. Her emerald eyes flickered over Eden in an attempt to dismiss her. "Joost is very adept at that, my sweet. Haven't we often spoken of his genius for pleasing His Majesty?"

"Yes," Max replied rather absently. Keppel, who was of more than average height, could be seen halfway across the room, but William had been swallowed up by the crowd. "Excuse me," Max murmured, letting go of Eden and Harriet. "Watch me, then follow." The command was intended for Eden, but Harriet kept to her side, more gaoler than companion.

Having committed herself, Eden wasn't about to let Harriet distract her. Anxiously she glanced down at the coppery silk of her gown and the matching petticoats. Her high, pleated *fontange* cap was in place, and its copper streamers floated down her back. Max had deemed her satisfactory, but Eden knew she was much more. Even now several men were turning her way, making no attempt to hide their admiration both for her and for the aristocratic Lady Harriet Villiers.

Eden was forced to concede that Max simply didn't find her attractive. His opinion might be valued, but it wasn't important. The only opinion that mattered was the King's. Every word, every gesture, every glance must be directed at winning William of Orange. Eden took a deep breath as she and Harriet paused at the edge of the group of courtiers clustered around Max, Keppel and the King.

Eden must also try to ignore Harriet's ominous presence, despite the conciliatory manner the other woman had assumed.

"La," Harriet remarked in a subdued voice, "note that my good uncle, Milord Bentinck, tries to capture the King's attention. How Uncle Wilhem hates his young rival, Keppel! They are like a faithful old lion and a skittish young tiger."

More surprised by Harriet's sudden change of attitude than her disclosure about William's feuding rivals, Eden was momentarily distracted. "I forgot," Eden confessed, "that Milord Bentinck was related to you." She tried to pick out the Dutch statesman among the churning covey of courtiers. A serious man with graying red hair was standing to one side, his face puckered in an expression of bewildered rejection. "Is that Milord Bentinck?" Eden asked under her breath.

Harriet's fine eyebrows shot up. "What? Where?" She seemed inexplicably obtuse.

"There," replied Eden, nodding toward the older noble, whose attempt at fashion was ill-suited to his stolid demeanor.

Harriet held a slim white hand to her eyes. "La, I seem bat-blind! To think I espied the dear man only a moment ago! Pray point with your fan, Mistress. The room grows hazy with smoke."

Trying to check her impatience, Eden jerked her fan in Bentinck's direction. "He's no more than ten feet away, Milady. I' faith, your sight is—" She stopped abruptly, startled as much by the sudden shocked expression on Harriet's face as by the unexpected immobilization of her fan. Turning slowly, her eyes widened and her mouth fell open. "Good God almighty and seven hands around!" Eden cried as, to her horror, she discovered that her fan was lodged in the unpretentious furls of King William's wig.

"We beg your pardon," came a gruff voice with a foreign accent. "By your leave, Mistress, please liberate our wig."

Woodenly clutching the fan, Eden felt dozens of eyes boring in on her. She was dimly aware of Max looming over the rest, his sharp features frozen in dismay. To her astonishment, it was Harriet who rushed to the rescue.

"Your Majesty!" she exclaimed, sweeping a practiced curtsy, "it was an accident! Mistress Eden was trying to point someone out to me, and she gestured with her fan." Her hand glided through the air like a white dove, then deftly extricated Eden's fan from William's wig. "Allow me, Sire," she exhorted, gingerly smoothing the waves of artificial hair into place. "Perfect! Your Majesty's imposing appearance makes King Louis tremble with envy!"

Mortified, Eden watched Harriet's eyelashes flutter like an insect's wings and realized that even the King was not immune to the insidious woman's charms. A large open space had formed around Eden, Harriet and William as the other courtiers withdrew. Max stood rooted nearby, his visage showing signs of a gathering storm.

For Eden, no door had ever seemed as far away as the nearest exit in Inigo Jones's banqueting house. Mercifully, the King was ignoring her. Instead he was murmuring his gratitude to Harriet and bestowing a perfunctory kiss on her hand. Then he turned to the dais where Bentinck brooded and Keppel pranced like a pony.

"Max!" exulted Harriet, her smile sweet as sugarplums. "Haven't we had the most extraordinary incident? Eden got to meet the King! "

"So I saw," Max muttered, eyeing Eden with barely controlled fury. "It's time to leave. Indeed, it's already too late."

But again, Harriet seemed to intercede. "Now Max," she countered, a graceful hand at the tiny spray of violets that sprouted from the bosom bottle she wore in her décolletage, "don't let a minor gaucherie spoil your evening. We must share a dish of early strawberries and thick cream."

Max vacillated, inadvertently giving Joost van Keppel time to approach the trio. "Zounds," exclaimed Keppel, studying Eden with an inquiring eye, "can this be your protégée, Max? She's kin to Marlborough, I hear."

With a fuming glance at Eden, Max turned to Keppel. "Don't blame Jack," he muttered. "The poor man has troubles enough."

Keppel pivoted just enough to show off the handsome embroidered clocks that adorned his silk stockings. He was a handsome young man, with well-defined features and an excellent physique, but for Eden, his attributes were lost under the heavy powder and elaborate wig. More to the point, she wished she could lose herself among this hostile company and flee London. Even the Berengers seemed congenial by comparison.

"Marlborough deserves a better fate," Keppel remarked, though Eden wasn't sure whether the Dutchman alluded to the Earl's imprisonment—or her.

Speculatively, Keppel gazed at Harriet, who was looking vaguely belligerent. "His Majesty receives poor advice. Perhaps I should test the wind and put in a word on His Lordship's behalf." With a careless motion, he withdrew an ivory snuffbox from his red damask coat. Inserting a pinch in each nostril and sniffing with consummate delicacy, Keppel eyed Bentinck across the room. "It seems to me that it's time for a breath of fresh air to blow through these stale old walls."

"Cheek," breathed Harriet, rising to the bait. "Have you ever seen a new foal run at Newmarket?"

Keppel regarded her with a bemused expression. "No, but I've seen an old fool try to run the King." Ignoring Harriet's ire, he sneezed twice, bowed to both women and nodded to Max before sauntering away in the direction of the royal dais.

"Boor!" cried Harriet. "He hates my uncle because the King relies so much on Uncle Wilhem's expertise! And because His Majesty and Uncle Wilhem were boys together in the Gelderland! Joost is a mere popinjay, a dancing doll!"

Several courtiers were turning to see why Lady Harriet was so annoyed, but Max put a firm hand on her arm. "You forget that your uncle has done much to persecute Jack, who happens to be my friend. I had hoped that our engagement might persuade him to leniency."

"Oh, pooh!" retorted Harriet with a wave of her hand. "Our union doesn't include the entire English peerage, half of which seems bent on regicide!" Abruptly, she composed herself and turned those mesmerizing emerald eyes on Max. "Take me home, my sweet. I'm most fatigued."

Eden, who had been standing in miserable isolation, tried to look at Max, but faltered. He had already motioned to a lackey and was dropping a coin in the lad's hand. "I have a rented coach," he said, then jerked a thumb in Eden's direction. "Will you see this ... young lady into it?" With only the most cursory of nods, Max sent Eden on her way.

Blindly, she followed the lackey out of the banquet hall. The ride to Clarges Street seemed to take forever. But as she dragged her elegant silk skirts up the steps and let herself in as noiselessly as possible, Eden's resolve hardened. The evening had been a disaster, there was no use avoiding the fact. But the gaffe she had made wasn't irreparable. Nor, she was convinced, had it been her fault.

Harriet was a nasty creature whose uncle happened to be the King's closest adviser—and an adversary of Marlborough's. Harriet had embarrassed Eden not only out of spite, but also to hamper the Earl's cause. Surely Max could understand his fiancée's motives. Eden could almost appreciate the other woman's petty jealousy. But Harriet's interference with Marlborough's fate was another matter. The Earl's life was not a trifle to be jeopardized by a spoiled chit's whims.

Quite worked up into a frenzy of righteous indignation, Eden headed not for her upstairs bedroom, but to the little parlor with the paintings she admired so much. She lit the tapers in the sconces that flanked the Venetian mirror, then she collapsed onto a tufted ottoman. She shed her dainty silver slippers, peeled off the spidery gloves and tossed her cloak onto the Italian harpsichord. In the flickering candlelight, Max's snow scene took on an eerie brumal cast. Frowning, Eden tried to relax and overcome her sense of failure.

After an hour passed she grew sleepy, but willed herself to stay awake. She hoped Max would not while away the night with his spiteful fiancée. To her surprise, no more than another five minutes passed before she heard his footsteps in the hall. Summoning up both courage and dignity, Eden called to him just as he put one foot on the bottom stair. "Max, I need to speak with you. Please."

Max peered into the gloom, his hand on the balustrade. "*Schoft,*" she heard him mutter, but he reluctantly complied. "Don't tell me you're going to make a tearful apology at this time of night," he grumbled, going to a small cabinet inlaid with mother-of-pearl and jet. "There's not much you can say to excuse your ridiculous behavior." Removing a grizzled glass decanter, he poured himself a drink, pointedly making no offer for Eden to join him.

"Max, you're an ass." Eden was bracing herself against the harpsichord, but her gaze was level. "No—it's that you're easily duped. Harriet makes you dance like a marionette, and I'll be halfway to heaven before I can figure out why. The woman has all the charm of rust."

Towering over Eden, Max held the tumbler of gin in one hand and drummed the fingers of the other on the burnished harpsichord lid. "You're insolent. You have no right to criticize Harriet. Or me. Here you are," he went on, his voice rising steadily, "trying to shift the blame for your own stupidity! When all you had to do was curtsy nicely and say a few pretty words and look completely dazzling. But instead," he roared, the gin sloshing over the brim of his cup, "you humiliated yourself—and me! You played the diddlewit! It was a farce!" Max gulped at his gin, then made a visible effort to get his temper under control.

His harangue had made its impression, yet only one word mattered to Eden. Max had called her dazzling. Not satisfactory, but dazzling. She felt the beginning of a smile on her lips, yet knew she must remain serious.

Tossing down the rest of the gin, Max shook himself like an enormous pup. "This is worthless blather. It's late, I'm to bed." He set the tumbler on the harpsichord and started for the door.

"Why didn't you tell me before?" Eden's question was phrased softly, yet with portent.

He turned, one foot on the threshold. "What?"

Trying not to betray her nervousness, Eden pushed an errant curl from her temple. "You refused to tell me how I looked. You threw me into the lion's den without a weapon. Did you truly think I was confident or sophisticated enough to survive on my own?"

Max's face contorted with annoyance. "Don't be silly! I complimented your appearance. What did you want, for me to grovel at your hem like Charlie the Lout?"

Eden lifted her chin. "You're not Charlie. Nor are you a lout. Why," she asked, and a sudden, jarring note of despair pierced her voice, "don't I hate you?" Eden began to cry, loud, racking sobs that convulsed her body and forced her to cling to the harpsichord like a shipwreck victim clutching at flotsam.

"God." Max's composure was jolted, and he took three long strides across the little parlor to her side. "Stop!" he commanded, shaking her bare shoulders. "You're overwrought! Here …." He reached for the decanter, remembered that he'd put it away and instead patted Eden's back in a soothing gesture. Her sobs subsided, though tears still coursed down her cheeks. Perhaps he should call for *Vrouw* de Koch and let the housekeeper put her to bed. But the jumble of curls that nestled in the curve of Eden's shoulder, the agitated rise and fall of her soft breasts, the wounded misery in her ebony eyes made him pause. For all her insouciant ways and ebullient manner, she was a vulnerable little thing, a fish out of water, an innocent country lass lost in the corruption of city and court.

Staring into her dark, sorrowful eyes, Max felt goaded to make an apology. But the words he was carefully forming never came out. Instead, his mouth claimed hers in a kiss that was as inevitable as it was impassioned. Eden's knees buckled and her fingers clutched at Max's chest for support. He was holding her close, lifting her off the floor, searing her lips with his, drawing the breath from her, and somehow reaching down into her very soul. She was limp in his embrace; the evening's catastrophe faded into insignificance.

Max's mouth crept down to the hollow of her throat while one hand lost itself in the tumble of curls at her neck. She pressed her fingers into the fine fabric of his shirt sleeves, savoring the taut strength of his arms. Max's touch on her breast evoked a gasp of delight, stirring emotions that Eden had only glimpsed at their first kiss. In the jumble of her mind, Marlborough's words came back to her, about differentiating between wants and needs. With Max, Eden knew no difference—want and need were one and the same. Without the slightest hesitation, she drew back just enough to permit Max's hand to roam at will, her eyes closed in sweet surrender.

With an agonizing slowness born of awe as much as pleasure, Max's hand all but swallowed up one breast, his thumb poised against her nipple as if willing its bud to burst with desire. All of Elsa's carefully concocted handiwork had now come undone, and shimmering claret tresses spilled over Max's arm. He lifted his mouth from hers to make a strange growling noise deep in his throat, and Eden purred in response. So, she thought hazily, this was love—or was it? Max was betrothed to another, and for Eden, love was a stranger.

But her mental processes failed her. Max was loosening the bowknots on her gown, slipping down the lace and silk and ruffles to reveal her sheer lawn chemise. This, Eden realized in some still rational part of her mind, was the moment of restraint. Should the dainty chemise with its edge of fine lace yield to Max's covetous hands, instinct told her, all was lost. Opening her eyes, she stared into the chiseled features with their steep plains and rugged angles. The hazel eyes were smoky, a parody of Max's usual cool detachment. He seemed almost helpless, a willing victim of Eden's spell. She felt strangely powerful, and the smile she gave him was as luminous as the April moon.

"Dazzling," he murmured, his long mouth twisting into a grin to match her own. "Is that what I said?"

"Yes." The response was hushed. "Did you mean it?" The hazel eyes sparked, but he didn't reply at once. Instead he slid the chemise over her breasts and groaned with pleasure. The rich fullness invited his caress, incited his kisses. Max buried his face in the sweet ripeness, and Eden cried out with rapture.

"I meant," he breathed, lifting her into his arms, "that I was dazzled. Bewitched, even." He was still grinning as he lowered her onto the faded Persian carpet. "We're insane, you know."

"Yes." Eden's eyes danced as she watched Max drop down beside her and yank off his shirt. The broad chest made her tremble somewhere deep inside, and the muscles of his upper arms rippled in the candlelight. "I thought you thought I was ... drab," she said, wrapping her arms around his neck.

"Drab!" Briefly, Max glanced into a dark corner. "Having you under the same roof is enough to drive a man into exile. Why do you think I went to Brabant?"

"Brabant? Where is that?" Eden tipped her head back so that he could kiss the curve of her throat. "I'm very poor at geography."

"I'm very good at it," replied Max, propping himself up on his elbows. "See here," he said, placing his palm against the bare flesh just above the waistband of her skirts, "this is a gentle plain. It ascends into this intriguing valley," he went on, trailing his fingers between her breasts and making her giggle, "and flanked by the most beautiful mountains in England." Playfully he kissed each breast in turn, then suddenly sobered. "*Schoft.* I sound like a giddy schoolboy! I haven't talked like this in five years!"

"You're wonderful," Eden countered, ruffling his hair with her hand. "Don't stop. I want to learn more."

But Max had moved away from her, though his arm still encircled her waist. "We are mad. At least I am." Pulling free, he got to his feet with scant evidence of his usual natural grace. "Eden, I'm sorry. I almost made fools of us both. You're right, I'm an ass."

"Max!" The wail in Eden's voice made her flinch.

"Please!" he begged, his voice showing pain, "help me to stop wanting you!"

"But I don't want you to stop!" Putting a hand to her head, she tried to regain her composure. Too much had happened to her too quickly. She waited almost a full minute before she looked at Max. "You're right, of course," she said dully. "There must be no scandal to hamper Jack's cause. Help me up."

"Here." Averting his eyes from her naked breasts, Max brought Eden to her feet. "Truly," he began, staring at the top of her head and sounding quite miserable, "I've behaved like a villain. You asked why you didn't hate me. Frankly, you should. I'm reprehensible."

It occurred to Eden that she ought to be embarrassed by her partial nakedness. But the fact was, Max's demeanor disturbed her more. He blamed himself for his desire, yet their lovemaking had seemed so natural, so spontaneous, so predestined, that Eden felt no guilt, only disappointment. "I understand that the King prizes virtue, but what of you?" she finally asked. "Do you hold back because I'm not Harriet? Or because I'm not your wife?"

The bleak expression that crossed his face made Eden's heart sag. But he recovered quickly and reached out to pull up her chemise. "Both." He spoke with anguish. "Or," he added stiffly, adjusting the sheer fabric as if he feared it would burn his fingers, "neither. It's not just a question of your honor, Eden, but of my own, as well."

Puzzled, Eden peered at him. She was about to insist that he explain himself when Max leaned down and brushed the top of her head with his lips. "We'll pretend this never happened," he said, then picked up his shirt and flung it over one shoulder before heading out the door.

In the dying light, Eden watched him disappear into the hall. She didn't understand Max. He seemed to want her, to admire her, even to bend to her will. The moodiness that so often beset him had momentarily fled, turning him into a carefree boy, no longer distant or detached. She had glimpsed another side of Max.

But Eden had no right to offer him help—or love. He was betrothed to Harriet Villiers; she was destined for the King. Whether or not the evening had been a debacle, her father remained in grave danger. Eden's chances with William were fragile, at best. But giving herself to Max would destroy all hope.

For now, it was the only hope her father had.

Chapter Eight

A SWIRL OF ACTIVITY IN THE house on Clarges Street the following morning provided a mask for any tensions that might have surfaced between Eden and Max. Two masons replaced loosened bricks in the kitchen fireplace, *Vrouw* de Koch and *Heer* Van de Weghe almost came to blows over a stray cat, the brewer's weekly delivery had come up short, and a priggish parson called seeking alms for the destitute.

Eden, whose troubled mind had not allowed her to sleep until almost dawn, woke sometime after ten. She still felt weary, but sat up in bed with a pot of hot chocolate and a plate of sugar buns, distractedly perusing the latest edition of the *London Gazette*. The stalled war on the Continent, the Royal Treasury's recall of all monies, and the anti-Catholic hysteria resulting from the assassination attempt on the King all commanded Eden's attention, yet she failed to grasp more than the bald facts. A brief item at the bottom of the page noted that the Earl of Marlborough had been imprisoned in the Tower for over two months. The veiled suggestion that he should be released unless concrete evidence was produced against him evoked heartfelt agreement from her daughter—and rubbed at the wound of her failure.

She had just set the tray aside when Max strolled into the room, his demeanor determinedly casual. Unnerved at the sight of him looking so unruffled, Eden clutched at the neckline of her jade-green robe. "Here—have a sugar bun," she offered, trying to conceal her unease.

Max glanced at the tray, but shook his head. "I've eaten," he replied, going to the window and pulling back the drape to savor the bright spring morning. "I hoped you'd be dressed. We're going to see Jack."

"Oh!" Eden's anxiety fled in the wake of this announcement. "I'll call Elsa. I can be ready in minutes."

Letting the drape fall into place, Max turned to Eden. "Good." He gave her a smile that seemed a mockery of the openness he had shown her the previous night. "I've hired a coach, which should be arriving at any moment." Max was at the door, rearranging the *steinkirk* at his neck and acting with a nonchalance that somehow didn't quite ring true.

"Will you tell Jack about last night?" Eden inquired anxiously.

"Last night?" For a brief moment, Max's color darkened. "Oh! Tie wig!" Relieved when he realized she wasn't referring to his lapse of self-restraint, he shook his head. "I think not. Jack needs to hear only good news."

Gratified, Eden watched him wheel away. Within fifteen minutes, Elsa had helped her into an amethyst silk gown with black velvet panniers falling into a short, graceful train. Eden adjusted the long lappets of her *fontange* cap and added a lace-trimmed manteau, should the breeze be up from the river. Reasonably satisfied with the results of her harried toilette, she descended to meet Max for the ride to the Tower.

Inside the coach, Max sat across from her, his long body awkwardly jammed into the corner. Eden tried not to notice that he was avoiding physical contact with her, but she couldn't ignore his manner in such close confines. It was also impossible to resist the man himself. He was again dressed in his comfortably frayed coat and full-sleeved shirt, and his virile magnetism was more apparent than ever. Deliberately Eden turned away to lift the window's little canvas flap and gaze out at the magnificence of Somerset House with its splendid setting about the Thames.

"You owe me a treat," Max said unexpectedly. "I've been anticipating a veritable pyramid of apple pastry for days."

Eden swerved on the rough-hewn platform to stare at him. "Oh! I forgot! So much else has happened," she explained, twisting her fringed silk parasol in her hands, "and you were ... vexed with me, besides."

Max had assumed a magnanimous air. "Don't fret, I was teasing you." He smiled, but again it was a halfhearted effort. "Indeed, though I beat you at basset, I thought I'd prove myself a good winner and we'd dine at Pie Corner."

Trapping the parasol between her knees, Eden clapped her hands. "I'd like that! I've never eaten in a London public house!"

"I know." Max's smile softened, and grew more genuine in the process. He hoped his invitation would be taken in the spirit it was given, as recompense for his harsh treatment of Eden at Whitehall. As for his reckless attempt at seduction, it was better left ignored. Eden could blame the gin he'd consumed, or his irascible mood. If he tried hard enough, maybe he could believe in such excuses, too. As long as Eden was still under his roof, he had to make every effort to treat her as naturally as possible. Ignoring her had proved disastrous—his lack of praise for her meeting with the King had undermined her self-confidence, and thus seriously damaged Jack's chances. Max could demonstrate his approval by going out with her in public, to Pie Corner and the Tower. But he must avoid being alone with her in private, or the game would be lost.

"The roast pork is excellent," he remarked as the coach turned into Giltspur Street. "And the Cheshire cheese is as mellow as you'll fine in any tavern. It's almost as good as the Dutch imports."

"You're partial," Eden countered, but her eyes sparkled. They were turning away from the river at Black-friars, heading toward the Smithfield markets. Eden could hardly believe that Max was escorting her to dinner. With a little smirk, she wondered what Harriet would think if she found out.

The coach ground to a halt outside the cookshop, where a throng of would-be diners had already gathered for the noon meal. Gripping Eden's elbow, Max steered her through the crowd to the entrance, where a harried host tried to instill patience in his prospective customers.

"Mayhap we should have gone to visit Jack first," Eden remarked, despairing at the crush of people.

But Max, who towered over the others, had signaled to the owner and was already being waved inside. Keeping close to his elbow, Eden quickened her pace to match Max's long strides as they entered the noisy eating establishment. The table found for them was not much larger than a tea tray, inconveniencing Max's long legs.

"It's a very popular place," he said with a little grimace, his voice raised above the din. "I also recommend the chops."

But Eden was too mesmerized by the raucous crowd of diners to consider the menu. Prentices with cropped hair and broad, bold hats laughed under the archway; gentlemen in brocade plundered haunches of port; ladies mingled with whores, and from Eden's perspective, it was hard to tell which was which. She was trying to determine the virtue of a dimpled redhead in peacock blue satin when Max suddenly stiffened in his chair.

"*Schoft!*" he swore, "it's Rudolf!"

Eden pivoted and immediately saw Rudolf, who had just gotten to his feet by the fireplace across the room. "Are you avoiding him?" she asked Max.

"Not precisely." Max, in fact, looked as if he was about to signal to his cousin, but at that moment another man emerged at Rudolf's side, his auburn wig askew as he exuded perfect smoke rings from a long clay pipe. "He has company. Perhaps later …."

Eden put a hand on Max's arm, but was unaware that he flinched. "Who is the other man, the thin one? I know him."

Max watched the pair move toward the door. "Why ask me, if you know him? I can hardly see his face under that damnable wig."

She gave Max's sleeve a little shake. "I don't mean I know him, I mean I recognize him. At least the smoke rings. Now where …?" She withdrew her hand, cursing herself for showing such familiarity. "Smarden!" she exclaimed as Rudolf and his companion bowed themselves out of the cookshop. "He was at the Bell and Whistle with a redheaded man the day I came to see Jack."

At first Max gave Eden a puzzled look, then the hazel eyes snapped with enlightenment. "Holy St. Hubert, I wonder …." He leaped to his feet, almost knocking over the little table. "Let's go," he urged, grabbing Eden by the wrist. "We're going to follow those two. I have a feeling we may have found John Fenwick."

Dimly, Eden recalled that Fenwick had been one of the ringleaders in the conspiracy to assassinate the King. Eden felt a pang of regret for the roast pork and Cheshire cheese, but she understood the importance of apprehending Fenwick. Surely he could—and would—exonerate the Earl of Marlborough.

In the bright spring sunshine, Eden and Max saw their prey climb into a hired hackney coach. Impatiently Max bellowed to their own driver, who was leaning against a timber, exchanging anecdotes with a burly cooper. By the time Eden and Max got underway, Rudolf's conveyance had already turned out of Giltspur Street.

"Damn," cursed Max, leaning out the open door, "we'll have to take a chance that they're heading for the obvious route, toward the Strand." Up ahead, Rudolf had been stalled by a calèche with a broken wheel. When the Count's vehicle finally turned, it headed east, into Cheapside.

"Why is this Fenwick with your cousin?" Eden asked breathlessly as they clattered past the Guildhall.

"Who knows? Rudolf loves his little intrigues, but the company he keeps is dangerous. I presume that ugly wig was meant to disguise Fenwick."

"It would have," Eden admitted, "if he hadn't blown those smoke rings. I remembered more the manner than the man."

"And a good thing," Max said, giving her a little nod of approval. "Assuming, of course, that it *is* Fenwick. I've only seen him once, and that was in a sweating house where the steam obscured my vision. Ah! They've stopped!" Max pounded on the coach, ordering the driver to follow suit. "They've gone into the Exchange." He looked thoughtful and rubbed his long chin. "Harmless in itself, probably."

Eden barely heard Max. She was too caught up in the bustle of English commerce. Everywhere she looked there were knots of people. Dour Scots vainly tried to wring investment tidbits from each other. Spaniards with drooping mustaches and unfashionable short cloaks mingled with Dutchmen wearing thrum caps and earnest expressions. There were Jews with ringlets longer than a woman's, and Irishmen loud with drink and bluster. Serving girls, some fresh from the country and wide-eyed with wonder, scanned advertisements tacked to a pillar, while energetic hawkers peddled all manner of wares, from mandrake and balsam to cordials and tobacco.

Eden's dazzled concentration was broken by Max's sudden descent from the coach. "Wait here," he called. "I see Joost."

Eden saw him, too, a riveting figure in a crimson cape over a gold brocade coat, black shoes with red heels and a gray beaver hat adorned with an ostrich feather. He held a tall walking stick festooned with crimson ribbons and was accompanied by a trio of young men who were only slightly less ostentatious. As Max joined them, she thought he looked like a hawk among peacocks and couldn't help but smile.

The smile faded as Rudolf and his companion emerged from the courtyard of the Exchange. Max prodded Keppel, who turned to stare at the Count and the alleged Fenwick. Leaning from the coach's little window, Eden strained to hear, but she could pick up only a few fragments, mainly from Max.

"That wig … Fenwick … have him arrested!"

Keppel craned his neck, but Rudolf laughed and waved a hand, obviously repudiating Max's charge. As the Count moved into the little circle, speaking in low, confidential tones, Fenwick began inching away, attempting to melt into the crowd that milled around the Exchange.

"Max!" Eden cried, flinging open the coach door. "Fenwick! He's escaping!"

Dodging past Keppel, Max started to give chase, but Rudolf hurled himself at his cousin. "Fool! That's no more Fenwick than I am!" he yelled.

Max pushed at Rudolf, but the two men were so evenly matched in size and strength that neither gave ground. Keppel, meanwhile, had taken action, calling for the guards, who were already pursuing Fenwick. Mindful of their fine attire, Keppel and his companions backed off from the brewing storm between Max and Rudolf.

"We'll tell the King what's happened," Keppel shouted, making for a set of sedan chairs. "I've no doubt those men will capture Fenwick."

If Max was less sanguine, he had no opportunity to say so, for Rudolf had drawn his sword. "You dare meddle, Max?" he sneered as a crowd began to gather. "For all you know, Fenwick's dead!"

Max's reply was a thrust of his own weapon, which just missed Rudolf's upper arm. Horrified, Eden tried to push through the pack of spectators, but she was hemmed in. She could see only Max's and Rudolf's heads, bobbing and weaving as the sound of steel on steel rang out. Irish voices called boisterous encouragement, Spaniards exclaimed in excited foreign accents, Englishmen

cheered lustily, and the Dutch kept silent. Just as Eden was about to surrender
to the crush and din, a buxom orange seller came to her aid.

"H'ain't nobody stops Bruisin' Babby," the woman declared, juggling her
crate of oranges and knocking over a spindly Italian. "Blimey, look at 'em, a
reg'lar pair o' Vikings! Who's yer money on, luv?"

Breathless from her battle through the crowd, Eden put a hand to her
breast. "I have no money," she replied, dismayed at the sight of Max and
Rudolf engaged in what looked like mortal combat. Rudolf was armed with a
lethal four-foot blade of tempered steel; Max had only his ceremonial sword.
The contest was clearly a mismatch.

At their feet a pair of mongrels yapped loudly while the crowd's cheers and
jeers grew increasingly shrill. Rudolf kicked at one of the dogs, momentarily
breaking concentration. Max lunged, his blade tearing his adversary's shirt
sleeve. Incensed, Rudolf aimed a flurry of thrusts in Max's direction, nicking
his right shoulder. Eden cringed, but her companion called for more blood.

"Carve 'im up, Curly!" she shouted, eliciting a protesting cry from Eden.
Bruisin' Babby shrugged her wide shoulders. "Aw right then, kill Curly,
'Andsome! Wot do I care," she remarked in a conversational tone, "they both
be furriners, if ye arsk me."

Trying to ignore the orange seller, Eden winced as Rudolf caught Max
off balance and tried to disarm him. Max's grip was firm, but Rudolf pressed
his advantage with a series of vicious stabs, two of which grazed Max's other
arm. Max was backed up against a pillar, and the crowd behind him refused
to budge.

Eden could endure no more of the unfair battle. Grabbing two oranges
from Bruisin' Babby's basket, she hurled them at Rudolf with all her might.
One missed entirely, but the other glanced off his hip, causing just enough of
a distraction to allow Max to escape from the pillar. Eden snatched up more
oranges, and Babby, titillated by the idea of joining in the fray, began flinging
her wares with deadly accuracy. At least four oranges bounced off Rudolf,
whose face was turning crimson with fury. The spectators were cheering even
more lustily, guffawing and shrieking as if they were in the stalls at Drury
Lane. The superiority of Rudolf's weapon was markedly diminished by the
thudding oranges, which were joined by apples, pears, plums and even a
shower of mackerel.

The missiles were being thrown indiscriminately, however, and Max was
being pelted as well. But the smashed pulp of a pomegranate proved Rudolf's
undoing. His foot slipped, and though he didn't go down, his sudden loss
of balance gave Max the opportunity to send his blade cleanly through his
opponent's right shoulder. A howl of pain escaped Rudolf's lips as his sword
clattered onto the debris-strewn cobbles.

"Pick it up," Max ordered, kicking some of the garbage out of the way. "We're not finished yet!"

The crowd was pressing forward, and Eden had to stand on tiptoe to see Rudolf clumsily reach for his sword, only to jam it in its scabbard.

"Better you should hang from the ramparts at Vranes than die by my sword!" an enraged Rudolf shouted. "You don't have the courage to kill me!"

With the court sword still in his hand and a red stain spreading across his shirt, Max shook his head. "Whatever else you are, Rudi," he said in a level voice, "you're still my wife's brother. Sophie Dorothea's soul wouldn't rest if I killed you. You know how she hated cruelty."

Rudolf made a disparaging gesture, then fumbled with a kerchief to stanch the blood at his shoulder. "It would have been better for her if she'd hated you," he muttered.

But before either of them could speak again they were interrupted by the arrival of a slightly flabby middle-aged man to whom the crowd showed a certain amount of deference. "I say," the newcomer offered in a tentative voice, "this won't do. You're disturbing Sir Isaac Newton. He's trying to count all the old money before he takes it off to the mint."

With a scathing look, Rudolf whirled and shoved his way toward Threadneedle Street. Max wore a stormy expression, but he spoke to the man with a trace of apology. "Forgive me, sir," he said, sheathing his sword and wiping his forehead with his sleeve, "but I think my cousin, Count Rudolf, has been sheltering Sir John Fenwick." The newcomer's heavy dark brows shot up. "You don't say! Now why would he do a thing like that?"

For once Max threw caution to the wind. "Because he's a thieving traitor, that's why! He's been kissing King Louis's arse, and James Stuart's, as well! Make no mistake," he went on heatedly, waving a fist in the general direction of Rudolf's departure, "that villainous cousin of mine is up to his ugly nose in this Jacobite business!"

Eden, who had edged closer and was trying to inspect the blood stain on Max's shirt, was surprised at his invective. So, it seemed, were the remaining onlookers, who began to chatter and argue among themselves. At last Max noticed Eden's presence. "By St. Hubert," he growled, "I would have thought you'd have had sense enough to leave!"

"How could I leave you?" Eden asked in hurt surprise. "You might have been killed." Just uttering the words made her blanch. Though the melee had lasted no more than five minutes, Eden felt as if she had lived a lifetime on the brink of despair. Nothing, she had realized, would be worse than having Max die. As she looked at his scowling face, Eden knew that she not only needed and wanted Max, she loved him. The insight made her feel weak at the knees and slightly dizzy.

Their companion recognized her anguish as well as Max's distress. "Come, let us find a table at the tavern in the courtyard and partake of some drink. You two have had a most disturbing afternoon." His smile was for Eden, but the question in his voice was for Max. "I don't believe I've been ...."

Max had already started to turn away, but stopped to make belated introductions. "Eden, this is Lord Sidney Godolphin, a very dear friend of Milord Marlborough." He looked faintly chagrined as he presented Eden. "Mistress Berenger is kin to Jack Churchill. Perhaps he's mentioned her?"

To Eden's gratification, it was clear that Marlborough had. Godolphin beamed, his round face lighting up in a most endearing fashion. "Of course! I'm delighted! Jack has praised you most highly, and now I see why! Oh, my dear," he went on, taking her hands in his, "Jack is such a fine fellow. I only wish I weren't so powerless to help him. Let us pray that this Fenwick is brought to justice and tells the truth about the conspiracy."

"Surely he will," Eden replied, studying Sidney Godolphin. His dark wig set off an unremarkable face and his brown button eyes seemed to wear a look of perpetual surprise. There was nothing about his unprepossessing appearance to suggest financial acumen or political prowess. If Marlborough was understated, Godolphin was positively bland.

"We were on our way to visit Jack when—" Eden made a sweeping gesture at the filthy cobbles "—this happened. Come, Max, we must tend to that wound. It worries me."

"Nonsense, it's only a scratch," Max scoffed, but he moved swiftly enough toward the tavern, where tables and chairs were set out at the edge of the courtyard under the arches.

"I tried to see Jack last week," Godolphin remarked as several pairs of curious eyes followed the trio. "Alas, I was refused admission. Not only is he more closely guarded, but my alleged disloyalties of the past have tainted my reputation as far as William and Bentinck are concerned. It's a wonder I still have my post with the Treasury!"

"I may not be an Englishman," Max said, dropping into a rail-back chair, "but my betrothed's uncle does a disservice to everyone by excluding you English from real power. I' truth, I blame Bentinck more than William. The King does his best, I think, with two countries to rule and Louis forever at his heels."

"Sage words," remarked Godolphin, as Eden carefully folded a napkin into a bandage for Max's arm. "And you, Mistress, have you met His Majesty?"

"I?" Eden flushed, then busied herself with rolling up Max's torn shirt sleeve and cleansing the wound with a cloth dampened in ale. At least Max wasn't trying to resist her ministrations. "In a way, yes," she answered vaguely, noting with relief that Rudolf's sword had not gone as deep as she'd feared.

Swigging ale and accepting an eel pie from a freckled serving wench, Max didn't even glance at her handiwork.

Noting Godolphin's puzzled expression, Eden quickly changed the subject. "I'm told," she said rather breathlessly, "that you own magnificent racehorses, sir."

Godolphin's face went through a startling transformation. "Indeed, I have brought to this country a most superb animal, the Arabian breed, known for its speed and agility," he said enthusiastically. "Other horses pale by comparison. 'Pon my word, there is nothing as breathtaking as this fabulous equine specimen. Lord Challenger, foaled this first day of February, promises to be a great champion. He is already strong, determined and incredibly fleet. Jack was with me at Newmarket when this excellent animal was born, and he predicted a great future even then." Godolphin paused, his face sagging a bit. "Would that Jack were here to enjoy the upcoming season ...."

He sat in silence for a moment, his eyes wandering toward the Royal Exchange, then he straightened abruptly, one hand gripping his ale mug tightly. "I say, what's that?" He leaned across the table and spoke even more softly than usual. "Max, dear boy, would you consider beating a hasty retreat through the rear door of this tavern?"

Eden and Max both followed Godolphin's surreptitious gaze. A dozen uniformed soldiers with rifles at the ready were marching under the main archway. Casually, Max rearranged his torn shirt, took a drink of ale and spoke over the rim of his mug. "Eden, go see Jack as we planned. That is, if they'll let you in. Tell him about Fenwick. I'm sailing on the next tide." Without apparent haste he got to his feet as the soldiers continued their precision step across the courtyard.

"Max," she breathed, feeling her heart turn to ice, "are you going to Brabant?"

He never heard the question. In a lightning move, he leaped high into the air and grabbed at the carved facade of the building's upper story. In another second he had gained enough leverage to haul himself over the balcony. The stunned soldiers halted on command while their leader boomed out an order for Max to halt. But it was too late. A glance upward revealed only a pair of giggling maids. Max was gone.

Chapter Nine

THE DAY, WHICH HAD BEGUN with uncertainty, then righted itself with Max's invitation, had deteriorated into catastrophe. Sidney Godolphin accompanied Eden to the Tower, only to be rebuffed by a grim-faced guard, who asserted that fresh troubles in the city made it impossible for prisoners to receive visitors. Assuming that word of the scene at the Royal Exchange had already raced through London, Eden and Godolphin made their weary way home.

With a self-deprecating gesture, Godolphin bade her good-bye in front of the blue door in Clarges Street. Assuring Eden that he would do anything he could to help, the nobleman plodded off toward his house in Piccadilly.

Eden was faced with delivering the bad news to *Vrouw* de Koch and the others. The housekeeper, however, took the announcement of Max's departure with at least a hint of good grace.

"And so? Is that one not always in some scrape or other?" she said with a huff, over an armful of comforters she was putting away for the summer. "Dueling with Count Rudolf! Those two never got along, not from the cradle! Mark my words, you heard it here!"

Eden was less inclined to dismiss the whole affair, however. While she sensed that *Vrouw* de Koch had spent much of her life watching Max come and go, Eden knew only one thing—Max had gone, but there was no assurance that he'd come back. Even though Eden didn't understand the subtleties of court politics, she recognized that Max was in serious trouble. That his dilemma somehow involved Sir John Fenwick, Count Rudolf, Milord Bentinck and the King was obvious; why he should be persecuted by the likes of his cousin and perhaps the Crown was considerably less clear. But then

Eden didn't understand why her father had been subjected to such unfair treatment, either. All she really took in was that without Max, her life seemed suddenly empty.

Nor was she able to unravel the reasons for Max's predicament from *Vrouw* de Koch, who was admittedly mystified. Eden did, however, press the housekeeper about Max's wife. It was no longer possible to restrain her curiosity, and when *Vrouw* de Koch brought up a supper tray with plump chicken and feathery dumplings an hour later, Eden put her query bluntly:

"What happened to Sophie Dorothea?"

Only the tightening of the housekeeper's jowls betrayed her surprise at the question. "Well, now," she said, uncovering one of the silver dishes, "it's been a while, some four years." She ran a hand over the starched white cap that covered her graying hair. "It's simple enough—she died in childbirth. So, alas, did the babe. Prince Max was inconsolable."

"That's her picture in the other bedroom, isn't it?" Seeing *Vrouw* de Koch nod, Eden continued quickly. "She was Rudolf's sister, I know that now. Max must have loved her very much."

"Oh, he did!" For a brief moment, the housekeeper's round face took on a nostalgic air. "She was so lovely, all pink and white and golden! Graceful as a gazelle, gracious as an empress, pious as a saint! In other words," she added, sounding more like her usual brusque self, "as unlike her dreadful brother as humanly possible. Still, to give the devil his due, Rudolf was very fond of her, having helped raise her after their parents passed away. He carried on like a wounded bear when she died, and blamed Max for getting her with child. Unreasonable, but that's Count Rudolf, and his grief didn't keep him from trying to take back her dowry, which happened to include Vranes-sur-Ourthe, a pretty place in Brabant. Or at least it was, before everyone got to fighting over it."

Eden sampled a chicken wing and wiped her fingers with a napkin. Strangely enough, she felt no jealousy toward Sophie Dorothea, only pity for the man she and her child had left behind. Max's tragedies far outweighed the snatches of happiness he'd known. Eden's greatest wish was that she might somehow have the chance to give him a future that would put the past to rest. Yet she knew that hope was impossible. "Then Vranes is the inheritance Max talks about?"

Vrouw de Koch tipped her head to one side and helped herself to a slice of chicken breast. "Not precisely. Being second cousins, Max and Rudolf somehow got into a squabble over some property left by a great-grandfather. He was one of those German Electors—not Max's grandfather from Saxony, but Frederick of the Palatinate. The land's in Germany. Dillenburg, in fact. Max's grandfather inherited, but was lazy and left the governing up to his sister's husband, a Hohenstaufen who was Rudolf's grandfather. They shared the revenues, most agreeable on both sides, but the arrangement didn't suit Max's father, or Rudolf's, when their time came. They quarreled, there was litigation, the matter was settled in favor of Max's side of the family."

"That sounds fair, considering it had gone to Max's ancestor, not Rudolf's," said Eden, hoping she'd kept the line of inheritance straight.

Vrouw de Koch nodded, her lacy cap askew. "Everything seemed peaceful, especially after Sophie Dorothea married Max. But even before she died, Rudolf went to war over Vranes, her dower lands. Max didn't take the field—he stayed at Sophie Dorothea's side while she was bearing the babe."

"You mean he fought against Max?" Eden paused, a fluffy dumpling speared on her fork.

"Not so much as he fought for King Louis, who had marched into Brabant." She gestured at her heavy bosom with her thumb. "Who knows, maybe Rudolf thought he could cast his lot with Louis and get both Vranes *and* Dillenburg. But now the whole war is stalled, Dillenburg barely managed to escape Louis's rampage and Vranes dangles between the allies and the French. Or so I gather. This military intrigue is so much chess to me. I prefer cards."

"So do I," murmured Eden, swallowing the dumpling and wishing she had more appetite. "Well," she sighed, leaning back on the chaise longue, "at least Max has found love with Lady Harriet." The glance she shot *Vrouw* de Koch was both anxious and probing.

"Huh!" huffed the housekeeper, snatching up a chicken wing. "That's not love, that's enterprise! Poor Max, he's never stopped mourning Sophie Dorothea. Why, I'd hardly heard him laugh until …." She stopped and stared at Eden. "You make him laugh, you know. That's good for him." Abruptly, she wiped her mouth with a napkin and straightened her apron. "I must be off. Already there have been inquires about Prince Max, and no doubt more to come." With that familiar listing posture, she bustled toward the door, then paused, her hand on the knob. "Why," she asked not so much of Eden but of the room, "are men so dense?" As Eden started to respond, the housekeeper wagged a finger. "Never mind," she admonished, "you *didn't* hear it here!"

THE ROUTINE MUST BE KEPT, Eden told herself, for with Max gone and Sidney Godolphin admitting his helplessness, she remained her father's only hope. There was Keppel, of course, and it was possible that he would rally to their side. But so far there had been no word from him, nor was there news of Fenwick. He had apparently vanished somewhere in the vicinity of the Bank of England.

Forcing herself to meet the May morning, Eden was not entirely displeased to learn that Master Banks, her riding instructor, had come down with an unseasonable ague. He had, however, sent instructions through Elsa that Eden should take a brisk canter through Green Park so she would not lose what little skill—as well as confidence—she had thus far acquired.

Without enthusiasm, Eden put on a rust-colored brocade riding jacket over an amber sidesaddle skirt. Within twenty minutes, she and Elsa were walking their mounts through the park. Though her bay mare was so docile as to be almost inert, Eden's manner was timorous, her seat unsure. Elsa, however, rode easily, a skill acquired on her stepfather's farm. Naturally, she was eager to hear more of the momentous events of the past two days, from the King's levee to Max's flight. Eden tried to relay some of the highlights, but her efforts at sign language were hampered by her need to cling to the reins.

"But the King's wig! It's so amusing!" insisted Elsa, laughing merrily. "Our William, he is not angry, only embarrassed." She paused as Eden's mare came to a stop. "But Prince Max, that is not amusing. Count Rudolf is not a nice man, and he lies about many things."

Eden was inclined to wax eloquent about Rudolf's perfidy, but the words would have been wasted. She had already cursed the Count over and over, blaming him for Max's hasty departure. The portrait of Max was being filled in, and Eden was both touched and dismayed by what she saw. Prince or not, his childhood had not been particularly happy, with his parents making rigorous demands and very likely not showering him with much affection. Indeed, she reflected, flicking the riding crop, his upbringing was not so different from her own. It was no wonder that he had fallen hopelessly in love with his pretty cousin, who no doubt returned his feelings with a fervor that was foreign to him. As a young bridegroom, he had his wife's property at Vranes and at least a claim to his inheritance from the Elector of the Palatinate. Max's life must have held the promise of order and security, with an heir on the way to cement the future.

And then Sophie Dorothea and the child had died. Max had suffered Rudolf's recriminations and fought his cousin's greed. War had come to the Low Countries, tainting Max's claim to Vranes and ravaging the land. It was no wonder that Max was moody and distant. What little love he'd known had been brutally snatched away. Nor, Eden supposed, was it so hard to understand why he'd consider marrying a woman like Harriet. At least she was wealthy. And her family influence would be a boon to a pauper prince, especially a foreigner.

But these perceptions didn't make it any easier for Eden to deal with her own emotions. In fact, Max's very vulnerability moved her, making her want to protect him from future hurt. And, Eden knew, life with Harriet would be full of hurt, for it would be devoid of love. Yet he was determined to marry the wretched woman, while Eden set her sights on the King. It was an impossible situation, made far worse by Max's absence.

Eden sighed again and shook her head, grateful that Elsa was riding a few yards in front of her and could not see the doleful expression on her face. Maybe Elsa was right. Maybe King William had actually been amused, but was unable to show it in front of the courtiers. Or was Eden fooling herself as she had when she was a child and had tried to believe that Charles II had not wanted to single her out in front of his courtiers on the road to Tunbridge Wells?

She was still meditating on the problem when she heard a coach rumbling behind them at a perilous speed. The conveyance was traveling far too fast for the leisurely roads in the park, and as Eden turned, she realized it wasn't going to slow down or swerve to avoid them. Knowing that Elsa couldn't hear the ominous thud of hooves or the menacing creak of wheels, Eden steeled herself and guided her horse straight into Elsa's mount. The startled animals reared, throwing both riders. Ignoring the pain, Eden frantically scrambled to the side of die road and was astonished when the black coach ground to a halt just ten feet away.

Staggering to her feet, Eden quickly surveyed Elsa, who was leaning against a gnarled tree, brushing off her clothes. Their horses had fled, and Eden swore softly under her breath. *Heer* Van de Weghe would be displeased.

Just as Eden started toward Elsa, the door of the black coach opened and a plainly dressed man with a blunt face stepped down. He moved purposefully in Eden's direction. Keeping a wary eye on him, she bent to pick up her high-crowned hat but didn't put it on. His apology, she told herself, ought to be most abject.

But the first words out of his mouth were anything but penitent. "You don't belong here," he growled in a guttural voice that might have been of foreign origin. "Go home, go back to Kent, or find yourself at the bottom of the Thames."

Eden stood her ground, though the man was so close she could have counted the hairs growing out of the mole on his chin. Elsa cowered by the tree, obviously sensing the man's menace. From somewhere nearby, children's laughter could be heard, and church bells were chiming the noon hour.

"Who are you?" demanded Eden, hoping she sounded far braver than she felt.

The man shook his head. "Never mind. Just heed me." He opened his hand, revealing a gleaming stiletto. "You follow?"

Eden suppressed a shudder. He spoke well enough, though not with the voice of a gentleman. Yet the coach was handsome, and its stolid driver wore tasteful gray-and-white livery. Daring to peer beyond the intimidating figure before her, Eden saw that the coach door was hung with a black drape, probably to cover the telltale coat of arms. She thought she saw someone moving inside.

Eden forced her gaze back to the blunt face. "You don't happen to be a friend of Lady Harriet's, do you? I can't think of anyone else I've annoyed lately."

The man found no humor in Eden's remark, nor did he seem to recognize Harriet's name. "It's not easy to laugh when your throat's slit," he warned, balancing the stiletto in his hand. "You follow?"

The wheels of another coach reached Eden's ears. "I follow my inclinations," she said with bravado, "and will do as I please." Her effrontery surprised them both, but Eden knew that the second coach was almost upon them. Cutpurses and pickpockets might roam London's parks after dark, but she doubted that even a belligerent fellow such as this one would murder her in broad daylight. The mere possibility reminded her of Captain Craswell's fate, and Eden's courage nearly evaporated.

But her adversary had heard the other coach and quickly pocketed the knife. "This is no game," he warned Eden, a stubby finger almost touching her nose. "You want to be carved up like a hunk of beef? Eh?"

Eden refused to give him the satisfaction of a reply. The black coach was pulling over to one side to let the second vehicle pass, no mean feat on such a narrow pathway. But a woman's throaty voice called out, ordering her driver to stop. The blunt-faced man lunged, took in the imposing satin and sable-clad woman leaning from the window, and scurried to the haven of his own conveyance.

"Rudi!" called the woman in that husky voice, "are you in there, you big poxy ape? Come out, or I'll have my man shoot your horses!"

Fascinated, Eden took Elsa by the hand and led her away from the tree. Someone gave muffled orders to the driver of the black coach. With great difficulty, the horses picked their way past the other conveyance and took off at a trot.

"Coward!" shrieked the woman, waving a fist. "I'll see you rot in hell, you Swabian noodlecock!"

"What are they saying? What is happening?" gasped Elsa.

But Eden didn't hear the maid. Instead she was staring unabashedly at her bawdy savior, trying to figure out why she looked vaguely familiar. Heavily painted and rouged, laden with rubies at ears and neck, the woman stopped cursing long enough to take a swig from a gold and garnet-encrusted flask.

"Well?" Her tongue flicked at a drop of liquor that clung to her reddened lip. "Where's your manners, Baby Ducks? Or didn't Count Rudolf's lackey offer you enough?"

Eden disengaged herself from Elsa and approached the woman in the white coach with its purple plumes and golden crest. "I'm not a baby duck," she asserted, disinclined to be put off by a sharp tongue any more than by a gleaming knife, "nor do I sell myself in Green Park."

"Then St. James's Park is the other way, Baby Ducks." Laughing richly, the woman sucked at the gaudy container, then leaned farther out the window to scrutinize Eden. "You'd do well there, or my teats aren't two but four." She started to laugh again but sobered abruptly, a hand at her mouth. "Mother of God," she murmured, staring at Eden, "if you're not Baby Ducks, who *are* you?"

Blowsy old bawd, thought Eden with indignation; she probably runs a brothel in Cheapside. A profitable one, Eden guessed, considering the rubies and satin and furs. Eden sniffed and drew herself up very straight, not the least bit diffident about giving her real name to this prying strumpet. "I'm Eden Berenger Churchill," she announced, and was startled when the woman's fingers went slack and the bejeweled flask fell to the ground.

Ever the diligent servant, Elsa ran to restore it to its owner. The woman blinked in a bleary fashion, then tried to focus on Eden. Her eyes, which were an extraordinary shade of dark violet, slowly cleared and grew vivid with some secret, intense emotion that completely baffled Eden.

"Mother of God," the woman repeated, and reached out her hand. "Get in," she commanded, the husky voice almost inaudible.

But Eden took a step backward. "Oh, no, Mistress. I mislike meeting strangers in the park."

Something like a chuckle erupted from the woman's throat. "A stranger!" She put a hand to her hennaed hair and shook her head. "Hardly that," she declared, the painted face suddenly softening. "I'm Barbara Castlemaine. If you're Eden Churchill, I'm your mother."

EDEN RODE IN A DAZE to Barbara's house in Arlington Street. Next to her on the cushioned coach seat, Elsa could hardly contain her curiosity, but had to be satisfied with trying to read Lady Castlemaine's lips. Though Eden could hear perfectly, she still had trouble accepting this raddled strumpet's words. For all Barbara's scandalous reputation, Eden was not prepared for the reality.

The house in Arlington Street was remarkably subdued in style, except for the bold purple front door. Lady Castlemaine's arrival was slightly unsteady, but her voice was strong and she shrieked at her pink-cheeked maid and cursed at a blackamoor wearing a green satin turban. The maid was ordered to tend to Elsa; the blackamoor was charged with bringing refreshments.

"Servants!" she grumbled, collapsing on a red velvet chaise longue and yanking off her big straw hat. "Holy Mother, you'd think they'd show more deference to a duchess!" She kicked off her shoes and put her fingers to her mouth, emitting an ear-shattering whistle. To Eden's amazement, a little monkey wearing a miniature guardsman's suit leaped from the top of the brocade draperies and landed in Barbara's lap.

"Cromwell! At least you don't bite the hand that feeds you," Lady Castlemaine said, proving her point by proffering a dish of Spanish nuts to the little animal.

Eden, who had slipped into an ornate chair, wondered if Barbara had forgotten her presence. But as soon as the blackamoor brought a tray of current cakes and almond biscuits, Lady Castlemaine whipped out her flask, drank it dry and fixed Eden with her piercing deep violet gaze.

"So you're Eden." She looked more bemused than elated. "At least you inherited some of my looks." She waved a hand at a portrait that reposed in shadow at the end of the room. "See for yourself. I was magnificent as Minerva when Sir Peter Lely painted me. Gin?" She held up a bottle, mustered from a small paneled table next to the chaise longue.

Still unnerved, Eden declined the drink, but got up to admire the portrait. Barbara had not exaggerated. The artist had captured the glory of her youth— streaming auburn hair, a fine full figure and those wonderful eyes, sharp, clear and seductive. Even as Eden admired the vivid strength and beauty, she recognized the similarities between herself and the woman who had given her birth. It was in the eyes—not the color, but the spark; in the mouth, full, mobile, prone to laughter; in the skin, radiant with health, sleek with youth. But more than coloring or features, there was a verve about the young Lady Castlemaine that all but leaped from the canvas. Eden was drawn instinctively to that zest for life, and realized it was a quality she shared with this dissipated courtesan who was her mother.

To Eden's embarrassment, her eyes had filled with tears. "Milady," she began, turning to Barbara, "I never imagined this moment would come!"

"Holy bat bottoms, you never imagined I existed!" The monkey yanked off his gold-braided hat, but Barbara slapped it on his head. "Behave yourself, Cromwell, or you'll get no gin. Sit, sit, sit," she ordered Eden in much the same tone she'd used on the monkey. "Enough of sentiment—along with guilt it's the most useless emotion in the world. Now tell me why Count Rudolf's henchman was trying to scare you off. Is it because of that handsome Flemish prince, or something to do with Jack?"

Trying to pull her thoughts together, Eden sat and took a deep breath. The drapes were shut against the May sunshine, and the room smelled heavily of jasmine. Eden was tempted to buoy her spirits with a sip of gin, but glanced at Barbara's ravaged face and decided to abstain.

"Prince Maximilian was forced to flee England yesterday," she began, but

Lady Castlemaine shook her head, the rubies glinting at her ears.

"God's teeth, I know all that—there's not much I don't know. Gossip travels like fog, seeping into every nook and cranny. Is Rudolf conspiring against Jack? Or is he doing our cousin's dirty work for her?"

Eden stared at Barbara. "Cousin? You mean Max's cousin."

"No, no, our cousin." Lady Castlemaine dropped a Spanish nut down her considerable cleavage, delved for it without result and shrugged. "Harriet," she averred, leaning forward on the chaise while the monkey grabbed the gin bottle. "Don't look so dense, Baby Ducks. Much as I hate to claim the grasping baggage as my kin, Harriet, like us, is a Villiers."

Eden gaped. Marlborough had made some passing mention of Barbara's ancestry, but it had come in such a flood of other more devastating revelations that Eden had forgotten.

"All these new—and generally loathsome—relatives must be a strain to sort out," Barbara remarked, sampling a dish of Morello cherries. "Rudolf has always been thick as thieves with that moldy old wedge of cheese Bentinck, so of course he and Harriet have much more than their appalling dispositions in common. I marvel that Harriet didn't choose Rudi over Max, but at least her vision works better than her brain." The deep violet eyes sparkled momentarily. "He's quite a specimen, that tall, blond prince. Would that I were twenty years younger—or even ten," she remarked a bit wistfully. "Have you bedded him yet?"

Aghast, Eden pulled back in her chair, "Of course not! He's betrothed, and I'm ... I'm ...."

"Disappointed." Barbara popped another cherry into her mouth and washed it down with more gin. "Never mind, he'd only distract you. Once you've seduced the King, you can do as you please where Max is concerned." Lady Castlemaine spoke with the blasé attitude of one for whom intimate feelings were but a garnish to the main course of life. "Tomorrow, William sails for the Continent. You must go, too, as he'll probably be away all summer, and Jack will be growing restive in the Tower. Worse than that, Jack's enemies may find the necessary pair of witnesses to testify against him. It's not inconceivable that Parliament could act in William's absence."

"But what of Fenwick?" Eden asked, jarred by her mother's suggestion of following the King abroad.

Lady Castlemaine brushed at the monkey, which was tugging at her petticoats and cheeping imperiously. "Here, Cromwell," she said, relenting and tossing him a cherry, "now be a good lad and go entertain the Persian cat." The animal scampered off, and Barbara turned to Eden. "Fenwick? Oh, he's a slippery sort, married to that moonfaced Carlisle chit who probably put him up to trying to kill William in the first place." She swung around on the chaise, gesturing toward the door with her gin bottle. "He's upstairs, trussed like a beef roast. Shall I ask for ransom or do my duty, Baby Ducks?"

Almost speechless, Eden wondered how many more shocks she could take in one day. "Here? How? You captured him, Milady?"

"Not exactly. I found him." Barbara looked supremely complacent. "After that melee with Prince Max, Rudi had to find a better hiding place for Fenwick than under an outlandish wig. He tried to foist him off on Harriet, but she refused to soil her dainty skirts—not to mention her uncle's shaky reputation. And then, proving himself to be the idiot I'd always claimed, Rudolf had the nerve to approach me!" Her indignation seemed genuine, though the effect was diminished by her slightly crossed eyes. "I abstain from court these days, not caring to bore myself senseless with those Dutch toadies William has plastered to his side, and I suppose Rudolf thought no one would dream of questioning me about harboring a traitor. But," she added, drawing herself up straight on the chaise, "I have my principles. Happily, they have nothing to do with my virtue, but when it comes to treason, I draw the line. All the same, who should show up on my doorstep last night but this ill-advised Fenwick. I had him locked away and went haring after Rudolf this morning, which is how I happened to be in Green Park chasing his coach when you suddenly popped up like a milkmaid in a haystack." Eden sat very quietly, trying to absorb everything her mother had told her. "But wouldn't Rudolf know you wouldn't shield a man who'd implicated Jack?"

Barbara gave an airy wave of her hand. "God's teeth, if I lent my support to every man I ever bedded, I'd be a veritable charity! Not that Jack wasn't remarkable between the sheets. Never let it be said that I'd carp about any of my children's fathers, at least not about the method that got them born in the first place. But when it comes to intrigue, I've retired."

"What will you do with Fenwick?" Eden asked, still a bit breathless from her mother's disclosures.

"There's a reward, I suppose." She tipped the gin bottle to her lips, discovered it, too, was empty, and swore. "Frankly, he's negligible. The main thing is to keep him from making accusations against Jack. I'm more concerned about your role in all this. William is a puny being, and when he dies—" she stopped to cross herself in a haphazard manner "—Princess Anne will take the throne, and Sarah Churchill will run that poor sow like a pig to market. But in the meantime, Jack must keep his head attached to the rest of him, which could prove tricky. See here, Baby Ducks," she said, lowering her voice and leaning forward to reveal a bulge of bosom above her bodice, "you're quite a splendid piece. That hair, that face, that lovely body! If only I could climb inside your skin for just one night, I'd ...."

To Eden's surprise, the violet eyes had misted over and the red lips trembled. "Yes?" Eden encouraged, embarrassed by her mother's show of emotion.

But Barbara resumed her brittle manner as her maid entered, announcing that Count Rudolf of Swabia had called and left a note. "That blundering ox!" exclaimed Lady Castlemaine. "Has he come for Fenwick? Or," she added, with a speculative glance at Eden, "for you? Nora," she commanded, turning to her maid, "you must put on Mistress Eden's clothes at once and do as I tell you! Hurry!"

Nora and Eden were both flummoxed by Barbara's orders, but they obeyed. As Eden exchanged her clothing for an Oriental shawl, Barbara scanned Rudolf's note. "As I suspected," she said, crumpling the missive and tossing it into the dish of nuts, "it's a request for me to send Fenwick to France where your sister can hide him. She's a nun, you know."

Though Marlborough had mentioned another child by Barbara, Eden still found the idea incredible. That her sister should be Catholic and in a religious order was virtual anathema from Eden's Huguenot point of view.

"You look shocked," Barbara remarked to Eden as the mystified maid struggled into the rust and amber riding habit. "God's eyes, I'm a Catholic myself." She crossed herself again, pausing to retrieve the Spanish nut that had fallen into her bodice. "Young Barbara's not exactly a saint, having borne one bastard already, but now that she's a Mother Superior she seems to have settled down." Getting to her feet, she righted the high-crowned hunting hat on Nora's chestnut curls and nodded with approval. "Be brave. Just start walking for Clarges Street. Your reward will be ample."

"Whatever is going on?" Eden asked as the puzzled maid headed out of the house.

Barbara had found a fresh bottle of gin. "I may be mistaken," she replied, "but I think Rudolf's threats to you aren't inspired by Harriet's jealousy so much as by Bentinck's. Pretty Keppel is rival enough for the dreary old mutt. The last thing he wants is a beautiful young virgin engaging the King's affection. And that's why you must go abroad with the court."

Eden considered briefly. "But how will I find Max?"

"Max! Holy goat balls!" cried Barbara, moving somewhat uncertainly to her daughter's side. "Forget Max! Only the King matters! You can be his mistress, you could even be his wife! Why do you care about that impoverished prince?"

In truth, that was the one question Eden would have thought her mother could answer. She stared at Barbara with bleak ebony eyes, hugging the Oriental shawl close. "But I love him!" she blurted, and realized that not only had she proclaimed the truth out loud, but for the first time in her life she had confided her deepest secret to the most natural recipient in the world—her mother.

But Barbara's maternal instincts were unorthodox. "So?" She shrugged, the large ruby winking at her throat. "Eden, the world is full of men! You can love them all! Why waste yourself on just one? Handsome Max may be, but he's poor! What could be worse, unless he were diseased as well?"

Max's poverty might seem pernicious to Lady Castlemaine, but it held no threat for Eden. She was about to say as much when shrieks could be heard from the hallway. An instant later Nora flew into the room, a smudge on one pink cheek, a rip in the rust-colored brocade of Eden's riding jacket.

"Milady!" she screamed, falling at Barbara's crimson hem. "They tried to make off with me! They had knives! They meant to kill me! Help!"

Lady Castlemaine turned to Eden with a knowing, satisfied expression. "You see? Rudolf followed us, the pawky great stews-monger! Now will you go abroad?"

Staring at the shaking, sobbing figure who knelt before Barbara, Eden couldn't suppress a shudder. No real harm had befallen the maid, but that was because she was Nora and not Eden. A vision of flashing knives wielded by blunt-faced men merged with the clash of swords at the Royal Exchange. Max's blood had already been shed; this time it could have been her own.

Nora's screams had subsided to whimpers while Barbara plied her with gin. But Lady Castlemaine's eyes were fixed on her daughter. "Well?" she demanded in that husky voice.

Eden drew the shawl even closer; she felt chilled despite the fine May weather. "I'll go," she breathed. "I'll follow the King."

Barbara raised the gin bottle in a makeshift toast. "Of course you will! You wouldn't be my daughter if you didn't! I was beginning to think Jack had made a mistake!"

Inwardly, Eden winced. Lady Castlemaine was hardly the sort of mother she might have envisioned. Yet despite the ravaged face, overblown figure and unabashed vulgarity, there was some elusive sense of kinship that Eden couldn't deny. Even as Nora removed the riding habit and handed her the items of clothing, Barbara confirmed Eden's belief.

"You'll find him there, too," she said, with a trace of the youthful sparkle Eden had seen in the Lely portrait.

Eden blinked as she adjusted the ruffled *steinkirk* at her neck. "Him?"

Barbara flipped the last cherry at Cromwell, who had appeared from under the chaise longue. "Holy rat's bung, don't be dense, Baby Ducks! I have the most dreadful feeling that for you, kings and crowns don't matter a ha'penny! There is only one him, and you'll let the rest of the world go to hell in a handcart before you'll give him up! How," she wailed, a hand to her head, "could I have had the misfortune to bear such a faithful daughter?"

Chapter Ten

Fʀᴏᴍ ᴀ ʀɪsᴇ ᴏᴠᴇʀʟᴏᴏᴋɪɴɢ ᴛʜᴇ valley of the Ourthe, Max gazed at Vranes and swore aloud. The House of Hohenstaufen's banner fluttered from the ragged castle keep. The French mercenaries remained in place, no doubt in the pay of Rudolf. Max knew that even if he could rally his villagers and tenants, they would be no match for a fortified castle guarded by professional soldiers.

He was enraged by the Frenchmen's presence, and saddened by the desecration of Vranes. The weathered stone castle that sprawled on a hill in the curve of the river had been Sophie Dorothea's marriage portion, passed on through her Flemish mother and given with Rudolf's grudging goodwill. Max and Sophie Dorothea had made their home within those ancient, mellow walls, with the village clustered around the castle and the farms spread out across the valley. In happier days Vranes had been a gladsome sight, prosperous and peaceful, with the tinkle of cowbells and the scent of newly mowed hay borne on the soft meadow air.

But now the castle walls were smoke-scarred, weeds sprouted from the roofs of village homes, and tangled vines trailed out of jagged windows. Chimneys had fallen down, and some of the narrow streets were strewn with rubble. Even the ancient Church of St. Hubert seemed to exude an aura of defeat.

Squinting against the sun, Max could make out the wing of the castle where he had lain with his bride and where the nursery had been prepared for their child.

Then Sophie had gone into that ghastly, torturous labor. For almost three days her screams had knifed through Max's brain, and the walls of Vranes had reverberated with her sobs. When at last the child was born dead, Sophie had looked straight into Max's dazed face and said, "Forgive me." With her hand stretched out to him in helpless appeal, she had closed her eyes forever.

Forcing himself to look away from the bedchamber's broken window, Max conjured up an image of Eden. While he dared not hope for the future, he knew it was useless to dwell on the past. He touched his spurs to his mount and turned his back on Vranes.

HER FACE DRAINED OF COLOR and her hands trembling on the reins, Eden sat stiffly in the saddle, awaiting the signal for the hunt to begin. Sidney Godolphin, who had complied with Lady Castlemaine's request for Eden to join the court, watched benignly from his place on a spirited gray gelding. Amiable and avuncular, he had insisted that Eden take part in the hunt at Dieren if she hoped to remedy her initial impression at Whitehall.

"I've seen boars," she whispered in a shaky voice as blue and gold-liveried lackeys passed around cups of ale. "They're horrid ugly creatures with big tusks. As for the stags, they're too handsome to kill. I'd rather eat fish."

"At the moment you look as if you've eaten something nasty." Godolphin smiled, raising his voice to make himself heard over the barking of the shaggy *kuishunds*. "See how good-humored William is in the saddle. Why, he even tolerates my tainted company. He'll certainly look more kindly on you after the hunt." Godolphin motioned with his riding crop toward the King who was exchanging jocular remarks with Keppel and Ned Villiers, Harriet's obsequious brother. "His Majesty looks younger in his homeland, don't you think?"

"Younger than who?" grumbled Eden. "Moses?" Yet it was true, and she was immediately contrite. Her kindly mentor didn't deserve such impertinence. Not only had he made arrangements for Eden to join the court in the United Provinces, he had augmented the purse from her mother by paying for her passage from Margate to Oostende. She had landed two days after the royal party, discovering that they had already left the Hague for William's favorite hunting ground at Dieren. Now, less than twelve hours after her arrival at the lodge, she was in a fever of anxiety. "I'm sorry I was rude," she apologized, an unsure hand at her mare's neck. "It's just that I'm so worried about ... my father."

Sidney Godolphin was a perceptive man. "And Prince Maximilian, as well." He gave Eden a sympathetic look as the Master of the Hunt readied his horn. "No news is good news, Mistress. He's probably in Brabant, pursuing his properties."

"Is Brabant far from here?" Eden scanned the horizon, as if she could see beyond the Gelderland to wherever Max might be.

Godolphin considered. "Two days of hard riding. Vranes is in the Ardennes Forest."

Two days in the saddle definitely daunted Eden. Yet if she could hire a coach …. She jumped as the horn sounded. The *kuishunds* were released, King William raised his arm, and the party was off.

With a maximum of reluctance and a minimum of confidence, Eden prodded her mare, Circe, into a walk. The morning dew still clung to the grass, the sun slanted in shafts of light through the trees, and the wood smoke from the foresters' stone chimneys lingered in the air. As Eden and her mount picked their way across an ancient bridge that led into the Veluwe Forest, she was alarmed at how swiftly the other members of the party were disappearing among the tall trees. Fortunately she could still make out Godolphin's portly form. But to keep up with him, it was necessary to spur Circe into a trot. Gritting her teeth, Eden urged the mare into the next gait as they approached the Warnsborne thicket.

Sunlight, shadow, glossy shrubs, spiky hedgerows, white blossoms on green leaves—the dense spring growth surrounded Eden, cutting her off from the others. Desperately, she tried to remember the route Godolphin had sketched. It was filled with strange, foreign names for swamps and copses that meant nothing to her.

Distraught, she reined in the mare, then cautiously turned her around. Once again, Eden knew failure. There would be no opportunity today to make a favorable impression on the King. The most she could hope for was to find the lodge and avoid the humiliation of having a search party sent after her.

There must, Eden thought, be a way to skirt the thicket. Her blue riding habit had already been caught by brambles, and there was a rip in one kidskin glove. Carefully she dismounted, leading Circe to the left of the clearing. The sound of rushing water guided them to a tumbling brook, which formed a shallow pool among moss-covered rocks. Eden let Circe stop to drink, and her gaze wandered downstream where she saw movement in a little copse of birch trees. The mare also sensed the unknown presence and pricked up her ears. A moment later, a magnificent six-pronged stag emerged. The animal paused, stared suspiciously at both horse and human, then moved toward them with stately grace. Eden could scarcely believe the stag's boldness and smiled in spite of herself.

"I'm not in the least bit a hunter," she said in a low, soothing voice. "I don't even like horses." With a pang of remorse, her eyes darted toward Circe. "Though as horses go, she's rather nice. We won't bother you." The mare blinked uncertainly at the stag, then resumed drinking.

Remembering that Keppel had given her some paper twists filled with sugar in case she needed to win her mount's goodwill, Eden withdrew them from her riding habit. She had no idea if deer liked sugar, but it wouldn't hurt to try. Carefully bending down to sprinkle the contents of the twist onto a fallen leaf, she frowned. The substance looked too coarse to be sugar. Eden licked her finger. "*Zut!* 'Tis salt!" She gave both animals an apologetic look.

But the stag was ambling toward Eden, its dark nose twitching eagerly. He stopped by the leaf, lowered his head with those wonderful antlers and began licking at the salt with enthusiasm. It was devoured in seconds. The stag raised great pleading eyes to his benefactress and waited patiently.

Eden had an inspiration. She kept the paper twists in one hand and grasped Circe's reins in the other. "Come along, my four-footed friends," she said in a gentle voice. "We shall return to Dieren. I much prefer bringing home live animals." With a triumphant little hitch of her tall riding hat, Eden led the way across the brook, around Warnsborne thicket and in what she prayed was the direction of the royal hunting lodge.

She was passing the edge of a meadow dotted with orange and crimson poppies when both animals stopped and tensed. Eden followed suit, hearing hoofbeats nearby. The hunting party, she thought, and wondered if the stag would take flight. But a moment later three soldiers rendezvoused across the meadow. Retreating into the thicket, Eden watched the men confer. No doubt they were on a scouting expedition, though it occurred to her that King William would hardly hunt in a vicinity where the enemy might be lurking. He'd just missed being assassinated on such an outing in England.

A single phrase, uttered with a laugh and carried by the gentle spring breeze, made her stiffen with alarm: "Prince Maximilian is too tall to hide under beds ...."

Fear enveloped Eden like a hostile hand. The men were going off in different directions. Clearly, they were searching for Max. Godolphin had said he was probably in Brabant. He might be wrong. He must be wrong.

Eden led her mare into the meadow. To her surprise, the stag followed, apparently craving more salt. Suddenly it dawned on Eden that if she sent both animals into the woods, it would create a diversion. If Max were hiding nearby, he might be able to slip away while the soldiers pursued the false quarry.

Wincing as she raised her crop, Eden whispered an apology to Circe. "I'm grateful for your gentle mien, but I really must spur you on. I'll find a dozen apples for you at Dieren."

One slap was all the mare required before she bolted off across the meadow and into the woods. Eden sighed with relief, then turned to the stag. "Go!" she commanded. "Run! The hunters are coming!"

The stag stood motionless, the huge dark eyes reflecting Eden's anxious gaze. She was afraid to take the crop to the animal lest he retaliate with those dangerous antlers. Eden shook out another twist of salt. The stag lapped up the contents, then followed Eden as she began walking again.

After several false starts, Eden found her way back. The servants goggled when she walked over the bridge with the big stag ambling behind her. William was just as astonished when he rode toward the hunting lodge and caught sight of Eden approaching with her new pet. Indeed, she thought with a flash of foreboding, he looked out of sorts. Judging from the paucity of game, she could guess why. Except for half a dozen rabbits and two scrawny boars, the hunt had not been a success.

"Mistress," said William, waving away a groom who would have helped him from the saddle, "what is this?" The King brandished his riding crop at the great stag, which, at all the commotion, hesitated for the first time.

Out of the corner of her eye, Eden saw a disgruntled Bentinck, a curious Keppel and a bemused Godolphin. But before she could reply, the stag leaped, streaked past the assembled company and escaped through an opening in the stone wall.

"Oh!" exclaimed Eden with dismay. "I had hoped he would make friends with the rest of you!"

William took a labored breath and a considerable amount of umbrage at Eden's candor. "We don't make friends with animals, Mistress! We hunt them, as sensible men and women do if …" he broke off, suddenly assailed by a coughing fit.

Keppel bounded to his master's side, proffering an elegant lace kerchief. "Enough, Mistress! You've upset the King!"

Unsettled by Keppel's reproach and William's severe hack, Eden bit her lip. "I apologize for causing any harm, but His Majesty's accusation isn't quite fair." Shaking off her distress, she boldly interjected herself between the King and Keppel. "Here, Sire," she urged, firmly gripping William by the elbows, "lift your arms and breathe deeply."

The courtiers murmured with a mixture of amazement and censure, but the coughing stopped almost at once. "There," said Eden with relief, " 'twas only a *cris de nerfs*. Triggered here," she added, tapping her temple, "rather than in the lungs."

William eyed her with reluctant gratitude. "You practice medicine better than some of our doctors, especially that fool of a Radcliffe in London." The voice was gruff, the brown eyes narrow. "Though you speak as bluntly as he. What do you mean about not being fair? We are known for our fair-mindedness."

Eden avoided flinching under the intense dark gaze. "I meant with regard to the animals, Sire. Your Majesty is famous not only for hunting them, but for nurturing them in your tame zoo at Honselaardijk. What is the difference between capturing an elephant and a stag?"

The brown eyes went very still, then the hint of a twinkle surfaced. "The difference? My dear, have you ever tried to eat an elephant?"

At that sally, the entire company burst out laughing. Eden did, too, as merrily as the rest. With obvious diffidence, William took her hand. "We don't know your name. We have met, though we can't recall where or when."

Eden felt the color rise in her cheeks. This was a critical response, and the only way she knew how to phrase it was with the bald truth. "I'm Eden ... Churchill, kin to Milord Marlborough. My fan met Your Majesty's wig at Whitehall."

"Ah!" William put a hand to his graying hair. "Of course! You have a penchant for the extraordinary!"

Eden was encouraged by the faint smile on William's face. "What sort of mixture do your doctors prescribe for your cough?" she politely asked.

Before William could answer, Keppel put a hand on his master's arm. "Doctors be damned, Your Majesty. What you need now is a strong, cool drink and a lively game of cards."

William of Orange seemed to shrivel as he leaned on his young favorite. "Excellent advice, my good Joost. There is, we fear," he went on with a melancholy look at Eden, "nothing that helps, but we thank you for your concern."

"I beg to argue," Eden said quickly as the King and Keppel started to turn away. "There are many beneficial plants and herbs I've seen on my short visit to your homeland. You must let me brew up some of them."

Over his shoulder, William's gaze was skeptical. "Mayhap," he said with a heavy sigh. "We shall consult with Dr. Bidloo when we return to the Hague." His step dragged as he walked away with Keppel toward the ancient lodge.

The rest of the hunting party dispersed, leaving Eden alone in the courtyard. Despite William's apparent dismissal of her medical knowledge, she felt the faintest flicker of optimism. She had helped him stop coughing, she had made him laugh, and she had discovered that he did not hold her in contempt for the episode at Whitehall. While Eden could hardly chalk up these little accomplishments as a conquest, at least she felt less gloomy.

Or did, until a dozen soldiers rode up, one of them leading her horse. "We have a message for Milord Bentinck. Has he returned?" the captain called as Eden hurried to meet her mare.

"Only minutes ago," she replied, patting the animal's neck and marveling that for once she was glad to see a horse. "Milord Bentinck may be with the King," she hedged. "His Majesty was unwell. I wouldn't disturb either of them right now."

The captain, a tall, solidly built man of thirty, looked chagrined as he juggled his decision. "We'll wait. The news of our failure will not be warmly received in any event." He dismounted and motioned to his men. "Come, lads, let's brace ourselves with a few cups of usquebaugh."

The captain's words disconcerted Eden, but she did her best to keep her emotions hidden. "Your search party failed then?" The ebony eyes were deceptively innocent. "Perhaps Prince Maximilian has returned to Brabant."

The captain studied Eden, clearly surprised that she knew their mission. Then his frank visage registered approval. "If he had any sense that's where he'd go, especially with half the court racing through the woods to add to the confusion. But there's no doubt he's close by. At least two farmers reported seeing him yesterday near Apeldoorn."

Eden tilted her head as Circe nuzzled her shoulder. "Oh? Are they sure it was him?"

"Aye, and why not?" Removing his helmet and wiping the perspiration from his forehead with his sleeve, the captain paused as two grooms came to take the horses away. "There's no mistaking the likes of that one. Who else looks like Prince Maximilian?"

Eden kept her expression blank as the soldiers began to amble off. "Nobody," she said softly. "Nobody in the world even comes close."

THE LUXURY OF HOT AND cold running water in a tiled bath was a novelty to Eden. William of Orange had installed the most advanced plumbing facilities in the world at Honselaardijk and was having similar baths built into the renovated wing of Hampton Court Palace outside London. While her fellow countrymen might scoff at such an obsession with cleanliness, Eden enjoyed relaxing in the warm, scented water.

Across the room, Elsa was laying out a quilted green silk robe and a pair of satin mules. "Ach," the little maid exclaimed, "I forgot your petticoats." Dispensing with a curtsy, she hurried out of the bathing room, her gold curls bounding under her stiff lace cap.

With her chin just above the water, Eden stretched out full length and admired the Jordaens frescoes that adorned the ceiling. She had seen William twice since they'd returned to the Hague, and on both occasions he had been polite, if distressed by Keppel's fawning attentions. Eden could almost sympathize with Bentinck.

At least, Eden reflected as she applied rose-scented soap to her breasts and shoulders, the King looked sturdier in the fresh air of his homeland. Yet she still believed that her gift of healing would provide the opportunity to win William's affection. And now, she knew, her efforts must be exerted not only on her father's behalf, but on Max's, as well.

She was deep in thought, soaping one raised ankle, when suddenly the door flew open. Expecting Elsa, she stood up. But it was Max who flung himself into the room, slamming the door behind him. Eden noted that he was dirty and unshaven, and that his riding clothes were torn. Yet somehow, he had never looked more handsome.

"Max! Thank God! What's happening?" Her heart was pounding, and she was oblivious to her nakedness.

Max, however, was jolted by the sight of those lush curves shining with water and dappled with soap. "Eden you're ..." he began, but quickly regained control. "It's Bentinck's men! I must hide!"

Eden scanned the tiled chamber, but there was no place to conceal a man as big as Max. Noting the helpless expression on his sunburned face, she fought off a wave of panic. There were footsteps in the corridor, men on the run, and heavy pounding on nearby doors. "Here!" She waved him to the bathing pool. "Can you hold your breath?"

Still rattled by the sight of her naked body, Max gave Eden a puzzled look. "Can ...?" He managed to tear his eyes away long enough to glance at the bath. "If it's deep enough." Without further preamble, he cast off his ripped cloak and stuffed it under Eden's dressing gown, then stepped into the bath, dirty boots and all. The water immediately turned color, and Eden winced. Perhaps the men wouldn't notice. With any luck, they'd refrain from bursting in on a lady in her bath.

But Eden had not given Bentinck's followers credit for thoroughness. Just as Max disappeared beneath the surface and Eden slid into the water, a trio of soldiers burst into the room. Their leader was the captain Eden had spoken with at Dieren; he, along with the other, blanched at the sight of Eden casually lathering her arms.

"*Zut!*" she cried, bobbing deeper into the bath and feeling Max's shoulder nudge her hip. "What is this outrage?"

"We seek a fugitive traitor," the captain replied, growing very red around the ears. "Prince Maximilian, you remember?"

"Shame! Seek your rebels elsewhere! Are you intent on rape, as well?"

"We're honorable men! We are obeying orders!" the captain declared, trying to hide his embarrassment behind bluster. With a final furtive glance around the bathing chamber, the trio backed out.

Only when the door was firmly shut behind them did Eden kick at Max to signal their departure. Sputtering and thrashing, he bolted erect, uttering a stream of garbled oaths. "Swine! I was trying to see the King! Bentinck not only intervened, he sent these villains to arrest me!" One by one, he lifted his boots from the bath and tossed them on the tiles to drain.

"What happened?" Eden asked breathlessly, still submerged up to her neck. "I knew you were at Dieren."

Max was stripping off his tattered shirt. "I've been everywhere. I now have proof that Rudolf has been dealing with King Louis. That's why I must see William." He stopped, the hazel eyes on Eden's damp curls and anxious face. "*Schoft*. You look like a Lorelei on the Rhine."

Eden's mouth curved into a smile. "Is that some sort of siren? Where is the Rhine?" she asked. "I've never been quite sure."

Kneeling in the water, Max moved closer to Eden. "You mustn't ask about geography," he said in a faintly hollow tone. "Don't ask the impossible of me."

Her eyes shimmered as she gazed at the broad shoulders, now bronzed by the sun and sleek from the bath. He reminded her of a powerful, tawny lion. Eden knew she must not tempt Max, but could not help reveling in her power any more than she could stop from yielding to him.

Yet William of Orange was no longer an unattainable goal. Her virtue was the most powerful weapon in the defense of her father. And of Max. Eden backed away until she felt her bare shoulders touch the tiles.

Max's hazel gaze bore down on her, poignant with desire. "I ask you again," he begged. "Stop me."

But Eden knew he didn't mean it. "How can I when I'll wither away?" Her chin trembled, but her eyes were steady.

"You don't know the difference between love and lust," he said, deliberately putting a hand in the masses of her wet hair.

"Yes, I do." The reply was simply stated, yet carried deep conviction. "I know the difference between you and Charlie Crocker."

Slowly he tipped her face up to his. Her cheeks were pink from the bath, her eyes wide with anticipation. Through the murky water, he could just make out the delectable curves of her naked body. "You don't know the difference," he insisted, his other hand at her back.

Eden inched forward, awaiting his kiss. "But I do," she murmured. "It's you who doesn't know." Without hesitation, she pressed her mouth against his, her fingers clasped behind his head. She paid no heed to his unshaven chin or the wound on his arm, which was all but healed. Nothing mattered except the fervor of their embrace and the hunger of their kisses.

Max's hand slid down to her waist and then to the rounded flesh of her buttocks, and Eden sighed. The yearning sensation that welled up shattered reason as well as ideals. Caressing the muscles of his upper arms and shoulders, Eden felt the water mingle with his touch and laughed with delight. Not all the kings in Christendom, not all the wealth of Araby could have brought her as much pleasure as Max, hurtling into the room with his sunburned face and ragged clothes.

Max lifted her just high enough out of the pool to bury his face between her breasts and outline the slim waist with his ardent fingers. Locked together in the scented water, they touched and kissed, beguiled by their mutual enchantment. The waters danced around them.

Max held Eden lightly with one arm, while his other hand went to his belt. "I'm a fool," he said, with a crooked grin. "And an ass as well, and you ought to hate me. But I can't stop. I warned you."

Eden's instinct told her what was about to happen. She took a deep breath and offered a token resistance by straining against his grasp. But the ebony eyes shone, and her heart raced with excitement. "No one need know. I could tell the King I was ravished in Smarden."

Max's grin spread across his face as he unhitched his belt. "You wouldn't lie. Yet knowing you, he might believe it. God help us that he—"

The sentence was cut short by the opening of the door and a sharp cry from Elsa. "Lord have mercy! Forgive me, I've come to warn you, Mistress! Your Highness, I didn't know …."

Clutching at his breeks, Max released Eden and turned to Elsa, who was standing by the pool, a froth of petticoats over her arm. Both master and servant had flushed, and it was hard for Eden to tell who was the most embarrassed. Discreetly, she submerged herself in the bathing pool and felt her spirits plunge along with her body.

"The soldiers," Elsa began, setting down the petticoats and gesturing animatedly with her fingers. "They are still looking for Your Highness and have the palace surrounded. I had no idea you were here."

"I am." Max spoke tersely as he pulled himself out of the pool and grabbed his shirt and boots. Eden watched him as he dressed, then beckoned for Elsa to bring her robe. Outside, darkness was settling in over Honselaardijk. She saw Max at the French windows, looking for a way to open them. "If I could slip out onto the dunes," he said more to himself than to Eden and Elsa, "I might be able to get to a boat." He turned and spoke slowly to the little maid. "Where is Bentinck?"

Elsa's color had faded from crimson to its normal rosy hue. "He's with the King. His Majesty is ill again. He suffered another coughing fit while listening to his musicians rehearse in the *oranjezaal*."

"I'll create a diversion," said Eden, decorously wrapped in her silk robe. "See, the moon is already going down."

Max glanced dubiously at Eden, then looked outside. It was true; the luminous half-moon was already hanging low over the scrollwork gardens. "What will you do?" he asked, a hand on her arm.

Pushing the wet hair off her forehead, Eden gave a little shrug. "I'll hunt for turtles. The soldiers will have to help me."

Max's chiseled expression briefly registered puzzlement, then he grinned and squeezed her shoulder. "I'm sure that makes perfect sense."

"Of course it does," Eden replied seriously. "But where will you go?"

The grin evaporated as Max pulled Eden close, and Elsa discreetly withdrew to a cabinet at the far end of the room. "Not far," he said. "Putting distance between us doesn't seem to work, does it?" Before Eden could respond, he kissed her mouth, a quick, fierce kiss that made her tremble.

"You'd best get dressed," Max growled, sounding much like the moody stranger she had first met. But, as she stared into the hazel eyes, she knew he was a different man.

Chapter Eleven

A SIMPLE PLOY HAD EFFECTED MAX'S escape. Out on the dunes, Eden informed the guard that she needed him to hold a torch while she hunted for turtle eggs in the sand. The King, she said, required a steaming soup, and the eggs that went into the making of it had to be procured after dark. Bored by his long watch and charmed by Eden, the guard stood at her side while Max crept out of the palace.

Eden was relieved that Max had gotten away, but she was desolated by loneliness. The next morning she awoke dispirited, wishing that she had fled with him instead of staying behind with the court. Trying to overcome her lassitude, Eden sought solace among the rows of blue and white lupin, of red and pink carnations, of gold and purple iris, all laid out in a perfect scrollwork pattern behind the palace.

Yet every sight somehow reminded her of Max. The statue of Cleopatra embracing the asp evoked lost love; Momus's mocking countenance taunted her with his cynicism; Narcissus, like Keppel, was self-absorbed, gazing at his reflected stone image in perpetual admiration, and oblivious to the rest of the world's troubles.

Eden had just reached the wrought-iron gates of the royal menagerie when Sidney Godolphin called her name.

"Mistress," he began, bustling up to join her and lowering his voice, "is it true that Prince Maximilian was in the palace last night?"

"He was." She couldn't hide her forlorn expression. "He tried to see the King, but Milord Bentinck ordered his arrest."

Concern was stamped on Godolphin's round face. "Bentinck is in a frenzy. The King is very ill," he explained as a pair of camels stalked the paddock and eyed their human counterparts with suspicion. "Alas, His Majesty's health is much worse than Dr. Bidloo had first suspected."

"Oh, dear." Eden frowned at a strange animal with twisted horns. "Mayhap I should seek out some of my more extreme remedies. Is it mainly his lungs?" Godolphin didn't reply until two maids in flaring Dutch caps had passed by with an assortment of cleaning utensils. "I'm not sure. Usually he's happier and thus healthier in the United Provinces. But not this time."

Eden was scanning the gardens. "There are cures within these very precincts," she announced, as a long-necked, long-legged creature strutted toward the fence. "Will you help me? I must see the King."

Godolphin inclined his head. "Of course. But are you sure you can be of aid, my dear?"

Eden was moving briskly down the path. "If what you say is true," she said over her shoulder, "I can hardly make him worse."

As MAX STOOD BESIDE HIS bay gelding and looked up at the steep curtained walls of the castle at Hohenstaufen, he forced his mind to dwell on every scrap of painful memory. Only now, after all these years, could he confront the tragedy of Sophie Dorothea and their stillborn son. First at Vranes, and now at Hohenstaufen, he had faced his past. Resolutely his hazel gaze scanned the ancient gray stones, so like the face of the mountain that it was almost impossible to tell where Nature's work left off and man's began.

Max's long mouth tightened as he caught sight of a single figure moving down the winding path that lead from the castle.

"Max!" called Rudolf, his voice echoing off the mountain.

Max said nothing. He had been standing at the edge of a little stream while his horse cropped at the short, thick grasses. With deliberate indolence he strolled to a linden tree and sat down with his long legs stretched out before him. It would take Rudolf another five minutes to get to the bottom of the mountain. Max wasn't going to waste his breath until he was face-to-face with his cousin.

To the casual observer, it appeared as if nothing could please Rudolf more than to find his kinsman lounging under the linden trees and taking the late summer sun. "How fit you look!" he exclaimed, vaulting the stream and dropping down beside Max. "Who could guess you've been running for your life!"

"You, for one, being the cause of my flight." Max spoke wryly, his expression wary. "I want it to stop, Rudi. Your persecution serves no purpose. In the end, everyone will suffer. If I were you, I'd worry more about William's wrath than about what happens to me."

Rudolf locked his hands behind his head and leaned against the tree trunk. "Is that why you came all the way to Hohenstaufen?" His bogus smile was trained on Max. "Sooth, I thought you wanted to kill me. Otherwise, why not come up to the castle?"

Max glanced at the invincible fastness that clung to the cliffs of the Swabian Jura. "I'm not quite the fool you take me to be," he replied. "As I recall, at our last meeting, *you* tried to kill *me*."

Rudolf's smile never wavered, its false cheer more sinister than a frank show of hostility. "It was mutual. Indeed, had you not been so squeamish, I'd be dead."

Max started to respond, then gave a little shake of his head. Rudolf didn't understand any motive that wasn't self-seeking. "It's pointless for us to carry on this feud. I'm willing to compromise," Max said at last. "I'll give you Dillenburg for Vranes."

Overhead, a hawk soared among the trees. The bay gelding looked up, then resumed its earnest cropping. The smile ebbed on Rudolf's face as he plucked up a fallen leaf and chafed it between his fingers. "That's a generous offer," he allowed, looking not at Max, but at an outcropping of rock halfway up the mountainside. "But it won't do." His blue eyes slid in his cousin's direction. "Come, come, why should I settle for half? Dillenburg should be partly mine in any event, we've always known that."

Max held his patience in check. "It was never yours, nor would there have been any questions, had it not been for my grandfather's indolence. In any event, a court of law decreed that Dillenburg belongs to me. You've been stealing the revenues, bribing the tenants, cheating me blind for years, all because you've had French troops to back you. But I would still rather have Vranes than Dillenburg, for the sake of Sophie Dorothea's memory."

Rudolf's lip curled. "You eloped with my sister. Abducted Sophie, as it were. It was only because I doted on her that I weakened and let her have Vranes as her dowry. But that was to please Sophie, not you. And when she died, the reason for my generosity went with her." He shrugged, and for a fleeting moment almost looked sincere. "You speak of memories! Who could blame me for wanting Vranes back? It's little enough recompense for the loss of my sister."

Max leaped to his feet in an incredibly swift motion for a man so large. "Damn your eyes!" he exploded, towering over Rudolf. "You talk as if she had been a piece of goods! She may have been your sister, but she was my wife!"

Rudolf made a leisurely effort to get to his feet. "More's the pity. But," he went on, reading the storm signals that played across Max's chiseled features, "there's still room for your precious compromise. If you sign the separate peace with King Louis, he will reward you amply. After all, except for Maastricht and a couple of other negligible outposts, he controls the entire frontier. What will you? Phillipsburg? Huy? Mons?"

Max's hand shot out to grab Rudolf by the front of his ruffled lawn shirt. "I want Vranes. That's my home." He spoke between clenched teeth, all but lifting his cousin off the ground. "I'll sign no traitorous treaties with the French. If you do, William will have your head. If," he snarled, shoving Rudolf away, "I don't take it first."

"Really!" Rudolf's aplomb was shaken, but he refused to be cowed. "You're much mistaken, Max. I have the Duke of Savoy as my ally and the Archbishop of Liège as my adviser. William can't touch me."

Max growled an old Flemish oath that made Rudolf flinch. "Both are in Louis's pocket—and purse. When William takes the field again, you're enough of a turncoat to sing a different song."

Tucking his shirt into his riding breeks, Rudolf sneered. "The English and Dutch won't go to war this year. They don't have the funds. The treaty must be signed in a week. Come back within four days and we'll ride together to Liège to meet with the archbishop."

"The hell we will!" Max had grabbed the reins of his horse and swung into the saddle. "You'll be an old man—or a dead man—before I ever sign such a piece of perfidy! There's nothing you can do to coerce me, either."

He was about to spur his gelding into a canter when he heard Rudolf laugh softly behind him. "But there is, Max." His hands on his hips, Rudolf planted himself in the shade of the linden tree. "You once took the woman I held most dear. Now I shall do the same to you."

Max's hands froze on the reins, causing his horse to startle. Surely Rudolf couldn't mean what Max thought he did. Warily, he finessed his response: "What are you talking about, you depraved swine? Harriet is safe in England."

"Harriet!" Rudolf spat out the name with an air of scorn. "I speak of your little peasant, of course. She is on this side of the North Sea. And, I've observed, she's much dearer to you than your fiancée."

Max felt the blood drain from his face even as his rage began to boil over. He was armed with his combat sword, but Rudolf wore no weapon, at least not one that was visible. The only solution was to find Eden before his cousin did. William, in his state of restless ill health, was moving the court at will. Rudolf had the advantage; he could make his inquiries openly. Max would have to track Eden down by stealth.

Turning in the saddle, he glared at Rudolf with an antipathy that would have withered a lesser man. "If you touch her, I'll not be squeamish next time. Upon the soul of Sophie Dorothea, I swear it."

Whirling, he dug his heels into the sides of his mount and galloped against the wind into the dark silence of the forest.

*

THE WHISKERED SWISS GUARDS IN their blue cloaks and flat caps had instructions not to let anyone but Joost van Keppel and Dr. Bidloo into the King's room. One glance at their stolid faces put Eden off, but Sidney Godolphin's self-effacing manner concealed a determination that would have done his thoroughbreds proud. With a polite nod to the guards, Godolphin turned to Dr. Bidloo.

"See here," said Godolphin, maneuvering around the rigid guardsmen who flanked the antechamber door, "Mistress Eden has some excellent remedies. Shall we be candid, Sir? Should—God forbid—anything happen to His Majesty, would you want to take the blame?"

Bidloo, a swarthy man with shrewd dark eyes, cast a disparaging look in Eden's direction. "If you're implying that this slip of a girl can help the King when I can't—"

"Slip of an *English* girl," Godolphin interjected. "Your London vis-à-vis, Dr. Radcliffe, is not here for consultation."

Bidloo's clever eyes darted around as he weighed Godolphin's words carefully. "Ah, yes," he finally conceded. "I've always said Radcliffe was an idiot." The doctor scrutinized Eden's collection, which included two jars, a wicker basket, three bottles, a cast-iron pot and a tea kettle. "I suppose she can do no harm. And if the worst should happen, the English shall bear as much responsibility as we Dutchmen."

William of Orange lay like a rag doll in the big canopied bed, his eyes closed and his breathing labored. The damask draperies were tightly shut, and though outside the summer sun shone from a clear blue sky, the room lay in deep shadow. The air was stale; the atmosphere oppressive. Keppel, attired in a brightly colored Indian banian, had been trying to feed his master puff pastry from a blue ramekin while a pair of Dutch pugs dozed on a rumpled blanket.

"The guardsmen were told to keep everyone out," Keppel said in a querulous tone. "His Majesty is very ill."

"Precisely," agreed Godolphin. "Which is why Mistress Eden is here." He forestalled Keppel's objections with a wave of his hand. "Dr. Bidloo has given his consent."

Keppel regarded Eden with skepticism as she hauled back two of the drapes and opened the tall French windows. "We must have air. It's stifling in here. And I need a fire, but only enough to boil my kettles." She glanced at Keppel. "Will you build it or shall I?"

Keppel stared at her peevishly. "This is nonsense. His Majesty should be bled. Where is Bidloo?"

Eden pulled aside the fender with its decoration of Grecian nymphs. "Milord Godolphin told you, Dr. Bidloo has given me permission to try my cures. See?" she said, standing up and showing him the contents of her wicker basket. "Poplar buds, which I shall mix with mutton fat for a salve to apply to His Majesty's nose. Camphor, to put into the boiling waters to ease his breathing. Elderberry, to eliminate ill humors."

About to scoff at her concoctions, Keppel was diverted by a rattling sound that came from the King's chest, followed by a series of gasps. The young favorite and Godolphin hurried to the bed, but Eden remained at the hearth, using a pestle to mix the salve and keeping her ear cocked for the bubbling of the pot.

"God help us," murmured Keppel, turning frantic blue eyes on Eden, "he can scarcely breathe! I told you he ought to be bled! Think of it—if His Majesty dies, Princess Anne will rule!"

Godolphin's round face betrayed only the slightest change. But Eden, in the process of putting the teakettle on the hob, stopped and stared at the shriveled figure in the bed. If William died ... Anne would be queen, Sarah Churchill would have more influence than anyone else in the realm, Marlborough would go free, and Eden would not be asked to sacrifice her virtue—or her love.

Searching Godolphin's face, she marveled at his lack of malice. Like Marlborough, he was a fair-minded man who respected the opinions of others. But unlike her father, Godolphin was also a gambler. Was it possible that he was betting on her failure?

Slowly she moved toward the bed. If William died, so many of Eden's problems would be solved. No one would blame her if she announced that having seen the King, there was nothing she could do.

William coughed twice, squirmed fitfully and with effort opened his watery eyes. He blinked and coughed again before fixing Eden with a gaze that was both pitiful and potent. "Mistress," he gasped, "why ...?"

Eden felt the power of those eyes and squared her shoulders. "Why, indeed, Sire," she answered brightly. "I'm here to make you well. Let me apply this salve." Bending over the bed, she deftly put the poplar and fat mixture around his nostrils. Too weak to offer resistance, William shrank back into the pillows. The iron pot boiled noisily, and Eden hurried to pour in the camphor. A sharp medicinal tang wafted over the room, mingling with the fresh, scented air from the gardens. Eden leaned against the ornate fireplace and offered a swift prayer. If all went well, the King should improve within the hour. Given her gift for healing, she had done what she had to do. No matter what the consequences, it would have been impossible for Eden to let William die.

*

To KEPPEL'S AMAZEMENT AND BIDLOO'S relief, the King was resting much easier by suppertime. The doctor refused to endorse Eden's methods, but allowed that she had somehow been lucky. "The moon, or the stars," he had muttered, "have much to do with life and death."

Keppel was less grudging. "The only thing more astonishing than your magic is the fact that His Majesty became so ill in the first place. He always prospers in his homeland. This summer, alas, has been different. He frets too much about his lack of money to fund the war against Louis."

Godolphin glanced at William, who seemed to be asleep. "Allocating funds for military purposes is not in my power. Having recalled the old coinage, Parliament seems loath to spend the new."

"Spending money is one of life's great pleasures," Keppel asserted, letting the pugs nuzzle his velvet house slippers. "His Majesty ought to clap Parliament in the Tower."

"Those days of divine right are gone forever, praise God," murmured Godolphin. He gestured at Eden, who was busily brewing her elderberry tea. "Let us not talk of the Tower," he whispered. "It upsets our good nurse."

Eden had been summoned to the bedside by Dr. Bidloo. "Our patient is waking up. I can scarce believe it," the doctor said, too grateful to show further rancor.

William was not only awake, but struggling to sit up. "What is all this fuss? Are we holding a levee in our bedchamber?" His voice was hoarser than usual, but the dark eyes were alert as he scanned the room. "Why do we have paste on our nose?"

"It's salve," said Eden, putting a soothing hand on his arm and straightening the covers. "Now you shall have some hot tea."

"Tea!" snorted William. "We despise tea!"

Eden gave a little shrug. She was weary after her long day, her curls were limp, and her skin was pale. But in her saffron skirts and amber petticoats, she looked like one of the French marigolds from the palace garden. "As you will, Sire. In consequence, we shall not reveal our plan to get money for your war."

The King's eyes narrowed. Bidloo frowned, while Godolphin and Keppel turned in surprise. "What nonsense is this now?" William demanded, a hand on his chest. "Do you mix money with medicine, Mistress?"

"Health and wealth don't always go together," Eden allowed, inspecting the china tea dishes that Keppel had set out on a teak table by the bed. "One year when my foster father needed money to repair our oasthouses, Master Peavey, the richest man in the village, refused him credit." She paused to pour tea from the steaming kettle.

William was growing restive, his face tight with impatience. "My point, Sire," Eden continued quickly, "is that if you can't get funds from one source, go to another. If Parliament declines, the next logical source is a money lender—in this case, the Bank of England. It's new, and ought to be more than eager to please you." She shrugged again, as if the solution were so obvious as to defy rebuttal.

William's brows drew together. "Do you mean a loan?" He heard Keppel snicker behind a lace-edged handkerchief. "But that's unprecedented! No King of England has ever asked a bank for a loan!"

"That," interjected Eden without so much as a deep breath, "is because until now there was no Bank of England to ask."

The sharp brown eyes flickered over Godolphin, then fixed on Eden. "Is this really your idea, Mistress?"

To Eden's surprise, she thought there was a tug of a smile at the corners of William's thin mouth. "If a bank has vaults filled with gold, why should it not be put at His Majesty's disposal? How will these bankers fare if Louis defeats the allies and overruns England? They'll be counting sous instead of ha'pennies."

William fingered his chin while Keppel gave Eden a bemused look. "Sidney," the King said at last, turning to his oft-maligned minister, "what think you?"

"It's brilliant, Sire." Godolphin beamed at Eden. "To be blunt, it's an idea that I or Bentinck or Shrewsbury should have introduced before this."

Reflecting briefly, William grimaced. "Mayhap. We will consider dispatching you and Milord Bentinck to England to meet with the bank's governors." His glance went from Godolphin to Bidloo and finally rested on Eden. Keppel had moved to the bed, the pugs at his heels. The young favorite started to speak, but for once, William ignored him. "You're a surprising young lady, Mistress. We've seldom known a member of your sex to be so widely accomplished." The King beamed at Eden. "Now, is it teatime?"

Chapter Twelve

To everyone's amazement, the King went haring two days later. While he was far from robust, his cough was better and his color had improved. Eden had no trouble plying him with fresh fruit, for unlike the English, William shared his fellow Dutchmen's belief that the summer harvest was more than tasty, it was healthful as well. She had less success, however, in keeping him from strong spirits.

The stratagem she'd outlined took more time. Several courtiers spurned the idea of seeking a loan from the new Bank of England, and there was much heated debate. But William, having accepted the proposal, refused to be talked out of it. As summer spun its green-and-golden web across the United Provinces, the King ultimately badgered his courtiers into a consensus. In early August, Bentinck and Godolphin sailed for England. Anxiously, Eden awaited word of their mission's outcome.

This obvious concern masked her greatest worry, which was for Max. Except for rumors that he'd been seen at various points along the Meuse, and as far east as Liège, there were no messages, either to the King or to her. The long, sunny days only emphasized her loneliness. Sitting in the seashell grotto at Het Loo, Eden could imagine walking hand in hand with Max up to the little pavilion on the hill above the palace, or drifting down the canal that wound between the formal gardens.

Reality was a string of empty days, like a necklace without jewels. Eden sent a long letter to her father, trying to cheer him—and herself—with accounts of her remedies for the King. She also scribbled a brief note to her foster family in Kent, should they be curious as to what had become of her since she had left London. Eden doubted that they'd care, and was certain they'd never believe her. That Eden Berenger, foster daughter of a Smarden cider maker, should be nursemaid to a king would strain the credulity of the entire village. Nor could Eden blame them.

But in fact she was traveling between Honselaardijk and Het Loo and Dieren and the House in the Wood, mixing salves and stirring elixirs that more often than not seemed to make William of Orange feel stronger. While His Majesty displayed an appropriate amount of appreciation for her skill, he made no attempt to go beyond the boundaries of strict etiquette. Keppel was always at his master's side, preventing any private interludes. Eden was relieved, yet felt guilty over not making more headway on her father's behalf.

The King had just returned from hunting at Het Loo when Eden saw him wave to her from the courtyard. Quickly she descended the broad brick steps and was about to make the obligatory inquiry after his expedition when she noticed that he was accompanied by a travel-weary Wilhem Bentinck.

Seeing Eden approach the sky-blue and golden gates, the King called out to her in an unusually animated voice, "Praise God! Wilhem has the money! Our thanks is infinite, Mistress!"

As grooms and servants scurried to help William and the other nobles dismount, Eden noted Keppel's ironic expression. She was surprised when he approached her, loosening his lawn cravat and perching on the edge of the courtyard fountain.

"It's a tainted victory," he said, keeping his voice low and abandoning his usual excessive mannerisms. "Your idea was clever, but it is Bentinck who has made it work. He wishes both of us ill, and now reaps his reward from the King's grateful hands." Keppel's blue eyes snapped, revealing a harder core than Eden would have suspected. "You'll notice Godolphin didn't return, thus letting Bentinck hog all the glory."

Eden looked beyond the marble dolphins that frolicked in the fountain. Keppel was right; Godolphin was nowhere to be seen. "But why did Sidney stay behind?" she asked, watching William and Bentinck share a stirrup cup.

Keppel reached inside the taffeta lining of his hunting coat and pulled out a sealed letter. "A friendly member of Bentinck's entourage gave me this outside the gates. It's for you, from Milord Godolphin." Noting that the King had finally disengaged himself from the jubilant Bentinck, Keppel leaped from his place by the fountain. "Sire! We must celebrate! Let us rally round the palace punch bowl!"

Springing to his master's side, the young favorite nimbly helped William up the broad stairs and through the dark green front door. Bentinck's efforts to follow had been thwarted by several excited courtiers, eager for news of the Bank of England's patriotic generosity.

Eden remained by the fountain, its cascade of waters drowning out the nobles' voices. Carefully she broke the seal on Godolphin's letter. She supposed she should not be surprised that Keppel had managed to insinuate one of his cohorts into Bentinck's party. Intrigue was not her metier, yet she knew it was necessary in order to survive at court.

Godolphin's handwriting was much like the man himself—plain, round and without pretension. He began with a brief account of the satisfactory business he and Bentinck had concluded: "Grocers' Hall rocked with Enthusiasm, once we made it clear that the Danger of Louis invading our Beloved Realm was quite real." The Bank's board of governors had been eager to show their loyalty, Godolphin related. They wished not only to help defend their country, but to demonstrate their stability over the Land Bank, which had failed the previous year. "It is known only to Providence and a Fortunate Few how much of a Debt is owed to you," he continued, "but I assure you, your dear Father is very proud of his Daughter."

Eden beamed when she read those words, and tried to imagine Marlborough, in his prison cell, exulting over her ingenuity. Godolphin's next lines were less sanguine: "I remain in England, for varied Reasons, not the least of which is your Father's Predicament. Since his Arrest, F. has made the most libelous Allegations to certain Members of the House of Lords, and I fear they will act swiftly in passing Judgment against M. All that prevents them from moving ahead in His Majesty's Absence is the lack of a second Witness. But such a one will be found, as enough Silver will eventually grease the right Palm."

Disturbed, Eden reread the letter more slowly, then started to tuck it away in the pocket of her lace-edged pinner-apron. She paused, noting that most of the courtiers and attendants had drifted away. Intrigue might be foreign to her nature, but it was essential. With a deft motion she unfurled the letter and submerged it in the pool. The paper's lifeblood dissolved in tiny rivulets of blue ink. Eden crumpled the sodden remnant and threw it into the water, where it disappeared beneath the dolphins' dancing fins.

THE ANTECHAMBER IN THE KING'S apartments was hung with tapestries depicting cavalry exploits. It was here that William received Eden, who carried a blue crock filled with steaming applesauce.

"Delicious!" he announced, taking in a heaping spoonful. "One of my Grandmother Amalia's cooks made a sauce that almost—but not quite—equaled yours."

Eden gave him her most beguiling smile. "It was always a treat with fresh apples this time of year in Smarden," she said, casting around for a way to steer the conversation in the direction of Marlborough's plight. "Merry come up, last summer I never expected to be in the Gelderland! What a difference it has made to find my real father!"

William's sallow skin darkened, and Keppel suddenly seemed absorbed in winding a tall mahogany clock across the room. Eden stiffened slightly, awaiting the royal displeasure. But she was relieved that she had finally broached the subject.

"We've never been quite clear about all that," the King remarked, setting down his porcelain dish and taking a sip of beer. "The Earl of Marlborough betrayed our trust."

Eden bridled, but tried to conceal her anger. "He's loyal, Sire. He's been the victim of jealous rivals. Could anyone have served you better than he did in your wars on the Continent and in Ireland?" She glanced at Keppel, hoping for an endorsement. But the young favorite was tapping the clock's case, intently listening for a ticking sound.

William stifled a cough and regarded Eden with a stern expression. "We expect Parliament to act before long. Then justice can be done." Seeing her shocked expression, the King made no effort to soften his words. "We are more merciful than most, Mistress, but traitors, especially in time of war, must not be spared."

"Sire!" Eden was aghast at William's harsh stand. "I beseech you, His Lordship is no Jacobite! He had nothing to do with the assassination plot! Someone has been filling your ears with vile calumny!" She paused, aware of William's affronted look and Keppel's odd stare.

The King's thin lips clamped together, emphasizing the aggressive beaklike nose. "Enough, Mistress. We are preoccupied today. Dynastic issues demand that we go a-courting."

Eden gaped at William. "You've found a bride?"

The King's thin lips all but disappeared. "I ... we seek one in Germany," he replied, his brown eyes no longer so piercing. "More politics." The glance he gave both Eden and Keppel was defensive as well as apologetic.

Having finally found the courage to mention Marlborough's detention, Eden was dismayed by William's obstinacy. But she was not prepared for his announcement about a new consort. Her own prospects had never looked more dismal.

Before the King could expand on the subject of his proposed trip, Bentinck entered, his ruddy face blazing with outrage. "God's fish, Willi," he cried, heedless of etiquette, "the Duke of Savoy and Count Hohenstaufen have signed a separate peace treaty with King Louis!"

What little color William had acquired drained from his face. "Damn all!" he breathed, his hand trembling on the beer mug. "Such treachery! And even though we have the money now, it's too late in the season to fight!"

With a malevolent glance at Keppel, Bentinck paced the antechamber, hands clenched behind his back. "This pair has sold us out, Sire. Louis will see their defection as a general weakening of our frontiers, from Southern France to Flanders."

Bewildered, Eden watched Keppel, who seemed to be displaying previously concealed inhibitions. He made no attempt to join in the political discussion, but merely glanced at Eden and gave a little shrug. She was not so inclined to dismiss this latest calamity. Eden knew it affected Max as well as the King.

"Excuse me," she began in a hesitant voice, earning William's frown and Bentinck's scowl, "but has Count Rudolf signed the treaty alone, or with his cousin?"

Both men eyed her quizzically at first, then comprehension dawned on Bentinck. "Maximilian, you mean? No," he said, his jaw jutting, "his name was not mentioned. What does that Judas plot now?"

To Eden's surprise, Keppel rose to Max's defense. "His Highness would never agree to such a thing. Count Rudolf has not acted in concert with his cousin. I would guess that the treaty is invalid."

William considered while Bentinck mulled. "Perhaps," grumbled the statesman. "Though there is another explanation." He waited, savoring the trio's attention. "Prince Maximilian may be dead."

The antechamber grew too warm in the August air. The frescoed ceiling seemed to bear down, and the paneled walls pressed in. Eden swayed, crashing into the table that held the blue clock of applesauce. Keppel caught her arm, but though he kept her from falling, the crock slid onto the floor, breaking into a dozen pieces and spilling its contents onto the tiled floor.

EDEN RACKED HER BRAIN TO figure out a way of joining the royal party at least as far as the Rhine. She finally resorted to asking Keppel's help. Luring him away from the bowling green at Het Loo, she stated her case in a way that sorely tried her unhoned skills at subterfuge.

"Prince Maximilian is a friend of my father's, as you know," she began, standing in the shade of an oak tree. "I feel an obligation to find out if he is indeed dead or alive."

Keppel glanced at the green, where his opponents, led by Bentinck, were having a sudden streak of phenomenal success. "Lovely Eden, your guile is unquestioned, but your deceit is appallingly heavy-handed. You and Max spent months under the same roof. Do you think I'm an imbecile?"

Eden's cheeks flushed, but she drew herself up very straight. "Prince Maximilian is betrothed to Lady Harriet Villiers. Do you think he and I would behave in an improper—"

Keppel's response was a hearty guffaw. Away from the King, his mannerisms were not only more genuine, they were considerably less effete. "Knowing Max and seeing you, I think you'd behave the way nature intended you to," said Keppel, quelling his laughter, but still grinning at Eden. "As for Harriet, the betrothal is off."

"What?" Eden was dumbfounded.

"That's right." As a cheer went up, Keppel craned his neck to see Bentinck accepting congratulations from the King and most of the courtiers. "Damn the old fool's eyes," muttered Keppel, "he can still bowl like a boy when it comes to pleasing William." He turned to Eden, unable to hide his amusement at her startled expression. "My friends in London have informed me that Harriet threw a terrible tantrum when she heard about the separate peace. It was shameful enough that her fiancé got himself exiled, but that he should be associated with such perfidy overwhelmed the delicate creature. She is said to be consoling herself with a spineless viscount whose pater owns half of Sussex."

Eden fanned herself with her hand, though the September afternoon held the crisp tang of autumn. "I didn't know. Does Max, I wonder? You don't really think he's dead, do you?"

Keppel shrugged, his attention once again diverted by the little scene on the bowling green. "Now where did that repellent relic get to? Toadying around William, I suppose. No, the King is over there, with Bidloo and Secretary Huygens."

Eden had the feeling she wasn't going to get much more out of Keppel. "If I could just ride with you as far as the Rhine, please. His Majesty needn't know I've come along."

Conscious of the King's approach, Keppel struck a pose, letting the slight breeze ruffle his lawn shirt and standing with one foot in front of the other to show off his well-turned calves. "I'll see to it," he said quickly, giving Eden a hasty bow. "And don't worry," he added in a low voice, "Max is alive. He's too damnably perverse to die."

EDEN AND ELSA PARTED COMPANY with the others outside Nijmegen late on the first day of the journey. Keppel had been as good as his word, seeing them into the last coach and bribing the attendants into silence. It was only after the dust had cleared behind the royal party that Eden realized she had no clear plan for finding Max.

"We'll head south," she announced vaguely, not looking at Elsa. Though she had pored over the maps in William's study the previous day, she still had only the sketchiest notion of where Vranes-sur-Ourthe was located. A town called Liège was impressed upon her memory, for there the Meuse and Ourthe rivers converged. But how far away, how long it would take, what they might find when they arrived were all questions Eden couldn't answer.

By sunset of the following day they were following the Meuse, and for the first time, Eden witnessed the ravages of war. Farm buildings lay in rubble, entire villages had been burned, once-fertile fields were choked with briars. Beggars huddled by the roadside while children in tattered rags chased after the coach, calling for coins. Eden tossed a handful from the window, and felt guilty that she could not give more. The personal funds supplied by Barbara Castlemaine had been generous, but Eden's tutoring had not included managing money.

"We shall stop at the next town," she announced to their driver. "It grows dark, and frankly, I find this war-torn countryside depressing. I wonder if Vranes-sur-Ourthe has suffered so?"

Elsa lifted one shoulder. "King Louis's soldiers burned much of the land they left behind them, all along the frontier."

As spires, battlements and rooftops rose before them in the pale September twilight, Eden tried to recall what Gerard had said about the war. The fact was, he had rarely mentioned his experiences at all. Eden suspected that he had not wanted to remember.

Following a placid river that seemed to lead into the town, the horses slowed in front of a ramshackle inn. Set off from the side of the road was a weatherbeaten shrine shielding a figure of what appeared to be a bishop. The old-fashioned lettering at the statue's base read St. Servatius. For Eden, such religious ornaments once would have smacked of idolatry. Yet here, in this part of the world known as the Spanish Netherlands, the little shrine seemed fitting. "Where are we?" she asked, wondering who St. Servatius might have been.

The driver, a bearlike man with curly red hair, was alighting from the platform. "Maastricht," he replied, kicking at a feisty mongrel whose speckled coat was bare in patches.

"Maastricht!" The name echoed in Eden's brain. Her father had won a great victory there, one of the few the allies had wrested from the French. Despite the inn's dilapidated appearance and the sense of gloom that hung over the city, Eden had the unaccountable feeling that she was being welcomed home.

Elsa, however, had no reason to share her enthusiasm. "Perhaps we should go farther into town," she suggested, picking her way over the debris that littered the small courtyard. Broken axles, discarded wagons wheels, rusted tools and shattered crockery covered the barren ground. Two gaunt-faced children huddled by a crude pen where a half-dozen scrawny chickens had gone to roost for the night.

But Eden had made up her mind. " 'Tis only for a few hours. We can leave at dawn." She turned as a pair of horsemen stopped at the edge of the road. "Don't be frightened, Elsa," she said, using sign language to make herself perfectly clear. "See there, more guests are arriving."

Elsa turned anxious eyes on the newcomers, but could see no more than the outline of their cloaks and hats. "They could be thieves," she mumbled.

Eden turned to the coachman, who was trying to find a trough for the horses. "How far is it from here to Liège?" she asked.

He cocked his head and considered. "Half a day."

"And then to Vranes?"

His forehead creased as he pulled on his ear. "I'm not sure. I've never been there. Ask the innkeeper, Mistress." His tone was polite, but his manner was impatient. "There's no water. I'll have to lead the horses down to the Meuse." Annoyed, he grabbed the reins and guided the thirsty animals toward the road.

Elsa had gone around to the side of the inn, searching for a porter. Eden waited with a vague sense of regret; perhaps she should not have been so stubborn about staying at the edge of town.

"Mistress!" the shorter man called in English, "do you speak the local dialect?"

Eden had no idea what the local dialect was. "Alas, no. I use French here mostly." She smiled politely, then let out a little gasp. The men were bearing down on her, and while she was sure she had never seen the short one before, she recognized Rudolf's blunt-faced henchman from Green Park. "What are you doing here?" she demanded, then saw that something gleamed in the palm of his hand.

Whirling, she started to run toward the inn, but tripped over a splintered shovel. Eden cried out as she fell, at first from pain, then in desperation. Elsa, of course, couldn't hear her, but perhaps their driver or someone inside the inn would race to the rescue. But before she could scream a third time, a heavy boot pressed down on her back and a rough hand went over her mouth. Squirming in the dirt, Eden tried to free herself, but her efforts were in vain. Something sweet assailed her nostrils, and the world was plunged into darkness.

WHEN EDEN AWOKE, SHE THOUGHT she was in her room above the Queen's garden at Het Loo. But as she struggled to clear her mind and focus her eyes, she realized that her surroundings were as unfamiliar as they were elegant. In the pale light of dawn, Eden could see a walnut armoire, a tall clock inlaid with marquetry, a Chinese screen decorated with peonies and a table covered with an ornate tapestry. The bed on which she lay was hung with blue damask, and the marble fireplace was accented with rich mahogany. Eden would have been charmed had she not been so terrified.

Slowly she sat up and surveyed herself for any serious damage. Her knees were bruised and her hands were scratched, apparently from the fall at the inn. The peacock-blue traveling costume was soiled and ripped at the hem. Her perky hat with its egret feather had disappeared along with her gold earrings, but she still had her necklace and bracelet. Robbery was not the motive; the involvement of Rudolf's henchman indicated that. Her coach must have been followed, probably all the way from Het Loo. Drumming her fingernails against the silken counterpane, Eden cursed aloud.

She should never have trusted Keppel. He was totally self-serving. He had betrayed her to the enemy and, in the process, gotten rid of a potential rival. What other reason could there be for her kidnapping? She could not believe that Max had ever called Joost van Keppel his friend.

But Keppel was no comrade of Rudolf's. Eden couldn't think of any reason the young favorite would ally himself to a man who had just alienated the King. Rudolf had cut himself off from the House of Orange by signing the peace treaty with Louis of France.

Deep in thought, Eden got up from the bed and went to the door. It was locked, as she had expected. Only Keppel—and Elsa—knew she was going to search for Max. Elsa, sworn to secrecy, was utterly trustworthy. Going to the nearest window, Eden noted that she was two stories above the ground. She looked out across an orderly gold and bronze autumn garden to a densely wooded parkland fenced off by a high brick wall. The house—or mansion— seemed quite large, with a creamy sandstone exterior. Her prison appeared to be very beautiful, but a prison nonetheless. Eden noticed a bowling green beyond an oval fish pond and was reminded of her fateful conversation with Keppel at Het Loo.

And then she knew. Bentinck had disappeared after the match. By chance or by design, the statesman must have overheard her confide in Keppel. And the wily old devil had somehow contacted Rudolf, whose men had followed Eden from Nijmegen. It was almost as impossible to think of Bentinck conniving with Rudolf as it was to consider Keppel—except that the older man knew his days of influence with the King were numbered, and he was desperate. Eden with her miracle cures and ingenuous schemes, created a double threat for Bentinck. He might be able to contend with one rival, but not two, and it was far easier to get rid of Eden than Keppel. Perhaps it was Bentinck who had ordered Captain Craswell's death, though somehow the deed smacked more of Rudolf's handiwork. Either way, that grim reminder was deeply disturbing.

Eden was shivering and shaking her head when she heard the door open.

Turning swiftly, she saw Rudolf glide into the room, dressed for the hunt. The perpetual smile was plastered on his face, and he carried a riding crop.

"Welcome to Zijswijk," said Rudolf, using his hip to close the door. "Have you breakfasted yet or would you rather wait for Max?"

Eden moved away from the window to stand by the tapestry-covered table. "Don't joke about Max," she snapped. "Where is he?"

Rudolf made his way to the table, where he perched on the edge and swung one booted foot. "Let me think—The Hague, mayhap, or the House in the Wood, or any one of the places William frequents when visiting his homeland." The smile widened. "Unless, of course, Max has found out that His Majesty has gone a-wooing to Moylandt. Then your beloved may still be in Germany, combing the Rhine for his Lorelei."

Eden edged away from the table. "What are you talking about? Max was my … protector, helping my father."

"And helping himself to your father's daughter, no doubt." Rudolf's leer was just short of parody. Before Eden could protest, he waggled the crop in her direction. "Let us not quibble over terms. Besides being your father's daughter, you are your mother's, as well. And everyone in Europe knows how she whored her way to fame and fortune. Do you expect anyone—especially King William—to believe that you're a virtuous maid?"

"But I am!" Eden cried. "No man has ever had me!" Skepticism was rampant on Rudolf's face. "That's utterly incredible. Unless, of course, Max is a greater fool than I thought." The smile had finally faded, replaced by a pensive expression. "There's one way to find out," he said with a little smirk. As he saw Eden recoil, he laughed in an artless yet insinuating manner. "No, no, not now. We have plenty of time, and right now my Master of the Hounds awaits me." Rudolf slid off the table and started for the door.

"Wait!" Eden was still shuddering at Rudolf's innuendo. "Why am I here? And where am I?"

Rudolf paused at the threshold. "I told you, Zijswijk. It's my estate outside of Liège. The reason you are here, you silly wench, is obvious—you are the bait to lure Max. You are my guarantee that he will add his signature to the treaty with King Louis." He shrugged carelessly, confident of his success. "Don't try to escape. The grounds are well guarded by mercenaries I've hired from the French army. They're a nasty lot, but very efficient. And," he added with a savage little smile, "I wouldn't proclaim my virtue too loudly, if I were you. They are particularly ravenous for virgins. All of them." With a flip of the crop, Rudolf exited the room.

FOR THREE DAYS EDEN REMAINED in her elegant prison. The days dragged, for she had only a few old books to help pass the time. Rudolf did not return, and Eden wondered if he had left Zijswijk. She was still stupefied by the reason for her abduction. Even if Bentinck had not been the instigator, he had willingly gone along with Rudolf to eliminate a rival. But Eden would never have guessed that she was being used as a pawn to coerce Max into signing the peace treaty. She would not have thought that he cared about her so much. The idea that he might filled her with a warm glow—until she remembered that if it was true, they were both in grave danger.

It was late the third day, with heavy gray clouds gathering on the horizon, that Eden saw Rudolf and a small party ride up to the manor house. Anxiously she peered down to see if Max was with them. But Rudolf was the only tall man among the riders, and Eden dejectedly wandered to the hearth, where a fire had been laid for the night. Perhaps Max would never come; maybe Rudolf had overestimated his feelings for Eden. Or he couldn't find where Rudolf was keeping her, or he had been killed or arrested …. In a fit of frustration, she clawed at the pages of a book she'd been trying to read, scattering them like torn petals on the counterpane. The destructive gesture appalled her; she felt no better than an animal. Yet that's what she was, trapped, held captive, shut away from the world like the exotic creatures in William's tame zoo. Giving in to despondency, Eden hurled herself onto the bed and began to cry.

She had sobbed into the pillows for almost a quarter of an hour before she acknowledged the futility of her despair. Trying to compose herself, she poured a glass of Moselle wine from a decanter by the nightstand and took a sip. When the door opened, she jumped, spilling wine onto the counterpane and cursing herself for being so nervy. Expecting the surly lout who usually brought her supper, Eden was surprised to see Rudolf, dressed in his bright blue traveling costume, a beaver hat set rakishly on his blond curls.

"You've been crying! Did you miss me?" He was grinning like a nasty cat.

Ashamed of her tears, Eden blinked several times and made a heroic effort to compose herself. "I wouldn't miss you if you flew to Araby on a magic carpet!" She scooted off the bed and went to light the tapers on the mantelpiece. Outside, the rain started to fall in straight, steady sheets.

"I've been conferring with the Archbishop of Liège," Rudolf remarked in a conversational tone as he tossed his hat onto a marble wig stand near the bed. "If he were a pious man, he'd pray that Max will be sensible when he gets here."

"If Max is sensible, he won't come," Eden retorted, turning away from the fireplace.

Rudolf strolled over to Eden and planted both booted feet not more than six inches from her hem. "You're not at all like Sophie Dorothea," he said, a furtive glint in his eyes. "She was delicate, all gold and apple blossoms, and pure as St. Agnes. Until Max came along." With a startling swift movement,

Rudolf grasped Eden's cravat and yanked it so hard that her head snapped back. "You claim to be pure, you dirty little trollop!" He was leaning down, his face almost touching Eden's, his blue eyes sinister and cold. "We will now discover the truth!"

"No!" Eden pummeled him with her fists, but he grabbed both wrists, swung her around and held her hands behind her back.

"Why the fuss?" Rudolf asked with a malicious chuckle. "If you're telling the truth, think of what delights I can teach you! And if you're not, consider the mutual sport we shall enjoy! Mayhap you can teach me!" With a vicious thrust, he kneed Eden in the small of her back, knocking her off her feet and pulling her arms painfully taut. She screamed, but Rudolf only laughed and sat down on a brocade-covered bench, hauling Eden across his lap. He held her wrists together above her head with one hand while the other stripped away the cravat at the neck of her lingerie shirt.

Eden's breath was coming very fast, and her mouth had gone dry. She felt drained from crying, yet knew she must somehow stop Rudolf's assault. Her unshod feet kicked out, striking nothing but air. She screamed again, but it would do no good. There was no one at Zijswijk who would lift a finger to help her.

"You're too loud!" Rudolf exclaimed, no longer making an attempt at his customary bonhomie. "Be quiet!" He slapped her hard across the face, then ripped shirt and chemise to the waist in one rabid gesture. The sight of Eden's breasts sent him into a frenzy. Rudolf threw her onto the floor and fell on top of her, making low, growling animal sounds in his throat. Fighting for breath, Eden writhed under him, as terrified by the shocking transformation as by his intentions.

He was tearing at her skirts and pressing wet kisses on her neck and breasts when a loud knocking resounded at the door. To Eden, struggling to keep her legs locked together and clawing at Rudolf's face, the pounding seemed to go on forever before Rudolf noticed. At last he paused in his feverish pursuit and called out, "Go away! Damn you, go away!"

But the knocking persisted, followed by a dull voice that Eden presumed to belong to her surly keeper. "It's the Prince. He's here."

Eden felt her entire body turn weak. Rudolf tensed, his weight crushing her. For several seconds he remained motionless. "Later!" he finally called. "Hold him below!"

Eden let out a terrible wail of despair, but rallied when she heard a swift series of thumping sounds in the hallway, just before the door flew open. Twisting her head, she saw Max not ten feet away, a double-barreled pistol in his hand.

"Get up!" he thundered at Rudolf. "Now, before I blow you to hell and back!"

Slowly, Rudolf eased himself off Eden, but remained on his knees near her. The room was eerily silent for a long time, with Max's gun trained on his cousin, Eden trying to recover her senses, and Rudolf undergoing a change in reverse, from ravening beast to worldly nobleman.

"Come, come, Max, the little peasant wench and I were just playing farmer in the barn. You'd hardly shoot me over *that*."

The gun exploded with a deafening roar, rocking the furniture and illuminating the room as if it was high noon. Rudolf jumped and rolled over. His smile was rather shaky when he saw that the wig stand had been blown to pieces. "You're done for now, Max!" he spat, hauling Eden to her feet. "My men will come running, and if you fire your other shot, you'll hit the peasant!"

Max's mouth was set in a grim line as Eden wriggled in Rudolf's grasp, her wide eyes both frightened and furious. Max had never hated Rudolf more than he did at that moment. But he could not kill his kinsman, though the opportunity was there. Either in arrogance or stupidity, Rudolf had miscalculated. Eden's head only reached midway up his chest. Max raised the pistol, took aim and fired.

The ball struck Rudolf in the shoulder, knocking him backward onto the hearth. His head hit the fireplace fender with a sickening crack. Eden stifled a scream as she reeled sideways to collapse against the mantelpiece. When the smoke cleared, she made a trembling gesture toward the recumbent figure on the hearth. "Is he ... dead?"

Max moved quickly to kneel by Rudolf. "No. I didn't shoot to kill. It's only a flesh wound, but he knocked himself out on this." Tapping the fender, he stood up and grabbed Eden's arm. "Let's get out of here. He was right about one thing, his men will be here any minute."

They were, in fact, already tromping down the hall. Max froze at the door. "*Schoft*," he muttered. "Here," he said, yanking off his suede jacket and throwing it over Eden, "cover yourself."

Eden obeyed, all but swallowed up in the big garment. "How can we get out? The windows are too high—I've already looked a hundred times."

Max chewed his lip. "We'll have to negotiate, I suppose, although our prospects aren't particularly rosy with a crew of French mercenaries."

Rudolf's men were at the door, pounding loudly. Max was loading his pistol and looking worried. On the hearth, Rudolf began to stir. The door caved in, splintering halfway across the room. Max raised the pistol but was confronted by a dozen soldiers, all armed with swords or harquebusses.

"Hold!" he shouted. "Your master is unconscious! Tend to him and let us go. He needs a surgeon more than he needs to keep us prisoner."

"*Sacre merde!*" cried the apparent leader, barging into the room. "How do we know he is not already dead? Drop your gun!"

Max didn't comply, but instead gestured with a nod of his head at Rudolf. "He's groaning even now. Do as I say, or he won't live to pay you."

The man's mouth curled in a snide smile. "Then we must steal our wages. Meanwhile, we will ransom you *à deux*, eh?"

In desperation Eden snatched one of the tapers from the mantel and hurled it onto the brittle pages that were scattered across the wine-soaked bed. The counterpane exploded, sending flames shooting up into the heavy hangings. Max looked away from the soldiers for an instant but never let his pistol waver.

"Come get the Count!" he ordered, as Eden rushed to his side.

But the flames had already enveloped the bed and were licking at the draperies. The soldiers pressed closer, saw the burgeoning inferno, and all but their leader turned tail and fled.

Smoke was filling the room, making Eden and Max cough. Shoving his pistol in his belt, Max bent down to tug at Rudolf's feet in an effort to drag him to safety. But Rudolf was awake.

"You pig," he growled at Max, his voice barely audible over the crackling of the flames, "do you expect me to be grateful to you for saving my life?"

Max was motioning to the soldier to help him move Rudolf. "Save your breath. We're all suffocating."

"Let go!" The scream was torn from Rudolf's throat. "Don't touch me with those hands that soiled Sophie! Killer hands! Swine!" Kicking at Max, Rudolf began to cough, a horrible, strangled noise that made Eden cringe.

Max backed off. "*Schoft*," he muttered, waving at the smoke and grasping Eden by the hand. "Get him out of here," he called to the soldier, whose form by now was almost obscured. The fire was scorching the far walls, and two of the windows had shattered from top to bottom. Eden put one of the long sleeves of Max's coat over her face as they fought their way out of the room.

The hall was full of smoke, but here the heat was far less intense and the sound of the flames was muffled. Max was propelling Eden down a staircase when they heard the shot. Both jumped, and Eden would have fallen had Max not held her arm.

"What was that?" she gasped, her voice hoarse.

Max gave a fleeting look up the stairwell. "I don't think I want to know," he said, and swiftly crossed himself.

Chapter Thirteen

MAX AND EDEN RODE DUE west at breakneck speed, and neither spoke for the first half hour. The rain, which had blown in from the sea, was behind them, and the September night was surprisingly mild. The landscape was flattening out, the horizon broken only by a few trees, windmills and the square outlines of tiny farmhouses. To Eden's relief there was no sign of recent devastation in this part of the world.

At last Max slowed their horse to a walk. No one at Zijswijk had tried to stop them. The French mercenaries had been too busy looting the estate, the servants engaged in saving their own possessions. Nevertheless, Max had been intent on putting as much distance as possible between them and Rudolf's country home.

"Do you think he's dead?" Eden finally asked.

Max's shoulders sagged. "I suspect so. His hirelings preferred plunder to wages, which is predictable of mercenaries. Rudolf was a fool to recruit such a villainous lot. But it was typical."

From behind spent gray clouds the moon made coquettish appearances. "But won't that soldier be arrested? Surely he'll hang for killing a count!" Despite Rudolf's brutality, Eden couldn't suppress a shudder at the thought of cold-blooded murder.

Feeling her tremble as she clung to him, Max gave Eden a wry glance over his shoulder. "You're such an honest little maid that you tend to believe in justice and integrity and all those other upstanding virtues. The fact is, Eden, that mercenary will never be charged with his master's death. He has a dozen witnesses who will testify in all honesty that I shot Rudolf first. And for a price, that same dozen will swear that I shot him again."

"Oh, no!" Eden buried her face in the back of Max's shirt. "But I know you didn't!"

She felt rather than saw Max shrug. "And who will believe the woman that half the world takes to be my … uh, paramour?"

"But I'm not," Eden attested staunchly. And with a pang, she wished the rumor mill hadn't been grinding in vain. It was only then that she remembered what Keppel had told her about Lady Harriet's defection. But this was not the time or place to speak of such matters. Instead, Eden asked Max how he had found her.

"Simple enough," he replied as a dog howled at the moon from the edge of a ditch. "Rudolf broadcast the news of your abduction far and wide. I was nearby, in Liège, when I heard. Indeed, I'd just missed him as he called on his accomplice, the archbishop." Though Max had spoken with resentment, his tone abruptly changed. "Holy St. Hubert, as much as he hated me, I never wished him dead! He was, after all, part of Sophie Dorothea."

"And, of course, she was perfect," Eden retorted, and was immediately sorry. "Oh, Max," she said quickly, squeezing him around the chest, "I didn't mean that the way it sounded. I know how much you loved her!"

Max stopped the horse at the rise of a narrow bridge over a canal. Eden froze, her arms still around Max but her heart thumping with anxiety. She must have infuriated him.

But after a long, dreadful pause, Max said in his most casual manner, "We'd better stop for the night." He urged the horse into a trot, they crossed the bridge, and he scanned the horizon. "The next town is Louvain, but it's some distance. Let's hope we can find a fanner who keeps late hours."

Eden could see a cluster of buildings just ahead. "What about that village? Can't we find a hostelry to take us in?"

Max chuckled. "You, perhaps, but not me. That's a begijnhof, rather like a convent, except it's a village in itself. And though the women who live there are deeply religious spinsters and widows, they aren't nuns. As you can guess," he added grimly, "there are a great many begijnhoven, thanks to the wars with King Louis."

"Max!" Eden exclaimed, "If Rudolf's dead, does that mean you'll get Vranes and Dillenburg back?"

She saw him incline his head. "Perhaps. That's up to King William … and Louis. I must still prove my loyalty to our sovereign. Dead men can't lie, but they can't tell the truth, either."

Eden was about to vent her indignation at such a potential injustice when Max espied a feeble light glowing behind a window in a cottage set off from the road. The iron gate creaked as he led their horse up the path and rapped on the door. Eden stood next to him on the stoop, as pleasantly surprised as ever at the tidiness of Fleming and Dutch alike, even in the remote countryside.

A bearded fanner, candle in hand, cautiously opened the door. Eden could not understand the language Max used, and discreetly tried to peer around them both to see inside the little house. A woman was cradling an infant, while two older children grappled with each other in a sleepy, halfhearted manner on a trundle bed. At last Max handed over a bag of coins. As Eden crossed the threshold, she realized for the first time since they left Zijswijk that she was not only extremely tired, but ravenously hungry, as well.

"The baby is teething," Max said in a low voice to Eden, "which is why they are up so late. They have a loft. I told them we were a married couple who'd been set upon by marauders so they wouldn't refuse us common quarters." He made a droll face at Eden. "These are fine folk hereabouts, and they take their virtue seriously. Their name is Boeykens."

Their hospitality was as faultless as their virtue. As if by magic, the good vrouw or madame—Eden wasn't sure which country they were passing through—produced spicy sausages, brown bread and three kinds of cheese, washed down with a tasty pale beer.

Replete, Max and Eden ascended to the loft. Pallets were already laid on freshly strewn straw, awaiting the arrival of relatives from Louvain, who would be passing through the next day on a journey to Lille.

The slant of the cottage eaves made it impossible for Max to stand up. "I hope my feet don't hang over the edge of the loft," he whispered, as with a final admonition for the two young boys to settle down, the Boeykenses blew out the candles below.

Eden blinked in the sudden darkness as she tried to rearrange herself in a comfortable position. Directly above her was a tiny oval window where she could catch a glimpse of sky. Now that she and Max were safe and in relative privacy, she felt unaccountably tense. "Where are we going?" she whispered, for want of a more pertinent remark.

Max was having even more trouble getting situated than Eden. "Oostende, then to England. William will be heading there as soon as his visit with the Elector is finished. If I'm to exonerate myself and you are to help your father, we must see His Majesty as soon as possible."

"Yes," Eden agreed on a rueful sigh. "I've lost track of time. What day is it?"

"I'm not sure, either. Third week of September, as I recall." Max kicked his boots aside and made yet another attempt to stretch out, this time on the diagonal. His feet struck Eden's calf, making her giggle. "Sorry. This is the damnedest barracks I've ever been assigned to. In truth, it's not—I slept in a pigsty once, near Ath."

"You wouldn't have to stick your head in the corner if you moved over,"

Eden suggested, trying to roll up the stiff sleeves of Max's jacket.

"I'm fine," Max replied abruptly, forgetting to lower his voice. He paused, leaning on one elbow. The reassuring sound of snoring floated up from the main floor of the cottage. "Good night, Eden." Grappling with the single coverlet, he sat up and banged his head on the rafter.

As he stifled the curse that leaped to his lips, Eden put out a hand. "Max!" she cried softly, "Are you all right?"

"Yes. No," he corrected himself, rubbing the top of his head.

The moon had come out, sending silver shafts of light into the little loft. Eden could see Max quite clearly, the sun-streaked hair awry, the lawn shirt torn at both sleeves, the bare feet sticking out from the coverlet. Eden found his dilemma both pitiable and endearing. "Is there a bump?" she whispered, sitting up. "Let me see."

"Don't!" Max retreated, though he could move no more than a few inches. "Go to sleep, Eden," he ordered in a stern voice. "You'll wake the Boeykenses."

"Judging from those snores, the French army couldn't wake them," Eden retorted, annoyed by Max's sudden shift in mood. Somehow, she had hoped that the recent candid rapport between them would have quelled his need to put up barriers. Maybe he didn't know his betrothal to Harriet had been broken off. Perhaps he was angry because she had spoken sharply about Sophie Dorothea. As he lifted his chin above the covers and grimaced slightly, Eden had to press her hands against her sides to keep from touching him. She had no right to want him. But neither could she repress her love for him.

Timidly, she made an attempt to mend the unexpected breach between them: "Max—I didn't mean to criticize your wife today. I was tired and frightened, and the words came out all wrong." Eden twisted around on the pallet, trying to keep the bulky coat in place. "Vrouw de Koch told me what a wonderful woman she was. I know Sophie must have been perfect."

Max had been staring into the rafters, his face devoid of expression. He raised his head and turned slowly, his chin on his hand. Eden was a scant three feet away, the claret curls a-tumble, the ebony eyes shadowed by the long lashes, the enchanting features made poignant by distress. Shoeless, with torn silk stockings and a bruise on her cheek, she was all but enveloped in his big coat. The childlike quality he had at first found captivating and irritating had never been more apparent, yet she had changed in these past months. As with a great painting, he discovered something new every time he looked at her. Today he had been struck by her courage and daring, as well as her ability to rally from adversity. Each fresh quality made her more priceless and unique. He reached out to brush the bruise on her cheek.

"Sophie wasn't quite perfect," he said quietly. "She wasn't you."

Eden's eyes widened with wonder, and she grasped his fingers in hers. She could not believe what he had said, nor could she take in the frank expression in his gaze. Wordlessly she pressed her face against his hand as joy spilled over her.

"I may never again have a chance to tell you how much I love you," Max said, speaking in a low, husky voice. "But you ought to know. You've given me strength and joy and hope. My life was empty until you popped out of that gate with Jack, all but falling down onto the cobbles." His smile was bittersweet as he caressed her cheek, ever mindful of the bruise from Rudolf's blow. "I didn't know it then. In fact, I refused to recognize the truth until a few weeks ago, when I went to Hohenstaufen. My memories of the place were so painful that I could never have gone there at all if you hadn't given me the fortitude to face the past."

Eden put a tentative hand in his rumpled hair. "But I didn't do anything. I wasn't even there," she protested with a little shake of her head.

Max pulled her closer and rubbed his nose against hers. "But you were. That's the wonder of it—you are always with me. You were even there when I left you the first time, to go to Givet last spring. And that's the way we must leave it." The pain in Max's eyes gave the lie to the resolute tone of his words. Slowly, he took away his hand. "Let's go to sleep, Eden. It grows very late."

Eden took a deep breath and closed her eyes. His declaration was more than she could have hoped for, yet it was what she had known for a long time. Guided by an instinct as old as Eve, she'd tried to tell him she knew the difference between the lust she had seen in Charlie Crocker's eyes and the love she had glimpsed in his own. But his denials had shaken her faith. She was young and inexperienced; perhaps she had been wrong.

"How could I have doubted what seemed so plain?" she murmured, as much to herself as to Max. "Do you know about Harriet?"

"Harriet?" Max was once again wrestling with his coverlet. "Oh—yes. She ran off with some rich peer from Suffolk."

"Sussex," Eden corrected him. Clearly, he didn't give a fig about Harriet. Eden should have felt triumphant. Instead she grew melancholy. Turning on her side, she looked at Max, his rumpled hair silvered by moonlight, his bare chest exposed under the open, ragged shirt, the sharp cheekbones taut with emotion. Her love could not be stifled any more than his, but she owed it to both her father and Max to keep a rein on her desire.

"I'm glad you don't have to spend your life with that virago," Eden remarked quietly. "She would have made you miserable."

"I already was." Max gave a rueful laugh. For some moments he was silent, and Eden wondered if he was drifting into sleep. Then he shifted on the pallet and turned to look straight into her eyes. "Did Rudolf really … harm you?"

"No." Eden shivered at the memory of his violent attempt. "He would have, though, had you not come in time."

Max nodded once. "For that, I would have killed him." His gaze traveled from her pale face to the curve of her throat and the opening of the bulky suede coat, which revealed the merest hint of the cleft between her breasts. "I can't get comfortable," he said rather testily. "Maybe I should sleep in the cheese house."

"The cats will keep you awake," Eden responded, a trifle too loudly. She tensed, awaiting some sound from below, but heard only the Boeykenses' contented snoring. Outside, an owl gave its nocturnal call and a chorus of frogs replied. Eden suddenly realized she was staring at Max and that he was staring right back, their gazes holding each other hostage.

Max willed himself to break the enchanted gaze, but even as he moved to sit up and leave the loft, his arms reached out to pull Eden close. No mortal man could go on resisting a maid as enchanting as Eden, especially when love joined forces with desire.

"I've no more fight left in me," he muttered, just before his mouth came down on hers. Eden drank in his kisses with a hunger fueled by self-denial. She felt his tongue in avid exploration, inviting her to respond with an eagerness to match his own. Their kisses grew more greedy, each devouring the other with the pent-up passion they had fought so hard to suppress. Max slipped his hand beneath the big coat, seeking her bare flesh.

"This is madness," he whispered, crowning one breast with his hand.

"No, it's destiny." Eden seized his hair in her fingers and planted fierce little kisses on the chiseled planes of his face. Her breasts ached at his touch, and she wriggled impatiently as he stripped the coat from her shoulders.

"These past few weeks I was haunted by the memory of how you looked in the bathing pool at Honselaardijk." Max spoke in a whisper, a crooked smile playing at the corners of his mouth. "I can't stop now, Eden. I should have known that before we came up to the loft."

Eden gave him a look that smoldered with a sensuality she would never have recognized in herself. "Maybe you did." Her thighs quivered as he kissed each breast, then flicked his tongue over her nipples, turning them into fiery buds of longing. She moaned softly, her hands at his chest, pushing away the tattered shirt. Max shrugged the garment off, his hand trailing from the nape of her neck to the waistband of her skirts. She knew as well as he did what folly they were about to commit. But wrapped in each other's arms, under the eaves in a shaft of silver moonlight, Eden could only follow her heart. She offered no resistance when Max pulled away the riding habit and placed the flat of his palm on her silk-clad thigh.

The hands that imprisoned her senses and freed her spirit crept up to caress that most secret part of Eden's being. Even through the filmy undergarment,

Max's touch was like flame on frost. She melted into him, urging his fingers to work their will. In a slither of silk, she lay bare before him, elated by the expression of awe upon his handsome face. Almost worshipfully he ran his long fingers through the rich ebony triangle that promised the fulfillment of his quest.

"God help me, I love you so!" he breathed, one hand at his belt. "Is love so wrong?"

Eden swallowed hard, then gasped as she saw Max in the virile glory of his nakedness. All the strength, power and intensity she had recognized in him overwhelmed her. As he knelt above Eden, she locked her fingers behind his head and arched her back. "You are godlike," she murmured, trembling at the sensation of his touch between her thighs.

Max's head was buried between her breasts even as he explored the untouched terrain of her womanhood. Eden tightened her grip on him, as if holding him captive. Her entire body seemed driven to a destination she understood in only some vague, primeval way. For one brief moment, it seemed as if her goal was elusive, an impossible attainment no earthly force could achieve. The unexpected pain vanished in a flash of ecstasy as he thrust slowly yet surely, his arms cradling her shoulders. Together they moved as one, their rapture lifting them above the clouds, over the moon, somewhere among the glittering stars. And like a comet, Eden's world blazed with light and warmth until she gasped with wonder and went limp in Max's embrace.

Max had also gone very still, his chin resting in the masses of her tumbled hair. He had known great happiness in Sophie Dorothea's arms, he had not lived a celibate life since her death, and his experiences with women had been momentarily pleasurable. But despite Eden's innocence, he had found such bliss as he could not have imagined. "You are aptly named," he said softly. "You are Eden."

Still dazed by the marvel of their mutual discovery, Eden looked at him with a smile that was as wide as her ebony eyes. "No matter what happens, we belong to each other," she whispered. "Forever." Her face was damp with tears.

STILL IN A STATE OF euphoria, Eden and Max set out the next morning for Brussels. The sun shone with the burnished gold of autumn, and the leaves were turning to copper on the poplar trees that lined the road. They spoke very little, content to ride pressed close together and to let their love flow between them like a sprightly mountain stream.

It was in a tiny, nameless village that the spell was broken. Max had stopped to water their horse at the trough in the rustic town square when he overheard the local blacksmith exchanging the latest gossip with a mendicant friar.

"William stayed only two days at Moylandt," Max told Eden after he had questioned the monk closely. "The Elector's daughter is a prissy schoolgirl of fourteen who smoked so much she set His Majesty to coughing up his lungs. To make matters worse, Keppel raced Bentinck's coach halfway to the Rhine, and the two men almost came to blows. The King has already sailed for England."

Eden blanched at the news. She had almost hoped that William would find a new bride, thus absolving her of the need to continue her pursuit. But that was thoroughly selfish. Besides, William's marital status had nothing to do with his acquisition of a mistress. Worst of all, his departure for England signaled danger for Marlborough. The trial would no doubt begin as soon as William reached Whitehall.

"How far is Oostende?" she asked in a hollow voice.

Max's face was grim as he surveyed the sun hanging low in the sky. "If we ride like the wind, we can make it by sunset. But we'll have to wait for the morning tide."

Eden nodded. She could scarcely believe that their idyll was over. "Max, when I get to England, where shall I go?"

For some time he could not bring himself to look directly at Eden. When he finally did, his eyes were filled with pain. "Your mother's, I suppose. We dare not stay together in Clarges Street." His attempt at a smile was a failure. "For many reasons."

Eden started to nod, then shook her head. "No, Max," she said in a choked voice. "Just for one."

Chapter Fourteen

Barbara Castlemaine was cursing like a pirate at Cromwell, who had ruined a Pieter de Greber still life by trying to rip the banana out of the painting. "Poxy wretch!" she screamed, swatting at the monkey and missing by a hair. "No more nuts for you!" As Cromwell grasped the draperies and swung onto the Italian chandelier, Barbara collapsed on the settee. "Why didn't I get a dog, like a sensible widow?"

Eden, who had been keeping her distance from the fray, cautiously sat down in a bergère chair opposite her mother. "I'm sorry, I didn't realize your husband died."

Barbara's finely plucked brows arched. "He didn't. It's just that I haven't seen the poor sod for so long that he might as well be dead. In fact, we might as well never have been married. If memory serves, I had no children by Roger. I felt more married to Charles than to all the rest put together."

"Even Jack?" Eden couldn't resist the question.

Over her gin tumbler, Barbara looked mildly surprised at her daughter's temerity. "Yes. Even Jack. Though he was the best of the rest, Baby Ducks, I'll give him that." She grew silent, one eye on Cromwell, swinging from the chandelier, the other resting on the Lely portrait at the far end of the room. "You've changed," she said at last. "Max, I presume."

Eden knew it would be fatal to admit she had given herself to Max. Yet she trusted her mother with a faith as old as time. More to the point, Barbara Castlemaine had an unerring instinct when it came to men and women. Eden's silence was the only answer her mother needed.

"Stupid of you, but inevitable," remarked Barbara. "At least he's well-rid of the Villiers baggage. Where is he, by the way?"

Eden assumed that Max was in Clarges Street. By chance, they had reached Oostende in time to sail on the midnight tide. Their journey from Margate had been made at a furious pace, bringing them into London on the first Monday of October. With a fervent and hasty farewell, he had deposited her in Arlington Street with a promise to let her know what was happening with Marlborough as soon as he could ferret out accurate information. Four days had passed, and there had been no word. Eden was more than worried, she was working herself into a frenzy of concern. Max, after all, was still nominally an exile.

But Barbara, who had expressed only the merest suggestion of surprise over the arrival of her bedraggled daughter on her doorstep, was well-versed in the rumor mill. John Fenwick would go to trial before the House of Lords before the week was out; Marlborough would follow.

"You must return to court," Barbara said, her mind on Marlborough. "Fenwick will not recant."

Eden got up and wandered restlessly around the room. "I don't understand why he's so obstinate. Why does he persist in such lies?"

Barbara popped a piece of marchpane in her mouth and washed it down with a swallow of gin. "A simple motive. Revenge."

"For what?" Eden regarded her mother with a puzzled expression.

Cromwell leaped from the chandelier onto the back of the settee and gave Barbara's neck a series of wet smacking kisses. "Off with you, your lovemaking reminds me of at least six men I regret I ever bedded." She paused, eye to eye with the monkey. "Well, three at least. Regrets are such a waste."

Eden was growing impatient. "Revenge for what?" she repeated, sidestepping Cromwell, who had come to chatter at her hem.

Lady Castlemaine blinked in a futile attempt at innocence. "Why, for being one of the three I regret, of course." She saw Eden's brow furrow. "Fenwick and Jack fought a duel over me years ago. Jack won." She shrugged. "It's simple enough. Why do you think Fenwick came here in the first place?"

Eden's shoulders drooped. She should have known that Fenwick's motives were personal. She was beginning to realize that the business of nations, like villages, was often conducted from the human heart.

"So you must go to court," Barbara was saying, trying to lure a suddenly coy Cromwell back with an almond sweetmeat. "I learned only an hour ago that a second witness has been produced to testify against your father." Barbara's glance turned rapier sharp. "Harriet found him. Isn't she sweet?"

RIDING IN HER MOTHER'S WHITE coach with its purple plumes, Eden felt conspicuous, but at least she was spared the discomfort of a hired Hackney Hell Cart. She could not resist stopping off in Clarges Street on her way to Whitehall. Her excuse was the need to collect some of her clothes: The garments loaned by her mother were too large and too ostentatious. In borrowed plum brocade and rose velvet, ornamented with gold fringe and embroidered pretintailles, Eden felt more decorated than dressed. Directing the coachman to wait around the corner, she hurried to the bright blue door and knocked.

Vrouw de Koch all but fell over her. "Mistress! Elsa was sure you'd been murdered by foul thieves! She's been crying ever since she got home! You disappeared from Maastricht as if by magic!"

Gently, Eden extricated herself from the housekeeper's smothering embrace. "Black magic is more like it. I'm glad Elsa managed on her own." Eden was well aware of the difficulties and fears the deaf girl must have faced when stranded by her mistress in a strange land.

"The coachman was very gallant," *Vrouw* de Koch offered. "And worried, he was, too, having misplaced his charge."

"With good cause, all things considered," murmured Eden as the little maid appeared along with *Heer* Van de Weghe and what seemed to be the rest of the household staff. A chorus of welcome echoed in the hallway, led by Elsa, who had burst into tears, this time, presumably, of joy.

"It's a long story," said Eden, touched by the servants' concern, but suddenly struck with an onslaught of anxiety. "I would have assumed Prince Maximilian explained what happened."

Her comment evoked blank expressions from the entire group. "But isn't he still on the Continent?" asked *Vrouw* de Koch.

Eden started to reply, but clamped her lips shut. Elsa, the housekeeper and the *hofmeester* were all eminently trustworthy. But Eden could not be sure of the rest, particularly the two or three new faces that had been added in the months she was away. "I thought he might have returned ahead of me," she answered a trifle lamely. To cover the awkward pause, Eden spoke again, explaining quickly that she had gone to live with her mother and needed to have her belongings sent to Arlington Street. *Vrouw* de Koch put Elsa in charge of another half dozen servants, who whisked up the stairs to Eden's bedroom.

Dismissing the rest, *Vrouw* de Koch and *Heer* Van de Weghe insisted that Eden come into the small parlor to wait. The housekeeper closed the door and turned to Eden with a somber expression.

"Himself was here, like a thief in the night," explained the housekeeper in a voice barely above a whisper. "No time to talk, to eat, to rest, mind you. Then he was off, and only the good Lord knows where." She glanced at *Heer* Van de Weghe, who nodded in stolid agreement. "Only the two of us knew he was here, but this house is being watched. Why did he ever come back?"

Eden plucked at the gold embroidery of her borrowed plum gown. "To make matters right with the King. He had no opportunity in the United Provinces, being hounded by Bentinck's lackeys."

"They'll hound him here, too," the housekeeper replied with a deep frown. "Is it true that Count Rudolf is dead?"

"Yes." Eden closed her eyes for a brief moment. "Alas, that doesn't solve Prince Max's .problems. Or Milord Marlborough's."

Vrouw de Koch was pacing the room, her chunky body listing more than ever. "I don't like it, I don't like it one bit. At least he's rid of the Villiers chit." She wheeled, fixing Eden with a shrewd eye. "He didn't come back because of you, did he?"

Dismayed at the accusation, Eden stiffened in the high-backed chair. "Certainly not! It was something to do with Vranes and that treacherous peace treaty."

Vrouw de Koch turned faintly sheepish. "Of course, of course." Ambling over to Eden, the housekeeper patted her satin-clad shoulder. "I wish it were because of you, to tell the truth. But I fear for him. He is star-crossed, that one."

Again, Eden saw *Heer* Van de Weghe's unhappy nod of agreement. Slowly she stood up. "No, he's not. He's had some bad luck in the past, that's all. But in the end, he will be happy." She gave both the housekeeper and the *hofmeester* a long, hard look. "Remember, you heard it here."

WILLIAM OF ORANGE WAS NEVER as content in England as he was in the Gelderland; he was never as happy at Kensington Palace as he was at Hampton Court; and he was always more irascible at Whitehall than anywhere else in his island domain.

Unfortunately for Eden, it was at Whitehall that the King was residing while he waited for the House of Lords to debate the charges against Sir John Fenwick and the Earl of Marlborough. Keppel met Eden outside the Holbein Gate in the late afternoon, while the fog came creeping up from the river.

"Sooth, His Majesty is testy today," Keppel complained, his own usual cheerful demeanor absent. "Secretary Huygens has resigned, Bentinck mopes, and Milord Shrewsbury refuses to come back to court after being exonerated in the Jacobite plots."

"Why," demanded Eden, "are Shrewsbury and Godolphin forgiven, but not Milord Marlborough?"

Keppel gave an impatient shrug. "It's Fenwick's doing. The man's a convincing liar, and now there is this other witness, an Irish bounder named Roark. To make matters worse, Sir John Vanbrugh, who is a good friend of

Marlborough's, has written a risqué play that has proved to be the toast of the London season."

Eden made a perplexed face at Keppel. "*Zut!* And what can some silly mummery have to do with Jack?"

Keppel avoided Eden's gaze. "Nothing directly, but its subject matter has offended His Majesty." He paused, then offered a sheepish little smile. "I suppose I should be offended as well. The play is called *The Relapse, or Virtue in Danger*. It's about men who ... prefer men."

Eden rolled her eyes in disbelief. The tapestry of life seemed to be made out of the most unlikely skeins. But she would not be stymied. "I've brought a new syrup that will soothe His Majesty's throat in this damp weather. Won't you let me see him, if only for a minute?" She turned a plaintive gaze on Keppel, but wondered if she could trust him. At least he had not betrayed her to Rudolf. On the other hand, for all his vaunted influence, he had made no headway in freeing Marlborough.

Keppel was mulling over her request, the garnets twinkling on his baldric sash. "It can't hurt, I suppose," he allowed, "but be prepared for an unpleasant meeting."

The King was sitting by the fire, a brocade quilt muffling him to the chin and the omnipresent Dutch pugs at his feet. He looked even thinner than when Eden had last seen him, but his dark eyes had lost none of their sharpness.

"Well!" he grumbled, as Eden dropped a graceful curtsy. "We thought you had abandoned us! Wherever did you run off to after Het Loo?"

"I'm not sure," Eden replied truthfully. "I spent some time in the country, near Liège."

Both William and Keppel eyed her with curiosity, but Eden wasn't about to enlighten them further. "Here, Your Majesty," she announced, extracting a small porcelain jar from her studded handbag, "this is berry syrup, with rare herbs. Not only will it help your throat, but it tastes delicious."

William took the jar and removed the lid, sniffing at the contents. His scowl softened, then he handed the syrup to Keppel. "Very well, we shall try it tonight at bedtime. We thank you for your concern."

Eden refused to acknowledge the ring of dismissal in his words. "You ought to take some now," she suggested. "You also ought to have a camphor kettle going, don't you recall? And," she added, picking up a decanter of gin that rested on a table next to the King, "you ought not to be drinking these strong spirits. You wish to get well, not fermented."

The King's brows drew together in a dangerous fashion. "You ought not to lecture your sovereign! Where were you when that Brandenburg brat smoked her chalk pipe like a sailor and I had the worst coughing fit of my life?"

Eden fought to keep from laughing as she envisioned the tribulations

William must have suffered at the Elector's summer house. She also noted that the King had forgotten himself long enough to dispense with the royal plural. Assuming a serious air, she tapped her chin and appeared to reflect.

"Your Grace has never permitted smoking in your presence before," she said with the faintest hint of reproach. "Why would you allow a fourteen-year-old boarding-school miss to give you asthma? Surely her charms could not have been so overpowering!"

"Not as much so as her pipe," William retorted, a glint of humor surfacing in his dark eyes.

"The truth is," Keppel chimed in, "Louise Dorothea of Brandenburg is a bony, gauche girl with neither wit nor allure. And," he added, spooning out a measure of Eden's syrup, "His Majesty thinks it unseemly to consider acquiring a second wife while he still mourns his first."

"Well put, Joost." William smiled wanly at his favorite, then docilely swallowed the medicine. "You're right, Mistress," he remarked with a wrinkle of his long nose. "It's quite tasty." He licked his thin lips and fumbled with the quilt. "The truth also is," he went on, leaning back in the chair, "we not only missed your ministrations on our journey, but ..." William stopped, glanced at Keppel, whose expression was impassive, and then looked at Eden. "The truth really is," he repeated after clearing his throat, "we missed *you*."

Eden's smile lighted up the gloomy chamber. She could hardly believe the King's admission. Even Keppel seemed favorably disposed. Yet she agonized over mentioning either her father or Max's plight. Perhaps this was not the right moment; maybe she should consolidate her victory first.

The decision was made for her by the bumptious entrance of Wilhem Bentinck. His glance at Keppel was filled with contempt; his reaction to Eden was disbelief. Still, he wasted no time on either of his despised rivals, but came straight to the point. "Prince Maximilian has been hunted down! He is hiding out at St. James's!"

The King wiped his mouth with the edge of his hand. "So he did come back to England."

Eden covered her distress by picking up one of the Dutch pugs. Lounging behind the King's chair, Keppel shot Bentinck an insolent look. "How, Milord, would you describe 'hiding out' at a royal palace? Surely His Highness is under the protection of Princess Anne."

"My point, exactly!" Bentinck fumed. "Is the Princess permitted to defy His Majesty's wishes? Maximilian is both a traitor and a murderer!" He glanced at William, waiting for approval.

The King emerged from the quilt and tossed it onto the floor. "Prince Maximilian must answer these charges. Let the soldiers search the palace, if necessary."

Eden exchanged apprehensive glances with Keppel, then put the dog down. "If you will excuse me, Your Majesty, I'm sure my presence is intrusive at a time like—"

"Your presence is suspect," interrupted Bentinck. He glared at Eden, then turned to William. "Sire, this strumpet follows in her mother's depraved footsteps!" His stubby fingers jabbed at Eden's plum and gold finery. "She even robes herself like that licentious bawd and has formed an infamous liaison with Prince Maximilian. May I suggest that she be arrested at once?"

The King scowled at his elder statesman. "God's blood, Wilhem, you do Mistress Eden a grave injustice. Apologize, or earn our extreme displeasure."

But tenacity was inbred in Wilhem Bentinck. "Don't be misled by a pretty face and a captivating manner. She's Marlborough's bastard and Maximilian's whore! They lived together for months, man! The trollop's a Jacobite spy!"

Anxiously, Eden watched William's reaction. His thin face was working painfully, and his eyes were a weary mirror of his soul. "Marlborough's daughter, yes," he said heavily. "But Maximilian's ... er, whore and Jacobite spy are serious allegations." He beckoned to Eden. "Come here, my dear. How do you answer Milord Bentinck's charges?"

Behind the King, Eden saw Keppel's unusually somber face. She felt Bentinck's hostile stare and tried to take courage from the earnest expression in William's dark gaze. But the fact was that Eden could not lie to her sovereign. She could, however, hedge.

"I swear to you, Sire, I am no spy. Nor do I understand politics, being barely able to discern a Whig from a Tory." She gave a little shake of her head. "As for living with Prince Max, that's so, everyone knows of it. But I can also swear that we never engaged in the slightest impropriety all the time I was under his roof." That much, at least, was true. She could look William of Orange straight in the eye and not flinch.

The King visibly relaxed, while Keppel gave Eden the merest suggestion of a wink. Bentinck, however, was not appeased. "You're too kindhearted, Willi! You'll regret this surge of sentiment!"

William of Orange rose from the chair, trembling with wrath, a bony finger pointed at Bentinck. "You go too far! We're not lads in the Gelderland anymore! Get out! Get out, before I have Joost throw you out! "

The stunned Bentinck jumped, but Keppel stepped beside his monarch. "My pleasure," he said with an exaggerated bow and a toss of his golden wig.

"Impertinent whelp!" Bentinck snarled at Keppel between clenched teeth. His face was a perilous shade of purple as he returned his attention to the King. "Am I discharged from Your Majesty's service?"

William, who was struggling for control, ran a hand through his sparse hair. "No. But you are dismissed from our presence."

Bentinck started to wheel out of the room, but tripped over one of the pugs. Stifling a vile oath, he turned to the others. "You'll regret this day," he snarled, then slammed out of the room.

Eden stared at the quivering door and wondered if Bentinck's threat was meant for her or all of them. The one thing she knew for certain was that Max was in terrible danger.

EDEN USED ALL THE COINS in her purse to bribe the coachman to make great haste between Whitehall and St. James's Palace. The distance was shorter than Eden had expected, but she wanted to arrive before Bentinck's orders could be executed. The carriage came to a grinding halt off Birdcage Walk. Glimpsing a group of soldiers through the coach window, Eden calculated her chances of gaining admission.

Eden Berenger Churchill would no doubt be denied entry by Bentinck's men. But no lesser entity than the Archbishop of Canterbury would dare to challenge the arrival of Barbara Castlemaine, the Duchess of Cleveland. Rummaging in one of the smaller boxes she had brought from Clarges Street, Eden took out a fashionable mask she had never worn, hid much of her hair under the ribbons and lappets of her *fontange* cap and found a pair of ruffled silk shoes with four-inch lacquered heels. Taking a deep breath, she plunged her hands inside a sable muff and sailed out of Lady Castlemaine's coach.

"Make way, make way," she shouted in her huskiest voice. "The Duchess of Cleveland to see Her Royal Highness. By my arse, bend those backs or I'll have your ears for supper!"

The startled soldiers edged away, some sniggering, others gaping. One, however, was bold enough to challenge the bawdy visitor and held out an unwavering hand. "Stay, Your Grace, we're under orders to admit no one. We have a criminal trapped inside and are awaiting further instructions from Whitehall."

Eden sniffed with disdain. "Most of the criminals in this realm are already at Whitehall, in my opinion." She tapped the man's hand with her muff. "Step aside, I've no patience with politics. Whig, Tory, Tory, Whig—Twigs and Whories would do as well; then at least I'd know which side I was on. Move, Lambchops, Her Highness is expecting me."

The soldier regarded Eden more keenly than she would have preferred, but she had no choice other than to brazen out her performance. "Well?" she cooed, pursing her lips. "Do you find me less dissipated than has been rumored? Would you care to find me later, say, on the cushioned seat of my fine coach?" Her effort at a lewd wink was partially frustrated by the mask, but the heaving velvet bosom turned the tide.

"Zounds!" exclaimed the soldier, his eyes lighting up with a mixture of excitement and apprehension. As Eden wafted the muff like a fan and waited, the man snapped to attention. "We know you by your ... reputation, and Milord Bentinck is your kin by marriage. Pray enter, Your Grace." As Eden marched past him, he spoke out of the side of his mouth: "How much later, madame?"

"The later the better," she retorted, throwing a coquettish glance over her shoulder. "I'm always better when it's later."

Inside the palace, Eden paused to collect herself. The masquerade had taken its toll. She had not thought further than getting past Bentinck's soldiers and was dismayed by the gaggle of guardsmen, footmen and servants who confronted her as soon as she crossed the threshold.

"Madame," intoned a liveried official of considerable dignity and ample girth, "may I have the honor of your acquaintance?"

Having decided to dispense with her disguise, Eden started to remove her mask. "Indeed, I'm—"

She was interrupted by a shriek that seemed to emanate from the chandelier but that in fact came from a pretty, honey-haired blonde who was standing halfway up the spiral staircase. "It's the Castlemaine! Throw the harridan out!"

"Madame," Eden began as the palace staff exchanged agitated glances, "I'm not Lady Castlemaine! I'm her daughter!"

If Eden had expected a swift reprieve, she was sorely disappointed. The blonde flew down the stairs, her color high, her eyes flashing. Within closer view, she was not as young as she had seemed, but probably almost forty. She was also furious.

"Harlot!" she cried, her hands clenched. "How dare you come here! Go back to your wanton mother!"

At a distinct disadvantage, Eden tried to becalm the other woman. "Madame, I have urgent business with Her Highness, the Princess Anne." Eden racked her brain for a suitable excuse. "I have come from Whitehall, with a message from His Majesty."

The blonde hesitated, but lost none of her pugnaciousness. "Do you know who I am?" she demanded with a menacing little gesture.

"No," replied Eden frankly, "though you seem to know me. I'm perplexed."

The other woman drew herself up in a sea of petal-pink lace and creamy satin. "I'm Sarah, Countess of Marlborough." Behind her, the household staff nodded in a chorus of approbation. Sarah held her head high and looked down her upturned nose at Eden. "Even after twenty years, I cannot imagine how my dear Lord Marl consorted with a concubine!"

"How?" echoed Eden, "or why?"

Sarah's pink cheeks blazed with anger. "Impertinent! How did you get in? Why, you even look like your mother!"

Having absorbed the fact that this strong-minded woman was her father's wife, Eden resorted to drastic measures. "Milady," she pleaded, dropping to one knee, "for the sake of your dear Lord Marl and my beloved Sire, hear me—and help me. May we speak alone?"

The Countess of Marlborough's stance remained rigid, but the blue eyes softened ever so slightly. "You bring a message from the Dutch Abortion? What can it be if not to send his horrid henchman's soldiers packing?"

"Unfortunately, it's not that," said a rueful Eden. "Please, madame, there is not much time."

Sarah pressed her lips together and snapped her fingers at the servants buzzing surreptitiously behind her back. "Very well. But you impose upon my charity. To think that I would ever consent to meet with the Castlemaine's bastard!" With a swish of satin she whirled, the household staff scattering in her wake. Moments later she led Eden into an imposing antechamber filled with the most elegant pieces of the last three Stuart reigns.

Eden came straight to the point. Without digressions, she recounted the interview with William, Bentinck and Keppel. She emphasized the King's continued intransigence in the matter of Marlborough, then shamelessly inquired after Max.

Sarah listened to the recital with a set face. But when Eden concluded, the Countess's lips quivered with emotion and her eyes flashed with indignation. "All of this is so needless! It's nothing more than jealous Dutchmen meddling in English matters! To be frank, I wouldn't give a fig for Prince Maximilian if my dear Lord Marl hadn't befriended him during the war. As for you," she went on, getting up from her chair and pacing the Persian carpet, "you may be my husband's daughter, but you're only an embarrassment to me. Why should I trust you?"

Eden's answer was swift and soft. "Jack does."

The blue eyes stared at Eden for a long time. "Lord, Mistress, it must be so." Sarah sighed, a hand at her fine bosom. Eden noted that the Countess's middle-aged charms attested to her reputation as one of the great beauties of the previous generation. The Earl of Marlborough had indeed been lucky in love to win the favor not only of the era's most famous courtesan, but of the lovely Sarah, as well. That both were women of incredible determination and strength was further evidence of his own inner character. Patiently, Eden waited for Sarah to respond.

"Prince Maximilian is with the Princess Anne and her consort, playing cards," the Countess finally confided. "He's bored to tears, but otherwise quite sound. Bentinck's men can tear the palace down, but they won't find him because they are not allowed to invade Her Highness's sanctuary."

Even as the Countess spoke, footsteps could be heard in the corridor.

Voices were raised and protests rejected. Sarah lifted an eyebrow in contempt but made no move toward the door.

Eden was frankly distrustful. "Are you sure they won't find him?"

Sarah's eyes turned to steel. "Of course I'm sure. Besides," she went on, securing a diamond earring, "the Princess is about to give birth." As she noted Eden's surprised expression, Sarah's mouth twisted in a bitter smile. "I know, the poor thing is always giving birth. The pity is, she has only sickly little Gloucester to show for it. May God be good to us all this time."

THREE HOURS LATER BENTINCK'S SOLDIERS were still searching St. James's Palace. Eden remained with the Countess in the antechamber, for all appearances enjoying a convivial supper and exchanging the latest gossip. The two women were, in fact, picking at their food and discussing the possible outcome of Marlborough's trial. A certain guarded cordiality was beginning to emerge between them.

"This Roark is a liar and a cheat," Sarah insisted. "He swears he was with my dear Lord Marl at Cupid's Garden on the first day of February, when the plot to kill the King was hatched. Nonsense, of course. Milord never goes there. The proprietor caters to a distinctly common sort of clientele."

"Last February," mused Eden. "That's when I met Jack, but it was later in the month, on my birthday. It seems so long ago."

"I found his plan for you harebrained," Sarah said frankly. "And so it has proved, since he's still in the Tower."

Eden turned defensive. "I've done my best, Milady. I' truth, His Majesty likes me."

"Obviously not enough," snapped Sarah, as a loud knock resounded at the door. She called out, and the liveried official who had greeted Eden entered the room with a deferential bow.

"The soldiers have completed their search," he announced, "but they are insistent upon going through Her Highness's chambers. What shall we tell them?"

The inference that Her Highness would tell them precisely what Sarah Churchill commanded was not lost on Eden. "I shall speak with these wretched animals," she said, moving resolutely to the door. "Wait here," the Countess added for Eden's benefit.

Eden did, but she was uneasy. She felt utterly useless, condemned to sit idly by while the Countess and people she had never met contended with Max's adversaries. To make matters worse, Eden had not managed to further her father's cause. She felt gloom come over her like fog, heavy, blinding and all-encompassing.

The palace had grown unnervingly silent. The fire sputtered fitfully in the grate, and the dancing shadows cast a macabre aura over the room. Her mother's coach must still be outside the palace. Indeed, Lady Castlemaine must be wondering what had happened to her daughter. Or else her efficient spy system had brought a full report. Eden was learning not to underestimate either her father's former mistress or his lawful wife.

Wearily she unpinned her *fontange* cap and shook out her hair. The long day had given her a headache. It was hard to imagine that somewhere within these walls Max was sitting comfortably playing cards, quite unaware that she was nearby, fretting over his fortunes. As she stared into the dying fire, her head began to nod and her eyelids drooped. She really should stay awake, she supposed, but the Italian marble clock on the gilded pedestal said it was after ten. Surely a brief nap would restore her flagging spirits ….

But her eyes were still half open when she saw the vision. The paneling next to the fireplace moved, as if by magic. The wall opened inch by inch. Eden stared incredulously as Max ducked into the room. A conjurer's trick, she thought dizzily, letting out a little shriek.

"Eden, hush!" he ordered, brushing cobwebs from his shirt. He stood quite still, listening for any sound of pursuit.

Struggling to focus, Eden half staggered from the chair. She stood poised on one foot until Max was finally satisfied that no one had followed him. "I've been so worried!" she exclaimed, remembering to keep her voice down. "How did you get here?"

Max had taken her in his arms. He didn't answer immediately, but drank in the piquant face, the tumbled hair and the frightened eyes. "The soldiers are searching Her Highness's apartments, much to her royal chagrin. Thank God for these secret passageways Charles II had installed to facilitate the comings and goings of his harem." He stroked the long tresses and savored the sensation of her body pressed against his. "I've sent a half dozen messages to the King. I didn't expect his answer to be a small army."

Puzzled, Eden looked up. "I'll wager none of your missives reached His Majesty." She straightened Max's *steinkirk* and brushed at the tousled blond hair. "There was a terrible scene today between the King and Bentinck. I'd guess that His Lordship's days are numbered. Max," she urged, lightly touching his face, "why not go to the country and wait things out? It's too dangerous for you to stay in London."

He ran his hands down the rose velvet that covered her back. "No. I've spent the summer running halfway across Europe. I'm going to settle this matter once and for all." With his arms still around Eden, he turned. "I heard something. In the hall."

Before he could duck into the passageway, the door opened, revealing the Countess of Marlborough. Sarah sauntered into the room, a portrait of self-possession. After she closed and locked the door behind her she collapsed onto a chair and poured herself a generous glass of wine. "Those pesky vermin have finally left. They even searched the Princess's garderobe! Imagine the nerve! If she miscarries again it will be William's fault!" Her shrewd blue gaze took in Max and Eden, standing close together. "Highness, you must remain here. Mistress, you must leave. All must appear as normal as possible. Half of London is no doubt already abuzz about the Castlemaine calling on Princess Anne."

At least, Eden thought, if the soldiers were gone she wouldn't have to face the bedazzled young guardsman with whom she'd flirted so outrageously in the guise of her mother. But she had no desire to leave under any circumstances. "I don't want to go," she blurted, staring longingly at Max. "I'd rather stay here."

"And I'd rather my dear Lord Marl weren't in the Tower," said Sarah in a cross tone. "We must do what needs to be done. This dire situation calls for more than duty, it demands discipline. Hie yourself off in your mother's awful coach and head for Arlington Street." Leaving her wine glass half drained, she stood up and put out a hand to Max. "Come, you may stay in the room next to the Prince Consort."

Max's shake of his head was eloquent. "Your hospitality is most generous, as is that of the Heiress Presumptive and her husband. But I'm off to see the King."

Both Eden and Sarah started at his announcement. "That's madness, Max!" Eden cried. "You'll be arrested before you get inside the palace!"

Max brushed her nose with his finger. "Not the way I plan to enter it." He went to the nearest window and pulled open the drape. "See there? Fog as thick as *Vrouw* de Koch's pudding. I'll manage it like a Wapping Wall smuggler." Bending, he kissed Eden's forehead. "Don't fret. Do you want me to spend the rest of my life hiding in women's boudoirs?"

Eden felt like telling him that he could hide forever in hers, but held her tongue. She could see by the set of his jaw and the steel in his eyes that there would be no stopping him. For one irrational moment she considered begging him to take her with him. But that would only undermine his already slim chances. The Countess was right. Each of them had a part that must be played to perfection. As Eden watched Max salute Sarah and stride out of the room, she prayed that the drama in which they performed was not cast in the tragic mold.

MAX APPROACHED WHITEHALL THROUGH ST. James's Park, pausing every ten feet to check for danger. His plan was to cross the old tennis courts, slip into the small privy garden and gain entry by using the heavy vines that clung to the ancient palace walls. Once inside, he would find Keppel, who would no doubt cooperate in getting Max in to see the King.

Moving with caution, he felt his way along the hedge that separated the enclosed garden from the kitchens. The fog that concealed Max also confounded him; he could make out nothing beyond arm's reach. In the distance he heard the muffled call of a late-night oarsman, delivering passengers at the river's edge. Max took another careful step, trying to avoid a patch of late-blooming herbs. He smiled, reminded of Eden and her catalog of cures. She had a knack for making him smile, even when she wasn't at his side. She also had an extraordinary way of tackling problems from an oblique angle.

Max froze in place. Eden's presence was almost tangible. She was right, he was going about this business all wrong. Inspiration struck like a blow. As he made his way out of the garden, Max was smiling again.

Chapter Fifteen

Eden spent the next day in an agony of suspense. Lady Castlemaine did her best to calm her daughter, but was distracted by a bandy-legged young colonel who arrived with a dozen bottles of Portuguese wine and a fatuous expression. It was only when Barbara emerged from her bedroom three hours later that she addressed her daughter's plight.

"If Max didn't get to the palace until almost midnight, he may not have seen the King until morning," Barbara reasoned over a plate of steamed mussels.

"But it's after four!" Eden cried, going to the window for the twentieth time that afternoon. "We should have heard something by now!"

Barbara plucked the last mussel from its shell and fed it to Cromwell. The monkey chewed warily, then spat the delicacy onto the carpet. "Poxy ape! You'll get no trifle for dessert!" Lady Castlemaine railed. She swatted at the animal, missed and turned to Eden. "I can't abide your doleful face. I'll send someone around to find out what's happened."

"I ought to go," Eden said, trying to ignore Cromwell, who was yanking at her skirts and protesting the indignity attempted by his mistress.

"Not now," asserted Lady Castlemaine, reaching for the bellpull. "You can perform your heroics later, when Jack goes on trial. From all I hear, he's going to need them."

An hour later, Barbara's lackey returned from Whitehall. The court was agog over a letter William received from Bentinck, insinuating that the friendship between His Majesty and Joost van Keppel was sordid and unnatural. Bentinck had chastised his sovereign for casting off steadfast comrades for the sake of a self-serving pup. William of Orange was crushed by the accusations and had taken to his bed.

As for Prince Maximilian, he had never reached the King. In fact, the Prince had not been seen by anyone since he'd left St. James's the previous night.

SIR JOHN FENWICK WAS A spare, dark, dapper man with a thin mustache and wary black eyes. To Eden he looked more like a shrewd tradesman than a conniving politician. His stance before the House of Lords was confident and he had an air of self-righteousness that invited credibility. Watching from the gallery with Joost van Keppel, Eden felt a surge of despair come over her.

Again and again Fenwick named Marlborough, Shrewsbury, Godolphin and Ailesbury as his fellow conspirators. When it was pointed out that Milords Shrewsbury and Godolphin had both been cleared, Fenwick merely sniggered. "Does faulty judgment make them less guilty?" he asked with a disdainful shrug.

A flurry of comments circled the chamber. Eden used the distraction to whisper a question. "Joost—are you certain there's been no word of Max this past fortnight?"

"Nothing." Keppel's face grew serious. "I can't understand it. Once Max's mind is made up, he never wavers. It isn't like him to change course."

"What of Bentinck?" Eden asked as the presiding Lord Justice called for order.

"Faith, he expects William to apologize! The silly old fool genuinely believes that the King should repent of his so-called sins."

"And William?"

"He broods." Keppel's expression was droll. "I'm not sure His Majesty comprehends the accusation."

The interrogation droned on. Fenwick repeated his tedious charges, finally pointing out that only one witness had been found to testify against him.

"True enough," whispered Keppel behind his kerchief, "since Lady Fenwick spirited the other off to the Continent."

"Why is Fenwick so adamant?" Eden asked in vexation. "Surely this can't be over a silly duel he fought with Jack twenty years ago!"

Keppel waited until Fenwick had stepped down and a recess for the day was announced. "No." He tucked his ivory walking stick under his arm as he helped Eden rise. "Fenwick is protecting the real perpetrators, that's obvious. The question is," he went on, with a watchful eye on their fellow observers, "who are they?"

THE EARL OF MARLBOROUGH WAS brought before the Lord Justice in the second week of November. England's highest magistrates, along with the entire membership of the House of Lords, were in an irascible mood. They were stymied in handing down a verdict in the matter of Sir John Fenwick, having failed to find a second witness to testify against him. Debate raged in Parliament, with Fenwick's supporters demanding that he be set free under a writ of habeas corpus, while his enemies tried to rally support for a Bill of Attainder, which would convict him without further testimony.

Eden wasted little time on the Fenwick controversy. She was far too distressed over Max's disappearance and her father's trial. Her efforts at talking to the King had been frustrated—William of Orange was in virtual seclusion, deeply offended by Bentinck's scurrilous charges. Yet he procrastinated in dismissing his chief minister. After a lifetime of service and friendship, Wilhem Bentinck was not easy to cast aside.

Keppel had tried to cheer Eden, but even his buoyant spirits and keen wit proved useless. She was convinced that something horrible had happened to Max, and that a similar fate awaited her father. Twice she had gone to the Tower to see Marlborough; twice she had been turned away. Only the Countess was allowed to visit the Earl during these dark days of his long confinement. By the time the Lord Justices were called back into session, Eden had worried herself sick and was unable to attend the first day's sitting.

"You missed nothing but libelous bilge, Baby Ducks," Lady Castlemaine informed her as they rode together to Westminster the following day. "Fenwick repeated his lies, and his whey-faced wife kept nodding her silly head. I kept hoping that the redoubtable Sarah would march up and hurl her from the gallery."

Eden was shocked when she caught her first glimpse of the Earl. His face had lost its freshness, his physique seemed to have shriveled, and even his step was slowed.

"Lord help us," Eden murmured, leaning over the rail. Her emotions were already in turmoil, since the constant agony over Max's disappearance never left her mind. She had not been prepared for Marlborough's deterioration and suddenly felt light-headed in the overcrowded chamber. "Is he ill?"

Barbara squinted through the mask she wore in a fruitless attempt to conceal her identity. "I think not. He's been mewed up too long. And he hasn't bedded his wife in months. Such deprivation would ruin Hercules."

But Marlborough's bearing was flawless. He stood in the dock with his shoulders squared and his visage unperturbed. At one point he glanced into the gallery, offering the hint of a smile to Eden and a nod to Lady Castlemaine. It had been over six months since father and daughter had spoken. For Eden, it sometimes seemed as if Marlborough were as much of a fantasy as King Charles had been.

She watched with pride as the Earl refuted charge after charge. After almost two hours, he was allowed to step down. Glancing across the ancient hall, with its great hammer-beam ceiling and its carved angels holding up Richard II's coat of arms, Eden saw Sarah sitting with Sidney Godolphin. Somewhat diffidently she waved. The Countess responded with a curt nod; Godolphin beamed unabashedly.

The Lord Chancellor pounded his staff, calling for order. With some reluctance, the assembly grew quiet. As the burnished autumn sunlight filtered through the high clerestory window, the announcement was made that a second witness was to testify in the matter of John, Earl of Marlborough. "Major Liam Roark," blared a clerk of the court as a stalwart figure in uniform entered the hall.

Eden leaned forward, almost bumping into the tall wig that adorned the gentleman in the next tier. There was something familiar about Major Roark—his carriage, his build, his coloring. Eden didn't realize what it was until he turned to face the gallery.

Liam Roark was Rudolf's blunt-faced henchman.

FANNING HERSELF WITH HER MINIVER muff, Eden sat back and tried to take in what Liam Roark was saying. So far he seemed to be reciting his personal history, which had nothing to do with Marlborough. Lady Castlemaine was swearing like a sailor and evoking signals of displeasure from their neighbors.

"That Swabian noodlecock Rudolf's lackey from Green Park," she hissed when her spate of invective had finally run its course. "I thought Max had killed the oversized idiot!"

Agitatedly, Eden shook her head. "I told you, Max didn't kill Count Rudolf, some French mercenary did. But who has bribed this wretched knave?"

A ring of angry faces glared at Eden and her mother. Both women became silent, listening for Roark to say something pertinent. Another ten minutes passed before he summed up his career, which had been primarily devoted to Irish Catholic and Jacobite causes, and his recent visit to the Continent, where he insisted he had studied German architecture.

"Architecture, i' faith! I'll wager he was studying Zijswijk's treasures," Eden said in a low, furious tone. "The man says nothing about Rudolf!"

Barbara sneaked a gin flask from her orange plush muff and swigged furtively. " 'Pon my arse, he doesn't. I wonder …."

Eden waited for her mother to finish her thought, but Barbara was jamming the flask into the muff and watching Roark with contemptuous violet eyes. It was as well, for the Irishman had begun his account of Marlborough's alleged complicity in the attempt to assassinate the King. The onlookers had edged forward, some with chins on the restraining rails, others standing on tiptoe at the far end of the hall. In an attempt at calm, Eden folded her hands in her lap and concentrated on every syllable.

" 'Twas February first of this year, as decent a day as the saints will allow, and I'd gone with some cronies to Cuper's Gardens. That's the place on the river across from Hungerford Stairs known to some as Cupid's Garden, being well-patronized by young lovers." Roark paused, assessing the effect of his testimony thus far. Among the audience, Marlborough remained composed, his irate Countess was being soothed by Lord Godolphin, and Lady Castlemaine was dabbing at the corners of her mouth with a silk kerchief. Eden, however, was suddenly having trouble paying attention. Not only was Roark lying, but he had said something that stirred the vaguest of recollections. She twisted her fingers together and tried to remember what it might be.

"Now I'm thinking, what is Milord Marlborough doing over in yon arbor with Sir John Fenwick and the rest? But by the Mass, I'm told he's cheap, and Cupid's Garden is a bargain, all things considered." Roark gave the crowd a crude smile, revealing at least two broken teeth. "But then we can hear the nobs talking—careless, of course, but they were in their cups. And what do they say but that there's a plan afoot to kill the King!"

Roark spread his beefy hands theatrically, and many of the observers gasped. Others made scoffing noises. Barbara delved for her flask, and Sarah had to be forcibly restrained by Godolphin.

The Lord Chancellor rapped for order. Marlborough stood calmly in the dock, wearing his air of detachment like a battle decoration. Roark was asked for the particulars of the conversation, but Eden paid little heed. Nothing the man said could be believed; she would not give him the courtesy of listening further. Westminster Hall was too warm, too close-packed, too filled with perfidy. Jumping to her feet, she snatched up her cloak and excused herself to Lady Castlemaine.

Out in the crisp November air, she stood on the terrace of the old palace that Edward the Confessor had built so that he might watch the progress of his great abbey nearby. The leaden gray sky was relieved only by that strange pale streak of sunlight nature offers as a reminder that winter is not quite settled in. Eden watched the traffic on the river with unseeing eyes and wondered which was worse—knowing that Marlborough's fate was in the hands of a perjurer or not knowing what had happened to Max.

She let out a little cry when Joost van Keppel touched her arm. "I saw you leave," he said, his blue eyes sympathetic. "I was in the crowd standing at the far end of the hall. Incognito, as it were." He gestured at his relatively plain garb, and for once he wore no wig. "Roark's story isn't believable, but how can Jack prove he wasn't at Cupid's Garden?"

Eden shook her head. "It's far easier to say where you were than where you weren't." She shoved her hands into her muff and realized that her lashes were wet with tears. "I feel so helpless—and stupid. Oh, Joost," she wailed, not caring if she cried in front of him, "where is Max? Nobody can disappear into thin air!"

Keppel's face grew unwontedly grim. "Something—or somebody—made him change his mind. I've made inquiries, I swear it. But nothing has come to light."

Eden wiped at her eyes with the muff. "It's been over a month. Do you think he went abroad?"

"It's possible." Keppel leaned on the stone wall, gazing down at two wherrymen who were arguing over a disputed fare. "The Princess Anne is giving a ball tonight in honor of William's birthday. Will you come?"

Eden's initial reaction was to refuse, but the strangeness of the event made her hesitate. She fumbled inside her miniver-trimmed vestee for a handkerchief. "Anne is feting His Majesty? How odd!"

"Not really. Despite the lack of affection between them, she is his official hostess in the absence of any other lady of royal rank. You must remember, too, that William is very fond of his nephew, little Gloucester. It makes at least a tenuous family bond."

It occurred to Eden that the occasion might provide her with an opportunity to speak with the King. Not, she reflected, as the luminous streak of light across the river dimmed to a pallid rose, that her pleas on Marlborough's behalf would do any good. But Bentinck should be on hand, as well. She would confront the villainous Dutchman and see if she couldn't wring from him at least some scrap of information about Max. Her eyes dry, Eden turned to Keppel.

"I'll go," she said, her chin set. "I can't just sit waiting. If I do, I'll lose my mind."

HER ROYAL HIGHNESS, PRINCESS ANNE, was a tall woman who would have been great of girth even if she had not just suffered yet another stillbirth. Her plain if somewhat doughy face wore a bovine expression, and only her regal carriage graced her with any personal magnetism. Her consort, Prince George of Denmark, was equally obese, and though he was markedly cheerful, his fair skin was blotchy and his blue eyes unfocused. Eden was frankly appalled at the pair upon whose star her father and his wife had affixed their dreams.

St. James's Palace provided a contrasting backdrop of glittering candles, banks of bronze and gold chrysanthemums and liveried retainers. Despite her restless fears for Max and her father, Eden stood resolutely at Keppel's side in deep green velvet and ivory brocade, with satin ribbons in her hair and a collar of pearls at her throat. The King was across the room, engaged in what appeared to be a morose conversation with the Venetian ambassador. William of Orange did not look like a man celebrating a birthday, but like one who was mourning the whole spectrum of his life.

"His Majesty's mood grows darker by the day," said Keppel in a low voice as a servant passed with a tray of Rhine wine in tulip-shaped glasses. "The Elector of Brandenburg has violated their kinship by selling several battalions to the Venetians. No doubt the Elector's daughter felt snubbed by our King."

"Perhaps." Eden was dubious, wondering why a fourteen-year-old maid would want to marry a man nearing fifty, King or not. Lady Castlemaine had suggested that Eden consider becoming William's wife instead of his mistress, yet Eden couldn't bring herself to contemplate either option. Next to the tall, swarthy Venetian with the lush mustache, William looked particularly puny.

But it was pity the little Duke of Gloucester evoked as the Prince Consort brought his son forward to greet William. Eden touched Keppel's sleeve and suppressed an exclamation. The child was dressed in the most splendid of court regalia, but his head was too big for his spindly body, one of his eyes was bloodshot, and his fair hair stood up in patches.

"Poor child!" Eden said under her breath.

Keppel's compassionate gaze watched the little Duke make a formal bow before the King. William's face brightened as he bent to admire the jeweled Order of the Garter, which had been presented to the child the previous summer. Uncle and nephew became absorbed in an animated exchange that clearly delighted them both.

"A shame His Majesty had no children of his own," remarked the Countess of Marlborough. "He might have made a better father than he does a king."

Keppel struck an indolent pose. "Your charity is markedly lacking on this of all happy days," he said with a toss of his huge wig. "I shall take into account your extreme distress over Milord's trial."

"Impudent rogue!" snapped Sarah with a wave of her French fan. "You've never lifted a finger to help my dear Lord Marl!"

Keppel's pose remained intact, but his gaze grew icy. "That's not true. You have no idea what I've tried to do, but all my efforts have met with failure." He glanced meaningfully at Bentinck, who had just entered the hall with Lady Harriet and a young man who was tall in stature and short of chin.

Sarah transferred her hostility to the older Dutchman. "Bentinck! Can it be that our idiot King wants to pension him off with properties that should go to the Prince of Wales?"

"There is no Prince of Wales," Keppel replied with irony.

Sarah's gaze flickered over little Gloucester, who was playing with William's court sword. "Not yet," she said grimly.

"I assume," Eden began, hoping to smooth over the ill will between the

Countess and Keppel, "if Princess Anne inherits the throne, Gloucester would be given that title?" Her query went unanswered. Lady Harriet, leaving both uncle and suitor in her wake, had approached in a sea of silver tissue and blue lace. With a halfhearted curtsy to the Countess and an equally unenthusiastic nod to Keppel, she spoke directly to Eden.

" 'Struth, I hear you've misplaced your paramour." The emerald eyes glittered with malice. "Or did he tire of your peasant ways?"

Eden assumed a wide-eyed stare. "Did you say *pleasant* ways?" Before Harriet could reply, Eden shook her head. "No, no, of course not, since you'd know nothing about them." Unperturbed by the fire in Harriet's eyes, Eden took a step forward, her chin set. "It's occurred to me, Milady, that you may know where Max has gone. Would you be kind enough to enlighten the rest of us?"

Indignant, Harriet tossed her dark curls and gave Eden a contemptuous look. "You're a fool, Mistress. How should I know where that feckless foreigner went? I was only too glad to be rid of him."

"Only because he was poor," countered Eden, oblivious to Sarah's disapproving expression and Keppel's unconcealed discomfiture. "Yon viscount may be rich, but at least Max has a chin."

"And you have cheek!" cried Harriet, jabbing at Eden with her fan. "As for Max, he may have lost more than his chin!"

Eden damped down the sudden chill of fear that Harriet's words evoked. "The best thing he ever lost was you," she snapped, gesturing angrily at Harriet. "Please put that fan down. I've suffered enough from your antics."

"Oh, really?" Harriet advanced on Eden, and their hems meshed on the floor. "You spiteful little strumpet, why don't you go back to Kent—or better still, straight to hell!"

As other courtiers edged closer to the contentious pair, Keppel intervened. "Please, ladies," he begged, taking each by the arm, "you'll upset His Majesty. It's his birthday, after all."

Furious, Harriet shook off his hand. "Don't touch me, you viper! If it weren't for you, my uncle would be—"

But Harriet's uncle was at her side, his ruddy complexion dark, his brow furrowed with anger. "Keep your foul, perverted hands off my niece!" he almost shouted at Keppel.

Keppel, with a haughty toss of his head, merely laughed off Bentinck's vicious remark. Seeing the amused look on Keppel's face, the older Dutchman opened his mouth to speak again, but instead lunged at his enemy. Harriet screamed, Eden stumbled into the Countess, and a great gasp went up from the onlookers as Bentinck grabbed Keppel by the throat. The surprise attack caught the young favorite off guard. Keppel reeled under the ferocity of Bentinck's stranglehold until he regained sufficient balance to grasp his assailant by the arms. Though Keppel had youth on his side, Bentinck was as solid as he was fit. Moreover, he was armed with hatred; his hold was not easy to break. Under the dislodged wig, Keppel's face was beginning to turn an unhealthy color.

"Cease! Cease, in the name of the King!" William stood four feet away, his voice hoarse and his expression livid. Behind him, little Gloucester peered out with his keen mismatched eyes, half-frightened, half-thrilled.

Slowly, Bentinck let go of Keppel and dropped his hands to his sides. William glared at both men, his lips trembling. "A disgrace," he muttered. "Infamy! We are outraged at such uncivilized behavior!" The King started to turn toward Keppel, but began to cough. Bentinck, muttering what might have been an apology, lowered his head and stumbled from the hall with Lady Harriet trailing behind him.

"Your Majesty," breathed Eden, quickly remembering to bob a curtsy, "do you have your medications with you?"

William stifled his cough long enough to respond. "No," he said curtly. "We shall return to Kensington at once."

"Sire ..." Eden begged, but the King wasn't paying attention.

"Joost," he said, with a weary shake of his head, "you must have been rude to poor old Wilhem. Take us home, please. It's not been a pleasant party."

Thwarted in her attempt to speak to either Bentinck or the King, Eden watched despondently as William leaned on Keppel's arm and the assemblage made way for the royal exit. On the dais, Princess Anne and Prince George noted the departure with phlegmatic expressions, while the Countess of Marlborough put a finger to her lips in a quizzical manner. Among the guests, only one person seemed as distressed as Eden at William's abrupt leave-taking. Alone under one of the balconies, the Duke of Gloucester stood on the verge of tears, his homely little face wearing a crestfallen expression. His thin hands plucked nervously at the diamond-studded garter which was too heavy for his frail body and seemed to weigh him down.

Chapter Sixteen

E VEN IN THE STRICT HUGUENOT atmosphere of the Berenger house, Eden
could not recall a less festive Christmas season than that of 1696. Despite
Lady Castlemaine's garish decorations and the endless parade of callers,
nothing buoyed Eden's spirits. There was still no word of Max, and as snow
clouds gathered over England, Eden's last shred of hope began to fade like the
winter sun.

John Fenwick had been condemned to die on the block within the
month. And on Christmas Eve Day, the Earl of Marlborough's sentence was
to be handed down by King William. Eden rode to Westminster with Lady
Castlemaine, praying that, in keeping with the yuletide season, His Majesty
would be merciful.

The great hall was packed and held an air of excitement and dread. To
Eden's surprise, she and her mother were greeted by the Countess, who
pushed her way through a throng of prentices dressed in their holiday best.

"There are occasions," intoned Sarah at her most majestic, "when
the present eclipses the past. You and I are not friends," she said to Lady
Castlemaine, "but for today, we must be allies."

"We can be twins for all I care, Sarah Sweet-Sheets," Barbara agreed with
an amiable lift of her sables. "Just remember, as a duchess, I outrank you."

Under ordinary circumstances the Countess would have been angered.
But on this bleak December morning, her one-time rival's tart tongue went
unremarked. Lady Castlemaine's blackamoor made way for them in an upper
stall, just under the great durmast oak roof.

Fumbling with her mauve taffeta skirts, Eden perched on the edge of
her seat, scanning the crowded chamber. A sea of powdered wigs, hats and

fontange caps bobbed and swayed below them, while the gossipers hummed like so many bees in a summer garden. It was not summer Eden recalled when her father was led into the dock, but the previous winter, at the Berenger garden gate. There, under a sky as threatening as the one that hung low over Westminster, she had first spoken with the Earl of Marlborough, and then Max.

On that long-ago morning the future had suddenly unfolded with all the promise of spring. Yet before the day had run its course, Marlborough had landed in the Tower. And despite Eden's best efforts, he had remained there ever since. As she watched her father stand with his usual cool detachment, she longed to leap from the gallery and race across the hall and fling herself in his arms. Instead she sat like stone, vaguely hearing Sarah's heavy sigh and Barbara's lusty curse.

The King was not on hand to deliver the sentence. Eden was somehow relieved, but as the assembly began to quiet down, she winced at the intimidating expression on the Lord Chancellor's face. Across the way, she caught sight of Sidney Godolphin, accompanied by a young man whose resemblance suggested kinship. His son, thought Eden. Godolphin's bloodlines, his own foal ....

Jarred, she sat up very straight and was about to speak to the Countess when the Lord Chancellor banged his staff on the stone floor. Eden barely heard the words that echoed off the ancient stone walls.

"John Churchill, first Earl of Marlborough, shall be taken four weeks hence to Tower Hill where he will be executed for high treason."

She had to reach Sidney Godolphin. Staggering to her feet, Eden nudged Lady Castlemaine, then Sarah. But both women were leaning forward, their fingers gripping the rail in front of them. Tears welled up in the Countess's eyes, and Barbara was using words Eden had never heard before.

"Please," begged Eden, tugging at her mother's sables, "let me pass. I must get to Lord Godolphin! I must talk to him about his horse!"

Barbara swung around, grabbing Eden by the wrist. "Stop it! You're hysterical! Sit down!"

But Eden resisted, trying to pull away. "I tell you, I must see ...."

Her words were drowned out by the furor that erupted throughout the hall. A few of the onlookers were cheering, but most were shouting their protests or stomping their feet in objection. Several hats were tossed onto the floor, along with a few less savory items. Through it all, the Earl of Marlborough stood motionless, his face impassive, his bearing noble.

With one last glance at her father, Eden opened her mouth to scream in defiance. But no sound came out, for the great hall was spinning, the heavy beams seemed to be crashing down, and the crowd had turned into a clamorous blur. Eden felt herself sinking into a sea of sable and satin, and then she felt nothing at all.

FROM SOMEWHERE FAR AWAY, EDEN heard a voice calling out, "Hot chestnuts! A ha'penny apiece!" Church bells were ringing, and the aroma of roasting fowl made her nose tingle. The first image she saw when she opened her eyes was a green vase filled with holly. Everything was as it should be, she told herself hazily, for it was the yuletide season.

Then, slowly, reality dawned. The world was awry, and her father was going to the block. To make life even more worthless, Max was gone, perhaps forever. Putting a hand to her head, Eden groaned and tried to sit up. Somehow she must accomplish the task she'd started before she went to sleep. If only she could remember what it was ....

"Don't try to move," said Max, putting a hand on her arm. "You hit your head when you fainted."

The ebony eyes widened with disbelief. But Eden didn't need to pinch herself; her headache was sufficient to tell her she was conscious. "Oh!" she exclaimed, feeling the lump just above her temple. "Oh, Max! Thank God!" Her effort to embrace him fell short, and she collapsed against the pillows.

"Just rest, you'll be all right," he assured her, his hand on her shoulder, rubbing it gently. "You had a terrible shock."

"Two, in fact." She pushed the hair off her forehead. "One terrible, and the other miraculous." Her eyes weren't cooperating fully as she tried to scrutinize Max closely. Was the blurriness due to her headache, or was Max truly an apparition? After all the weeks of anguish, Eden had trouble accepting his reappearance. Yet she could feel his touch and hear his voice. She noted, too, that the sun-streaked hair seemed a little darker, the flesh over those high cheekbones a trifle tauter, and the shadows under his eyes more pronounced. "Max," she demanded in a high, thin voice, "where have you been?"

"To France to visit the King," he replied lightly, but the hazel eyes still showed his concern for Eden. "We'll speak of that later. Now you must stay quiet."

"But I can't," Eden protested, making another feeble attempt to sit up. "Jack is going to die! And I know how to save him!"

Max stroked her face and kissed her nose. "I'm sure you do. You'll save everyone. Now go to sleep."

"Will you stay with me?" Her voice ached with the fear of losing him again.

He lifted her hand and entwined her fingers in his. "I'll nail my boots to the floor. *Vrouw* de Koch can bring food at four-hour intervals. I'll prop my eyes open with hairpins." His grin, off center and engaging as ever, spread across his chiseled face as he gently squeezed Eden's fingers.

"You could sleep next to me," Eden suggested in a small voice. Her free hand waved limply at the empty side of the bed.

Max inclined his head to one side. "I could do that," he allowed. His gaze traveled slowly from her peaked face to the curve of her breast under the covers to the outline of her slim legs. "God knows, I've thought enough about it." He took a deep breath as he let go of her fingers. "A lot. But I don't want to disturb you while you're recovering. I'll keep watch right here, I promise."

Reluctantly, Eden shut her eyes. But a moment later she was staring quizzically at Max again. "I still think I've gone mad. I hear singing."

Cocking his head, Max listened. Out in the street a half dozen voices were raised in a chorus of ancient carols. Max smiled at her, his face touched with tenderness. "You do, indeed. And why not, Eden? It's Christmas."

FOR THE NEXT TWO DAYS Eden slept much of the time. In bits and pieces, she discovered Max had been at Westminster, trying to conceal his height behind several onlookers who'd managed to climb on a riser for a better view. He had spotted Eden without difficulty, along with the Countess and Lady Castlemaine. After the grisly sentence was handed down, Max had planned to slip away. But he had noted Eden's obvious agitation and her subsequent swoon. Scorning detection, he had climbed into the gallery and rushed to her side. When he found out that she had not only fainted but had struck her head on the rail, he'd insisted on bringing her to Clarges Street.

"Your mother put up no argument, being in a bit of a daze herself," recounted Max as he and Eden sat in her chamber drinking hot coffee and nibbling *Vrouw* de Koch's spicy Christmas *speculaas* biscuits. "As for the Countess, only her great strength of character kept her from attacking the Chief Justice. She went directly to Kensington, but William would not yield." Max made a bitter face that had nothing to do with *Vrouw* de Koch's strong coffee.

"But something can be done," Eden insisted, adjusting the lavender dressing gown she had first worn upon her arrival the previous winter. Meeting Max's skepticism with a level gaze, she wagged a finger in his direction. "You think I'm fanciful, but I'm not. With Lord Godolphin's help, I can disprove Roark's testimony. Then there is only the word of Fenwick—who also lied. And William will have to free Jack."

Max did not look convinced as he placed a big hand on Eden's cheek. "How can you and Sidney refute Roark's charges? You hadn't even met Jack then."

"That's not the point," Eden said impatiently. "Somehow I remember what even Milord Godolphin forgot." She leaned forward eagerly. "On the first day of February, Jack couldn't have been at Cupid's Garden. He was with

Godolphin at Newmarket. It was on that day Lord Challenger was born, and even I know a thoroughbred such as that one would have to be registered immediately." Her eyes danced and her breasts rose and fell just a trifle faster under the lavender silk. "Would you care to wager with me that along with Sidney, Jack also signed those papers?"

Max let out a soft, sharp whistle between his teeth. "I never thought of that, either!" He put his hand under her chin and gave Eden an admiring look. "I wasn't at Newmarket, but was paying court to Harriet at that time." He grimaced at his former fiancée's name. "But I know Jack was there. The date itself simply didn't impress me."

"I suppose it stuck in my mind because every detail about him was so important to me. I was hungry for every shred of knowledge I could glean about my father." Eden rested her cheek against Max's palm. "Strange, it was easier to fill in the portrait of Jack than of you. Even though we were here together for all that time, you were far more elusive."

The ebony eyes were wistful, and the lashes dipped artlessly against the pale skin. She could hardly believe that less than a year ago she had not known either Max or Marlborough. Except for Gerard, the Berengers had dimmed into a faceless montage of acrimony and spite. Conversely, Marlborough was fixed vividly in her mind's eye, his inner strength never more apparent than when he had been condemned to die. As for Max, he was where she had always sensed he should be—at her side, sharing an intimacy she had once considered impossible. "Oh, Max," breathed Eden, "I never thought I'd see you again. I was sure you were dead!"

Moved by her fervor, Max nudged Eden's cheek with his fist. "I could hardly let you down by getting myself killed, could I?" He grinned at her, then grew serious. "Do you want me to speak to Sidney on your behalf?"

Eden shook her head vigorously. "I must do it myself," she asserted. "Saving Jack has been my responsibility from the start. Until now, I've felt like a failure. I shall go to Lord Godolphin at once."

"He went to the country for Christmas," said Max, putting an arm around her shoulders. "In any event, you must stay abed until tomorrow. This time I'm the doctor."

Eden tried to put aside her disappointment at the delay in rescuing her father. Dejected, she leaned against Max. "A day or two will make no difference, I suppose. But Jack must be devastated."

Max gave her a little hug. "He has enormous equanimity. He also believes in luck."

"Perhaps he does." But Eden was dubious. Certainly the Countess and their children must be suffering dreadfully. At least she felt some sense of reassurance in Max's arms, and as the warmth and strength of his body flowed into hers, she felt those stirrings of desire that were never far from the surface. "Seeing as how I'm already in bed," she said with a pert glance, "what treatment do you prescribe, Dr. Max?"

Max flicked her nose with his finger. "Nothing strenuous. A caress," he said, running his hands down her back. "A squeeze," he continued, spanning her waist. "A kiss," he added, brushing her mouth with his.

Eden nestled closer, planting little kisses under his chin. "Your cure is most efficacious. You, too, must have a gift for healing. I feel better already." She traced a path from his lower lip to the mat of dark blond hair exposed by his open shirt. It was almost three months since they had made love under a harvest moon in the farmhouse near Lille. Now the snow was falling in big soft flakes over London's rooftops, while sleigh bells jingled on the winter air. Eden shifted in Max's embrace, her hair cascading over his arm, her eyes shining with anticipation.

"Max, why me?" she asked, a plaintive note in her voice.

Caught in the draft, the candle flame wavered, casting shadows across the planes and angles of Max's face. "I don't know," he answered honestly. "There are many lovely women in the world, and even a pauper prince can cut a wide swath among them." He felt Eden bridle, and his eyes twinkled. "So to speak, I mean. But I was never one for indiscriminate lovemaking. Maybe it's because I'm a private sort of person. Any attachments I've formed have had some sort of meaning for me." He was speaking more slowly, the twinkle gone, the words carefully chosen, as if he'd never thought them through till now. "You brought joy into my life. You made me feel alive again. There's no pretense in you, Eden." He paused to lightly touch her breast. "Your heart is honest—and open. I couldn't help but walk straight into it."

Almost shyly, Eden studied the vulnerable side he was exposing to her. "You make me feel humble. And powerful, too." She sighed and pulled his head down to kiss his mouth. "Oh, Max, I love you!"

"I ..." he said between kisses, "love ... you." Their breath and tongues mingled, making Eden feel dizzy all over again. Max laid her down among the pillows, then stretched out beside her. The fire was dying and the snow was coming down faster. "How do you really feel?" he asked, gingerly touching the place where she'd hit her head.

Eden glowed in the candlelight. "Wonderful." She clasped him to her, tugging at his shirt. "Superb." Her fingers plied at the muscled strength of his back and shoulders. "Healthy as Godolphin's horse." She tipped her head back, letting Max tantalize her throat and breast with slow, languid kisses. Every small aggression was made with deliberate care, each new exploration carried out with delectable restraint. Eden wriggled with delight, yet wanted to urge Max to bring them to completion.

"Are you coddling me or taunting me?" she gasped as his fingers leisurely stroked the flesh between her thighs.

"Both." Max flashed a wicked grin, then poised himself above her. "Taunting is well and good, up to a point. We've both waited too long, Eden."

She would have agreed with him, but he was already claiming her as his own, no longer patient and premeditated but full of fire and intensity. Eden cried out with joy, welcoming him with a surge of passion that rocked them both. Their union was sweet as a spring meadow yet wild as the winter wind as they transported each other to a place apart. Max and Eden, alone together, soared above the snow, beyond the clouds, and could have sworn they heard the angels sing.

EVEN AS HE SEARCHED HIS paneled library, Sidney Godolphin roundly berated himself. He could not believe that he hadn't connected Roark's perjury with the date of his Arabian's birth. Eden soothed him, expressed her gratitude for his meticulous record keeping, then headed out through a light snow flurry for Kensington Palace. To her elation, the Earl of Marlborough's signature was inscribed, along with the date, below that of Lord Godolphin's. No man could have been at Newmarket and Cupid's Garden at the same time.

Her sense of triumph faded when a somber Keppel informed her that His Majesty was in solitude at Kensington. "It's the twenty-eighth day of December," he said in hushed tones. "The anniversary of Queen Mary's death. He sees no one. Not," he added with a little shrug, "even me. Did you know he always wears a lock of her hair around his neck?"

Several of Lady Castlemaine's favorite oaths leaped to Eden's mind. But patience was required; she announced that she would wait until the morrow. Could Joost put her up for the night?

Keppel looked uncertain. "Well, mayhap. It's that important?"

Eden assured him that it was. She was tempted to take him into her confidence, but before she could decide if that would be a prudent idea, Keppel inquired after Max. "I feared he was dead. What happened to him during all these weeks?"

Eden hedged. "He went abroad." She'd learned that much, but the truth was, she still didn't have all the facts. The only thing she was sure of was that Max no longer had any qualms about being recognized in London.

It was this question that Keppel next addressed. "I'm most relieved that he's alive and well," he said. "But isn't he afraid that the King will have him arrested?'

"It seems not," Eden said dubiously. "Yet I must confess, I fear for him. Surely Bentinck will be hot on his heels again."

But Keppel demurred. "My sympathy is scant, as well you know, but poor old Wilhem has plenty of other problems these days. His scramble to retain any kind of power preoccupies him, thank God."

Keppel's assessment should have given Eden a sense of relief, yet she remained uneasy. Following Keppel down the elegantly decorated corridor of Kensington Palace, Eden could not shake off the feeling that she was still walking under a sinister shadow.

WILLIAM OF ORANGE STARED FOR a long time at the piece of paper bearing the signatures of Sidney Godolphin, the Earl of Marlborough and three unimpeachable Newmarket racing officials. The King's color was somewhat improved since Eden had last seen him at St. James's, but he was haggard after his day of mourning, and his mood was irascible.

"Are you accusing Major Roark of perjury?" he demanded in a gruff voice that always seemed to tax his weak lungs.

Eden didn't flinch. "I am. It's quite plain, Roark was bribed. He used to work for Count Rudolf of Hohenstaufen."

William's dark eyes turned sad. "We once regarded Rudolf highly. Perhaps God punished him for his betrayal. Yet Prince Maximilian had no right to take justice into his own hands."

"He didn't. Rudolf was shot by a French mercenary." Noting the King's rising skepticism, Eden waved an impatient hand. "I was there, Your Majesty, at Zijswijk. Rudolf kidnapped me."

Passing a hand over his forehead, William set the registry form on his inlaid desk. He had received Eden in the King's Gallery, his favorite refuge for private conversations. "What you say sounds quite incredible. We feel your imagination has gotten out of bounds."

Eden tried to check her exasperation. "What happened to me—and to Rudolf—has no bearing on this document," she asserted, tapping at the paper with her index finger. "I have come on behalf of my father. He is going to die because two men have not told the truth. You, Sire, are known as a fair-minded man. You told me so yourself."

William's scowl was fearsome. He shifted just enough in his chair to indicate that Eden had put him on the defensive. "Why would Sir John Fenwick, who is about to die, persist in his lies?"

Eden threw up her hands. "I have no idea. Unless whoever he shields is as sure to kill him for telling the truth. You must recall, Your Majesty, that Fenwick, unlike my father, *did* take part in the assassination attempt."

The King's fist came crashing down on the desk as he jumped to his feet. "Your father! Your father! You hardly knew the man! What is the cause of this unwarranted devotion?"

Startled by her sovereign's outburst, Eden faltered. "Do I need any other cause than our blood ties? Would you not have done the same for your father, had you known him?"

Faintly abject, William sat down with a heavy sigh. "But I didn't know him," he murmured, abandoning the royal plural. "I've known neither father nor child." He fingered his lower lip and gazed without appreciation at the finely wrought Grinling Gibbons carvings on the paneled walls. "Now, having found a young man who is like a son to me, I am the target of the most depraved charges. Is it a criminal thing to have esteem and affection for a fine fellow like Joost?"

For the first time, it occurred to Eden that the role she should have been groomed for was of daughter to William, not mistress. But it was too late. She was forced to play her only remaining card. In her mind, she saw a kaleidoscope of exquisite gowns, lavish furs, dancing masters, riding teachers, music lessons, Dutch grammars and notes on etiquette. It had all led up to this, a single moment with the King and the one chance to spare her father's life.

Eden tried not to think of what would happen to her own. The memory of Max's embrace remained on her skin, the taste of his mouth lingered on her tongue, the power of his possession made her dizzy. She was about to surrender everything she held most precious. In saving her father, Eden would lose Max. She had always known it, but somehow had hoped to avoid making a choice. Yet Eden had given her word to Marlborough, and now she must keep that promise.

"Silly theatricals and calumnious letters can be easily quashed." Eden's gaze was direct; any attempt to play the coquette was put aside in the face of William's frank manner. "If there was a woman in your life, the gossip would stop at once."

"A woman!" The King snorted at the suggestion. "We've said it before, we must say it again—it's still too soon for us to remarry."

"I wasn't speaking of marriage." Eden's voice was calm, though inwardly she quaked.

The heavy brows came together. "What do you mean? Are you implying …?" William of Orange actually flushed. "Mistress, we don't believe our ears."

Eden could hardly blame him; neither did she. Yet the situation was desperate, and this was the moment for which she had been groomed these past months. "Why not? If I may speak plainly, Your Majesty has a certain fondness for me. I am an accomplished nurse. What better way to squelch those vile rumors than to take a … mistress."

His color still high, William rummaged around in his desk, biting at his lips. "You're but a child. Innocent, naive. You have no idea what you're suggesting …. We can't imagine …." He stopped abruptly, his dark gaze keen. "Why would you do such a thing?"

The truth teetered on Eden's lips. But she was terrified of telling the King that she would surrender her body in exchange for her father's life. Conversely, she could not lie. Instead she said nothing.

William waited patiently, then clasped his hands together on the desk top. "We are told that you and Prince Maximilian have formed a liaison. Is that true?"

Eden could not avert her gaze. Those compelling dark eyes held her captive, plumbing the depths of her integrity. Somehow, the King's stilted description of the powerful, passionate, tender feelings she and Max had for each other sounded so at odds with the reality that she was tempted to deny his allegation. Yet that would be dishonest, too. Eden gave a small shrug and spoke in a quiet voice.

"I love him. He loves me."

The King did not blink. Admission of a mistake was repugnant to most men; in a monarch, to recant is often fatal. But inside William of Orange's frail body dwelled not only an extraordinary intelligence, but a fine strength of character, as well. At last he looked away from Eden to the paper that lay on his desk, then stared into the darkest corner of the room.

"You have the valor of a hero's daughter," he said. "It's possible that your father has your integrity. Fetch Joost. We will have him bring us the writ of execution." The King got to his feet and stretched out a hand. "We shall spare the Earl of Marlborough. We are, after all, fair-minded."

Eden's knees wobbled as she curtsied low and kissed the King's thin fingers. Though she had truth on her side, Eden had secretly feared that her cause might miscarry one last, fatal time. Indeed, Marlborough had always been armed with innocence; it had done him little good. Yet ultimately— incredibly—Eden had succeeded in a way that neither of them could ever have predicted. "Your Majesty … what can I say? This is a joyful day! I will bless you forever!"

William's mouth sketched a smile. "You would have done much more, had we asked," he remarked dryly. "Fortunately, we admire virtue more than its counterpart. But make no more petitions, Mistress. Your requests fly in the face of royal decree. Rush off to the Tower now, and give your father the good news." He paused, letting go of Eden's hand. "In particular," added William with eyes that shone a trifle too brightly, "remind him that his greatest fortune is being a father in the first place."

Chapter Seventeen

EDEN DID NOT GO DIRECTLY to the Tower, but to Clarges Street to tell Max what had happened. He could accompany her, and together they would present the gladsome tidings to Marlborough. But when she raced breathlessly through the front door, *Vrouw* de Koch announced that Max had left the house more than an hour earlier.

"Seeing as how you had already spent the night at Kensington, Himself probably thought you'd be there for the duration," said the housekeeper, shaking the wet snow from Eden's cloak. "He sent word a few minutes ago that he was in a coffeehouse, and he asked you to meet him there." She listed around the foyer, looking for the message. "Ach, here it is—Old Slaughter's, in St. Martin's Lane."

Having already dismissed her hired coach, Eden calculated the distance to St. Martin-in-the-Fields. "I'll walk. It's less than a mile, I should think." She glanced at *Vrouw* de Koch for confirmation.

"It's all of a mile and it's snowing. Let *Heer* Van de Weghe get you another coach."

But Eden didn't want to wait. She was too full of her news to waste a minute. "It's not snowing that hard," she insisted, retrieving her cloak. "Besides, I like the snow. I used to walk in it all the time in Smarden."

The housekeeper's disapproving look seemed to say there was probably a number of things that country folk did that would flabbergast a city dweller, but she made no further protest. Fifteen minutes later Eden was approaching Leicester Fields, an open area not totally given over to London's residential sprawl. Peering into the snow, Eden looked for the wreckage of St. Martin's.

Unlike many of the other churches destroyed in the Great Fire, it remained a gutted shell.

Never confident in her sense of direction, Eden hesitated. She had followed a straight course eastward; now she had to turn toward the river. The snow was light, the morning dark. Yet the usual Saturday bustle of London had not been slowed by the inclement weather. Children pelted each other with snowballs, dandies paraded their finest furs, and hawkers were doing a brisk business in fresh-baked meat pasties. Careful of her footing, Eden espied the old church and headed for the lane that ran behind the ruins.

Old Slaughter's had the reputation of catering to artists, which, Eden presumed, was why Max frequented it over some of the other more fashionable coffeehouses. Overhead, the sign was dusted with snow, but Eden could make out the rough-hewn lettering. Skirting a mound of snow that a half dozen children had shaped into the form of an enormous fat woman, Eden approached the entrance with trepidation. She knew that except for whores, unescorted women were not welcome in most coffeehouses. But she must persevere in finding Max so that they could hurry to the Tower with news of the reprieve for Marlborough.

Through the smoky haze she saw an eccentric array of men, young, old and middle-aged, puffing at clay pipes and drinking their steaming brew from little round dishes. Some of the patrons' cheeks were swollen with wads of tobacco, and the air reeked with the pungent odors of smoke and coffee. A hum of conversation filled the room, punctuated by staccato bursts of laughter and an occasional jarring oath. Though Eden scanned the crowd, she could see no one as tall as Max.

She was about to flee when a young man approached her with a knowing smile. "I'm not a whore," she asserted firmly, thankful that she was still wearing the pristine dove-gray gown and matching cloak she'd put on for her audience with the King. "I'm searching for someone."

"I know," the young man replied. "A tall blond foreigner, correct?"

"That's right," she said with relief. "Is he here?"

"He's upstairs, in one of our private rooms." Leading Eden to a narrow staircase, her host indicated a door at the top. "He's in there, conferring with a pair of noted painters."

Picking up her skirts, she ascended the stairs and rapped on the door. A voice called out for her to enter.

The room was curtained, with only a single candle in a pewter holder sitting on the square oak table. Three men in high-backed chairs were gathered round, apparently perusing some sketches. Eden's gaze flew to the blond head showing just above the back of a chair that was turned away from her. "Max!" she exclaimed, hurrying to his side. "I have wonderful news! Jack will live!"

Eden paid no heed as the other two men rose and moved quickly to the door. She was about to drop to her knees beside the chair when the blond head turned. "I have news, too," said Rudolf. "I also live."

By sheer force of will, Eden kept herself from collapse. The shock of seeing Rudolf alive was tremendous, but the fear for Max was overpowering. Her only coherent thought was for the safety of the man she loved.

"Where is Max?" she asked, clinging to the chair for support.

Rudolf's brow puckered. "A good question, that. Where *is* Max?" He gave Eden his exaggerated smile. "I expect that together we shall find out. Unfortunately, I lost him at the bottom of St. Martin's Lane. The snow was coming down much harder an hour or two ago."

Eden's shoulders sagged with relief, then she straightened and brushed the hair from her forehead. Obviously Rudolf, not Max, had sent the note to Clarges Street. Max might still be somewhere close by. In any event, he would discover where she had gone when he returned home. A sense of comfort began to wash over her until she realized that that was precisely what Rudolf planned. Once again she was the bait to lure Max into a trap.

This time she was determined not to let herself be used. "How," she inquired in as calm a voice as she could muster, "did you manage to survive at Zijswijk?"

Rudolf wore a self-congratulatory air. "The fire wasn't as disastrous as was first feared. The rain helped discourage the flames. See," he said, pointing to the sketches on the table. "Even now, I'm working on the restoration." Cautiously Eden lowered herself onto one of the chairs vacated by the men who stood guard at the door. "I thought your mercenary shot you," she said bluntly, her brain searching for a means of escape.

Rudolf gave a disparaging little laugh. "Zounds, no! He was the one who was shot. My dear old friend Major Roark arrived just in time." He paused to wag a reproachful finger. "Hadn't you wondered where he was?" She hadn't, of course, not in the intensity of the moment, with danger coming from all sides. Roark had not even crossed her mind until he had shown up at Westminster Hall to testify against Marlborough. She should have known then that Rudolf was still alive. It dawned on Eden that all the cunningly cruel plots had been hatched by Rudolf, no doubt going back to the abduction and murder of Captain Craswell.

"It seems," Rudolf was saying in an indolent voice, "that Max and I are finally about to resolve our little quarrel. A pity that the loser won't be alive to see the victor exult." He reached out his hand to touch Eden's dove-gray sleeve. "What think you, pretty Eden?"

Eden jerked her arm away. "I think you're a villain twice over! I think you're the person Fenwick has been shielding all this time! Only someone like you could put such fear into another man! You've always been a Jacobite—how could King William have been fooled for so long?"

Oblivious to Eden's rebuff, Rudolf picked up a pipe and examined the bowl. "All men are fools in some ways." He shrugged. "Take Max—he's a fool where you're concerned. That's why he'll come here. Soon, I trust. And when I've finally had my revenge, I'll slip out of London and head for the Continent and my reward."

The words *revenge* and *reward* monopolized Eden's attention. "Why revenge? What reward?" she demanded, leaning back in the chair enough to gauge the distance to the curtained window.

Rudolf produced an enamel box from which he extracted a pinch of tobacco. "Revenge for many things," he said, filling the bowl of his pipe. "You wouldn't understand." The blue eyes raked Eden with contempt. "He took my sister. It's as simple as that."

Eden started to say that Rudolf was obsessed, perhaps even mad, but then chose to keep silent. If only her sense of direction would not fail her. Casually, she got to her feet, undoing the ties of her cloak. "And your reward?" she asked, trying to maintain a show of interest that was also tainted with revulsion.

"Ah," sighed Rudolf, taking an experimental puff at his pipe. "I can speak of that now. For my services over the years, I'm to marry Elizabeth Charlotte, niece to King Louis. Think of it," he mused, tipping back his head and exhaling a cloud of smoke, "she was once offered to King William himself. Such irony!"

"My, yes," remarked Eden without enthusiasm. A glimpse at the two guards informed her that they were still very much on the alert. Carelessly she dropped her cloak on the floor, then wandered around the room. Behind her, she heard Rudolf's chair scrape on the floor. Eden stiffened, then moved without apparent haste toward the window.

"Max should be arriving soon," commented Rudolf, setting his pipe on the table. "Are you anxious to see him? What is the news about Marlborough?"

It occurred to Eden that Rudolf mustn't know that William had pardoned her father. Not that the Count could interfere with a royal decree, but this was a secret to be revealed only by her and Max. "Marlborough?" Eden echoed vaguely. "I spoke of Jack, not the Earl. Jack Bunn, a man I knew in Smarden."

With alarm, she saw that same strange glint in Rudolf's eyes that had terrified her at Zijswijk. The perpetual smile was gone, he was loosening his *steinkirk*, and his mouth had gone faintly slack.

"Liar," muttered Rudolf. "Lie with me, lovely liar." He moved toward her, his boots making the floorboards creak, his furtive gaze filled with lust. Eden prayed that she knew what she was doing, and yanked aside the curtains at the window. Whirling, she plunged her fist against the flimsy casement, shattering the glass, and scrambled onto the sill. Momentarily stunned, Rudolf hesitated just long enough to allow Eden to evade his grasp.

"I'd rather die than let you touch me!" she cried. And in a flurry of skirts and petticoats, she flung herself through the window, hurtling into cold, empty space. For a brief, terrifying instant, Eden thought she had misjudged. But suddenly her body struck something solid and soft. As children squealed and passersby screamed, Eden clung to the ruins of the fat snow woman and gasped for breath.

The first person to reach her was a young girl. "Coo," she exclaimed, reaching for Eden's hand, "it's alive ye be! Wot a bleedin' miracle!"

"What a bleedin' memory," murmured Eden, thankful that she had been able to recall where the upstairs window was in relationship to the coffeehouse entrance. Struggling to her feet, she brushed clumps of packed snow from her clothing and dabbed at a cut on her cheek. A crowd had gathered, coaches stalled in the lane, and a cartload of kindling was trapped against the opposite wall. Warily, Eden glanced at the front door of Old Slaughter's. As she expected, it burst open, revealing Rudolf, his two companions and several other coffeehouse patrons.

"They pushed me!" Eden screeched, pointing straight at Rudolf. "Snowball them! They're wicked foreigners!"

The children had recovered from the excitement of a young lady falling out of a window and the disappointment at having their snow sculpture flattened. They needed no urging to take up a different form of winter sport. Indeed, they were joined by some of their elders, who weren't precisely sure what had triggered this particular sensation, but hated to be left out. To Londoners, foreigners were always fair game.

But Rudolf was not daunted by child's play. Ordering his men to draw their pistols, he had them trained on the youngest of the merrymakers. "Halt or I'll blow you to Piccadilly!"

Several members of the snowball-wielding contingent froze with their arms in midair. Eden took advantage of the diversion to push her way through the crowd. But Rudolf spotted her. "Stay, Mistress!" His voice was harsh. "Would you have me slay one of your small warriors?"

Slowly, Eden turned. She was cold without her cloak, and her gown was soaked through. "Only you, Count Rudolf of Hohenstaufen, would threaten children! You're not just a Jacobite traitor, you're a murdering coward to boot!"

Through the light snowfall, Eden saw Rudolf's eyes narrow. "For that, you die at my hand." His voice was as cold as the ice that formed on the waterspout above the door. As the onlookers gasped, Rudolf grabbed the pistol from the man on his right and leveled it at Eden.

Her immediate thought was to fall to the ground in the hope that Rudolf would aim high—but the shot might kill an innocent child standing behind her. With a cry of terror she threw her hands in front of her face. Rudolf tugged at the trigger just as Max fell upon him like a great bird of prey.

The pistol went off with a shattering roar, ripping a hole in the nearest coach and startling the horses. Max and Rudolf were on the ground, grappling in the snow. Eden could only guess that Max had come out through another window and had somehow managed to leap from the sturdy oak coffeehouse sign. With all eyes fixed on Rudolf, and with the snow coming down more heavily, no one had noticed Max's unorthodox arrival.

As the two men rolled in the slushy lane, Rudolf's armed companion turned his gun on Max, but could not get a clear shot. Frustrated, he danced this way and that, the snow blurring his vision.

"'Ere!" a stocky bargeman shouted at Rudolf's men, "leave 'im be! 'E saved the little miss 'ere!"

The crowd responded with a unified charge at the two henchmen, who were swiftly subdued.

Eden, with three of the smallest children clinging to her wet skirts, tried to see what was happening to Max in the midst of the melee. At last she caught sight of the two combatants a few yards away. Max had Rudolf in a viselike grip and was trying to haul him down the lane. With one great heave of his body, Rudolf threw Max off, then went for his dagger. Still staggering from the force of Rudolf's defensive maneuver, Max unsheathed his rapier. The weapon Rudolf wielded was shorter by half than Max's swept-hilt sword, but its thicker blade and curved cross-guard made it equally lethal.

Except for the frightened horses, the crowd grew quiet as they watched the two big men duel. Eden held her breath when Max slipped on an icy patch and Rudolf tried to drive his dagger home. Max dodged just in time, the blade missing flesh but tearing his clothes. Righting himself, Max countered with a thrust that caught the baldric on Rudolf's sash, driving him to the wall. With a well-aimed kick, Max knocked the dagger from Rudolf's hand, sending it into a pile of slush-covered garbage.

As the wind howled down the lane, the onlookers huddled closer together, awaiting the outcome of what they were sure was mortal combat. The two blond giants were skirting the precipice of life and death and though both were foreigners, the London crowd seemed to know that one was good, the other evil.

Through the thick, swirling flakes, Rudolf glared at Max with a fanatical hatred. "Kill me! Kill me as you killed Sophie!" Taunting his adversary, he yanked off the sash, ripped open the brocade waistcoat and tore at his linen shirt. With chest exposed, he let out a stream of German curses, then reverted to English: "Do it! Let this foul multitude see what a murdering pig you really are, Max! They'll tear you to shreds!"

Breathlessly Eden waited for the fatal lunge. But Max stood riveted to the ground, the rapier poised at an angle. "I prefer the King's justice," he said at last. "Call me coward, but don't call me murderer, for that I am not." Deliberately he took a backward step, but kept his weapon at the ready. "You will come with me down the lane to the Eagle and Child. We will await the King's men there."

With surprising docility, Rudolf shrugged and moved toward Max. "I don't fear Wee Willie," he said in a pallid imitation of his usual amiable tone. "I have friends even more powerful than he."

"Really," remarked Max, glancing at Eden, who was giving the terrified children a farewell pat on the head. The crowd was already dispersing, driven away by the sudden severe change in weather as well as realization that the battle was over. Rudolf's henchmen were nowhere in sight, apparently having retreated into Old Slaughter's to lick their wounds.

Up ahead, the driver of the damaged coach was still trying to quiet his skittish horses. With Eden at his side, Max held the rapier at Rudolf's back. The trio paused by the coach, waiting for the vehicle to move out of the way.

"You'll pay for this," the coachman yelled, still struggling with his animals. "Milord Sunderland will see to that!"

"A pox on Milord Sunderland," Rudolf replied agreeably, pulling his shirt and waistcoat into place. "The man's a snake." Casually, Rudolf turned to look at Max. The small ivory-handled pistol he held in his right hand was pointed at Eden's abdomen.

"I'm going to walk down the lane alone," he said evenly, his terrible smile in place. "This little cannon would probably not kill your lovely trollop, but it would certainly spoil your pleasures with her. I'm disappointed in you, Max. You really ought to have searched me. Do you think I'd carry only a dagger in a dangerous city like London?"

Max's lean face had darkened with rage, directed not only at Rudolf but at himself, as well. He said nothing, the sword still held a tantalizing, impotent foot away from Rudolf. Eden knew she was shaking as much from fear as from the cold, and tried to move closer to Max.

"Stay where you are, all of you," Rudolf barked. "You didn't deserve to win. Victory goes only to the bold." His smile turned into a ghastly leer. "A pity there's only one ball in this little toy. It would be more of a pity to waste it." Slowly he raised the gun a few inches, squinted down the gleaming barrel and moved the weapon from side to side. "Which one of you will make the ultimate sacrifice for the other? How true is true love?"

Max threw his arms around Eden, offering her as much protection as possible. Rudolf's menacing figure was a blur. Eden cringed in Max's grasp, yet wanted to hurl herself between her beloved and his vengeful cousin.

Unable to watch the coachman while aiming at Max and Eden, Rudolf sensed rather than saw that the horses had finally quieted down. In the ensuing deadly stillness, he steadied the pistol and pointed it at Eden's breast. Bracing for the horrible explosion, Eden opened her mouth to cry out, but there was no sound, from her or from the gun. Lord Sunderland's irate driver had swung the whip at the horses. The big animals had reared up, hooves thrashing in the wind, then hurtled down, to send Rudolf flying against the coach wheel. The pistol dropped from his hand as he let out a terrible curse. The horses broke away, thundering in a circle and crushing Rudolf's body beneath the heavy wheel.

Max pulled Eden close, shielding her eyes with his hand. "Don't look," he breathed.

She didn't need the caution. The horrific grinding of the coach and the trampling hooves painted a grisly picture in her mind's eye. "He's dead?" she asked in a faint voice.

Max winced as he took a last glance at the blood-spattered snow and the crumpled form that had once borne the hopes of the House of Hohenstaufen. "Yes," he said, his voice unsteady. "This time he's really dead."

DESPITE EDEN'S INITIAL URGENCY IN getting to the Tower, she was unable to continue directly. Nor could Max leave the scene of the tragedy until the authorities had been summoned. "I owe Sophie that much," he explained as they sat in the Eagle and Child, drinking Nantes brandy and recovering their nerves.

Eden, who had been rendered speechless by the events of the past hour, noted with gratitude that the strain was beginning to ebb from Max's lean face. Sitting near the fire so that her clothes might dry out, she shook her head and at last found her voice. "You're an amazing man, Max. Half of me wanted you to kill Rudolf, the other half begged for mercy. I admire you more for your compassion than I would for what others might have called heroics."

"I'm glad," he said with a wry grin. "Harriet would have called me dismal. But," he noted, slipping his hand under hers, "Sophie would have sided with you, even if Rudolf hadn't been her brother. In some ways the two of you are more alike than I thought."

Eden smiled for the first time since she'd left Clarges Street some two hours earlier. "Perhaps we can be even more alike," she said with a mischievous glint in her eyes.

Max looked up as a serving man brought plates of Westphalian ham and buttered potatoes. "How do you mean?"

Eden waited for the server to leave. If Old Slaughter's had reeked of stale tobacco and overbrewed coffee, the Eagle and Child dispensed an aroma of roasting pigeons and sizzling mutton steaks and fresh-baked bread. Eden took knife and fork to her thick slice of ham and gazed at Max through her lashes. "Like Sophie, I can be your wife. The King has freed Jack."

Max choked on a piece of potato and had to cover his mouth with a napkin. "Holy St. Hubert!" he finally gasped, leaning forward in his chair. "What happened?"

Supremely pleased with herself, Eden tossed her head and toyed with a piece of ham. "Oh, I simply explained to His Majesty about Roark's perjured testimony and then I suggested he take me as his mistress and after he got over the shock I admitted that you and I were in love and he said, 'Fine, somebody has finally told the truth to a poor Dutchman.' Or something like that." She gave a little lift to her shoulders. "Well?" The ebony eyes were very round. "Didn't I perform admirably?"

Max let out a whistle and sank back in his chair. "It's incredible. Does Jack know?"

"Not yet. That's why I was so anxious to find you. I wanted us to go together to the Tower. But by now the news may have already gotten there ahead of us."

"Perhaps not." Max considered briefly, then gazed at Eden with open admiration. "I can hardly believe it! I don't think I ever thought we'd be free to be together." Still dumbfounded, he reached across the table to lightly touch the cut on Eden's cheek.

For a long moment they sat looking at each other, their smiles as wide as their eyes were bright. Max was the first to break the spell, placing a kiss on his fingertips and brushing Eden's lips with his hand. "We have plans to make, plans I never thought we'd have the chance to consider. But first, we must get to Jack, wherever he may be. I have some news of my own." He began to eat in haste.

Eden was about to ask what sort of news when Lord Sunderland's coachman approached their table. He had, as far as Max and Eden could tell, spent the past quarter of an hour explaining to the authorities how the accident with his horses had come to pass.

"Bloody nuisance," he grumbled, sitting down without waiting to be asked. "Milord is on his way to Kensington, I'm told, but from what I hear, King William won't grieve over a Jacobite spy."

"True enough," agreed Max, passing the man the brandy bottle. "We owe you our lives, you know. If this were the army, I'd commend you for your … assistance." He started to reach for some coins, but the coachman waved his hand.

"No, Your Highness, I needn't get paid for ridding the world of that traitor."

"At least let me pay for the damage," Max persisted.

The coachman snorted again. "Milord says he's having a new one made. It seems his son, Lord Spencer, is going a-wooing." The man halted abruptly, glancing around the crowded room. "Oh, blimey, it's no secret now. Young Spencer is courting Anne Churchill. The match looked dubious, don't you know, because her father was in the Tower." He leaned on the table confidentially. "All London's abuzz—Marlborough's been set free." The coachman sat back, waiting for an appropriate response. "What do you think of that, eh?"

"WE'LL HEAD FOR ST. JAMES'S," Max said as they hurried out into St. Martin's Lane. "Jack will undoubtedly join the Countess there."

Wearing Max's cloak, Eden blinked against the unexpected brightness of the afternoon. The snow flurry had passed, leaving London under a brilliant white mantle. Footprints already marred the pristine landscape, but a sense of peace had descended over the neighborhood. The aftermath of the storm not only concealed the drab and dirty aspect of the city, it also had erased the evil that had so recently pervaded the lane outside Old Slaughter's. Eden could not be sure exactly where Rudolf had been killed. Even the lumpy mass that had once been the fat snow woman was a sparkling mound, which the children were turning into a fantasy castle.

In the Strand, the winter calm was broken by shouts from a gaggle of Londoners who surrounded two men on horseback. Eden and Max paused, both shielding their eyes against the bright winter sun.

"It's Jack," said Max, grinning. "And Joost. They must be coming from the Tower."

Amid the cheers of his supporters, the Earl of Marlborough sat astride a handsome gray gelding. He wore the same brown cloak he'd had on when Eden first met him in Smarden, but had acquired a beaver hat with a turned-up brim etched in gold braid. Keppel was costumed in his usual style, a peacock blue embroidered cloak over an orange satin vest, fringed gauntlets at his wrists, with a black plush muff depending from a silver ribbon slung around his neck. The sleek bay stallion he rode was caparisoned to match its rider's wardrobe. But all eyes were on the Earl.

Taking Eden by the hand, Max led her up the Strand to join the festive crowd. But before they could reach the gathering, a calèche came crunching over the snow-covered street, its top folded back to reveal Sarah, Countess of Marlborough, and the five Churchill offspring.

To Eden's surprise, the smallest girl was no more than seven years old. It had not occurred to her that the Earl's other children could be so young. The boy was no more than ten, but his three elder sisters all appeared to be in their middle teens. Eden tried to scrutinize them for possible signs of kinship.

They were a handsome lot, but at a distance of some twenty feet, she saw little resemblance to herself. Marlborough had been right, Eden was definitely her mother's daughter.

Her father's wife did not see Eden and Max, so intent was she on the gladsome sight of her husband. As the calèche rolled to a halt near the entrance to Drury Lane, the Earl jumped from his horse, the crowd obligingly parted, and the Countess alighted from the calèche with her children at her heels.

The public reunion of husband and wife evoked a hearty cheer from the onlookers. Keppel beamed his approval while Max put an arm around Eden and inclined his head in a bemused manner. The young Churchills were being greeted one by one, with a special salute for the son and heir who stood at military attention before allowing his father to hug him close. Eden felt tears sting her eyes, and she put her head against Max's arm.

"I should be ecstatic," she murmured as all the Marlboroughs clambered into the calèche. "Why am I crying?"

Max's initial reaction was to tell Eden that she was shedding tears of joy. But another look at the delirious Marlborough family elicited a different opinion. Max phrased his reply as tactfully as possible. "You wanted to be the bearer of good news. It didn't work out that way, Eden." He gave her shoulders a little squeeze as he wiped her tears with his finger. "You'll see Jack later. I know he'll be enormously grateful."

"It's not that," Eden began, but stopped as the calèche turned around in the middle of the Strand and began to head for St. James's Palace. With her hand half raised, Eden thought of calling out to her father. But the procession, truncated as it was, suddenly reminded her of that summer day on the road to Tunbridge Wells, when she had wanted so badly to be noticed by King Charles. Even after more than a decade, Eden couldn't bear a repetition of the humiliation she'd suffered when the man she believed to be her father had ridden on without so much as a nod.

And then, as Marlborough and his children jostled for comfortable positions in the carriage, he turned toward Eden and Max. His refined features lighted up, and a smile as dazzling as the snow crossed his face.

"Max! Eden! Come here!" The calèche stopped again, the driver waiting patiently while still more Londoners congregated.

"Jack!" Eden cried as she ran to meet him. Her feet slipped twice on the fresh snow, but both times Max grabbed her arm. A moment later, she was leaning against the calèche, holding Marlborough by the hands. "I didn't think you saw me," she whispered, unaware that her cheeks were still damp with tears.

"I didn't," Marlborough replied honestly. His smile was as kindly as ever, his manner as self-deprecating as Eden remembered. "I'm not used to being out in the bright light of day."

Eden smiled through her tears. "I'm so glad you're free! I've been afraid ... of so many things."

"Here," said Marlborough with a mild glance of reproach at his younger children who were growing fractious, "come join us. We're a bit cramped, but we'll manage." He looked beyond Eden to Max who was standing with hands on hips amidst a clutch of well-wishers. "Max! Take my horse, ride with Joost. We're heading for St. James's."

Eden hesitated for only a moment, then climbed into the carriage. The Countess's smile held a hint of frost, but the rest of the family displayed unconcealed curiosity. As Eden watched Max swing up on the Earl's gray gelding, she became aware of the awkward atmosphere that had suddenly enveloped her fellow passengers.

Apparently, Marlborough felt the same sense of discomfiture. With Eden pressed between him and the side of the calèche, he bestowed a sympathetic smile on his family. "My dear children," he said in his imperturbable voice, "this is your sister, Eden. We all owe her a great debt. Indeed," he went on, while the five young Churchills gaped with varying degrees of disbelief, surprise and hostility, "she has saved my life."

"Our sister?" Anne blurted, taking in only the first part of her father's words. "Papa, how can this be? Do you mean that ...." Words failed the Earl's eldest.

"It means your father is human and had an unfortunate lapse," snapped Sarah, shoving her hands deep inside her ermine muff. "In fact, he had two of them. The other one is in France." The Countess's expression brooked no further remarks.

The Earl, however, was not quite as cowed by his wife as the rest. "We'll have a long talk about all this later, my dears. Indeed, we'll have plenty of time to talk and talk. Thank God," he breathed, and without regard for the sensibilities of the others, he reached out and patted Eden's hand. Her face glowed with happiness. After a lifetime of waiting, her father's carriage had finally stopped to take her in.

By the time the Marlborough entourage had reached St. James's, the crowd of admirers had grown into the hundreds. At the palace gates the Earl doffed his beaver hat and waved while a great cheer shook the afternoon's relative calm.

Members of Princess Anne's household rushed to greet Marlborough and escort his family to the Heiress Presumptive's apartments. Eden was propelled along with the others, though she would have preferred to wait for Max. She had last seen him coming down Pall Mall, trying along with Keppel to push through the surging crowd.

Once inside the palace, Eden caught Anne Churchill by the sleeve. "Milady," she said, not quite certain how to address her half sister when it came to rank, "I will rejoin His Lordship as soon as I can, but I must see after Prince Maximilian. He, too, would like to officially greet your—" Eden swallowed hard, then lifted her chin with dignity "—*our* father."

Anne, who closely resembled her mother, glanced at her parents as they proceeded down the passageway surrounded by old friends. When she was assured that the Earl and his Countess were out of earshot, Anne grabbed Eden by the arm. "Is it true that Charles's coach trampled a German noble today?"

For a moment, Eden had no idea what her half sister was talking about. "Count Rudolf?" She saw Anne give an ambivalent nod. "He was killed in St. Martin's Lane—oh! Is this Charles the son of Lord Sunderland?" inquired Eden.

Anne's eyes shone. "He is. And as brave as his father is guileful." Her feet sketched little dancing steps in the wet entry hall. "My parents despise them both. But I intend to marry Charles anyway! Are you really the one I have to thank for my good fortune?"

Taken aback by Anne's forthright speech, Eden tugged at the folds of Max's cloak. "I' truth, if you mean that His Lordship's release has removed a cloud from over your marriage prospects, then I may have been of some help. But," she added with a little tremor in her voice, "I owe your beloved's kin even more. The coachman may have saved my life, and that of Prince Maximilian, as well."

Anne accepted Eden's gratitude without emotion. "Well and good. Charles will be pleased." The sparkle ignited in her blue eyes. "He hates the nobility, you see. As long as this Rudolf was a count, the coachman no doubt will be rewarded."

"But ... Eden stared at Anne in bewilderment. "Isn't Charles a nobleman himself?"

Anne was already making her way down the passage. "Oh, yes," she called over her shoulder. "But Charles prefers to be known as Mr. Spencer. Don't you think that's rather brave? Imagine, such a fuss over titles! What's a name, after all?"

What, indeed, thought Eden as she watched Anne Churchill skip off in the direction of the royal apartments. For Eden, finding a name had been a lifelong search. After nineteen years of imagining who she might be, she had discovered that she was a Churchill and a Villiers. But for her half sister, who had never been shadowed by doubt, the prospect of becoming Mrs. Spencer put spring into her step. Marveling at the ironies of life, Eden departed the palace to find Max. And for the first time, she realized that though she knew his title, she didn't know his full name.

OUTSIDE, THE CROWD HAD DISPERSED, except for a handful of citizens who huddled together under the fading sun to discuss the consequences of Marlborough's release.

" 'E'll be our general again, mark my words," a pockmarked man of middle age admonished his listeners. "An' send them Frenchies 'arfway to 'ell, 'e will."

"No wonder Wee Willie Cheesemonger couldn't win the war," grumbled a tall woman. "Foreigners don't know how to fight except with each other."

Eden suppressed a smile at the running commentary as she walked through the newly trampled snow to Pall Mall.

No doubt Max had decided not to intrude on the family reunion. As for Keppel, he knew of the Countess's antipathy toward him and probably felt it tactful to withdraw.

Yet it was Joost Eden saw in the dying light, his stallion pawing impatiently at a bare patch of ground. "Where's Max?" she called, approaching with caution, for ice was forming a thick crust on the wide street that led away from the palace and into the Strand.

"Where have you been?" Keppel asked in a petulant tone, though it occurred to Eden that of course he must know.

"I was carried away by ...." The words died on her lips as she saw Keppel's unhappy expression. "Joost! What has happened? Where's Max?"

Keppel soothed his horse with a distracted hand. "I thought you knew. Didn't you see?" He waved his plush muff in the general direction of Whitehall. "The King's men have arrested Max. He's been taken to the Tower."

Chapter Eighteen

EDEN COULD NOT BELIEVE THAT her state of euphoria had evaporated so swiftly. As she rode pillion behind him, Keppel was doing his best to explain what had happened, though he was somewhat uncertain. "Soldiers bearing the royal insignia came up to us just before we got to St. James's," he said as they passed through Temple Bar. "I' faith, I wasn't quite sure of the charge. It wasn't treason, but rather conspiracy or complicity. It all sounded most vague to me. The strange part was, Max didn't argue. That's not like him."

"It's not." Eden was thoughtful as they crossed the road that led to Blackfriars. "I don't understand," she said fretfully. "Max seemed so confident that he wouldn't be arrested. Do you think this box of bees is Bentinck's doing?"

Keppel hesitated in answering while he guided the black stallion around the base of the tall pillar that commemorated London's great fire. "As much as it galls me, Bentinck retains much of his power. It's a sop, you see," he went on, giving Eden a faintly shamefaced look over his shoulder. "The King is going to make me Earl of Albermarle within the month."

"Politics!" Eden spat out the word. Indeed, it was not quite the epithet that had leaped to her tongue. But she dared not express her real feelings; she needed Keppel now more than ever.

As they emerged from Tower Street, Eden saw a group of workmen building a scaffold on Tower Hill. Several onlookers loitered in the Twilight to watch the construction. Timidly, Eden tapped Keppel's arm. "What ... who is that for?" she asked in a hushed voice.

"Sir John Fenwick," Keppel replied. "His wife came to beg the King for mercy today, but though William was kindly spoken, he remained adamant. Fenwick dies tomorrow."

Despite her antipathy for the condemned man, Eden could not look at the scaffold. The chilling thought that it could have served two prisoners instead of one stabbed at her brain. She wasn't cheered by the news that Lady Fenwick's plea had been in vain. William of Orange was a fair man, but he was also unbending.

Flaunting his position as King's favorite, Keppel demanded to see Sir Edmund Greene, the Lord Lieutenant of the Tower, at once. Five minutes later Eden was seated in the surprisingly cozy parlor, which dated from Elizabethan times. A gracious host, the Lord Lieutenant offered wine and sugar cakes, but his guests declined.

"I've done my duty, which is to incarcerate state prisoners," Sir Edmund explained in his forthright manner. "His Majesty's soldiers bring me criminals, I lock them up. Who they are or what they've done aren't my business." He shrugged his broad shoulders and devoured a sugar cake. "This foreign fellow has been here once before," he said, then gave Eden a searching look. "God's eyes, Mistress, weren't you with him?"

Anxious to make some sort of progress rather than exchange useless chitchat, Eden replied curtly, "Yes, and with as little reason then as now. Where is Prince Maximilian?"

Unruffled by her abrupt manner, Sir Edmund gestured over his shoulder. "The Bloody Tower, just beyond here, where the little Princes were murdered."

Eden's nerves jangled with fear and frustration. Jumping to her feet, she upset the plate of sugar cakes, spilling them onto the carpeted floor. "Joost, go to the King. Only you can convince him of this injustice. Bentinck be damned, William loves you best! I'm going to Max."

As both men gaped at her, Eden raced out of the room and out onto Tower Green. Darkness had descended on London, and on the ramparts the ravens tucked their heads under their wings and settled in for the night. Clutching Max's cloak more tightly around her, she felt a pang of longing flicker through her body. Only hours ago he had worn this same garment; indeed, his own arms had held her as close as the fabric did now.

Peering into the gloom, Eden tried to determine which part of the fortress housed the Bloody Tower. The name evoked horror. Across the Green a half dozen soldiers wearing the scarlet and gold uniforms of yeoman warders marched in formation, their boots making loud crunching noises on the crisp snow. Without hesitation, Eden approached the men.

"Take me to Prince Maximilian," she ordered boldly. "I'm here with Milord Keppel, who represents the King." The ambiguity of her words was lost on the soldiers, who stopped, glanced at one another then broke ranks.

"His Highness is right over here," said the tallest of the contingent, pointing to a square-shaped structure at least three stories tall. His honest brown eyes studied Eden more closely. "Where is Milord Keppel?"

Eden tossed her head in the direction of the Lord Lieutenant's lodging. "In there. Take me to the Prince at once, please."

The sheer audacity of her demand, and Keppel's reception by their commander, persuaded the soldiers to acquiesce. Five minutes later Eden was climbing up a narrow, winding staircase. Only two of the soldiers had accompanied her, and upon reaching Max's cell, they discreetly withdrew into a recess of the stone passageway.

"Max!" Eden cried as she peeped into the darkness beyond the barred door. "Max, are you there?"

There was no response. Eden called for the soldiers, who came at a run. The one who held the torch was the tall man who had spoken to her on the Green; the other, who carried a big hoop filled with keys, was much smaller but of a wiry build.

"He can't have escaped," muttered the tall man, turning the key. "This is locked."

"There's a window, but it's up high," the other guardsman said as he steadied the torch.

His companion shot him an ironic glance. "This foreigner is tall as a tree, though I doubt even he could reach that embrasure. He must be asleep."

Pressed against the cold stone wall, Eden could not endure the soldiers' musings another instant. "Open that door!" She pushed the guards aside and flung herself into the cell. The torch cast eerie shadows over Max's prison. It was a large room, chillingly suitable for two royal though blameless heirs in ages past, and now detaining a Flemish nobleman who was equally innocent. Trying not to remember the gruesome fate that had befallen the English princes, Eden scanned the chamber. Halfway up the wall an oak closet jutted out above the empty bed. At a right angle, a tall mullioned window was set about ten feet above the floor, while the sparse furnishings loomed out of the darkness like so many coiled creatures ready to pounce.

"The closet," breathed the wiry guardsman. "He may be in there."

Eden tried to focus her gaze on the wooden fixture, but something else caught her eye, and she screamed in shock. On the floor, near a table, Max lay on his back with one arm flung above his head. Next to him was a tray with broken dishes and the remnants of a meal.

Staggering across the room, Eden fell down beside him, calling his name in a panicked voice. "He's been poisoned! I know it!" she cried, groping for a heartbeat. "Fetch a doctor!"

The shorter of the two men handed the torch to his companion, then raced off to get help. To Eden's great relief, she found Max's pulse beating with surprising strength and regularity. She had to stifle a gasp of exhilaration when she saw him open one eye and wink at her.

Comprehension dawning, Eden stood, wringing her hands in apparent agitation. "He may be dead ... I can't tell. We must find an antidote!"

The tall guardsman joined Eden, leaning over with the torch held aloft, the keys dangling from his other hand. "Blimey," he mumbled, "it must have taken a whopping dose to knock out the likes of him!"

Eden was about to make an appropriate response when Max's legs lashed out, catching the guard around the ankles. The man let out an oath as he fell. His voice was quickly stifled when Max's fist crushed into his jaw. The keys clattered to the floor; the torch sputtered as it struck the cold stone.

Riveted to the spot in total darkness, Eden reached out with an anxious hand. "Max," she gasped, then suddenly felt him grab her around the waist and propel her across the room.

"Climb into the closet," he breathed. "We'll take our chances hiding there for now."

Stumbling, Eden had to regain her balance before her foot found the first narrow wooden step. At the top of the short flight, Max reached around her to open the door. "There's not much room," he whispered. "Keep close to me."

Eden needed no urging. She clung to Max, still overcome by the shock of the past few minutes. "It was a ruse?" she asked in a hushed voice, thankful to be in his arms despite the danger they faced.

"Yes." He sounded tense, and she could feel him stiffen as voices floated up from somewhere down the passageway. A moment later the voices had come much closer, probably into the cell. Eden recognized the voice of the wiry guardsman as he exclaimed over his unconscious comrade. Apparently the doctor had been found, for someone was asking that the tall guard be tended to immediately. In the ensuing interchange Eden could make out very little, for several people seemed to be talking at once. She held her breath, felt Max's heart beating in her ear and was faintly buoyed by the reassuring squeeze he gave her waist.

More noise followed, then the voices began to fade along with the hurried footsteps. Max let go of Eden and moved just a few inches away. Now accustomed to the darkness, she realized for the first time that while there was a small window set into the permanent wall, there was no ceiling in the closet. A man of average height would not have been able to look over the wooden partition, but Max was at eye level with the rough oak's edge.

"They're gone," he said, brushing at his forehead first with one hand then the other. "Thank God for assumptions."

"What do you mean?" Eden whispered as Max felt for something along the wall. "I was certain the closet would be the first place they'd look for us."

"Ah! There's the rope I purloined," he said, holding up a large coil. "Of course the closet was where they should have searched. But it was so obvious, they assumed nobody would be stupid enough to hide there."

"Oh." Eden's voice was very small as Max gestured for her to stand back. With a mighty swing he smashed the window, then waited for any sound of discovery. There was none.

Protecting his hand with the rope, he broke off ragged fragments of glass. The night air rushed in, making Eden quiver with cold. Wordlessly she watched Max secure the rope from a hook at one side of the casement, then throw the remaining length out the window. With a wry smile, he turned to Eden. "How's your climbing prowess?"

She took in a sharp deep breath. "*Zut!* How far down is it?"

He gave her his hand. "Never mind. Just keep looking up. You'll know when your feet touch the ground."

Her heart beating much too fast, Eden let Max help her over the casement. Clinging to the rope, she could look neither up nor down, but kept her eyes shut tight. With feet entwined and fingers grasping the swaying lifeline, she descended ever so slowly, certain that it was only a matter of seconds before someone would raise the alarm. In the long, grisly history of the Tower, few men, and no women, had ever escaped. The thought was sufficiently unnerving to make Eden feel suddenly dizzy. Bright lights flashed in her mind's eye, and her fingers started to slip.

For Max's sake, she must go on. Steeling her resolve, Eden inched downward as the rough hemp scratched her hands and the wind sent Max's cloak flapping around her body. From somewhere nearby, bells began to ring, a deafening sound that made her grit her teeth and grip the rope even harder. The ravens awoke with shrill cries, then soared into the air, circling the wall above the moat. Yet Eden persisted, knowing that for every moment lost, there was the chance that Max would be discovered.

Suddenly, blessedly, her feet touched solid ground. The bells had stopped ringing, and she opened her eyes. Above her, she could see Max descending the rope with the amazing agility that had always astonished her in a man his size. Briefly, Eden took in her surroundings. She was in a walled enclosure that held a half dozen barren trees. From the Green, she could hear soldiers running and shouting. No doubt the bells that had pealed just moments before had been a general alarm. Eden suppressed a cry of relief when Max jumped the last four feet to the ground and hurried to take her arm.

"Most prisoners would try to break out of the Lord Lieutenant's lodgings," he said, unhooking the guard's key ring from his belt, "but we're going to break into it."

Fascinated as well as fearful, Eden watched Max select the proper key and fit it into a door at one end of the stone wall. Slipping inside, they halted, trying to find their bearings in the darkened passageway.

"This leads to the lodging," he whispered, taking a tentative step. "We came out in the privy garden. We've no other way to go."

Eden absorbed the information without comment. She could still hear the sounds of soldiers outside, but the passage was deathly quiet. Creeping along in the darkness, they reached another door, which gave way at a touch. Light from several candles almost blinded them; Eden groped for Max, who put an arm around her shoulders.

Standing in the glaring light of the scullery were the Lord Lieutenant and Lady Harriet Villiers. Sir Edmund wore an expression of grim triumph; Harriet was a gleefully venomous vision in mauve satin and miniver trim.

"*Schoft*," muttered Max, pulling Eden closer. "Our luck ran out."

But Harriet waved a gloved hand at him. "Not a bit of it, my love. Indeed, there was no need for such heroics on your part. I've come to free you." Still wearing her spiteful smile, she extracted a sealed piece of paper from her muff. "My uncle made a slight mistake. It wasn't you, Max, who is accused of complicity in Rudolf's murder, but Mistress Eden. Aren't you relieved?"

Eden's outrage conquered her fear. "Viper! Neither of us killed Rudolf!" She lunged at Harriet, but Max held her back.

"She's right, Harriet," he asserted, trying to calm Eden. "This is a farce. Tear up that silly warrant or whatever it is and let us be on our way." He spoke with a certain weariness, like a man who has fought his way through a dense jungle and finally been stopped at the edge.

"It's not that simple," Harriet averred, the smile fading as she broke the seal and showed the paper to Sir Edmund. "You can't dismiss charges without some sort of evidence. I'm afraid you'll have to leave Mistress Eden here until the matter is resolved."

Still fractious, Eden fought against Max's restraining hands. "This is petty conniving! She wants you back Max, because she thinks now that Rudolf's dead, you'll regain your property and mayhap his, too. Harriet would rather be a princess than a viscountess, isn't that so, you nasty shrew?"

Harriet bridled at the accusation, but held her ground. "You forget, peasant, that Max and I were betrothed for some time. I've merely reconsidered and am willing to take him back now." She fluttered her lashes at Max and turned to Sir Edmund. "Well? Will you do your duty?"

"I always do my duty," the Lord Lieutenant replied, looking ill pleased as he spoke to Eden. "Milord Bentinck has signed this warrant and I must hold you here in the Tower until I receive further instructions. As for Your

Highness," he went on, trying to ignore the wrath on Max's and Eden's faces, "according to this document, you are free to go."

Max dug his heels into the scullery floor. "I won't leave without Eden. I've fought too long and too hard for what I want to give up now."

"Max!" Harriet's green eyes glittered dangerously. "We had an understanding! Would you bring the House of Villiers down on your head? Or," she added maliciously, "would you prefer to lose it out on Tower Hill tomorrow with John Fenwick?"

With both arms around Eden, Max eyed Harriet contemptuously. "I cared for you once, in my fashion, Harriet, but I didn't love you. Nor did you love me. We were convenient for each other. But I love Eden and I'm going to marry her. Tear up that warrant and make way."

Harriet snatched the warrant out of the Lord Lieutenant's hands. "You're an idiot, Max." The green eyes were almost black with hatred. "You'd give up everything for this bastard slut! I'll take this back to my uncle and have him charge you both with complicity." She gave a toss of her head, the single ostrich feather swaying ominously on her miniver hat. "I hope you die for your stupidity. To think your children could have been born of Villiers stock!"

"They still can." The husky voice emanated from the kitchen, and Lady Castlemaine emerged, her blackamoor manservant and a pair of Russian wolfhounds in tow. "Well?" she demanded, restraining the barking dogs. "My daughter's as much a Villiers as you are, Harriet. Why don't you take that warrant or whatever poxy pap you've trotted out and put it up your petticoats?"

Furious, Harriet almost flung herself at Barbara, but the wolfhounds held her at bay. "Strumpet!" shrieked Harriet. "Trollop! You've no right to meddle."

Lady Castlemaine tugged at the dogs' leashes, quieting them down. "Faugh, you're the one who meddles, Harriet. Call me what you will, at least I'm an honest whore—unlike you." Barbara turned to Sir Edmund. "The King's carriage awaits His Highness and my daughter. Joost van Keppel has made Wee Willie see reason. We thank you for your hospitality, but the hour grows late." As the blackamoor manservant made way through the kitchen, Barbara beckoned to Max and Eden. "Come, children, this place makes my backside twitch. Imagine, queens used to be beheaded for adultery! Praise the Virgin for modern enlightenment!"

Sir Edmund had stepped aside while Max guided Eden through the scullery, his hand firmly placed at her back. But Harriet was not quite ready to give up. Her face contorted with frustrated rage, she picked up a paring knife from a tiled counter and dove at Lady Castlemaine. "Drunken bitch! You won't get away with this!" she screamed.

With amazing reflexes, Barbara neatly parried the blow with one arm, while her other fist flew out to land with a resounding crack on her attacker's chin. Harriet groaned, reeled and fell to the floor, landing on a pile of flour sacks. At least one of them burst, spilling a white cloud from the tip of the ostrich feather to the miniver-trimmed hem. Thoroughly stunned, Lady Harriet Villiers lay with feet splayed and mouth agape as the dogs barked their farewell and Lady Castlemaine dusted off her gloves.

"Milady!" Eden breathed in astonishment as Max propelled her down the passageway that led to the main entrance of the Lord Lieutenant's lodging. "You were magnificent!"

"I often am." Barbara shrugged as they emerged onto Tower Green. "But," she added, taking a swig from a gin flask she carried in her muff, "what's a mother for, eh, Baby Ducks?"

WILLIAM OF ORANGE WAS ABED, the camphor kettle boiling on the hob, the poplar salve smeared around his nose. "We are following your instructions," he said, sounding more crotchety than he looked. "We may confound our enemies and survive the winter after all."

Outside, the parish church of Kensington chimed the midnight hour. In the King's chambers, Joost van Keppel lounged against the Grinling Gibbons mantelpiece, and Max stood near the head of the canopied bed while Eden blended a cough mixture in a crystal bowl. To the observer, it was a placid domestic scene, elegant in detail yet homely in execution.

"You have much to explain," the King reproached Max with the wag of a finger. "Not the least of which is why you didn't come to us directly after your return from the Continent."

Max shielded a guttering candle by the bed with his hand. "I had already tried many times, Sire, and was always thwarted by Milord Bentinck." He glanced at Keppel, who nodded in agreement. "When I was arrested today— yesterday, now—I decided that was all for the good and gave no resistance. If Bentinck thought I was safely imprisoned, he couldn't keep me from seeing you if I escaped and came to Kensington. I'd hoped to catch him off guard, you see."

Considering Max's words, William touched his long nose. "Ah. It makes sense—we think. But it was reckless."

"Not as much as Bentinck's attempt to try me for murder," Max said bitterly.

"I blame Harriet," put in Eden, spooning out the cough mixture. "Here, Sire, you like this, remember?"

The King raised his hands in protest. "We're not coughing," he said, shrinking against the pillows.

Eden persevered. "Not yet. Take just a spoonful and ensure a restful night."

Reluctantly, William obeyed. At the end of the bed, the Dutch pugs yawned and stretched, then rolled over and went back to sleep. Keppel poured himself a cup of usquebaugh and adjusted the sash on his damask lounging robe. "Zounds, Max, give us your news! Rumors are flying from here to Paris!"

Curiously, Eden looked at Max, who wore an unusually self-satisfied expression. She knew he had traveled abroad, but so far there had been little opportunity for him to confide in Eden. As the King indicated that Max should sit, Eden shoved a chair next to the bed. Resting one long leg on the other knee, Max unfolded his story.

"Originally, my plan was to see the King. You, Sire," Max said with a nod toward William. "Then, as I was sneaking about the garden at Whitehall, it occurred to me that I was calling on the wrong king. It was Louis I needed to see to settle the controversy between Rudolf and me. To pave the way, I began with the Archbishop of Liège, who had connived with Rudolf over the separate peace. I convinced His Excellency that betraying you to the French was not in his best interests. His political acumen exceeds his piety." A wry smile touched Max's lips. "As it was, I had to become forceful in showing him that Protestants aren't the only ones who are venal and grasping. Eventually, he gave in. The treaty, of course, is null and void."

William nodded with solemn understanding. "We are most gratified. It's still hard to believe that Count Rudolf was so treacherous. He always seemed such a pleasant fellow."

Eden turned her head so that the King could not see the face she made. She couldn't understand how William, who was usually an astute judge of human nature, should have failed in Rudolf's case. But then the King had also been wrong about Marlborough. Everyone, it seemed, was entitled to a margin of error.

"After Liège, I went to Versailles," Max continued, accepting Keppel's proffered glass of Moselle wine. "It was risky, yet I had to make it plain to King Louis that I had never at any time agreed to settle the dispute over Vranes-sur-Ourthe. To my surprise, Louis was in an affable mood. The yuletide season, perhaps." Without breaking stride in his recital, Max reached around to take Eden's hand and place it on his shoulder. "The French King is willing to continue peace negotiations. James Stuart has been offered the Polish throne, left vacant by the death of John Sobieski." He paused not only for effect, but to gently stroke Eden's fingers. "Thus, Louis will recognize Your Majesty, not James, as King of England, Scotland and Ireland as soon as the treaty is formalized."

"Ah!" William of Orange let out a great sigh of relief and closed his eyes. "Praise God! How long we have waited!"

"Max!" Eden grabbed him by the shirt and shook his shoulder. "You never told me! How could you?"

"I promised I'd tell you in good time," Max replied reasonably, trying to loosen her tenacious grasp. "It was His Majesty who needed to know first though I must admit, it was your inspiration that sent me racing off to the Continent." He gave Eden a wry grin.

"But, how?" she demanded, wide-eyed.

The grin grew crooked, "I tried thinking like you do, and amazingly it worked."

Eden was momentarily nonplussed. William, having savored his elation, was already back to business. "We must resume the peace talks," he asserted, reaching for pen and paper from the table next to the bed. "We will dispatch Dykvelt and Matt Prior to France immediately. We must also, I fear, prepare for war. If the peace talks should fail or bog down, we may be able to regain more of our lost holdings in the meantime."

Eden, who had stopped shaking Max and was standing next to him with her arm draped over his back, interjected a question. "Sire, who will lead this army if you need to fight?"

The keen dark eyes stared down the long nose at Eden. "We haven't yet made that decision, Mistress. Or," William inquired with a glint of irony, "would you make it for us?"

Eden put a hand to her claret-colored curls. "I wouldn't think I'd have to," she exclaimed, all round-eyed innocence. "The answer is obvious."

King William's gaze locked with hers while Keppel hid his smile and Max tapped his long chin. "Obvious, eh?" grumbled His Majesty. "That Marlborough fellow, we suppose?"

Eden gave the King a dazzling smile. "Yes, my father. Who else?"

William pulled the covers up to his chin. "Who else, indeed?" he muttered. "But the Lady Anne is getting married to that Republican rascal, Lord Spencer. We suppose the Earl will have to give the bride away first."

"Brides," corrected Eden, and turned to look into Max's hazel eyes. For one startling instant she saw her own image reflected, not as she was now, but as she had been a year ago, under the eaves at Smarden, wondering what the New Year would bring. Then the vision faded and she saw only love.

Elsa was twittering her way down the staircase while *Vrouw* de Koch chided the kitchen help and *Heer* Van de Weghe argued with a tradesman on the front stoop. Eden rolled over in bed and wondered why she felt so cold. Opening her eyes, she also wondered where she was—not in the familiar bedroom with the pansies on the counterpane, but in a much larger chamber, filled with oversize furniture and bold splashes of color. Eden sat up and savored the sunlight.

"What time is it?" she called to Max. "Oh, do close that window, it's chilly in here without you!"

"That can be remedied," said Max, moving across the room on his bare feet. "It's going to snow again. The clouds are moving in from the north."

Eden watched Max throw off the striped robe and get into bed. "I don't care if it snows for a month," she declared with fervor. "Let's not leave here until spring." Feeling the warmth of his body next to hers, she gave a little shiver of pleasure. "You know, I'd never seen your bedroom until now? It was too dark when we got back to Kensington last night."

"It was this morning," said Max, nipping her nose with his teeth. "It's past noon now. And I didn't give you time to see much of anything except me."

"Hmm," murmured Eden as he pressed kisses along her jaw and neck. "Which was fine, i' truth, though it is a very nice room. Are those your paintings?"

Max lifted his head just long enough to glance at the far wall. "Most of them. Except for two, they're not very good."

"I must study them," said Eden in a vague sort of way as she ran her hands up and down the hard muscles of Max's back. "Will you paint my portrait some day?"

Max was fondling her breasts, teasing her nipples with his thumbs, making her brain grow hazy with the return of desire. "Maybe." He grinned across the pillow at her, the sun-streaked hair rumpled, the hazel eyes agleam with longing. "I'll paint you nude."

"You will not!" Eden pulled away and almost fell off the bed. "Even my mother didn't pose nude!"

With little effort, Max hauled her across the sheets. "All right, I'll paint you with clothes on, but you must be naked for the sitting."

Eden's show of indignation dwindled into a giggle. "You're dreadful. Why do I love you so much?" With a sigh of mock surrender, she offered her face for his kisses.

Capturing her mouth, Max felt the smooth flesh from back to buttocks, lifting her body just enough to touch his own. His kiss deepened, turned greedy, devoured her, as if he could never quite satisfy his hunger for her. "*Schoft*, Eden," he breathed, "let's get married. Today."

Gasping for breath, Eden clawed at Max's chest. "Not yet ... I want a real wedding. I want ...." She moved her knee in such a way that she felt the full masculine strength of him pressed against her. "Dear God," she blurted, "I want—and need—only you!"

Moved by her ardor, Max studied the piquant face. The wide-set eyes, the full mouth, the inviting curves of her body, the splendor of her hair splashed across the pillow—in looks alone, she was truly fit for a king. The irony of his initial misgivings assailed him. Her forthright manner, her penchant for laughter rather than restraint, even the qualities that had once compelled him to call her a diddlewit and a bumpkin had turned into disarming assets. But most of all it was her open nature, her generous spirit and enormous vitality that had restored him to life. In return, he had given her very little; indeed, he had very little to give. The thought struck him with jarring suddenness, and he buried his face in the curve of her shoulder.

"Eden!" He uttered her name on a strangled note against her skin. "What did I do to deserve you?"

"What?" Grabbing Max by the hair, she raised his head so she could look into his face. With the weight and heat of him still upon her, Eden's brain was definitely fuzzy. But she saw the serious, even anxious expression in his eyes and knew she must give him an answer. Of course he was tall and strong and handsome and even had a title, foreign though it might be. He was smart, too, and brave and honest. Yet Eden probably could say as much for a dozen men she'd met in the past year, including Joost van Keppel. Taking a breath, she smoothed the hair from his forehead and looked him straight in the eye.

"You've made me feel as if I belong to someone. You took away the loneliness. Even Jack couldn't do that." A smile quivered on her lips. "I'm not just me anymore, I'm part of you."

An odd light shone in Max's eyes, and if Eden hadn't known better, she would have suspected he was on the verge of tears. He brushed her mouth with his, then sought the ripe flesh of her breasts, the flat of her stomach, the valley between her thighs. Her rational thoughts dissolved in a haze of longing. As Max found amazing new secrets to claim as his own, Eden responded with a zeal to please him as much as he delighted her.

Astonished by her spontaneity, Max rolled over on his back and groaned with ecstasy. "Where," he gasped as Eden's clever tongue and sprightly fingers stirred him to near frenzy, "did you learn to do that?"

Eden paused, her cheek resting on his hip. "Well …" her insouciant gaze darted up the length of his body, "I guess I am my mother's daughter, after all."

Max closed his eyes and surrendered to Eden's delicious attentions. "To think I ever thought ill of that woman. She's quite remarkable, actually."

"Unique," corrected Eden with a breathy sigh. Deftly she draped her body over his and, with a little shudder of anticipation, edged down to capture him between her legs. "Oh!" she exclaimed, bracing her knees. "Oh, Max, you're remarkable, too!"

His grin slightly awry, Max clasped Eden's buttocks and rocked her back and forth. Lost in the tempo of their passion, mindless of sunlight or shadows, unaware of anything but their mutual desire, they melded body and soul together until at last rapture first elevated, then depleted them. With trembling limbs, Eden tumbled off Max, sprawling next to him in the bed with one arm flung across his legs and her head on the flat of his abdomen. For a long time neither of them spoke, and though they weren't quite sure, they may have slept. The world was a hazy place, yet warm and comforting.

Eden was the first to move, scooting up toward the pillows and gazing at Max's chiseled profile. His eyes were shut, and she was certain that he had nodded off. "Oh, Max," she whispered, "you talk of deserving! No one deserves anyone else—we're gifts to each other, freely offered, gratefully taken. How I love you, Max!" Her face damp with tears, she pressed a kiss on his bare chest over his heart.

Slowly, Max opened his eyes and his arms enfolded her. "What a pretty speech," he remarked, kissing the top of her head. "With words like that, you might have coaxed a king."

Eden wiped at her cheeks with her fist and nestled closer. "I might have. But no one except you will ever hear them. To any other man they would be a lie."

The light was fading in the bedchamber and the wind stirred over the rooftops. "Ever honest is my Eden," murmured Max. "It's said, you know—" he sat up just enough to look at the Dresden china clock over the mantelpiece "—that whatever you do on the first day of a new year, you will do every day that follows."

Eden seemed to reflect. "What day is it? I've lost track."

"It's New Year's Eve." Max spoke with exaggerated indifference.

"Well." Eden pulled him down beside her. "In that case, we'd better stay here in bed until tomorrow. We can always get married next year."

Max did not argue.

Epilogue

THE SUN WAS LOW ON the horizon, promising a clear day despite the cold air that blew in from the North Sea. The dock at Margate was crowded with passengers and baggage, but attention was fixed upon the handsome party that had just emerged from a capacious coach bearing the Churchill ancestral arms. Prince Maximilian Augustus Frederick Wittenberg and Princess Eden of Nassau-Dillenburg, the Earl and Countess of Marlborough, Lord Sidney Godolphin and Joost van Keppel, Earl of Albermarle, were exchanging bittersweet farewells. On this first day of February, 1697, the newly married Nassau-Dillenburgs were sailing for the Low Countries to claim their inheritance at Vranes-sur-Ourthe in Brabant, where they planned to make their home.

"Don't let Max spare any expense," Sarah insisted in an aside to Eden as *Heer* Van de Weghe supervised the luggage. "From what I've heard, the castle is in shambles. Believe me, when my dear Lord Marl and I build in the country, I'll see to it that he loosens the purse strings for once. A woman has to be comfortable, after all, especially one in your condition."

Placing a delicate hand on her stomach, Eden smiled at the Countess. Marlborough's wife might never formally accept Eden as part of the family but she had thawed considerably. "After the child is born in the fall, we will return to England for a visit. Max has decided to keep up the rent on the house in Clarges Street."

"We're counting on that," said Marlborough, sidling up to Eden. "It's possible that we may visit you first, of course. Much depends upon Bentinck's success with the French negotiations."

"Bentinck!" Even in her present state of happiness, Eden could not hear the statesman's name without a sense of outrage. "If I'd been King William, I would have sent him packing to Holland!"

Marlborough's refined features tightened ever so slightly. "So would a number of others, my dear. But the fact is," he said, taking her arm and leading her away from the rest, "the King still needs Wilhem. Only a tough old nut like Bentinck can deal with Louis."

"Max did right well," declared Eden, observing her husband's amiable exchange with Keppel and Godolphin. "In fact, he played the diplomat to the hilt."

The Earl's fair eyebrows lifted a notch. "Somehow I have the feeling that while Max played at being a diplomat, he probably was not very diplomatic. It's not exactly his style. Or mine, if it comes to that. We are both better at deeds than words. And no one knows it better than William."

"William." Eden spoke the name with fondness as the breeze ruffled the ends of her silk kerchief. "Next to Max—and you—I think more of him than of any other man." She looked at her father with an ironic gaze. "Isn't that strange, since he caused all of us a great deal of trouble?"

If there was one person who could understand Eden's affection and charity toward William of Orange, it was the Earl of Marlborough. His wife might rave and rant and wish him dead, Godolphin could grumble about Dutch interference, and the Princess Anne could pray for "the sunshine day" when the English throne would be hers, but Marlborough, like Eden, held no grudge against the House of Orange.

"You're a good child," the Earl said, taking Eden's hand in his and watching the sails snap on the three-masted Dutch vessel that was waiting for the tide. "I owe you so much, yet have given you so little. I regret all these months we were kept apart while I was in prison—but there it is."

"Now, now, you sound like Max." Eden wagged the forefinger of her free hand at her father. "You gave me your name, which is all I ever wanted. And your love," she added more softly, committing to memory the fawn-colored hair, the finely molded mouth and the clear gray-green eyes. "In a more practical vein," she noted, "those shares in the Hudson Bay Company and the two thousand guineas for our wedding present were amazingly generous."

Marlborough's mouth dropped. "Two *thousand* ...?"

"Thousand, hundred, dozen, diddle, done," broke in Sarah, taking her husband's arm. "Eden has no head for figures, that's quite clear. Come, come, it's time for boarding. The captain has given his signal."

Eden glanced at the clinker-built upper works of their vessel and felt a pang of sorrow. "In so many ways, I hate to go. I'll write, I swear it, though my letters look like they were scribbled with chicken feet."

"Eden! We must board!" Max was striding across the dock, his hair blowing in the wind. Before he could reach his bride, a big white coach with purple plumes rolled up to the pier and the Duchess of Cleveland descended in a billowing cloud of blue and red stripes.

"Baby Ducks!" she called, "don't leave without a kiss for your poor old mother! I finally recovered from my excesses at your wedding!" Oblivious to deckhands, crewmen and voyagers, Lady Castlemaine swarmed over her daughter, planting loud, smacking kisses on each cheek. "There! I'm so proud of you, a princess and a wife and a mother! And all with the same man! It's enough to make me weep!" To prove the point, Barbara pulled out a lace-edged kerchief and blew her nose.

Eden glanced beyond her mother's huge rose-covered hat and saw an extremely tall man leaning against Lady Castlemaine's coach. Indeed, he appeared even taller than Max, and for one ghastly moment she thought Rudolf had again been resurrected. But the man removed his hat and Eden noted with relief that he was quite dark. And dirty, unless her eyes deceived her at such a distance.

"Who is that?" she asked, nodding toward the coach.

Barbara was exchanging belligerent glances with the Countess of Marlborough and giving a lewd wink to the Earl. "Who?" The violet eyes darted in the direction Eden had indicated. "Oh, him. No one, really." Barbara sniggered, then leaned forward to embrace her daughter a final time. "Not a word, Baby Ducks! It's my latest conquest, Czar Peter of Russia. He's here secretly to visit Wee Willie wheeze-'n'-cheese, whom he much admires, though I can't tell why. And yes, he's filthy but he *is* great. Where did you think I got the wolfhounds?"

Eden staggered slightly as her mother released her. Max had been distracted by Elsa's twittering litany about a lost trunk, which *Vrouw* de Koch had just miraculously found under the Marlborough carriage. He made a deep bow to Lady Castlemaine before hustling Eden up the gangplank.

"Oh, Max," lamented Eden as they reached the rail and looked down on their friends and family, "how, after so many years, could I find all of my family and now have to part with them?" She covered her mouth and tried not to cry.

"Eden," Max said quietly, placing his hand at her waist, "we are a family. You and I and the babe ...." His words were drowned out by the raising of the anchor and the shouts of the crew.

"I know," said Eden, more to herself than to Max. And she did, for this was what her dream had always been about—under the eaves at Smarden, enduring the harsh taunts of her foster family, comforting herself with stories of King Charles, trying to please her real father by capturing a king. But the search had ended in Max's arms, and now, with their unborn child, they were going to Brabant and his home in the Ardennes Forest. Nor were the Berengers completely forgotten. Gerard would join Eden and Max in another month, to take the post of Max's steward. In a new life, ironically near the source of his injury, Gerard might be able to make himself whole again. Or so Eden and Max hoped, for both were grateful to the only Berenger who had ever eased the burden of her childhood.

As the sails began to fill and the ship creaked out of its moorings, Eden saw her father, her mother, the Countess and the others wave with fond enthusiasm. "You're right," she said, and her face glowed at Max. "At last, we're going home." She shook her head as Max bent down to press his lips against her temple. "Max," she said against his chest, "I meant to look up Brabant on a map, but I forgot. Where *is* home?"

As the ship crested on the tide and sailed toward the rising sun, Max held Eden tightly. "You don't need to look at maps," he said softly. "For us, home is wherever we are together."

SEATTLE NATIVE **MARY RICHARDSON DAHEIM** lives three miles from the house where she was raised. From her dining nook she can see the maple tree in front of her childhood home. Mary isn't one for change when it comes to geography. Upon getting her journalism degree from the University of Washington (she can see the campus from the dining nook, too), she went to work for a newspaper in Anacortes, Washington. Then, after her marriage to David Daheim, his first college teaching post was in Port Angeles where she became a reporter for the local daily. Both tours of small-town duty gave her the background for the Alpine/Emma Lord series.

Mary spent much of her non-fiction career in public relations (some would say PR is fiction, too). But ever since she learned how to read and write, Mary wanted to tell stories that could be put between book covers (e-readers were far into the future and if she hadn't seen her daughter's iPad, she might not know they exist). Thus, she began her publishing career with the first of seven historical romances before switching to mysteries in 1991. If Mary could do the math, she'd know how many books she's published. Since she can't, she estimates the total is at least 55. Or something. See below—count 'em if you can.

At the time of her husband and mentor's death in February 2010, David and Mary had been married for more than 43 years. They have three daughters, Barbara, Katherine and Magdalen, and two granddaughters, Maisy and Clara. They all live in Seattle, too. Those apples don't move far from the tree ... literally.

For more information, go to: www.marydaheimauthor.com.

Discover Mary Daheim's other riveting historical romances

Serena Farrar dreams of being a journalist in Massachusetts. First she must obey her family and marry sea captain Brant Parnell. Her coldness drives him back to sea, so when an ugly scandal erupts, Serena has no choice but to flee to her sister in New Bern, NC. Brant arrives as conflict engulfs the city. Serena is not only a Yankee in enemy territory, but also a woman at war with her heart.

In the time of Mary, Queen of Scots, a young girl left destitute by her father's death meets a pirate in the service of the Queen. They make a bargain: he will marry her, giving her security, and she will not reveal his profession or curtail his freedom. By the time love begins to blossom, it may be too late. First they must survive the turmoil plaguing the court of their Queen.

It's 1585 at Gosford's End in the Scottish Highlands where 17-year-old Sorcha Fraser is impatient for life to begin. Graced with beauty and spirit, she doesn't have long to wait. While out riding, Sorcha meets a young man in priestly robes. From henceforth, as they negotiate the intrigues of the Scottish court, their lives will be intrinsically linked, though fate continues to tear them apart.
The sequel to *The Royal Mile*.

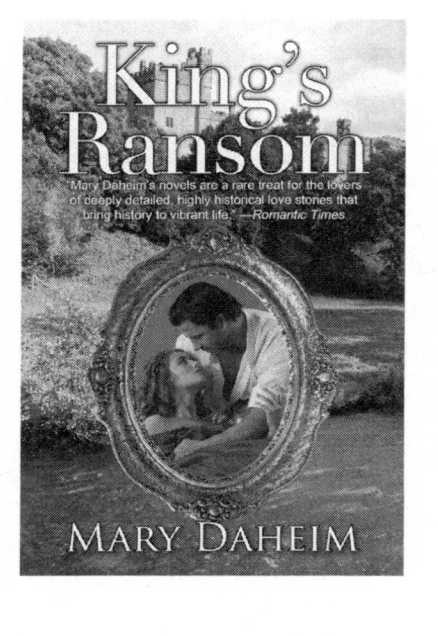

Honor Dale, niece to Oliver Cromwell, has good reason to hate the royalists. First they slaughtered her parents, and now the notorious Captain Hood has stolen her family's jewels to fund the restoration of Charles Stuart to power. Gradually he steals her heart as well. But what is Hood's true nature? Is he a charming, adventurous rake or a desperate nobleman fired by idealism?

In the court of England's King Henry VIII, Morgan Todd, the niece of Sir Thomas Cromwell, is a lady-in-waiting to the queen. An exotic beauty, she is mistaken for a willing servant and deflowered by Francis, the brother of the husband her uncle has chosen for her. Motherhood, war, and intrigue will come between them, but Morgan will never forget Francis, an honorable man in a land of schemers.

Made in the USA
Middletown, DE
28 May 2016